The POSTMISTRESS *of* PARIS

ALSO BY MEG WAITE CLAYTON

The Last Train to London

Beautiful Exiles

The Race for Paris

The Wednesday Daughters

The Four Ms. Bradwells

The Wednesday Sisters

The Language of Light

The
POSTMISTRESS
of PARIS

a novel

Meg Waite Clayton

HARPER

An Imprint of HarperCollins*Publishers*

THE POSTMISTRESS OF PARIS. Copyright © 2021 by Meg Waite Clayton. All rights reserved. Printed in the United States of America. No part of this book may be used or reproduced in any manner whatsoever without written permission except in the case of brief quotations embodied in critical articles and reviews. For information, address HarperCollins Publishers, 195 Broadway, New York, NY 10007.

HarperCollins books may be purchased for educational, business, or sales promotional use. For information, please email the Special Markets Department at SPsales@harpercollins.com.

FIRST EDITION

Designed by Bonni Leon-Berman

Library of Congress Cataloging-in-Publication Data has been applied for.
ISBN 978-0-06-294698-0

21 22 23 24 25 LSC 10 9 8 7 6 5 4 3 2 1

FOR ANNA TYLER WAITE,
who wasn't born an heiress, but built her own kind
of fortune in her own way

"Hope" is the thing with feathers—
That perches in the soul—

—Emily Dickinson

I have traveled through many countries and learned
to hide my thoughts in many languages.

—Hans Sahl

The POSTMISTRESS *of* PARIS

PART I

JANUARY 1938

Once back in Paris, I learned that most Americans were scurrying home. I decided to stay on. I had lived in France for eight years and felt a part of her. I had learned to love her people, her history, her landscapes, and her old stones. If the French could take it, so could I. Besides, too many extraordinary things were in the making, and I didn't want to miss out.

—Mary Jayne Gold, *Crossroads Marseille, 1940*

We should have left France after Max was arrested the first time, but we couldn't imagine a world other than Paris.

—Leonora Carrington, *Villa Air-Bel*
by Rosemary Sullivan

Monday, January 17, 1938

IN THE SKY OVER PARIS

The sky out the glass roof of her Vega Gull was as crimson as the airplane. Beyond the windshield and the gray whirl of propeller, ten thousand tons of iron stood laced against the setting sun. Nanée called over the roar of the Gypsy Six engine, "*La Dame de Fer à son Meilleur Niveau*—that's the kind of art *I* love," to Dagobert, her sole passenger, who wagged his unkempt poodle tail as they circled the Eiffel Tower. *The Iron Lady at Her Best.*

She flew on up the looping Seine, headed back to Paris for the Exposition Internationale du Surréalisme, three hundred artworks depicting gigantic insects, bizarre floating heads, and dismembered or defiled bodies she knew were meant to be thought-provoking but always left her feeling unsophisticated and far too American. Midwestern. Not even from Chicago but from Evanston. She loosened the white silk scarf at her neck as she initiated a controlled descent from a thousand feet to eight hundred, six hundred, five, to buzz her empty apartment on avenue Foch. She loved Paris, if only its winter nights weren't so long when you were twenty-eight and living alone.

She throttled back to idle and extended the flaps over the Bois de Boulogne, descending to two hundred feet as she approached the park's lake, its small cascade and charming little Emperor's Kiosk. Up here in the air, there was no grumbling about Prime Minister Chautemps excluding socialists from the French government, no brother killing brother in Barcelona, no Hitler claiming to be eager for peace while all of Europe trembled. She dipped a wing for a better view, to see the trickle of water over rocks into frozen lake and—

Oh lord! A span of black wings stretched to white-feathered tips at ten o'clock. A red bill opened in a call of warning inaudible over the engine as she slammed the throttle wide open and yanked back the yoke, snapping to the right and climbing to avoid crashing into the black swan already diving to avoid her.

But the nose of the plane was rising too quickly. Vertical speed fifteen hundred feet per minute. Through the windshield: nothing but sky.

The airspeed indicator plummeting toward stall speed.

The wings buffeting as the plane began to lose lift.

The stall horn sounding its alarming blare.

She pushed the yoke forward, rolling out of the turn, sending the nose dipping in an effort to recover from the stall.

Dagobert tumbled forward as the altimeter unwound and the plane shot downward, the view now pure propeller and frozen lake.

The ice!

So little room to maneuver.

Poor Dagobert whimpering.

The airspeed indicator at forty-five knots.

Fingers aching from her grip on the yoke.

"It's okay, Daggs."

Her whole body tensed, about to splinter.

Fifty knots.

Fifty-five.

She willed the airspeed indicator to move faster so she could pull up again without stalling before she crashed into the ice.

Faster, damnit!

Sixty.

Sixty-five!

Pulling back on the yoke again.

The pitch of the nose rising now.

The attitude indicator moving toward level.

So low she was nearly skimming the frozen lake.

Her knuckles pale with her tight grip but, yes, she'd stopped the stall. She was flying straight and level.

The airspeed indicator now at seventy knots.

She retracted a notch of flaps, the plane sinking a little and her stomach with it. She pulled back a bit more on the yoke, maintaining altitude.

Dagobert looked up anxiously from the floorboard.

Another notch of flaps. A little more on the yoke. Initiating the climb out.

Four hundred feet. Five hundred.

A last notch and they were in a stable climb to six hundred, with time now to recover from anything new that might go wrong.

Back at a thousand feet, she circled, waiting for her damn heart to stop trying to escape her damn chest. The Seine looped soothingly from the west to the south and on to the east, to another view of the Eiffel Tower, more distant now.

The frozen lake that might have been her cold grave, and that of Dagobert and the swan too, circled back into view.

"All right," she said to Dagobert, still crouched on the floorboard, as rattled as her own nerves.

She descended toward the lake again, this time to a less daring five hundred feet, to run along the length of the water, past the waterfall and to the left of the island and the Emperor's Kiosk, its little blue dome so hopeful.

And there he was, at the north tip of the lake—the black swan, settled safely on the ice.

She ought not to have been flying so low, but that was what she loved: the high, open sky, yes, but also the rush of earth.

That daughter of yours would rather be wild than broken. Don't you worry she'll end up alone?

"But I'm not alone, am I, Daggs?" She patted the bucket seat beside her, shaking off her father's words. "I have you."

Dagobert reluctantly scrambled back up, then hunkered down on the seat, head on paws. She tugged on one of his velvety ears, and he shook his head that way he did whenever she messed with them.

"I didn't mean to scare you, but I couldn't bear to hurt him," she said as she banked eastward, toward the landing strip at Le Bourget. "And this is his world. He belongs up here."

SHE BROUGHT THE plane to a stop on the tarmac and climbed from the cockpit onto the wing, already pulling off her goggles and leather helmet and shaking out her hair. She lifted Dagobert from the plane, the poor dog still trembling a little, and kissed him on his cold black nose. She set him on the wing, then pulled out her skis and her slim traveling case. Only then did she dare glance to the clock on the domed airport tower. She was impossibly late.

She slid down to the tarmac, leaned her skis against the wing, and set her case on it, beside Dagobert. He watched attentively as she popped it open to its mirror-lined top, swapped her flight jacket for a purple wool with gilded beads and buttons, and added her fur-cuff bracelet. Damn, it was cold, but at least there was nobody to see her. She looked in the mirror, then shrugged off the jacket and bracelet and tossed them on the wing. She dug out a reliable old black Chanel dress and pulled it over her head, slipped her blouse off underneath, and let the silk fall into place over her leather flight pants. Better. Not warmer, but better. She added her flight jacket again, for warmth. Could she just wear the leather pants and boots with the dress? It was a Surrealist exhibit, after all.

Dagobert settled in, resting his head on his paws as she swapped her wool stockings for silk ones. She pulled on heels. Added pearls. More pearls. Even more. She clipped the strands together with an oversize safety-pin brooch, silver with a red Bakelite accent, then unfolded a fabric crumple into an elegant hat. She touched perfume to throat and wrist and wrapped her flying scarf back around her neck. Not better, but warmer. She added the fur bracelet again, its brass underside cold. She applied lipstick, then took Dagobert's face in her hands.

"I don't want to go either, but it's for Danny." Danny Bénédite, her French brother; she'd lived with his family when she first came to study at the Sorbonne years ago. Danny did so much good for so many.

She kissed Dagobert twice in the French way, leaving red lipstick on his face. "All right," she conceded. "I'll drop you by the apartment."

Dagobert licked the fur of her bracelet.

"That's Schiaparelli, Daggs."

Dagobert's look: she could wrap him around her wrist any time she wanted, and at a fraction of the cost.

She lifted him from the wing and set him on the tarmac. "You *are* terrifically soft and beautiful," she said, "but you would never sit still on my wrist."

IN THE GALERIE des Beaux-Arts courtyard, Nanée eyed Salvador Dalí's *Rainy Taxi,* a vine-covered 1933 Rolls-Royce with a male mannequin-chauffeur wearing a shark's head and goggles in the driver's seat and, in the back, a gowned, sopping-wet female one covered in live snails. A gallery attendant handed her a flashlight and opened the grated door to a "Surrealist street" lined with more female mannequins dressed—largely *un*dressed—according to the fetishes of prominent artists, with a velvet ribbon gagging a mouth, a birdcage over a head. Unsettling laughter haunted the main hall, a dim, dusty grotto of a room with hundreds of coal sacks hung from the ceiling, a double bed in each corner, and a floor that was somehow all pond and leaves and moss without actually being wet. The source of the laughter was, she found, a gramophone devouring mannequin legs, titled *Jamais.* Never. Nanée was inclined to agree.

A crowd was gathered around a display of photographs hung on freestanding revolving doors at the dim room's center. And there was Danny, all neatly-slicked-back hair and round black glasses, long nose, tidy mustache over a narrow, dimpled chin, with T beside him even smaller than her husband, her boy-cut dark hair and huge hazel eyes more handsome than beautiful.

Nanée threw her arms around Danny, then exchanged bee kisses with T. *La bise.*

"Don't you look posh?" T said.

Nanée, who'd forgotten to take off the flight jacket and scarf, said, "Do you like it? I'm calling this look 'Aero-Chanel.'" She smiled wryly. "Sorry I'm late. The winds were fierce."

"When are the winds in your life not fierce?" Danny teased.

The French writer André Breton stood in front of the revolving-door photographs, clasping and unclasping his hands as he finished an introduction and asked everyone to join him in welcoming Edouard Moss.

"Edouard Moss!" The Edouard Moss photos Nanée knew were from newspapers and magazines: an adorable girl in pigtails enthusiastically saluting Hitler; a man having his nose measured with a metal caliper; a clean-chinned son taking scissors to his Orthodox Jewish father's beard, the forgiveness in the father's face heartbreaking and raw. Edouard Moss's photojournalism as well as his art would have set Hitler against him, forcing him to flee the Reich.

"I thought you would like Edouard," Danny said.

"'Edouard'? That's awfully chummy, isn't it?" Nanée teased. Danny took such pleasure in befriending the artists he helped, quietly using his position with the Paris police to arrange French residency permits for refugees like Edouard Moss.

T straightened the flap on one of Nanée's flight jacket pockets. "*I* thought you would like Edouard," she said.

Edouard Moss stepped forward then, his tie askew and his dark hair charmingly unkempt. A square face. A mole at the end of his left eyebrow. Thin lines etching his forehead and mouth. He held the hand of a two- or three-year-old girl with carefully braided caramel hair and a much-loved mohair kangaroo. But it was the photographer's eyes that caught Nanée off guard, willow-green and weary, and yet so intense that they left her sure it was in his nature always to be watching, to be aware, to care.

He frowned as he noticed one of the photographs on the revolving-door display—not the centerpiece merry-go-round horse at a frightening angle, distorted and angry, but a smaller print, perhaps the back of a naked man doing a push-up; Nanée so often couldn't tell with Surrealist art, except when they wanted you to know that they had, for example, chopped a woman's body in half. The photograph, improbably tender, left Nanée awash in something that felt like shame, or pity, or remorse. Grief, she might have said if that didn't seem so ridiculous. The sight of all that skin, the shadow masking his derrière . . . It felt so personal, like the back of a lover lowering himself to join his vulnerable body with hers.

Edouard Moss said something to André Breton, his voice too low to hear but his expression insistent. When Breton tried to respond, Moss cut him off, leaving Breton to nod his lion head for an assistant to remove the push-up man photograph.

As the gallery quieted, Nanée whispered to Danny, "I have champagne if you want to bring your friends to celebrate afterward." She couldn't say why she extended the invitation; she'd meant only to put in an appearance and duck out early, to go home to her apartment and fresh pajamas. But she always did have champagne.

She returned her attention to Edouard Moss.

"Mutti!" the little girl with him called out, her face lighting up in surprise and delight.

Nanée looked around, sure the child's mother must be right beside her.

She turned back to Edouard Moss, who was staring for such an impossibly long, disconcerting moment that the crowd turned to see what he saw. They were all looking at Nanée.

He offered an awkward, apologetic smile—to the people waiting or perhaps simply to her—then squatted to the girl's level and took her little face in his hands.

It ripped Nanée's guts out, that simple movement, a father lowering himself to his daughter's level. But maybe they weren't father and daughter. The girl might be a niece, or even the child of a friend. So many parents who couldn't or wouldn't leave Germany themselves were sending their children to live with family elsewhere.

"Non, ma chérie," he said to the girl, his voice a cello baritone with only a hint of German accent. "Souviens-toi, Maman est avec les anges."

Remember, Mama is with the angels.

"Mutti ist bei den Engeln," he said.

Monday, January 17, 1938

GALLERIE DES BEAUX-ARTS, PARIS

Luki pulled Pemmy close, soothed by the scratch of Professor Ellie-Mouse's kangaroo head, her wooly-warm smell. She wanted to go to the Mutti Angel, to hug her and ask her where she had been, but Papa's hands were warm on her face. Papa smiled at the Mutti Angel, but he didn't go to her either. Was the angel like in the storybooks? If you touched her, would she disappear? Luki didn't want her to disappear. Pemmy didn't either.

The angel looked like Mutti but different, maybe because she lived with the other angels now, like when they were in their old home with Mutti they spoke the old words, but now they only spoke the new words except when Papa wanted to make sure she understood. Luki usually did understand, but she liked to hear the old words, Mutti's words.

"Maman est avec les anges, Moppelchen," Papa repeated. "Mutti ist bei den Engeln."

"But Mutti could bring the angels here, to see your photographs, Papa," Luki said. "The angels could come home with us. They could have my bed. I could sleep with Mutti and you."

Tuesday, January 18, 1938, 5:00 a.m.
NANÉE'S APARTMENT, PARIS

It was coming up on dawn outside the elegant apartment's arched windows, but still Edouard had to speak over champagne corks popping into a cacophony of voices in French, German, English, and the shared language of laughter. "May I?" he asked Nanée, indicating the Meret Oppenheim–designed fur bracelet André Breton was just handing back to her. André. What the hell had the man been thinking, hanging *Salvation* in the exposition, calling it *Nude, Bending*, such a prosaic title. And even as the photograph was being removed, Edouard had turned to see this Nanée's face looking up at him, like Elza's ghost. God, no wonder Luki had been confused.

He reached for the bracelet, the brush of Nanée's fingers warm, the scent of her in his hands now. He touched the fur to Luki's cheek before he could think how inappropriate that might be.

"Meret says it was Picasso joking at Café de Flore about this bracelet that inspired her fur teacup," he said to Nanée.

T said, "That cup spoiled my tea-drinking for months. Even now, when I raise perfectly lovely china to my lips, I can't stop imagining fur in my mouth."

"And T is dreadfully cranky when she can't enjoy her Earl Grey," Nanée teased.

She looked less like Elza in the brighter light and without the hat she'd worn at the gallery—much fairer—but she did have the same arch of brow, charming little nose, slightly impish mouth, the same direct look in her eyes as she watched him watch her, the same obliviousness to her own charm.

"Yet that's what made Meret famous," he said. "The fact that you cannot now shake her fur teacup—"

"The point of Surrealism is to provoke," André interrupted, drawing Nanée's attention away from Edouard and back to him, as he'd been doing all night. The man was married to a stunning and talented painter, Jacqueline Lamba, his second wife, with a daughter even younger than Luki, but marriage was no barrier for a Surrealist, monogamy not being held in any great esteem by the movement for which André himself set the rules.

Edouard said, "We seek to overthrow the confines of society—"

"—to find the marvelous in the world," André again cut in. "Only the marvelous is beautiful. And beauty is convulsive. Beauty is a disorienting and shocking disordering of the senses. It will be veiled-erotic, fixed-explosive, magic-circumstantial, or it will not be."

Nanée smiled, slow and warm and yet challenging. "I might be more sympathetic," she said to André, "if someone could explain to me why 'the marvelous' has its women naked with their heads in cages or their bodies dismembered, while its men are invariably intact and clothed."

André, leaning closer to her, said, "Ah, I do think we should introduce you to our friend Toyen, who changed her name because in her native Czech the surname identifies a person as male or female, and she wishes simply to be a painter, not a female one."

"You avoid my question," Nanée said. "Why are the women naked and dismembered, while the men are full-bodied and fully clothed?"

"But of course the answer," Edouard answered before André could, "is that we are men."

Even André laughed, but Nanée only said "Pffft" that way French women did. She was American and not, just as he was German and not.

"You are thinking this is not an answer, that we are men," Edouard said. "But it is merely not the answer you wish to hear. Much like Freud, we're interested in exploring, without moral judgment, obsession, anxiety, even fetish."

She shifted uncomfortably—discomfort being what he'd meant to provoke, being a proper Surrealist himself.

André handed him a piece of drawing paper, suggesting he start them in a round of Exquisite Corpse—an André-invented game in which three players drew separately a head, a body, and legs or a tail, each without seeing what the others had contributed, to create, invariably, a bizarre composite creature. André justified all his Surrealist games as ways to unlock creative minds, but Edouard suspected they were his friend's excuse to drag out the shame of others for the world to see. Still, he handed Nanée back the fur bracelet and accepted a Waterman pen, moss-green agate with a gold clip and a single gold band on an oft-chewed cap, already looking for something to copy, to play André's game without exposing himself. He spotted two photos on a Louis XV desk by the windows, one a framed young Nanée at a shooting target with trophy and pistol in hand, her proud father beside her, and the other a snapshot atop an envelope, recent mail, of Nanée in flying gear. He uncapped the pen and set nib to paper, beginning with the long line of neck he imagined under the scarf in the snapshot, drawing poorly, but then he did have the excuse of Luki asleep in his lap.

"I believe you've both hit on something," Nanée said as he drew the bones of her eye orbits, the effect in the unrelenting black ink faintly skeletal. "I think the answer is that you men are unwilling to allow your own inadequacies to be set beside the ideal."

"The ideal being a woman's body?" he replied.

"The ideal being a man's perfect body, which is as 'marvelous' as a woman's," she said. "Anxiety, as you say."

Everyone laughed, the entire room attending now to this conversation as he drew her cheekbones, her unremarkable chin. Luki stirred, not from the noise but from the tension in Edouard's muscles.

He added a filigreed birdcage to his sketch so that Nanée's skeleton face peeked out through the open cage door—pandering, he supposed, birdcages being all the rage now among the Surrealist crowd, but also imagining stacking negatives to float Nanée's head alone in a birdcage, free of its mortal body.

"Yet if you examine your own words, Nanée," he said, "you will see that your argument supports my answer, that we are men."

"You *are* a Surrealist then? I didn't see any isolated female sex organs in your photos."

Edouard reassessed her—a woman who could say "sex organs" without embarrassment?—as he draped the neck of his caged paper skeleton in a scarf like the one she wore, letting it fly out as if caught in a mighty wind. The kinds of photos she spoke of simply weren't what interested him. What compelled him, or used to when he was still taking photos, was never the sin, original or otherwise. It wasn't even the central power, the tragedy, the disaster or violence. It was the watchers, those standing to the side, never imagining they were involved.

He refolded the paper along the crease and flipped it over—stunned to see not Nanée's skeleton eyes observing him from the page but Elza's. Elza's jawline. Elza's nose. Elza's cheekbones. Elza, his wife everyone described as "lost," as if she might be found somewhere other than enclosed in a tomb. She peered up at him the way she did in his dreams, demanding to know why he'd let their child die. Not charging him with her own death or even her sister's, but grieving for her unborn baby, the sibling Luki would now never have.

He picked up the pen and scratched a quick set of flight goggles over the eyes, refolded the paper, and passed it to André, who began blindly adding a body.

"Come to think of it," Nanée said, "I didn't see a single naked body in your photos, Edouard."

"*Nude, Bending,*" André said without looking up.

Edouard again bristled at this title for *Salvation*, but correcting André would only draw more attention to the photo he hadn't meant for anyone to see.

"Not a single *woman's* body," Nanée said.

André did look up then. "What did you see in that photo, Nanée?" he asked, the same question on Edouard's own mind.

"Well, it's . . . a man's shoulders curled forward? Doing a push-up, I thought."

"Sometimes the viewer doesn't see all that is in the art," Edouard said, silencing André. "Sometimes even the artist himself doesn't see."

"That's the best of art," André said, "the unedited subconscious expressing itself." He folded the drawing paper and handed it to Nanée. "Let's see what more you're hiding about yourself then, shall we? You've played Exquisite Corpse before? In this version, we draw *les petits person- nages*. Do not think. Simply draw whatever comes to your pretty mind."

Nanée, with the fur bracelet again on her pale wrist, hesitated, but took up the pen.

Elsewhere in the room, a fragment of conversation: "Revelation of the Jewish racial soul." The room went silent, even Nanée's quiet dog hiding under the sofa turned to the voice. "We're talking about Hitler's war on 'degenerate art,'" the man explained. Joking. As if he couldn't imagine this Nazi insanity might cross into France.

Revelation of the Jewish racial soul. The phrase was the caption painted on one of the walls at the Nazi exhibition *Entartete Kunst*— "Degenerate Art"—some six hundred modern and abstract works presented for the sole purpose of inviting ridicule, most removed from the walls of German museums on the excuse that they insulted German feelings or undermined public morals or simply lacked artistic skill. Edouard had no idea where they'd obtained the two of his photos included in the Munich "exhibition," one hung in a jumble of artworks under the words "nature as seen by sick minds," the other under "an insult to German womanhood."

"All that art will be destroyed now that the exhibition is over," Danny said.

"The art will be quietly sold outside of Germany to fill Hitler's coffers," Nanée said. "It's the artists themselves the Nazis mean to destroy."

"Which is why any of you with an ounce of sense has fled the Reich," André said, and they all laughed, the truth being so much easier to face with laughter. Half the artists in the apartment were German refugees.

Edouard, watching Nanée hand the folded Exquisite Corpse paper back to André, said, "You don't chew your pen."

"Chew my pen?"

He took it from her and turned it to show the barrel end, the bite marks.

"Oh!" She laughed lightly. "It was my father's. When I was a girl I would spy on him sitting at his desk in the library. He did chew his pen. I'd forgotten that."

"You spied on your father?" André asked.

Nanée closed her hand around the pen as if to hide it. "Is that so odd?"

"Did you spy on anyone else?" André asked.

Without waiting for her to respond, he opened the folded drawing paper and showed everyone the bizarre three-part creature: Edouard's skeleton head in flight goggles and birdcage with Nanée's scarf at her neck; André's octopus body wielding paintbrushes, guns, swastikas, and a severed Hitler head dripping blood; and Nanée's cartoon-man hips, legs, and knobby knees, a groin covered only with a fig leaf, shoes very like Edouard's but with the laces tied together, and on the ground beside the creature, a stuffed kangaroo.

As Edouard tried to digest the shock of that little kangaroo, André joked, "Ah, it appears I find myself in the middle of something."

Everyone laughed harder and harder as André went on about what appeared to be Nanée's head and Edouard's bottom half with his own many arms in between. The noise stirred Luki, who half woke, smiling sleepily.

"Mutti, will you sing to me?" she asked Nanée.

Edouard was glad of the room's laughter then, glad that no one but Nanée could have heard. He stroked Luki's hair until she settled back into sleep, this child who was all her mother and nothing of him, all that was left of Elza.

He stood to leave, saying to Nanée, "I'm sorry. You look so very like Elza. It confuses her." He stared at Nanée, knowing it was rude but unable to look away. It confused him too. "We ought to be going," he said. "Thank you."

At the door, Edouard held the sleeping Luki as Nanée helped him bundle her into her favorite red coat, then held his own coat for him. She handed him the hat Elza had so loved, his initials marked in the hatband as if he were the hat and the hat him.

"She doesn't have a baby," Nanée said. "The kangaroo. Her pouch is empty."

Luki's poor mohair kangaroo was strangled by her arm even in sleep. The joey (which Luki was quick to point out was what a baby kangaroo was called when anyone called it anything else) had disappeared somewhere between Vienna and Paris, and no amount of searching had uncovered it. Luki was distraught at the loss—"Did Joey go to the angels too?"—and Edouard was distraught at the frightening omen of the missing kangaroo child. But Luki's mother had already been taken from her; what worse fate could it portend?

"Goodbye then," he said to Nanée.

Nanée considered him, the question in her expression: Would he not speak of the baby kangaroo, or could he not?

"In France, we say *au revoir*," she responded in a gentler voice than he would have imagined. Not just quiet, but gentle. "Until we see each other again."

Tuesday, January 18, 1938, 6:00 a.m.
NANÉE'S APARTMENT, PARIS

As the party carried on behind her, Nanée watched Edouard appear on the sidewalk below and set off down avenue Foch, his daughter still in his arms. From up here at her window, what she saw was his back, with the child's head resting on his shoulder, and the gray felt fedora—a hat her father might have worn, with its matching Petersham ribbon and its fine leather sweatband embossed with his initials, ELM, like the sturdy, beautiful tree she used to climb when she was a child.

T joined her at the window, whispering, "I knew you would like this one."

"Do be serious," she said, still watching Edouard. "I may 'sabotage myself in love,' as you like to say, but I'm not fool enough to fall for a man who just lost his wife."

She touched her fingers to the glass, cool where the brush of Edouard's skin had been warm as he handed her back her fur bracelet after touching it to the child's vulnerable cheek.

"You're not humoring me," T said. "If you don't much care for a man, you always do humor me."

"Pffft."

"You push the good ones away. Men's egos are more fragile than you allow them to be."

"I pushed him away *how?*" Turning to her now that Edouard and his daughter had disappeared around the corner, toward the metro.

T gave her a look.

"How?" Nanée repeated.

T retrieved the Exquisite Corpse drawing abandoned among the champagne bottles and glasses: the head—Nanée's own head?—in the birdcage; the octopus middle; the fig-leaf groin and knobby knees she'd drawn.

"Edouard drew my head in a *birdcage*, for heaven's sake!" Nanée protested, but quietly, lest she draw attention. That was something she'd learned early: when to draw attention to oneself and when to avoid it. Evanston Rules.

EVANSTON RULES WEREN'T restricted to Evanston, of course. They applied at Marigold Lodge, their thirty-four-room Michigan summer home, Prairie style, with red-brick chimneys and dormers, two dining rooms, a library, sun porches. They applied in New York City. And they applied at Miramar, the Newport mansion built by a friend of her mother's who'd survived the *Titanic* while her husband and son had not, where Nanée spent her last months in America. The society pages reported her family's arrival in New York that June of 1927 "on their way to summer in Rhode Island rather than Michigan this year," but in fact summering at Miramar was the excuse and New York City the purpose of the trip—to consult a specialist about why Nanée's courses had stopped.

She'd not yet been intimate with a man, and it shocked her that her parents imagined she had been, that they'd committed an entire summer to protecting against the rumor that their only daughter might be pregnant. Yes, she shunned corsets, but corsets belonged to her parents' generation as much as did the idea that a woman ought not to vote, or if she did, she should vote as her husband did. Daddy had always encouraged her independence, and she'd emulated her big brother, Dickey, in all things, in learning to sail, to ride horses, to shoot. She read the stories of King Arthur and the knights of the Round Table because Dickey did, although she was alone in trying to piece together a suit of armor from nothing but cardboard, paste, and an exorbitant volume of silver US Foil Company food wrap that, despite her best efforts, she never could keep from crinkling. She followed Dickey in smoking. In nipping at Daddy's bourbon (illegal under Prohibition, but what was good for the workers wasn't necessarily good for the boss). And in sneaking out her window at night. Sure, she knew Mother would disapprove, but the car she drove was a gift from Daddy, and she never did leave it; she just drove the dark roads, sometimes stopping in the parking lot of a jazz joint to listen to the smooth notes of saxophones and clarinets, and women singing. Music that left Nanée breathing nearly as freely as she now did up in the Vega Gull.

The discreet doctor in New York City assured Daddy and Mother that she was "still intact." He couldn't say why her courses had ceased, or whether she would be able to bear children. She'd sat silently as he answered her parents' questions, imaging a future in which the most private parts of her body were forever opened up and examined by cold metal and cold hands. And she could still hear Daddy saying to her mother in their private train car from New York to Newport, "What I mean is, if Nanée might not be able to provide a man with an heir . . ." and Mother's response, too, "A debutante ball is not a business transaction, for heaven's sake. Your daughter's inability to have children, if it comes to that, will not ruin your reputation for reliable goods."

Still, within days, Daddy had made arrangements to send her to the Collegio Gazzolo, a finishing school in Italy run by a contessa they knew. Nanée had a proper brain in her head; she might have gone to Radcliffe or Wellesley or Smith, but she was given no choice. She was shipped off to Europe to master nothing more than good posture, how to wear a ball gown and set a menu, and the fine art of saying absolutely nothing of consequence while making the right kind of man feel important, so that he might marry her. "To work this wildness out of her system in private," Daddy insisted to Mother, as if Nanée's exile to a country where the family was less known might save him from shame. "That daughter of yours would rather be wild than broken," he said. "Don't you worry she'll end up alone?"

Nanée was, it turned out, the least wild of the contessa's girls, the only one who'd never gone the limit except in her imagination. Despite their influence, she behaved well enough that, when the year was over, her father wanted her to return home. She had in mind, though, to move to Paris—simply to defy him, he said. How did she imagine she would support herself?

But he agreed, finally, to a single year at the Sorbonne on the condition that she live with Danny's family. That's where she was when Daddy went into the hospital for a minor operation, and never recovered. November 3, 1928.

There was no Pan Am Clipper flying boat yet, no way to get home other than by a long sea journey to New York and a train on to Chicago. Mother told her not to come, that Daddy would be deep in the ground before she was halfway across the Atlantic. Nanée saw now that her mother had felt free for the first time since her wedding day, and didn't want her daughter to see that truth hidden behind her widow's veil. Perhaps Mother imagined Nanée would feel the same unseemly sense of freedom. Perhaps that was some part of what she *had* felt, some part of the reason she didn't rush home.

Mother instead came to Paris. She took rooms at the Hôtel Meurice, and Nanée moved in with her. Nanée liked it at first, dressing up in evening clothes and jewels, going to places like Bricktop's or Le Boeuf sur le Toit, where the headwaiter always found room for them. But she'd tired of it by the time her brothers joined them to ski that next Christmas. Or perhaps she'd tired of Misha, an ousted White Russian count looking for an American heiress to restore him to wealth, with whom her mother liked to go out clubbing and get drunk and fight.

They skied in St. Moritz, Nanée surprisingly taking to this sport that required her to be out all day in the cold. She stayed until spring, long after Mother returned to the States with her White Russian, who, being a count from a country that no longer allowed royalty, was welcomed into American society with a ball thrown by friends. That was when Nanée had taken her own first lover, after her mother's second wedding. She didn't return for that either. She continued skiing in the Swiss Alps while her mother and Misha settled into the comfortable life Daddy had made, and she climbed into bed with a fellow she imagined she loved. Nanée's taste in men was as bad as her mother's, though, and she lacked the sense Mother had to settle down with just one lout who, being a count, hadn't caused a scandal the way Nanée would were she to marry anyone other than a boy from the right kind of family, from Evanston or Newport or New York. But then Evanston Rules were more forgiving of the second love of a wealthy older widow than they were of a daughter with prospects on her first trip down the aisle.

T SET THE Exquisite Corpse sketch on Nanée's desk, beside the photograph of Nanée in her flight gear that another of her charming louts had sent her. *Was* it her head Edouard had drawn? The flight goggles and scarf, yes, but an artist as talented as he was could draw a head that was unmistakably Nanée's if he meant to. Not that she'd known that was what he'd drawn before she, with his part of the creature folded away, unmistakably drew Edouard's nearly naked lower half.

"He drew my head in a birdcage," she repeated, hearing his voice again, *obsession, anxiety, even fetish*. Yet what she'd felt when saw the sketch was, oddly, understood. As if he could see how she so often felt, looking out at the world through a gilded cage in which she'd managed to pry the door open but was somehow unable to leave.

"Anyway," she said, "you can't get a man by letting him believe you're attracted to him." It was the contessa's admonition—*Non puoi procurarti un uomo facendogli credere che sei attratta da lui*—invariably delivered with her insistence that the girls marry in their "own class," since only wealthy, socially suitable men could be presumed to marry them for love rather than for their fortunes.

"I wrote Danny every day from London," T said.

"But that's different—an advantage of an overseas love." Nanée remembered Danny hurrying home each day in hopes that an envelope from England waited on the little blue plate by the door. "He wants to be with you, but he can't. That's the ticket. Make him want something he can't quite reach."

"And certainly don't risk living happily ever after when there might be a truly horrible fellow out there whose sole attraction is that he won't cause a scandal in Evanston."

"I'm not the snob you imagine me," Nanée protested.

"Of course you are," T said, but with affection.

She slid the Exquisite Corpse drawing closer to Nanée as another cork popped behind them, laughter bubbling up with the champagne. The knobby knees might be forgiven, but the baby kangaroo—Nanée could see that through T's eyes now. She could see it looked carelessly cruel, although that wasn't how she'd meant it.

"He reminded me of Daddy." The confession surprised her more, apparently, than it did T. "The way Edouard Moss got down to his daughter's level. The way he spoke so gently."

"That's a gauzier view of your father than even your mother would claim."

"At Marigold Lodge, though," Nanée said, remembering the manicured peninsula of lawn and weeping willows stretching down to the waters of Pine Creek Bay and Lake Macatawa. *To my brave girl*, her father had written in his will, surprising everyone with his bequest of the family summer home to Nanée. "Daddy was a different person in Michigan."

"Even so, Nan, you need to let go of this quest for a man you imagine would have made him proud."

"I don't—"

"You do, though. You're so anxious not to be taken in by one of your 'terrific louts' that you won't pause to consider what might please *you*."

Nanée studied the birdcage head again, the knobby knees and the kangaroo she'd drawn herself, the much-loved creature abandoned on the floor lest her need for love reflect badly on her father. "The push-up man photograph—why do you suppose he made André take it down?" Thinking she might inquire about it at the gallery, she might buy it if she could. It too left her feeling understood in some way she couldn't begin to describe.

"He's leaving for Sanary-sur-Mer tomorrow," T said gently. "Edouard is."

They both looked out the window, to the broad, empty avenue and the lightening sky.

Nanée folded the Exquisite Corps back into thirds, then into thirds again, and closed it in her palm.

"Later today," T amended. "Tonight. On the overnight train."

"Sanary-sur-Mer," Nanée repeated. It was one of the sunniest places in all of France.

Wednesday, January 19, 1938
SANARY-SUR-MER

The train banked around a curve, and there in the dawn light the sea stretched endlessly blue and foamy white. Edouard opened the window to the smell of the train's coal smoke and, underneath it, the briny sea and pungent pines, and a hint of wild thyme. He fingered his Rollei as the train conductor called out, "Gare d'Ollioules, Sanary-sur-Mer." The little fishing village in Provence was a collecting place for writers and artists. Aldous Huxley had written *A Brave New World* there, joined by D. H. Lawrence and Edith Wharton, and anti-Nazi and refugee writers and artists had taken it up so enthusiastically in the last few years that it was being called "the new capital of German literature and art." André Breton had arranged a cottage for Luki and Edouard here at the edge of the Mediterranean, promising that sales from the exposition would cover the purchase price. Perhaps in the company of other artists, Edouard would photograph again.

"We're here, Luki," he said, jostling her awake as the train slowed into a little shed of a station, where a public bus waited to take them and their luggage to the cottage.

Luki looked up at him with a sleepy smile so like Elza's that he thought he would cry.

"Where's Mutti?" she asked.

He grabbed his Rollei and stood, then lifted Luki into his arms and folded them into the few passengers waiting to disembark, the weight of her sorrow so heavy to carry. How did you make a child understand that the mother who taught her to dance before she could walk would never dance with her again? How did you make a child understand that the loss wasn't her fault, that she'd done nothing wrong and no better behavior would bring her mother back?

"Mutti loves you more than anyone," he said, "but she has to stay with the angels. She's left me to take care of you. We're going to our new house now, remember?"

Luki said, "And I'm going to take care of you?"

Edouard blinked back tears. "Can you smell that, Luki? That's the smell of wild thyme."

Chanel N°5. That was the scent of that fur bracelet. The scent Elza wore, but then so many women did.

"But how will they find us?" Luki asked.

Edouard studied her expectant face, trying to understand what she was asking. "The angels?"

"Yes. How will they find us to bring Mutti to our new home?"

SOMEONE ON THE platform called Edouard's name. Lion Feucht-wanger?

"I've come to take you to your cottage lest the wood benches on that rattletrap bus leave you unable to sit and drink with us at Chez Schwob," the German novelist said.

"But you . . . How did you know we were coming?"

"Ah, but everyone knows everything in Sanary, unless they don't want to know."

"This is Professor Ellie-Mouse," Luki said.

"Well, how do you do, Professor?" Feuchtwanger said. "You look awfully like a kangaroo for a mouse."

"She *is* a kangaroo! She has a joey but we can't find him. He was only an inch big when he was born, but now he's bigger and he can sing. In Australia—which is different from Austria, where we came from—Pemmy and Joey would live in a mob of fifty kangaroos. If you're mean, they pound the ground with their big feet and kick you and bite you."

Feuchtwanger pantomimed fear. "Well then, I shall be very careful not to offend the good professor."

They loaded their luggage into Feuchtwanger's car and set off from the station toward Sanary Bay, Luki hanging out the window to better see the narrow streets lined with pastel-colored shops and bead-curtain doors, their shutters just opening to the morning: butchers and grocers, *laiteries* selling fresh milk and butter, a shoemaker, a hardware store, *bonneteries* offering stockings and thread, beach hats, espadrilles. The fishing boats were already unloading the morning catch—rock lobsters and sardines and sea bass—and setting it up for sale right there on the quay. Gulls circled and called as women mended nets in the sharp morning sun, chatting easily together as their children collected mussels into buckets.

"Papa, can I play in the sea?" Luki asked.

"After I teach you to swim," Edouard said.

"And Pemmy. Kangaroos can swim. They use their tails."

Edouard, imagining the stuffed kangaroo sinking into the Mediterranean, said, "We'll see."

In a public square across from the harbor and palm walk, a gnarled old man in clothes as wrinkled as his face stood in front of a pink stucco town hall, surrounded by crates of olives, apples and pears, oranges and clementines, cabbages and carrots and potatoes and endive. "I have twenty centimes, twenty centimes," he called out in a nasal voice, the produce, like the fish, to be auctioned and shipped to Paris or Brussels or London. Edouard would buy fresh fish and vegetables and bread here. He would take photos again, and Luki would go to school someday, and they would make friends and be healthy and free and safe.

Feuchtwanger drove slowly past the waterfront terraces of Café du Port and Hôtel de la Tour, where people sat over early coffee and already cards were being dealt. He occasionally offered explanations or answers: Sanary hadn't a full-size library, but Au Grand Tube had some decently stocked bookshelves and good-quality art and photography supplies. Edouard must try the big wheel of Gruyère at Chez

Benech, but for today Feuchtwanger's wife had made Edouard and Luki a *poulet à la crème.*

"Is there a cinema?" Edouard asked. Elza had loved the movies; why hadn't he brought her here when he could?

"A converted garage shows films on Sunday nights, but for anything filmed in this decade you'll want to go to Toulon."

At a spit of rocky beach backed by a palisade, they turned up toward steep cliffs and out to the point, then left onto a narrow lane. Across from a white two-story stucco house that was Thomas Mann's Villa la Tranquille, a driveway led to an ochre-yellow cottage with faded blue shutters and a sign on the wrought-iron gate: ATELIER-SUR-MER.

EDOUARD UNPACKED LUKI'S things in the room with the beautiful window, the view of the sea in the distance framed by a large pine and the remains of another fallen tree beside it, long dead and stripped of its branches. He placed a photograph of the three of them on the night-stand along with a page full of math equations in Elza's tidy script that Luki wanted to keep. He made them a big luncheon from the *poulet à la crème,* then left Luki to play while he settled his own things in the other bedroom—his cameras, prints, and negatives. He set *Salvation,* still framed for the exposition, on the desk, and he lay back on the bed and closed his eyes for just a moment, raking his heart over the spike of memory.

HOW LONG HAD he been sleeping? It was eerily quiet, with only the singing of evening birds outside the window in the red-gold of fading sun and the rhythmic lap of sea crashing on rock. Could Edouard live in so much silence? Could Luki?

"Luki?" he called with sudden alarm.

It was far too quiet. But surely Luki too had fallen asleep.

"Luki?" he repeated more quietly lest he wake her, but rushing to her room. She'd slept on the train while he lay awake almost all night, afraid she might wander from the compartment.

She wasn't in her room.

He called her name again and again, constantly, loudly, as he ran out of the house and toward the palisades.

Good god, what had he been thinking, taking a house on a cliff overlooking the sea with a child who wasn't yet three?

He tripped on a tree root. Went sprawling. Was up and running again, calling her name at the top of his lungs.

And there she was. Thank heaven, there she was, turning now to look at him.

He hurried to her, scooped her up from her perch on the fallen pine trunk. He hugged her to him for a long moment before sitting on the log, pulling her into his lap.

"Moppelchen," he said, trying to calm himself so he wouldn't alarm her. She had been nowhere near the steep fall to the rocks and the sea. "Moppelchen," he repeated, Elza's nickname for her chubby baby, her little fatso. He pulled her close, buried his chin in her soft hair, and whispered, "What are you doing out here by yourself?"

"I heard them singing. Did you hear them?"

"Singing," he repeated, wondering if he could find another house, one farther away from the Mediterranean. "Yes, that's the sound of the birds and the sea. It's beautiful, isn't it?"

"The birds and the sea, and the angels too."

He held her head back a little, to better see her brow that was her mother's, her tiny nose, her cherry lips. "Singing angels?" he said, trying to tease her out of another conversation about where Elza had gone. "Moppelchen, are you sleepwalking?"

"Listen. They're all singing with Mutti."

She began to sing then, the song Elza used to sing to her each night. He pulled her close, repeating "Moppelchen, Moppelchen," the thoughts crashing in with the crash of the sea and the red-gold of the evening sky, the soft, steely blue of the water in the late-day light, and the sweet pungent smell of Luki's hair pressed to his face. He tightened his arm around her and sang gently with her, "Wie ist die Welt so stille / Und in der Dämmrung Hülle / So traulich und so hold." *How the world stands still in twilight's veil, so sweet and snug.*

Yes, they would stay here, where perhaps the world would stand still. He would put a fence around the house. He would arrange it in the morning, and they would be safe here, listening to Elza and the angels singing with the birds and the sea as they sat together on this dreaming log.

Twenty Months Later: Tuesday, September 5, 1939
GARE DU NORD, PARIS

It was time. Germany had invaded Poland, provoking France and Britain to declare war. The miracle Nanée and everyone in France had thought would save them hadn't come. Instead, the "appel immédiate" posters calling Frenchmen to enlist—posters that had been taken down after the Munich crisis a year earlier—were up again. This time the call was real.

Nanée looked on as Danny knelt awkwardly in his new soldier's uniform, the bustle of his regiment already boarding as he pressed his lips to his two-year-old son's blond curls. Peterkin tipped his head back and looked up from under long lashes, an expression already identifiable as the boy's disgruntled stare. He dropped his new floppy-eared bunny to the dirty platform and pulled two toy pistols from a holster.

"I have two guns, Papa," he said. "One for me and one for Bunnykins."

Nanée took T's hand, drawing a glance from Danny. "You're more family than my own family," he'd told her when he asked her to come with them to the station. "T will need you to hold her hand after I leave."

"I wish you could come with me, champ," he said now. "You'd sure be a better French interpreter than I, but let's not tell the British Army."

It gave T some comfort, and Nanée too: that the only weapon Danny was to wield in this war was his ability with languages.

"You're such a brave boy," Danny said to his son.

What a brave girl you are, Nanée's father had once said to her. She had been seven then, old enough to remember, which Peterkin was not.

Danny wrapped Peterkin and T in his arms one last time, his chin grazing T's boy-cut hair.

"Nanée," he said, "I'm trusting you to return these two to me in just as good a shape as I'm leaving them."

T, wiping a tear, tried to muster the same note of humor and hope. "But who will take care of Nanée while she's taking care of us?"

"Nanée can take care of herself and then some," he said, and he grabbed his kit bag, and kissed T and Peterkin one last time.

Nanée watched him board the train and peer back out at them through the dirty window. As the train disappeared into its own steam, its *clack clack clack* fading into the chatter of the station, she stooped to pick up Bunnykins, then wrapped her arms around T and Peterkin both, like Danny had.

"You ought to leave too, Nanée," T whispered, a heartbreaking ache in her voice. "You ought to go home."

Nanée leaned back and looked into her friend's face. "Pffft," she said. "Just because Ambassador Bullitt commands me to?" Then, more gently, "I'm not leaving you, T."

"If I had a home in America to return to, I would go."

Nanée pulled the stuffed bunny's ears and snuggled him against Peterkin's little face, all the while trying to imagine living back in Evanston, or even at Marigold Lodge.

"If I had a home in America, T," she said, "so might I."

Saturday, October 14, 1939
SANARY-SUR-MER

Y̶ou are Edouard Moss?"

Edouard, watching from the whistle-stop station platform as his friend Berthe settled her daughter and Luki in the train carriage, turned to see two policemen.

"You will come with us."

"With you? No, my papers are in order." He pulled them from his jacket pocket. "I'm sorry, the train is just leaving. Give me a moment to see Luki go."

Luki, inside the carriage, was showing off her new yo-yo to her little friend, speaking in flawless French. At four now, she had lived all the life she knew in Sanary-sur-Mer, with no memory of Vienna or Berlin except through photographs and the stories Edouard told her out on their dreaming log. Now Berthe was taking her ahead to Paris, allowing him to finish packing up their cottage and prepare it for sale.

"You will come with us," the man repeated. "To the station."

Edouard, unable to hide his alarm now, stammered, "I don't understand."

He called to Berthe, "The kangaroo's name is Professor Ellie-Mouse. She teaches mathematics, like all good stuffed kangaroos." Trying to keep a lightness to his voice, to maintain his composure. One more day. That was all he needed. Paris would be a safer place for Luki and him. A big city. Anonymous. No paranoid neighbors. No one who, seeing his light on late at night, might suggest that his single steady bulb somehow signaled code to a Nazi ship. A single light behind old film he examined for some image he could develop and sell so he could feed them, only to print *Salvation* again and again, as if finding the right exposure time, solarizing, burning and dodging that single photograph into a perfect print might save him. Prints that brought in no grocery money, that he didn't even try to sell.

He called to Berthe, "Luki loves numbers." Like Elza had. "If she's upset without me"—Lord, she would be frantic if he didn't show up tomorrow as he'd promised—"run her through the multiplication tables; that soothes her." If he kept talking, Berthe might realize what was happening, so she could explain to Luki if he was delayed. "She likes to square numbers, too, and cube."

"Edouard?" Berthe said.

"A number multiplied by itself, and then by itself again." He nodded ever so slightly first to the one policeman, then the other.

Berthe looked startled as she registered the police.

Edouard said to the policemen, "My Luki—"

"It will only be for a few questions."

The train still there, in the station. He could take Luki off it. He could keep her with him. He could bribe his way through one more day, couldn't he?

He focused on the policemen, trying to stay calm. This was France. This wasn't Germany.

"You would want the child to accompany you?" one of the policemen asked.

Berthe had Luki in her arms now. She was holding her up to the open window, saying, "Wave to your papa. Wave to him, sweetheart."

Edouard called to the train, "Luki, I love you! I love you!"

Luki raised one small hand.

LUKI GRIPPED HER yo-yo tightly, wishing Pemmy wasn't hiding in the suitcase, wrapped in a towel. Tante Berthe's hands were at her waist, holding her up to the window. She waved to Papa. She tried not to cry. She was lucky, because she would see Papa tomorrow. Her friend Brigitte didn't get to see her papa at all because her papa was a soldier. And Pemmy didn't even have a papa, except Papa was like a papa to her even though he wasn't a kangaroo.

She waved to Papa again as he waved back.

"Tante Berthe," she said, "are those men Papa's friends?"

Tante Berthe didn't answer.

The men looked angry. Luki wanted to tell them to be nice to Papa, who never got mad at anybody, not even when Pemmy climbed into the bath with her for a swim and dripped water on his photographs. He said they were only photographs and Pemmy could drip on them any time she wanted, but they needed to get her as dry as they could because she wasn't as fun to hug when she was sopping wet, and also, maybe one swim in a lifetime was enough for a kangaroo.

Papa called out again that he loved her. Then the train was moving. It was taking her away from him. Papa was getting smaller and smaller. He got so small. Then he disappeared.

AS THE POLICEMEN waited outside the cottage, Edouard put a few things into a suitcase that had been Elza's. Nightclothes. Clean things for tomorrow. So much of his life was already packed in crates around him. Why hadn't he just thrown the things from his makeshift bathroom darkroom into a last crate and gotten on that train with Luki? He could have left a key with a neighbor and managed the sale of the cottage from Paris. But the French had long been so good to refugees. They'd accommodated a million as Spain fell to Franco, and even Daladier's decree authorizing the internment of "undesirables" on the excuse of national security had been nothing but words and posturing, with no actual internment camps involved. Yes, an August 30 circular called in the event of war for the gathering up of men from "the old territories belonging to the enemy," and now France was at war with Germany, but he was Jewish, a refugee from Hitler's brutality, for god's sake. How could anyone imagine him a spy for the Reich?

He pulled from a crate his Leica, set it in the suitcase, and rooted around for film as if this moment might free him to photograph again. He gathered what money he had, wishing he'd sent more with Luki. He grabbed a pen and the box of writing paper he'd gotten to write a thank-you note to Nanée Gold for that gathering in Paris so long ago. He set aside the half-written letter, the words he'd never been able to complete, and he extracted a clean sheet.

This would all be sorted out before his train left tomorrow. He'd be in Paris before Luki could miss him. But he quickly jotted a few words:

My Luki, I hope I will be with you even before this letter arrives.
But in case my train is delayed, or I am, I want you to know how
very much you are loved.
—Papa

He tucked the note into an envelope and addressed it to Berthe at her quai d'Anjou address on Île Saint-Louis. He put the box of stationery and pen into the suitcase, grabbed the photograph by his bedside— Elza and Luki and him at the Vienna apartment a lifetime ago—and the blanket he'd been told to bring. He locked the door, slid his key under the geranium pot, and rejoined the waiting police.

Sunday, October 15, 1939
CAMP DES MILLES

Suitcase and blanket in hand, Edouard climbed from the cattle car into a line herded by French soldiers toward a five-story red-brick tile factory outside Aix-en-Provence, its industrial smokestacks hard against an impossibly blue sky. He was prodded through a gate no wider than a car, past a caretaker's lodge, and into a factory yard so thick with brick dust that his feet kicked up a red fog. He turned to see, through a spiky iron fence topped with barbed wire, a little French village and hilly fields, olive groves, vineyards turning golden in the fall, and a distant aqueduct that would perhaps lead to Marseille, twenty-five miles away. It was a good fifty back to Sanary-sur-Mer, and hundreds to Paris, and Luki.

The gate clanged shut.

His train was not the first to arrive. Laundry hung drying along the fence, and at the far end of the yard a man sat in front of an easel, improbably painting. Long lines waited at latrines. Ahead, internees were processed at tables set between two flagpoles flying the tricolor flag of the French Republic, blue and white and red.

It was hours in the hot sun and the painter had long ago folded up his easel before Edouard reached the flagpole, the tables, and someone to whom he could plead his case.

He said, "My Luki—"

"Money?" the guard asked.

"I can't stay here. Luki. She's alone. She's only four. Her mother is dead." Remembering Luki out at the dreaming log, asking why they had to leave.

"Money," the guard repeated.

Edouard handed his money to the man, who turned to searching his suitcase with no attempt at thoroughness.

"I can't stay here," Edouard insisted. "Luki is in Paris with a friend who—"

"You are number one hundred and thirty-two. Next!"

"But you don't understand. I—"

He sensed, then saw in his peripheral vision, a well-armed guard, gun drawn.

He was not a prisoner. He could not be a prisoner. He was no danger to France. This was all a mistake.

He gathered his things and followed the line into the factory building, stopping to let his eyes adjust to the dim light, dust already lining his throat and burning his eyes. He crossed a floor so thick with brick dust that it was lumpy. At the back wall, dark wooden stairs led into the bowels of the abandoned factory.

THE CAMP WAS full of others Edouard knew by reputation or more—artists and intellectuals from Germany who'd settled in Sanary-sur-Mer and Arles and elsewhere in Provence. It had been Max Ernst at the easel in the courtyard, painting with supplies brought to him by his artist-mistress. Fellow photographer Hans Bellmer was here. Nobel Prize winner Otto Meyerhof. Lion Feuchtwanger, who must have been taken into custody in Sanary-sur-Mer while Edouard was too busy packing to join friends at the café. Along the whole long length of the hallway where the kilns had once fired tiles, hundreds of men tried to create art of one sort or another.

"Work staves off hunger and anger in equal parts," Hans Bellmer said.

Max Ernst added, "Lest we become brick debris ourselves."

The two were working together on an odd mural: two women hunched over two dead men, with one of the men's arms hanging out of a painted frame to grip the ankle of a surreal giant skeleton that was all pelvic bone and legs trying to escape to a high-heeled boot twice the size of the rest of the painting. Maybe art was a mirror held up to reality or maybe it was a hammer with which to shape it, Edouard wasn't sure. He thought art might serve any purpose, and at its best it did reveal the truth of our own individual hearts. But he wished in this moment to wrap his fingers around the grip of any hammer, artistic or not, and swing it in every direction, not to shape this reality but to smash it to bits.

If others felt this anger, though, they didn't show it. In a nearby cavern, actors rehearsed plays and even opera, while around them writers scribbled in journals, tiny print to preserve their paper. Poets. Playwrights. Translators. There were sculptors and architects here too. Film directors. Conductors. Songwriters and composers. Pianists and singers and musicians of every kind. University professors offered classes and lectures. Comedians shared jokes, although now everyone was a comedian, much of the art they created ironic. Art and intellect and humor—they washed away boredom, maintained morale, and allowed, somehow, a modicum of dignity. Only a few here weren't creating art of one sort or another, and even they sat easily on piles of bricks, absorbed in games of chess played with pieces carved from spare bits of wood on boards scratched into the floor, or stood in heated discussion in a kiln that bore a DIE KATAKOMBE sign, a nod to the Berlin cabaret that had been a hotbed of political thought until Joseph Goebbels shut it down.

That night, after Max and Hans set down their paints, everyone put on their best clothes, as if headed for a night at the theater, and gathered in the camp's hanger in the center of the tilery, where a makeshift stage, orchestra pit, and pseudo-seats had been set up. Even the camp staff came to watch.

Adolf Sieberth, who'd been head of Radio Vienna at twenty-four, waited for everyone's attention. "'Courage,'" he announced. He turned to the musicians, his back to the audience, and began to conduct his refugee orchestra with as much dignity as if they were in a real symphony hall.

"Courage always, and forge ahead," they played and sang, the beginning of a performance that would have been lauded in any of the world's most famous venues. Comedy. Parody. Theater. The man the performance was dedicated to, camp commander Charles Goruchon, gave the internees there as much freedom as he could: Observant Jews prayed in the central courtyard. Internees received letters and packages. They bought things from a little camp store and received visitors. They spent whole evenings creating and sharing, imagining for a few hours that crystal chandeliers illuminated their art in some world other than this French internment camp surrounded by a barbed-wire-topped iron fence.

WHEN THE DAY'S-END call sounded that first night, Max Ernst suggested Edouard set up next to him, and because everyone admired Max, the men shifted their straw mattresses on the hard factory floor—an entire level of the building dedicated to row after row of straw sleeping mats. Men contributed bits of their own straw to make a mat on which Edouard spread the blanket he'd brought. He opened his suitcase to his pajamas neatly folded on top. His day clothes were filthy, but warmer. *He* was filthy, his very pores filled with brick dust.

"Stay with your routine as much as possible," Max said. "It pays to remember we're human. Use your suitcase for a semblance of privacy."

Edouard took the framed photograph from the pocket of the jacket he'd worn since being taken from Sanary—Elza's impish mouth and direct gaze, Luki just six months old, and Edouard's face above theirs, looking to the camera. The photo had been taken more than a year after the German military stood by as Hitler conducted his Röhm Purge, murdering the military leaders and the prior chancellor, along with dozens or perhaps even hundreds of anti-Nazi journalists. Within weeks the military was swearing unconditional obedience not to Germany or its constitution but to Hitler. How had he not seen then that it was time to flee? How had he not seen how much he was putting at risk? He'd had this grand idea that his photos might bring the world to his country's defense, his one single camera, when all of Europe could not stop the madness that was Nazi Germany.

Edouard quickly stripped and pulled on his nightclothes. He carefully folded his day clothes and tucked them into his suitcase, under the clean things. He pulled out his Leica and stationery and pen, then set the suitcase like a low wall between Max and him. He placed the framed photograph atop the suitcase and sat on his straw mat, glad to be under one of the vast room's three bare bulbs, the only light the dim factory floor offered. He touched a finger to the photo, then to his camera, imagining Luki in Paris, wondering where he was. *My Luki*, he wrote. Perhaps it was just as well that she was far away. How very frightened she would be to see him like this.

"Lights off now," came the call from the bugler.

First one, then another of the three bare bulbs that lit the room were turned off with a pull of a string, leaving only the one above Edouard as a barrier against the dark.

"Lights off," the bugler repeated.

Edouard, unable to find words to explain to Luki where he was or why, how long it might be before he joined her in Paris, set the page beside the photograph atop the suitcase and settled the Leica on top of it, to keep it in place.

"All right, then?" Max Ernst asked.

Eduard nodded, and Max stood and turned off the light.

"Good night, Luki," Edouard whispered as he lay in the darkness, his eyes adjusting. Soon he could see the outline of the frame atop his suitcase. He could know it was there, even if he could no longer make out the shape of the family they had been.

Sunday, October 15, 1939
ÎLE SAINT-LOUIS, PARIS

Luki lay in the dark, holding tightly to Professor Ellie-Mouse as voices drifted up from outside the window. She said, "It's okay, Pemmy. Papa said he would be here today, but today isn't over." She nuzzled the pale-green ribbon at Pemmy's neck, smooth and slidey on her nose and lavender-and-olive-smelling from where she'd washed under Pemmy's chin with soap, but not with water, because even though Pemmy stayed wrapped in the towel in the suitcase all the way on the train, she was still damp from her swim. Luki wished she had Joey. She wished she could turn his key to make his music. Pemmy liked to go to sleep to Joey singing. Luki hadn't meant to leave him behind after they'd found him yet again, but surely Papa would bring him. "Papa only stayed to pack our things," she said to Pemmy. "It's easier for him to pack without you hopping all around, knocking things out of boxes."

Eight Months Later: Wednesday, June 5, 1940
AVENUE FOCH, PARIS

Nanée, with T, Peterkin, and a well-loved Bunnykins dragged by his ears, watched in the sweltering heat as French soldiers passed, uneven lines of exhausted and bedraggled men already shedding their French military uniforms lest the Germans catch up with them.

"We can't stay in Paris, T," Nanée began again. "It's been two weeks since the government prayed in Notre-Dame to save France from their incompetence, and pffft, still nothing. I'm afraid God has gone off on the French."

A shopgirl from a nearby boutique joined them, watching silently, a large silk bow smartly tied to her standard-issue gas mask. Nanée too had a gas mask. An air raid shelter had been set up in the basement of her building, and in T's as well. They'd all gotten used to throwing on their bathrobes and trooping down to join their neighbors, politely shaking hands and saying good evening. In Nanée's building, the concierge had at first served coffee and soup, and they chatted until the all-clear signal. But as the nights dragged on with the same sirens and no actual war arriving, fewer of her neighbors bothered, and eventually Nanée too simply pulled the covers up over her head. "The Phony War," they'd started calling it. But now it was real.

"No miracle is coming, T," Nanée said, serious now. "Even the soldiers retreating to safety aren't stopping here."

"How will Danny find us if we leave?" T whispered.

Nanée lifted Peterkin and tucked his head to her chest. "Everyone who made it out of Dunkirk is in England."

"But what if he didn't?"

Nanée tried to convey with a look words she couldn't say, that if Danny wasn't in England, he wasn't anywhere.

"Hitler will restore order," the shopgirl said. "It will be best for France."

Nanée wanted to take the little ninny to task, but there were far too many like her to take them all on.

She asked a passing soldier, a boy with a bandaged eye, where he'd come from.

"France is lost," he answered. "The German Panzers——"

"Yes, but *where?*"

"Up near Abbeville."

She said to T, "That's not a hundred miles away. The Germans took all of Denmark in four hours."

"No. Danny wouldn't be able to find us."

"But you have to think of Peterkin, T. Danny would want you to get your son out of danger. You have to think of your child."

Thursday, June 6, 1940
CAMP DES MILLES

Darkness, and the sounds of prisoners in restless sleep—barking coughs, snores, sleep-talking—interrupted by the rising signal, the bugler playing beautifully, as always. Edouard leaped from his straw mat, pulled on the bare overhead bulb, dressed as he said a quick good morning to the young Luki in his photo, and took the wooden stairs by twos to get outside. Hell. A long line already waited for the seven filthy latrines, men as thin and ill-kempt as he was, despite their best efforts. Others stood in nightclothes and nightcaps, debating in whispers; they'd been here for hours. It was crazy, all these refugees, anti-Nazi to a man, locked up as "enemy subjects" for no reason other than xenophobia and administrative incompetence. It was so absurd that it would make you a Surrealist if you weren't one already. Even Max Ernest, who'd been released in November with some of the more famous internees, had been brought back some weeks before, as if the approach of the German army might make the men here more dangerous to France, when in fact holding them captive simply made France more dangerous for them. Max had no answer to why he'd gone home to the Ardèche rather than fleeing France when he could have; it was so hard to imagine things could get worse until they actually did.

Edouard passed the time in line practicing English with another man, a way of looking forward, imagining that a future might exist in which all of France wouldn't fall to Hitler. The armored cars and motorcycles on the road beyond the gates—were they going toward the fight, or retreating? "My Luki is in Paris with a friend," he said to his line mate. He'd just received a letter from her the day before, this one not written by Berthe describing how Luki was doing but a few words in big loopy letters, with the K backward and numbers better formed. *I love you, Papa*, Luki had written, and she'd included a drawing of him with her on his shoulders, the way he often carried her to and from the dreaming log back in Sanary-sur-Mer. He'd slept with the letter beside him. He had it in his pocket now. "Luki is just learning to read and write," he said, swallowing back the sadness of Berthe rather than Elza or him teaching her. "She has a laugh like sheet lightning," he said. "She likes to pretend. She questions everything, like her mother did."

Just as he reached the front of the latrine line, several guards stepped in front of him. There was nothing to do but wait.

Some twenty guards were marching into the courtyard as Edouard emerged from the stinking latrine, the internees gathering for the morning roll call. Everyone stood bored as a sergeant in a red fez called numbers and they answered. "One?" "One." "Two?" "Two." "Four?" "Four." Lucky number three had been released in the fall and left France before the spring roundups.

Foreign legionnaires carrying barrels of latrine refuse across the courtyard set them down for a minute to rest. "Ice cream! Get your ice cream!" one of them shouted. They alone laughed.

"One hundred thirty-two?" the guard called finally.

Edouard replied, "One hundred thirty-two."

Back inside, Max Ernst smoothed his dirty white hair over his balding head, then ladled coffee from a bucket on which a thin layer of reddish dust had already settled. Edouard, holding his now-hot tin cup gingerly, dipped his bread and took a bite.

"The bread's better today," he said.

"That's last night's bean soup still in your cup you're tasting." Max lowered his voice to a whisper. "Tater will have his pork this morning, if you can get enough of your money from the rag-shop boss."

"He feeds our own garbage to his pigs and returns it cooked, sliced, and wrapped in old newspaper," Edouard said, not that he spent his own money on anything but postage for his letters to Luki. "The barber can get you today's paper, you know, and a folding chair to sit in while you read it."

"The news would only be worse, and I'd have to leave the chair behind when we go."

"Ever the optimist."

The man next in line grumbled that his cup wasn't full.

Max, ignoring him, further lowered his voice. "Feuchtwanger is again appealing to the commandant to give us back our papers and allow us a chance to be somewhere else before the Germans arrive. A train to the Spanish border."

He'd been talking about this scheme for days.

"I have to get Luki from Paris," Edouard said. "I can't leave France without her."

He took his cup and bread back to his straw mat. Across the room, dust motes reflected in a narrow shaft of light from a window. Closer by, a brick fell and broke, kicking up more dust.

Thursday, June 6, 1940
AVENUE FOCH, PARIS

Nanée set a last jerry can of gas into a two-wheeled trailer piled with belongings and attached to the back of her little Citroën, and she joined T, Peterkin, and Dagobert in the car. She adjusted the white scarf at her neck, threw the car into gear, and headed down avenue Foch, already crowded with fleeing Parisians, the Arc de Triomphe fading in the distance as they left. It was a long slog through heavy traffic to Châteauneuf-sur-Loire, eighty miles to the south, where she dropped T to stay with friends of Danny's family, accepted an offer of supper, then set off with Dagobert along a languid river, past meadows and orchards and vineyards to a rental in Le Mesnil. The cottage had a tiny bedroom, sitting room, kitchen, and bathroom, with something akin to a tub in the shape of a three-foot-wide circular vat to be filled with water heated on the stove. She unloaded her things from the car, leaning down last to retrieve from under the driver's seat the pearl-handled Webley revolver her father had given her, with which she'd won that first target-shooting contest—eighteens and under, short-barreled revolvers. She'd been the youngest, just fourteen, and the only girl.

"Well, Daggs," she said, "welcome to our new home."

Just a week later, though, they were in the Citroën again, picking up T and Peterkin and heading farther south. The Germans had marched into Paris, the city covered in soot and a choking fog of smoke from oil and gas tanks the French forces destroyed in their retreat.

"Good god, will this heat never break?" Nanée said.

And where the devil were they? They meant to cross the Loire at Sully to avoid a bottleneck at Orléans, then drive the two hundred miles south to La Bourboule, to stay the night with another friend of the Bénédite family before continuing on toward the Atlantic-coast ports and a ship to England. But the little dirt road ended in nothing but a muddy field and woods.

Perhaps that explained the lack of traffic.

She studied the map spread out over the steering wheel in the sweltering car, to the distant sounds of German airplanes and bombs. She backed up to turn around, succeeding only in wedging the trailer and car, the wheels digging more deeply into a rut. Even little Peterkin climbed out to try to unhook the cart, Dagobert sniffing and marking his territory lest any other dog claim it. They rummaged around in the trailer for a makeshift tool, then hammered and tugged, trying to unlatch a hitch that wouldn't budge, still to the sounds of bombs and airplanes. Were they closer now?

"If we get this apart," T said, "we might never get it back together again."

"Our gas will take us farther without the trailer," Nanée said.

"Our jerry cans are in the cart."

"Pffft. We'll put them in the trunk." Thinking through whether there was anything she particularly cared about in the trailer. Her books, yes, but she couldn't possibly get them all in the car. And beyond that? Even the single piece of art she'd brought was not the one she'd wanted—not the Edouard Moss push-up man she'd returned to the Galerie des Beaux-Arts to purchase that day after the Surrealist exposition, but a photograph by another artist she'd bought when that one wasn't for sale, a woman's face and naked breasts seeming to float in murky water. *On Being an Angel*, it was called. She'd never even hung it, and yet it was the only art she'd brought, as if it would bring bad luck not to leave the Paris apartment intact for her return at this insanity's end.

They gave up on the hitch, finally, leaving in the absence of their banging an eerie silence. Had the German attack, wherever it was, ended?

Nanée hopped into the driver's seat to try to turn the car again, Dagobert following lest he be left behind. She pulled the car forward a few inches, then backward and forward, backward and forward, cranking the steering wheel with each reversal. Again and again and again, an inch or two gained each time, until finally she moved forward, completing the turn even with the trailer still hitched.

T cheered, and Peterkin cheered with her, his bunny still held by its ear, as Nanée climbed out to bask with them in this small victory. Dagobert put his paws to the window and barked.

A terrific roar sounded overhead, the inverted gull wings of a German Stuka flying low. As they stood watching, it fired.

Surely it wouldn't shoot at them? Surely it wouldn't shoot a child? Disbelief flooded Nanée even as she saw that Peterkin was straight in its path.

She ran for him.

T ran too.

Nanée reached him first.

Scooped him up.

Ran for the tree line.

The roar of the planes—several now—was deafening, the rat-a-tat-tat of their guns pure hell.

One of the planes followed them, shooting as if in a carnival game. But not at all like that. Not pretend. Not a nightmare. Real screams filled Nanée's ears, real wails. T screaming, "Peterkin!" and Peterkin crying in Nanée's arms. Was he hurt? Was T?

Nanée, still running, glanced back to confirm that T was just behind her.

She dove for the tree line, the sturdy trunks and cover of leaves.

She would not cry. She would not cry.

T was beside her on the ground already, taking Peterkin from her and tucking him underneath her to shield him with her body.

Nanée looked out to the little car pointed in the only direction the road went, toward the German planes already disappearing. Dagobert watched her through the car window, shivering.

She was up again, running back to the car, T with Peterkin close behind her.

The poor dog climbed all over Nanée in the urine-smelling Citroën as she shoved the gearshift into drive, spraying gravel and dirt as she took off down the road, all the while saying to the whimpering dog, "It's okay, we're all okay, we're okay."

THE BRIDGE AT Sully was strewn with bodies caught in the German strafing. The line waiting to cross stretched forever: cars with number 75 license plates, the code for Paris; buses and tractors and bicycles; even old tumbrels, those two-wheeled open carts that once carried condemned prisoners to the guillotine. All were loaded with mattresses and dishes, clothes, food, children's toys, books, even fur coats, despite the desperate heat. But most people walked. If they were lucky, they pushed prams full of their belongings. Everyone was headed south, toward the sea.

They barely made fifty miles that first day, despite driving late into the night, the Citroën's headlights—dimmed by the wartime regulation blue paint—reflecting such a nasty drizzle that Nanée drove with her head out the window to better see. They gave up at a dark barn on a dark road somewhere near Vierzon. Nanée explored it, flashlight in hand, and returned to report that there was a hayloft, if they could get Peterkin up the ladder.

"A hayloft all to ourselves," she said. "That sounds rather deluxe, doesn't it?"

She set a flashlight, pointed up, at the bottom of the ladder, and they began to climb. They were nearly to the top, Peterkin on his mother's back, T choking under his grip around her neck as Nanée followed close behind to catch him if he fell, when a rung splintered under T's foot. Nanée called out, but already the wood was snapping.

A ghost face appeared above them in the shadowed light beam, as if her father had come to call her to the Lord.

"Mon Dieu!" a man's voice said, his arm reaching from the hayloft to catch T's wrist as another man reached to grab Peterkin's arm.

"Ne bougez pas." His voice firm and direct and surprisingly calm.

Nanée's mind froze, unable to process the French as the man scooted forward, hanging upside down from the waist, his wide, sturdy hands on Peterkin's little ribs, carefully lifting him.

T stepped up above the broken rung, a big step, and climbed into the hayloft.

The faces peered down at Nanée.

"Let me . . . let me get the flashlight," she said.

The faces puzzled.

"Le flash?" she said, searching for the word. "La lampe de poche?" Her hands shaking. Could she really climb down the ladder and back up again? "Et mon chien, Dagobert."

THE SECOND DAY, even the back roads were slow going, through endless fields and pastures that were hauntingly peaceful despite the retreating French soldiers and the detritus of war: rifles and machine guns thrown in the ditches alongside the roads; abandoned cannons; the occasional military vehicle, invariably empty of gas. That night they knocked on the door of a prosperous château outside Le Berry to ask if they might stay in the barn, only to be informed by a pompous butler that the countess did not take in refugees. Nanée hadn't thought of herself as homeless, but hearing it, she saw that she had been a refugee of some sort for a decade. She was filthy. She was starving and yet unwilling to take food that Peterkin might eat. It turned out her daddy was wrong; money couldn't buy everything.

They knocked at a modest farmhouse, where a girl not much older than Peterkin called gloriously to her mother, "Maman! Refugees!" as if nothing could delight her more than to finally see these odd creatures she had heard about on the radio. Her mother gave Peterkin a huge yellow bowl of warm milk, and fed them the first proper meal they'd had in two days. Even Dagobert slept well in their cozy house.

In thinner traffic the third day, they climbed hills wooded with broad-leafed chestnut trees, rocky soil, poorer towns. Just after noon, they entered Guéret to find the square filled with townspeople in intense conversation, scattering concern.

"What's happened?" Nanée called out the car window.

The gaggle of worriers peered at her. Could anyone not have heard?

"Maréchal Pétain has asked for an armistice."

The war was over. In a single month, France had not only given up, but also squandered any bargaining power it had in forming the peace by begging for it. This was how it started everywhere. In Austria. Czechoslovakia. Poland. People gave up without a fight. And in this little town in the middle of France, everyone seemed relieved.

Monday, June 17, 1940

DINARD

Luki woke to the startling sound of someone pounding. Brigitte still slept beside her in the bed in the big house by the sea, but Tante Berthe was already answering the door. Outside the window, it was still nighttime, but the end of it.

"It's okay, Pemmy, don't be afraid," Luki whispered, patting her pouch with the tiny folded-paper Flat Joey she'd made so Pemmy wouldn't miss Joey so much; he looked just like a piece of paper decorated with numbers, but Luki could fold him back into shape any time.

Madame Bouchère, who always said hello to Pemmy when they went to the butcher, said to Tante Berthe, "The Germans will be here in two hours."

No one liked the Germans. That was why Tante Berthe had brought Brigitte and her here, to the house she lived in when she was their age, because she didn't want to stay in Paris with the Germans. Mutti and Papa were Germans, and so was Luki, but they were a different kind of German than the ones everyone didn't like. When Luki had asked what kind of Germans they were, Tante Berthe went quiet for a long time, then said Papa was a photographer and not a soldier, and everyone who ever met Luki loved her.

Now Tante Berthe and Madame Bouchère were talking about a boat. A boat was sailing in two hours, and Madame Bouchère could get Luki on it.

"By herself? To England?" Tante Berthe asked. "But she's barely five."

"The Kleins would take her."

Pemmy whispered to Luki that she didn't want to go anywhere with the Kleins, and neither did Flat Joey. Old Monsieur Klein sometimes shouted things that didn't make sense.

"You can't keep her here," Madame Bouchère said. "It will put us all in danger."

But how would Papa find her if she wasn't with Tante Berthe?

Luki very quietly climbed from under the covers with Pemmy and Flat Joey. She opened the trunk at the end of the bed, climbed in, closed the lid, and pulled the sheets and blankets inside over her. She lay there in the muffled quiet, hugging Pemmy. She heard Tante Berthe calling for her, but she stayed completely silent, and Pemmy did too. She missed Papa. She thought maybe he had gone to be with Mutti. Tante Berthe used to remind her that Papa sent letters every week. "People in heaven can't write letters," Tante Berthe said. Luki didn't know why they couldn't, but it must be true, because Mutti never did write letters to her. But now Papa didn't write letters either.

"Brigitte, where did Luki go?" Tante Berthe demanded.

Brigitte didn't know.

Tante Berthe was frantic now, saying they had to find Luki. And still Luki lay silently in the trunk. Pemmy was scared, but not as scared as going on a boat with the Kleins to a place where Papa couldn't bring real Joey to her.

WHILE TANTE BERTHE watched out the window, Luki and Brigitte sat facing each other in the trunk, looping strings with their fingers to make cat's cradles and Eiffel Towers; Pemmy didn't have any fingers, so she couldn't play with string. Some men would be coming, Tante Berthe had said. They weren't nice men. When they came, Luki was to play the hiding game again.

"All right, girls," Tante Berthe said. "Now."

Brigitte climbed out of the trunk to go downstairs and wait until the men came to the door. Then she was to come get Tante Berthe.

"Remember," Tante Berthe said to Luki, "these men might be mean to me and maybe even to Brigitte, but don't you worry, you just lie quietly in the trunk, playing the hiding game. You mustn't cry or anything. If these men find you, they will take you away."

Luki lay back on the blankets inside. "Would they take me to the angels, to be with Mutti?" she asked.

Tante Berthe scooped her up out of the trunk then, and hugged her so hard it pressed Pemmy into her bones. "No, Luki, you mustn't think that," Tante Berthe whispered, kissing her head again and again. "You mustn't think that."

She lay Luki back into the trunk then, gently, like Papa used to. "You just lie here and think about nice things," she said.

"Like Papa singing to me?"

"Yes, exactly. Lie quietly and imagine your papa singing to you until I come back. But just your papa gets to sing. *Don't* sing with him."

"Pemmy won't sing either," Luki whispered.

"You are such a good, good girl," Tante Berthe said. "All right. No matter what you hear, you stay in the trunk until I open it."

Tante Berthe set sheets and blankets over her.

Luki held Pemmy tightly, and she touched one of the little flowers on the sheet as it settled onto her face. It was pretty fabric. It was soft. It smelled like Tante Berthe's laundry soap and also the salty air outside, where Tante Berthe hung the laundry to dry, and it smelled a little of the rocks along the shore here, where the sea sometimes splashed up in great spray clouds even bigger than the ones at the dreaming log.

"Don't be afraid, Pemmy," she whispered as the lid of the trunk closed them into darkness. "You're really fast, like all kangaroos. You could run away from anyone." Pemmy didn't like this hiding game, which wasn't really a game now.

She heard Brigitte's voice say, "They're at the door, Maman," along with some metal clicking just outside the trunk, above her ear. Then footsteps, Tante Berthe and Brigitte leaving.

The sound of the sea outside the window was wilder here than it had been with Papa at the cottage, but still Luki listened to it, like she used to listen in bed at night. She listened inside her head too, to Papa singing like he did at the dreaming log, *Wie ist die Welt so stille.*

Tante Berthe was speaking with some men. The men weren't quiet like she and Pemmy were. Their voices were loud and raspy. They didn't sound nice. Luki lay with her hand on Pemmy, trying to keep Papa's voice singing in her head.

Pemmy was very hot and very scared and wanting to know, silently, how long the song would continue, when the not-nice voices came close. Tante Berthe kept saying to the men that she would do whatever they wanted, but she was sorry, she didn't understand what they were asking. The words the men were using were some of the words of the song, Papa's words. Would these men know where Papa was? She wanted to ask them, but she'd promised Tante Berthe she wouldn't make a sound.

The men were asking about the trunk now, about the lock.

Luki felt a rush of fear. Was she locked inside? Didn't Tante Berthe know she would be good? She was a good girl and Pemmy was a good kangaroo and even Flat Joey was very well behaved.

"I don't understand, I'm sorry." Tante Berthe's voice was all wrong. Too high. She sounded like Pemmy when Pemmy was scared.

"Diese französischen Idioten," the man said.

A loud rattle sounded right near Luki's ear—an angry rattle and a man's voice demanding Tante Berthe unlock the trunk.

Luki wet herself. She didn't even know she had done it until it was done. She couldn't stop herself. But going tinkle didn't make noise.

"I'm sorry, I don't understand," Tante Berthe kept saying.

"Der Schlüssel!" the man insisted.

Luki understood. He wanted the key. Should she tell Tante Berthe that? The man sounded so angry, like he was about to hit someone.

Monday, June 17, 1940
LA BOURBOULE

Y ou can get out, Nanée," T said. "You can go to America. You
could take Peterkin with you. You could claim he's yours."

They were in La Bourboule, up in the salt peaks of Auvergne
where the Angladas, husband and wife doctors and friends of Danny's
family, ran a spa for children with respiratory diseases. The trees here
were full of birds calling to the morning sunrise, and Dagobert could
not be more loved by the children already, and there were no signs of
war—although whether that was because France had asked for peace
or because they were too far away, Nanée wasn't sure. As they prepared to go on, unhitching the trailer to save gas now that they had
help, she tried to imagine what it might be like if they stayed. But there
were still ships sailing from Bordeaux to England, or that was the rumor, and in just days, after the armistice was signed, a berth on a ship
to an enemy country might be impossible to get.

"From Bordeaux, we'll get a ship to England, T," she said. "All four
of us. You, me, Peterkin, and Dagobert."

T looked across the hitch to Nanée. "I became French when I married Danny. I'm no longer British, and Peterkin never has been."

Dagobert, sensing Nanée's alarm, nudged her arm and snuggled up
under her hand. She petted his just-washed fur as she tried to calm
herself. She had her American passport. Her American neutrality. She
would remain safe enough even in a Nazi-occupied France, at least for
a few days. But T was married to a man who had helped so many who
defied Hitler. Peterkin—Pierre Ungemach Bénédite—was the son of
a man who could so easily be on one of those lists the Nazis brought
to each country they conquered, to be arrested for defying the Reich.

T said, "I can petition to have my British nationality reinstated and
leave France only if Danny is . . ."

Is dead.

A desire to flee washed over Nanée. Even armed with her American neutrality, she was afraid of what was to come, what life would be like living under German occupation. It was an irrational fear, and it wasn't. She was helping Danny by helping his family, and the Gestapo were no kinder to those who helped their foes than to the foes themselves.

Nanée focused on the rough scratch of Dagobert licking her wrist, the soothing warmth of his love. She could take Peterkin. No one could fault her for helping a child. And taking Peterkin to safety in the United States would allow her to leave with her dignity intact.

Good lord, was she really concerned with her dignity?

She hugged Dagobert to her as if he were her child, hearing her father's voice, *What a brave girl you are*. She was seven again. At Marigold Lodge. They'd made a bonfire down by the lake, or the staff had made it for them, and she and her brothers were sitting on a fallen tree they called the log sofa, roasting marshmallows. The adults sat in chairs brought down for the season and a photographer from one of the Grand Rapids papers was taking photos for their society pages when the fire popped, spraying a magnificent spark cloud. A red ember struck Nanée's palm, so startling her that she only stared at the burn as Daddy stooped to her level, took her hand, and kissed the spot. "What a brave girl you are," he said. "You don't even cry." And the next morning, a photograph of the moment ran in the newspaper, with a caption suggesting Nanée was cut from the same strong cloth as Daddy was—a photograph he framed and set on his desk. He'd left Marigold Lodge to her too. The house and the land all the way to the log sofa and the lake. *To my brave girl*, he'd written in his will, as if what that newspaper had written about Nanée had ever been one bit true. Still, after Daddy died, she'd asked her mother to send her that photo. But the photograph Mother sent her was the one of Nanée with Daddy after she won that shooting contest when she was fourteen, and when she asked again for the newspaper photo, her mother had no idea what she was talking about.

Nanée looked from T's pleading face back to Dagobert, and pulled on his ears. He shook his head that way he did.

"We'll be okay, T," she said. "We'll get a ship from Bordeaux to England. We'll just lose your papers. No one can doubt you're British. No one can doubt Peterkin is your son."

EVEN COASTING DOWNHILL to conserve gas, they arrived at Brive on fumes, and waited an hour in line at a station only to have one of the cars ahead of them take the last of the fuel. It was early in the afternoon. There was, at least, a decent hotel where, at dinner that same night—all of Brive by then choking with refugees—T said she had bumped into someone she knew. "A rather vile woman Danny once nearly came to blows with. An archreactionary. Her husband has probably already settled into a high place in Pétain's defeatist government. But she has a car, and she has gas, and she's trying to get to her beast of a fascist husband in Bordeaux."

"Surely it hasn't come to that, all of us crowding into a car with a fascist," Nanée said. "We'll just buy some of her gas."

"She won't sell a drop, and she can't take all of us, or won't. She has room only for one more. And she's agreed to take you."

"Me? She doesn't even know me!"

"She sees an advantage to having an American passport in her car. There's room for you, and for Peterkin on your lap. Take him for me, Nan. For Danny and me. Take him to America with you."

"But . . . but we don't even have a passport for him."

"It will be chaos. With the French government falling, the Americans will be loading ships to get their citizens to safety."

"But T—"

"I'll take Dagobert with me back to La Bourboule," T insisted. "The children there already love him. We'll all take good care of him." She hugged Nanée fiercely, as if Nanée had already agreed.

"Thank you, Nanée, for saving my son."

Monday, June 17, 1940

A ROAD SOMEWHERE IN BRITTANY

Luki sat right up next to Tante Berthe in the car, which felt a little less scary; Tante Berthe was driving very fast. Luki was wearing Brigitte's white dress that she wore for her first communion, and Tante Berthe was saying again that Luki was to say she was Catholic, and yes, Pemmy too, Pemmy was a Catholic kangaroo professor.

"You're not going to be a Jewish girl, you understand that, right?"

Luki nodded even though she didn't understand at all, except that she knew it was important because Tante Berthe kept repeating it. Only Luki and Pemmy were moving this time, to live with Tante Berthe's sister, or all her sisters, at a church where Luki would kneel even though Papa didn't kneel. She was afraid if she said she didn't understand again, it would make Tante Berthe cry, but she didn't want to lie either. Papa said she was never to lie. So she just nodded, which she didn't think was a lie because a lie was words.

The car hurried along. Outside the window, cows ate the grass.

"If Pemmy was a cow," Luki said, "she would eat grass. But Pemmy isn't a cow."

"If Pemmy ran out of other things to eat, she could eat grass. Sometimes we have to pretend we're a little different than we are."

Luki giggled, imagining Pemmy eating grass right from the ground. Pemmy did not think this was very funny, but Flat Joey Letters giggled with her.

"Luki," Tante Berthe said, "if anyone asks you, you can tell them your papa kneels. He would want you to. It will keep you safer."

"Pemmy wishes Papa would come get us."

Tante Berthe hugged her close with one arm, her other hand still on the steering wheel.

"I tell Pemmy it's okay even though we can't take Papa's letters,"

Luki said, "because still he wrote them. He's not with the angels, be-cause he wrote us letters, even if we had to put them all in the fire."

Tante Berthe was quiet for a long time. Luki wondered if she knew about Flat Joey Letters and the photograph Luki wasn't supposed to have either. Luki made Flat Joey Letters before she put Flat Joey Num-bers in the fire. She told Pemmy it was okay because Flat Joeys were pretend; they were just a way to remember that Joey was safe with Papa, wherever Papa was.

"Luki," Tante Berthe said, "your papa is still writing to you. I know he is. Just like Brigitte's papa is writing to her. The letters can't get to us right now. But I promise you, your papa is writing to you."

Tuesday, June 18, 1940

BRIVE

Nanée dressed that morning in her favorite gray flannel slacks and some of her best jewelry—a diamond ring and her emerald earrings—but with her grandmother's pearls underneath her blouse and the diamond brooch that had belonged to generations of her father's family pinned inside her trouser pocket, the Schiaparelli fur bracelet that had only ever been hers there too. She packed nothing but a few toiletries, saving the space in the small satchel she could have at her feet for Peterkin's bunny and his clothes, while T moved through the motions of getting him ready, her voice, which had been so steady, now flat and toneless, necessary words and nothing more. T couldn't let any feeling creep in, or she would not be able to do this, and she had to do this; Nanée understood that.

At the car that was to take them to Bordeaux—a flivver no American would value particularly—its fascist owner eyed her with disappointment, no doubt wondering whether Nanée was really the kind of American who might open roads otherwise closed. The vile woman's maid sat in the back seat, surrounded by suitcases stacked so precariously that surely they would whack the poor girl in the head at the first turn. This woman valued her own possessions over other people's lives.

Nanée offered her most gracious smile. "Thank you for agreeing to take Pierre and me." Pierre. More upper-class than Peterkin. This silly woman would care about that.

T focused on Peterkin. She put one hand on each of his little cheeks and made him meet her gaze.

Nanée squatted down to Dagobert's level. She couldn't watch T saying goodbye to her son. She couldn't bear it. She could barely bear to say goodbye to Dagobert.

She took her white silk scarf—less clean than it once had been—from around her neck, and tied it around Dagobert's. It would smell of her. She kissed his little face twice, in the French way, leaving lipstick on his fur.

"I don't want to go either," she whispered. "But it's for Danny."

He licked her bare wrist, then her face. She petted the mess of his fur and kissed him twice again. "Surely even the Boches will love such a wonderful fellow," she said.

She was glad he couldn't understand her words.

She buried her face in Dagobert's then, her mouth open wide so that she would taste him, taste his fur and his little black nose, his eyes that had not stopped loving her even in her cowardice.

She climbed into the passenger seat then, and accepted Peterkin, and pulled the door shut so that T wouldn't have to close it. She refused to cry even as they drove off, Peterkin clutching the bunny and looking out the window at T and Dagobert.

Tuesday, June 18, 1940

AMBOISE

Luki didn't look up to the beautiful colored windows because there was a scary man up there who was bleeding from a crown of thorns on his head. The church had been pretty when she came with Sister Therese earlier, when the man in the robe talked and it was full of music and the nun held Luki's hand and sang in her beautiful voice. It still smelled like the pipe smoke of Papa's friends, and the Lady Mary wasn't scary, she was God's mutti, except Luki wasn't supposed to say *mutti* anymore. Reverend Mother said she must call even her own mutti "Maman," and nobody else was to know Luki was German.

"I know it's scary, but this is what good Catholic girls do," Luki said to Pemmy as she walked carefully up the side aisle where she knew she would find the Lady Mary, staying as far away from the wall and the scary paintings as she could. Pemmy was a Catholic kangaroo professor now and she was a girl too, and Catholic girls came to this place and prayed, which just meant you knelt down and talked to a statue. Luki didn't like the bleeding man, but the Lady Mary's face was pretty, so she came to pray to her.

She gasped: the bleeding man was lying here now, and he was reaching out, trying to grab her!

She turned and ran as fast as she could back up the aisle and through the door into the sunshine, which was so bright it blinded her.

IT WAS DARKER in the cellar even than in the church. Luki curled up with Sister Therese. She was so tired. She wanted to sleep, but every boom was so loud and shaking. She buried her face in Pemmy, feeling the edge of Flat Joey Letters tucked with the photograph in her pouch. "Don't be scared, Pemmy," she said, trying to sound like Sister

Therese. Sister Therese sounded scared whenever she said it, but her voice made Luki feel better.

Another boom came, and rat-a-tat-tats again and again, and more men's voices, not gentle voices like Papa's, but shouting. Mean. Some in the old words and some in the new ones, but even the voices using the new words were angry.

The booms again, one after another after another after another. And Sister Therese was pulling Luki into her lap, singing into her ear so she could hear even in the booms. The other nuns sang with her; Luki could hear their voices between the scary sounds. She tried to hear only their voices, tried to feel it was the angels the nuns sang about, the angels with Mutti, who used to sing her to sleep before only Papa did. "Il te couvrira de ses plumes; tu trouveras un refuge sous ses ailes." *He will cover you with his feathers; you will find refuge under his wings.*

Saturday, June 22, 1940
CAMP DES MILLES

Y ou have to come with us, I tell you," Max insisted, but Edouard only watched through the iron fence as the line filed out the Camp des Milles gate toward the waiting boxcars. He knew Max was right; you had to do nothing more than listen to the retreat, regiment after regiment, truck after truck, tank after tank. If the internees were in the camp when the Germans overran Aix-en-Provence, their circumstances would be dire.

Edouard had woken that morning to see Walter Hasenclever, who slept separated from him only by a suitcase, unmoving. Even in the dim light through the distant, dirty window, Edouard knew the Czech novelist was dead, that sometime in the night he'd taken the overdose of veronal he brought to the camp. More than two thousand of the camp's three thousand internees, though, had chosen to take their papers and board the train for the border, to try to get out before the Germans arrived. Camp commander Goruchon had made the decision to let the men go on his own; the subprefecture knew nothing about it.

Max called back to Edouard, "Don't be a fool! Come with us!"

"What, and leave the poor fleas and lice and bedbugs with nobody to feast on?" Edouard said.

He wasn't a fool, but the train would be sealed until it crossed the border, and once he was in Spain there would be no coming back, no way for him to reach Luki in France.

He'd been able to write her once a week and receive letters from Berthe and her before the Germans took Paris, but he hadn't had word of Luki since the letter she'd written by herself, which he kept in his pocket. He didn't know whether Berthe and her daughter had fled Paris, whether they'd taken Luki with them, or where they might be if they had. Luki living with Berthe under Nazi rule—the thought was terrifying. But so was the idea that Luki might be anywhere in France or even in the world without him knowing where.

He didn't wait for the train to leave. He didn't allow time for his own fear to tempt him to change his mind. He returned to his straw mat under the bare bulb and opened his suitcase. He took his Leica out and set it aside. He took the top sheet from the box of stationery and, with one hand on his camera, began to write in the tiniest script he could manage, *My Luki* . . . Another letter he couldn't send.

There would be a way out. There had to be. He wasn't so naive as to believe Goruchon would open the gates and allow Edouard and the others to walk out. The camp commander was taking a huge risk even with the train, but an entire locked train might be explained as prisoners in transit lost in the chaos of the German invasion. Anything more would seal Goruchon's fate when the Germans overran Aix-en-Provence. But in the chaos of the invasion, there would be a way out, just as there had been a way out of Germany.

Except there hadn't been a way out for Elza.

Saturday, June 22, 1940

BIARRITZ

Nanée sat at the American consulate in Biarritz for the fourth time in as many days, looking for permission to take Peterkin to the United States. Despite the connections of the vile woman they'd ridden with and her remarkable knack for backing up and speeding around roadblocks she couldn't talk her way through, there'd been no getting into Bordeaux. Nanée and Peterkin had ridden with her to a château outside Biarritz, where Nanée spent a single long night being appalled at the certainty of the woman's fascist friends that Hitler would bring order to France. The next morning she took rooms in a hotel in town where she'd stayed so often that the concierge remembered her. She hired a girl to watch Peterkin, bought a suit from her favorite boutique—regretting she'd left the Robert Piguet in which she could convince anyone of anything in the trailer back in La Bourboule—and set about trying to talk her way around bureaucrats.

"As my colleagues have already told you," the latest bureaucrat in the phalanx was now saying, "you may of course leave any time you would like. You have your American passport. But we cannot allow you to take this French child without his passport and a valid French exit visa."

Nanée wondered if there wasn't some way to back up from this beast of a bureaucrat and race around him.

"By the time I get permission from the French," she insisted, "the armistice will be signed. Any permission the French granted me today might be no good tomorrow."

The nasty little functionary responded, "Then you might ask yourself why you continue to sit here rather than hurrying on to inquire with the French authorities."

AT THE FRENCH prefecture of Bayonne, Nanée presented her single passport as if it were all that could possibly be needed for her to leave for America with a young French boy. The man across the desk examined it like a jeweler looking through a loupe at a fake.

"Of course you may have an exit visa anytime," he said.

Nanée gave him Peterkin's name with her own.

"I'll need to see the boy's passport," he said.

How was it that now, when they ought to be a mess of panic, the French authorities were showing a remarkable ability to stick to *no* as the answer to anything? But she couldn't risk offending this lout's fragile French pride.

She explained that Peterkin had been separated from his mother in the flight from Paris—a story she could tell with the confidence of a woman speaking the truth.

He would have none of it.

"Peter has an aunt in Maine who will take him in," she explained. "Surely you don't want to keep an American boy in France during a war."

"But the war is over, mademoiselle."

Nanée lowered her gaze, as ashamed as she could manage. She whispered, "The truth, sir, is that he's my son."

He eyed her ringless fingers.

"Only mine. The father has no idea of him." Avoiding the word *illegitimate*, which would leave him thinking less of her. Less sympathetic. Less willing to help.

"You will have to prove that also, mademoiselle." The last word spit out in distaste.

For heaven's sake, was she really stuck with the only absolute prude of a man in all of France?

She didn't wait for him to explain what she already knew—that even illegitimate children were issued birth certificates.

BACK AT THE hotel, she sent a telegram she hoped would reach T. She had failed. They would have to meet up somewhere so she could return Peterkin to his mother, although she had no idea how she would manage that. The trains weren't running, and she had no car, nor any certainty that she would be allowed to take Peterkin anywhere.

With nothing left to do, she woke the next morning, checked for the answer from T she knew could not possibly have arrived yet, and took Peterkin to stroll on the promenade and dig in the sand.

A week later, with no word back yet from T, a low rumble woke Nanée—a sound she knew without ever having heard it. She jumped out of bed, pulled on slacks, scooped up the sleeping Peterkin, and ran down to a lobby lit by a single lamp at an empty reception desk.

From here, the *stomp stomp stomp* of boots on pavement was deafening, and still the boy slept.

She joined the frumpy hotel clerk in the doorway, her back to the rooms where she had, in years past, danced and drunk champagne and flirted with men in tuxedos, with no idea that that time might ever end.

She held Peterkin more closely as she watched an endless stream of vehicles and tanks and German guns pass on the road, German soldiers marching in orderly formation, tall and fair, clean-shaven, and perhaps handsome if you didn't know they were horrid. She breathed in the slightly sour smell of Peterkin's hair and his scalp, this sleeping child who was not her own, who would never be. She nuzzled her face to his and whispered—to him or to herself or to whatever god might be watching over them, although that was hard to imagine— "And so they have arrived."

PART II

The Villa Air-Bel came into our lives, first as a house out of town for the Bénédites and myself . . . The Surrealists who found themselves in the region soon flocked around Breton for afternoons and evenings of talk and games . . . Strangely enough, we rarely referred to it as Air-Bel, or the villa, but called it the château, which was a gross exaggeration and had no business on the lips of such a democratic left-wing bunch, anyway.

—Mary Jayne Gold, *Crossroads Marseille, 1940*

Thursday, September 5, 1940
MARSEILLE

On the promenade in Marseille, where Nanée had always bought postcards, peanuts, and Eskimo Pies, a single peddler's hoarse voice offered a newspaper no one wanted to read. France had accepted peace under onerous terms: the Germans kept two million French prisoners of war, extracted heavy financial reparations, and split France in two. Germany controlled the north and the Atlantic seaboard while Vichy prime minister Philippe Pétain, as authoritarian as Hitler and beholden to him, called for a "new moral order" in the south, replacing the French motto "Liberté, égalité, fraternité" with "Travail, famille, patrie"—work, family, homeland—by which they meant to shame any woman who had ever dared bob her hair or take a drink or a job or a man to her bed. Nanée had taken advantage of the new Nazi interest in getting foreigners away from the Atlantic ports to finally return Peterkin to T, who was in Tours by then to find Danny's mother, having left Dagobert with the adoring children up in La Bourboule. Nanée caught a freight train to collect Dagobert, her car, which T had taken back there, and her trailer of possessions. But she couldn't bear to return to Nazi-occupied Paris, so she came instead to rat-infested, brothel-laden, relentlessly sunny Marseille.

She meant to arrange a Pan Am Clipper from Portugal or, failing that, a ship on which she would have to pray German U-boats would respect neutrality. When it came time to leave France, though, she couldn't fathom what she would do back in the States. Would she move into the Evanston house with Mother and Misha? Live alone at Marigold Lodge? Stay in New York in hopes of contributing somehow to the war effort despite her country's stubborn isolationism and her own complete lack of skills? So she renewed her foreign-resident permit and stayed in this city in which every language was spoken, all the refugees from Stalin's purges and Hitler's sweep through Europe crowding the city's hotels and cafés and streetcars, along with the Spahis and Zouaves and Senegalese soldiers who'd fought with the French, now trying to make their way home.

With the better hotels already full, she counted herself lucky to find a dark little room at the Continental, too near the old port's ugly transporter bridge and fishing boats to be elegant, even without its faded blue wallpaper flowers of a type never seen in actual soil. But the room did have—along with a tarnished brass bed, three torturously straight-backed chairs at a pale wooden table, and a single tired pink lamp—a private bathroom with that ultimate of luxuries: a claw-footed tub.

She set the photograph of her father and herself on the dresser, propped beside it the art photograph of the woman seeming to swim in murky water, *On Being an Angel*, and littered the room with her books. She stored tins of meat, biscuits and chocolate, and bottles of whiskey and wine in the armoire, on the top shelf of which she stashed her Webley. And she paid an exorbitant price for a three-band radio with a splintered walnut case, chipped Bakelite knobs, and a perfectly intact brass double-needle dial she could tune to the BBC news.

Her friend Miriam Davenport saw her name on a list at the American consulate, and in no time they were living in each other's pockets. Miriam couldn't be more different from Nanée. She wore her ash-blond hair parted from forehead to nape and plaited into two braids tied together atop her head like a cartoon milkmaid rather than a Smith College graduate in France on a Carnegie scholarship. Her laugh was too loud, and her clothes hung poorly. She was engaged; she'd come to Marseille in search of a way to get her fiancé out of Yugoslavia. Like Nanée, she'd lost her father, but while Nanée's daddy had left a fortune, Miriam's left only debts.

Still, they met every evening at the Pelikan Bar, where Miriam greeted Dagobert by exclaiming, "Hitler! Hitler!"—the name alone provoking him to bark like mad, which made everyone laugh. They ate dinners out, since the meat and bread rationing didn't yet apply to restaurants, then moved on to conversations in the local bars about when Germany would occupy all of France. Nights often ended with friends crowding into Nanée's hotel room to listen to the 1:00 a.m. BBC broadcast while taking turns soaking in Nanée's tub—a radio, booze, and a bath luxuries Nanée was happy to share.

Now Nanée walked with Dagobert on leash toward the Hôtel Splendide, where Miriam was going to introduce her to her boss, Varian Fry. Fry had recently arrived in Marseille, sent by the newly formed American Emergency Rescue Committee—in French, Centre Américain de Secours, or CAS—with a list of some two hundred notable artists and intellectuals: Picasso, Chagall, Lipchitz, and Matisse; writers like Hannah Arendt; Nobel Laureates; and even the journalist who'd bestowed on the German National Socialist Party the nickname Nazi, Bavarian slang for "bumpkin" or "simpleton," which became so ubiquitous that Hitler's only recourse was to embrace it. Fry was working behind the political cover of providing perfectly legal aid to refugees and a CAS "affiliation" with the respected American Red Cross to quietly arrange illegal escapes from France for those on his list. Surely this Fry fellow could use Nanée's help, and her money too.

But Varian Fry was reluctant even to meet Nanée, Miriam had warned; he didn't think people like Nanée existed.

"Does he imagine me a spy for the Gestapo or Vichy or both?" Nanée responded, and they'd laughed together as they laughed at everything.

Then Miriam replied matter-of-factly, "I'm afraid this *is* how Varian believes spies work, though—sending beautiful women to infiltrate."

Nanée wanted to do something to help, the same as any decent person in this newly terrible world surely must. Having failed at getting Peterkin out of France and at finding Danny, she was now intent on learning from someone who knew what they were doing. And the people on Varian Fry's list included many of the same people Danny had arranged French residency permits for before the war. If she couldn't help Danny or his family, perhaps she could help those he'd helped himself.

Nanée slipped through a lobby crowded with refugees, pale to a person despite the long Provence summer just ending, and desperate after so many days wearing the same clothes and hiding out in dirty little rooms. She took the stairs up to room 307, a single room filled with volunteers interviewing refugees from the edges of the bed or leaning on radiators or sitting on the floor—a cacophony of conversation carried on over giggles and squeals from a playground the makeshift office overlooked. And there was Miriam, interviewing at a desktop made from a mirror, its former placement visible in unfaded paint on a nearby wall.

They hardly had to move in the cramped room to reach a man in horn-rimmed glasses, rolled shirtsleeves, and a loosened Harvard tie. Decent posture. A lean if not hardy build, thinning hair, a domed forehead, and a broad nose. It was hard to fathom how Miriam found the bookishly earnest thirtysomething Varian Fry attractive, but then most women prefer their heroes to be handsome, and so often we see what we want to see.

Fry, speaking in a clipped Eastern Seaboard monotone, was showing a list of names to a refugee, asking, "Do you know the whereabouts of any of the others on my list?"

Who would have imagined the hardest part of helping famous refugees escape would be finding them? But the peace treaty with Germany required France to "surrender on demand" anyone requested for extradition by the Gestapo, which had in mind to hunt down every voice ever raised against Hitler, including most of the people on Fry's list. And the Marseille police were a mixed lot; some would look away, but others conducted mass arrests of refugees and hauled them off to internment camps. What any official did on any given day was a measure of the state of his own nerves. Some two hundred thousand refugees stayed in Marseille anyway, the chaos of temporary grape- and olive-harvest workers and organized crime making it possible to disappear here while at the same time searching for an escape. Nobody advertised where they lived, though, not wanting to end up in Camp des Milles or the hellhole of Saint-Cyprien, much less in Gestapo hands.

The refugee speaking with Fry pointed to a name on the list. "He's living at the Bar Mistral on Point Rouge." Another—an art critic and specialist in Negro sculpture—had hanged himself at the Spanish border when they wouldn't let him out of France.

"I don't want to be like him," the poor fellow said.

"There are ways to get people out," Fry assured him.

The man wept at Fry's offer of money for clothes, having not had a kindness in months.

Varian offered his handkerchief, apologizing that it wasn't fresher, then saw him off with, "I'll see you soon in New York."

An optimist, Nanée thought, but then Varian Fry had not been long in France.

As Miriam introduced her, Fry eyed the Robert Piguet suit Nanée had worn to impress him: a blue darker and less flashy than royal yet not quite the dull everyday of navy, with soft yellow pinstripes, a conservative midcalf skirt, and a short jacket that escaped boredom through its soft yellow lining and a stylish collar stretching to her shoulders. He frowned at Dagobert, who wasn't at all *that* kind of poodle, not prissy or clipped or even overbrushed, but she could see Fry adding him to the equation, somehow finding her as frivolous as Dagobert might look if he *were* pampered and chic.

"I'm sorry, Miss Gold, that Miriam has put you to the trouble," Fry said, "but we don't need—"

"I am not a dilettante, Mr. Fry," Nanée interrupted, but softly, regretting now the silk flying scarf she'd added at her throat for luck, white again but somewhat tattered from Dagobert's love.

"For Pete's sake, Varian," Miriam said. "Nanée gave her *airplane* to the French military long before you even *imagined* helping—"

Fry silenced her, then walked to the loo, motioning them to follow.

In the tiny bathroom, a fellow stretched out in the bathtub was dictating a letter to a woman perched with her typewriter on the bidet. The two looked up, not at all surprised to have company, and gathered their things and left, closing the door behind them as Fry turned on the tub faucet and the sink tap.

"We must assume we're bugged," he said, "and in any event, the walls are paper thin."

Nanée objected, "But you're interviewing—"

"We're extremely careful with our words," Fry said. "Those we're trying to rescue—Picasso, Chagall, Matisse—"

"Picasso has placed a sign on the door of his studio on Grands Augustins that reads simply 'Ici'—Here—with no intention of leaving Paris," Nanée said, her irritation getting the better of her. "Chagall is so focused on painting that he hasn't noticed the Germans have taken France. And Matisse insists that if everyone of merit leaves, France will not survive. You're intent on helping the famous, who often don't even want to be helped, when—"

Miriam interrupted, "What Nanée is trying to say—"

"Is that she is far too outspoken for a position that requires the utmost discretion," Fry said.

Dagobert chose that moment to put his paws on the edge of the tub and lick the flowing water. He shook his head, spraying Fry's pant legs. A look crossed Fry's face: *She can't even control her dog.*

"What I'm trying to say, perhaps inelegantly," she said more gently, "is that it's fine to help famous artists and thinkers escape France, but why is one life to be valued over another? Why spend scarce resources finding those who wish to remain hidden when there are refugees so desperate to get out that they line up at your very public door?"

"The Emergency Rescue Committee has sent me here with a list of people for whom we can arrange American visas," Fry protested. "They must be my priority. And while Vichy may not be Hitler, Hitler—"

Dagobert barked madly, startling Fry.

Miriam laughed her overloud laugh. "Hitler, Hitler," she whispered to Dagobert, sending him barking madly again.

"Dagobert is no fan of the man with the mustache," Miriam explained.

Varian, nonplussed, continued, "Our resources aren't unlimited."

"Your resources aren't," Nanée agreed. Miriam had told her he'd already spent the $3,000 he brought and, despite generous friends like Peggy Guggenheim and the *New Yorker*'s Janet Flanner, was strapped for cash. "And yet you pay Marseille's gangsters a percentage of your dollars just to convert them to francs, when the mafia have as much to gain in converting francs to dollars. Me, I have an American passport—"

"As do I," Fry said.

"Your passport shows you came just weeks ago, to help refugees. Mine shows I've lived in France for a decade. Which of us do you suppose can more easily move around France to, say, courier messages or even people?"

With the Marseille docks now closely watched by the Vichy police, the Spanish border was for most refugees the only way out. But to get to the border, refugees needed French transit visas, which they could not get without notifying Vichy of their whereabouts and making themselves vulnerable to a roundup. And to get across that border into Spain, they needed French exit visas, which Vichy no longer granted to former citizens of the Reich lest the French offend Hitler by allowing his critics to escape his wrath. Sometimes the border check at the Cerbère train station would look the other way. Some refugees used a map of a secret path over the Pyrenees. But stateless persons caught traveling without safe conduct passes risked imprisonment in France, or deportation to a German labor camp and the starvation rations and brutal work routine of a place like Dachau, or even a firing squad. Anyone, stateless or not, caught leaving France illegally risked the same, as did those caught helping them.

Nanée fingered the diamond brooch on her suit lapel and gave Fry her best attractive-heiress-who-might-convince-anyone-of-anything look. She lightly pulled Dagobert's leash so he stood pertly, and she took Miriam's arm. She pulled her own single set of documents from her handbag and offered them to Fry as if she were holding two sets of papers.

"Our transit visas, Officer," she said.

She'd meant to make him laugh. He did not.

"So you want to be our postmistress?" he asked.

What Nanée wanted was to feel useful, to have a purpose. "Perhaps your post*master*. *That* would be terrific cover. The Nazis never imagine a woman can do anything at all." She smiled meaningfully at Fry. "So few in the world do."

Miriam shot her a look. "Nanée wants to help bankroll our effort too."

"But any amounts I contribute would be used to save ordinary souls," Nanée said.

Fry frowned. "The refugees on my list have contributed—"

"I can take messages anywhere you need them taken," Nanée interrupted. "I can help your friends who don't have French transit visas get to the border. I can even help you change money without using the French mafia, but—"

"Really, you cannot—"

"The people you're helping—some have francs they want to change into dollars when they get to the States. They can leave that money here with you, to fund your operations, and I'll provide an equal amount in dollars for them from my accounts at home. *Voilà.* We effectively bring my money over from the States to fund your effort, without any transfer trail to alert Vichy."

Fry eyed her differently now, but said, "I don't believe you appreciate the effort it takes to obtain American visas for people we don't—"

Miriam opened the bathroom door to the room crowded with refugees Fry was already trying to help, even though they weren't on his list.

Fry watched them for a long moment, then improbably stooped to Dagobert's level, looked into his face, and whispered, "Hitler, Hitler."

Dagobert barked so enthusiastically that Fry recoiled before carefully offering the back of his hand. Dagobert sniffed it, then licked it.

Fry rubbed Dagobert's ears. "You aren't a bad fellow after all, are you?" he said.

He stood, adjusting his glasses as he frowned again at Nanée's suit. "We'll start a second list," he conceded. "People for whom we don't yet have the promise of visas."

"In honor of Nanée," Miriam said, "we'll call it the Gold list."

"I won't disappoint you, Mr. Fry," Nanée said.

"Varian," he answered, and he nodded to the open bathroom door, inviting them to leave first.

And already Miriam was introducing Nanée to the whole merry gang: Monsieur Maurice, a Romanian doctor, was Varian's consiglieri. German-born economist Beamish Hermant specialized in fake passports and black-market money swaps. Heinz Oppenheimer organized the interviews and kept the books. Charlie Fawcett, an American sculptor who spoke French with a thick Georgia drawl nobody could understand, allowed refugees entrance to the office while watching for Vichy police. Lena Fischmann took shorthand in French, German, and English, spoke Spanish, Polish, and Russian too, and was a master at hiding illegal expenditures. And Gussie, nineteen and Polish and Jewish, looked so like a skinny fourteen-year-old Aryan boy that he could carry coded telegrams to the central post office and go from *tabac* to *tabac* to buy blank identity cards for their forger without ever being stopped.

"We're moving to new space tomorrow," Miriam told Nanée. "A Jewish leather goods maker is vacating a floor of a building before the Vichy seize it, and he's given it to us. Number sixty rue Grignan. We interview from eight till noon, take lunch, then conference as long as it takes to decide which of the day's interviewees we might help."

Wednesday, September 11, 1940
THE CAS OFFICE, MARSEILLE

The new CAS office—up a dark stairway at the back of the building to a floor split into two rooms, with Varian's office at the back—still smelled of leather goods. On the wall across from the windows, in place of the shelves of handbags and briefcases and wallets, now hung an American flag. The rest of the front room was dedicated to square wooden tables and hard wooden chairs like the one from which Nanée was interviewing a charming young Austrian artist, hoping to get him through the bureaucratic nightmare that was the first step for a refugee escaping France.

"Do you have a usable passport?" she asked him, the next question from the script. With Austria now part of Germany, an Austrian passport got you exactly nowhere, and all German Jews had been stripped of their citizenship. But sometimes refugees had managed passports from other countries. "Other travel documents?" Sometimes a country issued a document in lieu of passport. "An overseas entry visa, preferably to the United States or Mexico?" "One to anywhere else?"

Well, that saved her having to ask discreetly if his documents were genuine. She marked the answers down in their code.

"Anyone in the US who might sponsor you?"

The artist had an agent who represented his work in New York. That was something.

Spanish and Portuguese transit visas? A temporary French residency permit? A work permit? Money? Again, no and no and no. He'd had a residency permit, but he'd destroyed it. He'd been on the ghost train from Camp des Milles, one of the two thousand refugees who'd nearly reached the Spanish border before the train turned back on news of a train of Germans arriving that might take them prisoner. They'd all destroyed their papers, better not to have proof of being a refugee of the Reich, only to learn that the rumored Germans were, ironically, their own refugee train. A few, like this fellow, had managed to open a boxcar and jump somewhere near Arles, but most stayed aboard to be returned to the camp, afraid that jumping would lead to being found and shot on sight by the invading Germans.

"All right. Can you tell me about anything you've done to oppose the Nazis?"

He'd designed anti-Nazi posters in Austria, which ought to be worth a ticket to freedom, but they were hard to come by. Still, if he had references, his name might make it onto the list for visa applications taken each night first to a police station in a blue-lit alley off rue Colbert for the needed police stamp, then to the night window at the post office behind the stock exchange, where the clerk who answered the bell would count the words and mark it in purple ink, make them sign to attest the words had no hidden meaning, and cable it to the States. The man listed several names, and Nanée noted them, but she didn't know any of them, and all references had to be people known to Varian or someone else at the CAS, lest they be duped into offering illegal escape to someone who turned out to be an infiltrator of the Vichy or German sort.

"Edouard Moss would vouch for me," the refugee suggested.

Edouard Moss. The photographer who'd held his daughter in his lap that entire night at her Paris apartment, even as he drew the head in flight goggles and a gilded birdcage that both was and wasn't her. She kept that sketch even still, tucked behind the art photo on her dresser at the hotel, of the woman swimming—the photograph she bought when the Edouard Moss photograph she'd so loved, the push-up man, wasn't for sale.

Dagobert hopped up from under her chair to greet Gussie, who said Varian wanted a moment when she was free.

"I'll be there in just a minute," she said, offering Gussie her best smile. The boy had such a crush on her that Varian mercilessly teased him, leaving her sure it would kill the poor kid's spirit and with it any chance he might have for love. But Varian insisted nobody had any real chance for love, so they might as well have some fun.

Nanée asked the refugee, "Is he in the States? Edouard Moss?"

"He was at Camp des Milles with me before the armistice."

"He took the train with you?"

"The ghost train? I don't know. He wasn't in my boxcar."

Edouard Moss could be anywhere, then, or nowhere at all.

"Anyone else who could vouch for you?"

"Maybe Danny Bénédite? He got me my residency permit."

"Great," she said. "We know Danny." She'd just gotten word that T had found him, thank heaven. He'd been evacuated from Dunkirk, but returned to France to carry on the fight with six hundred men from his division. He was in a railroad station in Poitiers when Pétain asked for peace, so he laid low in Meyrueis, avoiding the German roundup of French soldiers until word of T's whereabouts reached him through someone who knew someone who knew someone else, the way anyone knew anything in Vichy France. They were now quietly settling with Peterkin on an uncle's Languedoc farm.

Nanée finished with the interviewee and put everything properly in the file before making her way, Dagobert beside her, to Varian's office—a smaller room crowded with everything that had been cleared of the front room: empty shelves, packing cases, and stray inventory, briefcases and handbags and wallets. Varian, at an oversize desk spread with papers, nodded to Lena, who closed her steno pad without being asked and left, closing the door.

Nanée supposed she was in for it. But *she* wasn't the source of the rumors. She'd heard Varian was going to Portugal from the irreproachable Lena, who wanted to enlist her in convincing him to bring back soap; even honest Miriam had taken to visiting the American consulate for the sole purpose of nabbing bars from their ladies' room, there being no decent soap to be bought in all of France.

She stood waiting, Dagobert mercifully quiet beside her.

"I'll be away from the office for a few days," Varian said.

It was true, then, unlike most rumors circulating through Marseille: the Emergency Rescue Committee back in the States was insisting that Varian's time here was up and he needed to go home. He couldn't leave, but nor could he detail in a letter his reasons for staying, as the Vichy government read all their mail. So he was going to Portugal to argue his case. She wondered if the rest of the rumor was true too, that on the way he would personally escort four of his "protégés," as he liked to call the refugees he helped, over the border, and check on five who'd been picked up by the Gestapo in Spain. He would be risking imprisonment, a labor camp, a firing squad.

"I'm leaving Maurice in charge," he said. "Can I count on you to help him keep things moving along here?"

"Of course, Varian," she answered evenly. "Anything you need." Thinking he wasn't so very different from the new "work, family, homeland" French government, leaving one of the men in charge. But no, that wasn't fair. Varian was a prince compared to the disgusting den of defeatists that was Vichy. He was married to a woman who'd been an editor at the *Atlantic Monthly*. He gave both Lena and Miriam plenty of responsibility. It was only her he didn't trust with the details of what he meant to do—never mind that she'd already committed five thousand dollars to be swapped for refugee francs to fund this effort, never mind that she showed up each morning as early as anyone, and sat in the office all day doing interviews, and never once suggested that her freedom to move about on account of her American passport was being underutilized, even though it was.

"All right, then," he said. "Thank you."

"But it will be Friday the thirteenth," she said. If Varian left tomorrow, he and his protégés would arrive in Cerbère that evening and try to cross the border the next day, Friday.

"Gussie is coming with me as far as the border," he said. "No doubt he'll carry his copy of *L'envers et l'endroit* to keep us all on the right side of luck."

Nobody ever did stop Gussie, but Nanée chalked that up to his jacket and tie, his strawberry-blond hair, and his sweet young face rather than that lucky book of Camus essays.

"Why you, Varian?" Nanée asked on impulse.

Varian set down his pen and studied her. "You mean because I'm nothing more than an American journal editor, with no apparent qualifications for spiriting people wanted by the Nazis out of France? But I do speak French and German, and my very lack of skills leaves me unlikely to be the subject of a Gestapo file. And you, Nanée?"

His "very lack of skills," much like hers.

"How did you get our country to agree to give you visas for your list?" she persisted. "They're leftist or downright Communist, and mostly Jewish, and lord knows anti-Semitism is alive and well under the Stars and Stripes."

Varian leaned back in his chair. "The committee sent two representatives to appeal to Mrs. Roosevelt," he said. "It didn't hurt that, just days before, she'd seen a photograph of her friend Lion Feuchtwanger interned at Camp des Milles—and just weeks after he'd been received by then French president Lebrun. Before our deputation left her office, she'd called her husband to assure him that if he refused to authorize our visas, German immigrant leaders, with the help of American friends, would rent a ship to bring them to Washington and cruise up and down the East Coast until the American people, out of shame and anger, forced him and Congress to permit them to land."

Nanée waited, one of her few skills being an Evanston-bred ability to allow men permission to brag on themselves.

"I came because no one else would," Varian said.

Dagobert tilted his head, studying Varian, then trotted over to him. To Nanée's surprise, Varian set a hand gently on his head.

"I was in Berlin in July of 1935," he said, "and happened upon an anti-Jewish riot, Nazis brutally kicking and spitting on a man lying helpless on a sidewalk, his head covered with blood. The police did nothing to stop it, and neither did I. I went home and wrote about it, a piece almost no one read."

It was, she supposed, the same reason she had joined his effort—because she couldn't live with herself if she didn't help. He'd left a good job, a wife, a home, and friends to do it when no one else would. Perhaps there was a more interesting soul behind the Harvard tie, the I-don't-believe-you-appreciate admonitions, and the unrelenting optimism than she'd given him credit for.

"Well, travel safely, Varian," she said. "And do please bring back some soap."

Wednesday, September 11, 1940
CAMP DES MILLES

Edouard lifted one of the last bricks from a pile near a guard tower and passed it on to Max, who passed it to the next person, who in turn passed it on again, the men nearly as uniform as the bricks now, with their shaved heads and their ragged clothes, their bony bodies, bony faces. The line stretched all the way across the courtyard to a growing pile of bricks by the factory door, the camp full again now that most of the men who'd nearly escaped on the ghost train were back. The good old days of Commander Goruchon and relaxed discipline were over. Theoretically, Les Milles was now the camp for internment of "foreigners of the Jewish race" who intended to emigrate, and who among them didn't intend to leave France if only they had the chance? But the Vichy government had transferred the administration of the camp to the *gardes mobiles*, a particularly unforgiving branch of the French police.

Beyond the iron rails and the barbed wire, a woman walked by.

"Jumbo!" Max called out. "Your wife!"

Jumbo emerged from one of the latrines, already dropping his mop and looking toward the fence. His wife was no longer there; no passerby was allowed to stop to look in. Still, he ran full speed straight toward the wall she'd disappeared behind, and Edouard and Max gave him a boost up so he could peek over the top.

"Isabelle!"

Already, Jumbo was being pulled down by one of the guards.

Already, Edouard and Max were again moving bricks.

"Must be nice to have a French wife who comes once a week from Marseille just to walk by for a glimpse of you," Max said, his own Leonora having sold their house in France and returned home to Spain.

Edouard rolled the bit of straw in his mouth, the most solid thing he had to chew to stave off hunger now that the toothpicks he'd made last for days each were gone. Next week he would have kitchen duty, an entire seven days of collecting potato peels from the floor at the end of the day, scraps he would try in vain to make last for the intervening weeks before he had kitchen duty again.

"At least we're not on latrine duty today," Max said. "This exercise is good for my sleep."

"You sleep here?" Edouard joked, and they both laughed glumly.

"Me? No, I lie awake, trying to come up with distractions so I don't think of the bromides they put in our food eroding my memory."

As Edouard passed another brick to Max, he remembered waking in his bed in the cottage at Sanary-sur-Mer, soothed by the ocean as Luki slept in the room beside his. He still had no idea where she might be, whether she was living in hiding, or even if she was still in Paris. He'd had no word for three months. With the armistice, Germany had decreed there would be no mail between the free and occupied zones, leaving no way for Berthe to get word to him. Not that he could get there even if by some miracle he managed to gain release from Camp des Milles; even French citizens who were Jewish were forbidden to return to occupied France. The Nazis wanted free rein to seize their wealth for the Reich.

Edouard didn't even know what had happened to the cottage. Had Vichy confiscated it? It was tucked so far away from the world that they might not even know it was there, or that it was empty. He wanted to claim it to protect his property, the only thing of value he might sell to raise funds for passage for Luki and him to some other country, but to inquire about it would be to invite attention, to ask to have it taken from him. The Vichy government was grabbing property left behind even by French citizens like the Rothschilds and Charles de Gaulle. And there would be no release from Camp des

Milles for Edouard. The only way anyone walked out of this camp other than under armed guard now was if his paperwork to emigrate was in order, his passage paid, and his boat about to leave. And the only reason anyone's papers were in order was because the Gestapo hadn't yet organized the enforcement of Article 19 of the Franco-German armistice, the "surrender on demand" clause. No one was working for Edouard's release, and this reprieve would not last.

"I'm going to work on that fresco tonight," he said, trying to raise Max's spirits the way Max so often did for him.

"If we're still making art, we're still alive," Max said.

A guard called out, "Reverse!"

The men groaned, but they reversed the direction of the flow of bricks. In the high sun, Edouard set the one he'd just lifted from the pile back onto it, and accepted from Max the brick he'd just handed him, to be stacked right back where it had started.

EDOUARD PAINTED WITH Max that evening on a brick wall in the underground of the old tile factory. He ought to be capturing this all with his camera, the men at work and the art everywhere. Yet he couldn't. It was getting worse, his distance from his art. At first, he was able still to look through the lens. He framed shots. Set the f-stop. Focused. He rationalized: he had limited film and no way to develop it, even the water here too foul for rinsing film.

"I don't even know why we do this," he said to Max. "Why we keep creating art out of nothing while we devolve into brick dust."

Max studied him, then picked up a brick and began with a penknife to chip at a hole in it. Dust reflected in the light of the dim overhead bulb. Slowly, others gathered to watch as Max dug and dug at that brick, which began to take shape as a face.

"It staves off hunger, making art does," Max reminded him. "It's a balm for anger. You have a daughter, Edouard. I have a son. We're lucky. We have children for whom we must stay alive."

Max dug into the brick again. Edouard watched, wondering if it was Max's son he was sculpting—his son as the young boy who had never really lived with Max, or as the grown man the son now was, safe in New York. Edouard wondered whether Max ever doubted that he deserved to call the boy his son.

He said, "I have to get to Paris. I have to get to Luki."

"If your daughter is still in Paris," Max said, "I hope she's hidden from the Germans."

"I don't know," Edouard said. "I don't even know."

Max put a hand lightly on his shoulder, the way he sometimes did just for the assurance that they were still human, that they could still feel. "And yet you must know she is somewhere," he said. "You would feel it in your heart if she were not."

THAT NIGHT, LIKE every night, Edouard sat on his straw mat under the bare bulb and opened his suitcase. He took out his camera, set it aside. Then his box of stationery. He closed the suitcase. Opened the box. Extracted the top sheet, which was already filled on one side with his handwriting in the smallest script he could manage; he had so little paper left.

He turned it to the empty back side, and set his hand on the camera. He couldn't say why this routine was important. He closed his eyes, feeling the metal camera body cool on his fingers, imagining Luki on the dreaming log in Sanary-sur-Mer, Luki somehow being watched over by Elza. He tried to shut out the sound of the men around him, to replace it with Luki's voice singing and the splash of the sea, her mother joining her. He imagined Luki turning to see him. He imagined framing the shot. The smile on her face rising from a print so that he would always have it, always have her with him.

He took up the pen then, and began, *My Luki*—one more letter he could never send, but the writing of it kept him alive.

Monday, September 30, 1940
THE CAS OFFICE, MARSEILLE

N anée followed Varian into the CAS office's small washroom, where he set the water running for one of his conferences. Dagobert immediately put his paws up on the tub and took a drink, as had now become his routine, Varian always happy for his company.

"That click and buzz on the phone?" Varian said to Nanée. "It's a tap. A friend at the prefecture confirmed that."

He peered closely at her face, as if he suspected she'd set the bug herself. Did he imagine she would confess to it so easily if she had? He was under a lot of pressure. He'd been successful at acquiring soap on his trip to Lisbon, but less so at persuading the US government to leave him to his work here. A September 18 cable sent through the US consul general had been waiting on his return: "This government cannot—repeat cannot—countenance the activities of Mr. Fry, however well-meaning his motives may be, in carrying on activities evading the laws of countries with which the United States maintains friendly relations." His passport was valid until January, but everyone was pressuring him to leave France immediately, before he was arrested or expelled: the American embassy in Vichy, the American consulate in Marseille, the US State Department, the Emergency Rescue Committee that had sent him, and even his own wife. Varian ignored the efforts to recall him, and worked even more urgently to get refugees out of France. But that too was getting harder, the pressure from Vichy necessitating all communications be underground and anything sensitive communicated in person. They'd even taken to unplugging the phone between calls.

He said to Nanée, "I thought it might be time to have you try delivering messages for us."

She said, "Whatever I can do to help, boss," glad finally to be accepted as loyal, trustworthy, and fair, and in no way a spy for the US State Department or Vichy or anyone else.

"It's far more dangerous than you might imagine," he said.

"You don't have to flatter me by making this seem important. I'm happy to do anything you need."

"You will have information that will put you on the wrong side of the law. Information we keep here, yes, but we have Charlie watching the door to warn us. You'll be out alone, going to meet refugees wanted by Vichy. A courier of any sort . . . it's one of the most dangerous things I ask anyone to do."

"But Gussie—"

"Gussie looks like a beautiful schoolboy no one would suspect, but don't imagine he doesn't risk his life. And there are places Gussie would stand out, where his presence would be questioned." Varian hesitated. "Places like the Panier."

"You want me to deliver messages to the Panier?" The old city. Hideouts. Gambling dens. Killing floors. Basements linked from one building to the next, to hidden chambers attached to no buildings at all, to crypts in which one could find, sidling up next to the dead, gold bricks, jewelry, stolen art, and cocaine. It was an ideal place for a refugee to hide out, if he or she could stand it; you might disappear for weeks or months until you could escape. But while the Vichy police wouldn't likely bother you in the Panier, the Marseille mafia might. The district was said to be the source of every severed head found floating in the sewers of Marseille; the criminal element knew which sewers led to the harbor waters for easy disposal of those who ran afoul of their desires.

"A clean-cut boy like Gussie would draw attention there," Varian said, "whereas there are always women on the streets of the *vieux ville*. A certain kind of woman, yes, but . . ."

There was variety enough among the whores in the Panier that, as long as Nanée didn't dress too poshly, she would be less conspicuous than sweet-faced Gussie with his jacket and tie and his lucky copy of *L'envers et l'endroit.*

Varian said, "I understand if you can't—"

"I can," Nanée said. "I will."

She would get a cheap skirt or two at a secondhand shop, since she had just the one skirt from the suit she'd worn to impress Varian, far too nice to blend in there, and a woman in trousers was now frowned upon as a sign of inappropriate female emancipation, Vichy trying to push women back a hundred years on the excuse of not wanting "ladies" to look or act like men. She would enjoy appearing to buckle to Vichy expectations of femininity—behaving as a woman should, which was to do nothing of consequence—while actually defying them.

Varian said, "I'd like to get you used to making deliveries first."

He handed her an address at Prado Beach, on the opposite side of Marseille from the Panier, and told her the message. "You'll knock, twice, three times, then once. If you're in the right place, with the right person, and it's safe to deliver a message, they'll respond, 'Postmistress?' to let you know, and you'll respond, 'Indeed, yes.' If they say nothing, Nanée, or anything but that single word, *postmistress*, you leave immediately. Do not enter. Do not try to help them. Get word back to us as fast as you can, preferably to Lena or me. But don't do anything yourself. Is that clear?"

"'Indeed, yes.'"

"The fact that you're entitled to be here in Marseille won't protect you. Again, the people you'll be delivering messages to are not."

"I understand," she said. "I can't afford to be caught helping them."

And I won't be, she thought. But she didn't say the words aloud, not wanting to tempt fate.

"Memorize the addresses I give you. Don't take them with you when you go. Don't take anything that suggests what you're doing."

"'Indeed, yes,'" she repeated.

He smiled a little despite himself. She was rather proud of that. Prying a smile from Varian's lips was one of the hardest tasks in Marseille.

"You won't always be able to take Dagobert with you. You'll have to strike a balance between when he makes you look innocent and American and when he draws attention. If you need to leave him behind, he can stay with me."

Nanée, not sure how to respond, knelt to Dagobert's level and rubbed his ears.

Varian said, "You will likely be followed sometimes."

"The Postmistress motto: If you can't lose a tail, don't deliver the mail."

Varian actually laughed. It was such a surprising sound that she was sure half the office had turned to the closed bathroom door. It was a surprisingly warm laugh.

"All right," he said. "Thank you."

She and Dagobert were already through the bathroom door when Varian said, "You're not, it turns out, quite the typical American heiress I expected."

She turned back, astonished.

"Point to you," he said. "Good luck and Godspeed, Nanée."

NOT AN HOUR later, Nanée was climbing from a trolley at Prado Beach, the Saint-Pierre cemetery behind her and Dagobert at her side. She knocked twice, then three times, then once, her heart beating like that of a horse in the starting gate at Churchill Downs.

If a boy like Gussie could do this, certainly she could, she told herself.

She waited. Was she in the wrong place? Was she being watched?

She glanced around her. No one. Just Dagobert sitting ever so politely beside her.

It seemed such a long time to wait. Should she leave?

The door opened slightly, stopped by a chain. An eye peeked through the crack.

In a whisper, "Postmistress?"

"Indeed, yes."

The eye retreated. The door closed.

The sound of the chain sliding. The door opened slightly wider.

An old woman bent in half over a cane pulled her inside, into a room cluttered with art and antiques.

"He's arrived safely in Lisbon," Nanée said. "He'll be on the ship to New York tomorrow."

Not, she didn't think, a very dangerous message, since the protégé was already safely out of France. A trial run. But the woman wept with relief.

WITHIN TWO WEEKS Nanée was on the trolley for her thirteenth delivery, and on October 13 too, shrugging off the sense she ought to pull the plug this time. Was it just superstition? She chanced a glance at the man she thought had been following her all the way from the CAS office—watching the office or watching for her; it didn't much matter which. This message was for two refugees in strict hiding, the police far too interested in the couple for them to risk being found. She uncrossed and recrossed her legs, feeling the man's gaze on her, watching despite the inconspicuous gray trench coat she wore over her second-hand skirt. No, it wasn't just any man's admiring glance at a woman's legs. She wasn't mistaken. He was definitely following her.

If she had a little more nerve, she would manage to casually chat with him, to charm him. Put him off his guard. But she did have a plan.

She watched out the trolley as they reached the outskirts of Marseille. Varian hadn't yet sent her on a delivery to the Panier, but she'd ridden this route to Prado Beach so many times now that she knew every stop and doorway. She had managed to deliver every message Varian entrusted to her, and this one was urgent. Urgent good news. Not the best news. She never did get to bring the very best news: that someone was to be included in the next small group headed to the border. She liked to imagine doing so. She liked to imagine whispering through one of those cracked doors that it was someone's turn to escape. Would they throw their arms around her, or would they be so terrified now that the moment was upon them that they might begin to change their minds? She liked to imagine leading the mad dash over the border to Spain too, but only those directly involved in the convoys were allowed even to know when they were going, and that wasn't a task with which Varian entrusted her.

The trolley passed her stop, but she stayed on. She saw in her peripheral vision the man still watching her. She pretended to be absorbed in reading her book—Gussie's lucky book he'd loaned to her since it was her thirteenth delivery, and on October 13.

She had nothing incriminating on her, she reminded herself. The man might take her in for questioning, but anyone in the Vichy police would be daunted by her American passport. No one wanted to be the one whose actions toward an American might be the excuse for Roosevelt to shrug off the thin veil of neutrality and join the British in fighting this war. Roosevelt wouldn't, of course, make any decision based on what the French did or didn't do to Nanée—but what was logic in a war that began with a phony Polish attack on a German radio station, staged by Hitler's thugs so they had an excuse to invade?

After the trolley had completed its next stop, just as it was setting off again, she closed the book and hopped off as if just realizing she was missing her stop.

The tail, caught off guard, had to negotiate around a stout woman with shopping bags.

Nanée used the distraction to duck into the doorway she'd been waiting to pass.

Had the tail managed to get off? Had he seen where Nanée had gone? She chanced a peek around the edge of the portico. He stood in the street, searching as the trolley clanged away.

A woman from the trolley lumbered away down the street, briefly greeting a teenage boy who continued in Nanée's direction.

Nanée stepped farther back, watching the trolley tracks.

The boy appeared in her view, just feet away. He continued on a few yards, then stood waiting at the stop for the trolley to downtown Marseille.

After a moment, the boy, sensing Nanée's presence, glanced back over his shoulder. She fumbled for her keys as if she lived there, hoping the man tailing her wasn't looking in the boy's direction. Hoping he might have gone the other way.

She heard the clang of a trolley coming from the other direction, bound back to Marseille center.

She listened to the grind of it slowing.

Watched it pass her.

Watched it stop, the entire trolley now in her view.

Watched, still from her hiding place in the doorway, as an old woman with a young girl got off.

The boy alone got on.

She heard footsteps, now hurrying toward her just as the trolley began on its way again.

She ran for it. Hopped on just in time.

Too late for the tail to catch the trolley.

She did not look back. She didn't wave to him, tempting as that was.

At the address, finally, Nanée gave the code knock, two, three, one, at a hotel room door. It opened slightly.

"Postmistress?"

"Indeed, yes."

The door opened wider, her invitation into the room.

Two people looked expectantly at her—two people anyone with any interest in art would know.

"Your Czech passports are ready," she whispered.

Varian now had a deal with Vladimír Vochoč, the Czech consul in Marseille. Vochoč would provide a passport to any anti-Nazi Varian recommended, and Varian would supply funds to have them printed in Bordeaux, right under the Nazis' noses. The consul was entitled to have passports printed in France, which came with pink covers rather than green, but the pink Czech passports had become so common that the legitimate green ones were as likely to be questioned as the illegitimate pink ones, or more. Twice each week, Varian joined a friend of the Czech consul for breakfast in the friend's room at the train station hotel, where he exchanged an envelope of photographs, descriptions, and cash for one with the passports for prior applicants. Varian didn't give Nanée the passports themselves to deliver, out of concern for her own safety. If she were caught with forged documents, even her American passport would be no protection.

She said to the two artists, "Come to the office tomorrow morning to collect them."

They thanked her profusely, as if they believed their danger were ended rather than just begun.

Sunday, October 20, 1940
THE CAS OFFICE, MARSEILLE

D anny picked up an identity card from Varian's desk. Varian, alarmed, grabbed it back. This was not, Nanée thought, an auspicious start for a job Danny needed, since he and T and Peterkin hadn't been able to survive on the income from selling his uncle's grapes in the Languedoc markets.

"It's a forgery," Danny said.

Varian took him by the sleeve, pulled him into the bathroom, and turned on the tap. Nanée, with Dagobert right behind, followed and closed them in.

"How can you can tell the *cart d'identité* is a forgery?" Varian demanded.

"When Danny was working with the police in Paris before the Germans invaded," Nanée answered, "he quietly expedited naturalization papers and residency permits for German refugees. He can translate your correspondence into French officialese that will pass the authorities. He knows how to get permissions no one wants to give. And he knows where to find the people you're looking for."

Danny said, "Vichy doesn't advertise, of course, but I hear through the refugee underground that most are at an internment camp near Nîmes or back at Camp des Milles."

Obtaining American visas for people in the camps was complicated. US authorities suspected them simply for having been arrested, and yet if Vichy or the Nazis released them, that raised concerns they might be Nazi sympathizers or even spies. But Varian already had authority for visas for those on his list.

"Do you think you could get them out?" Varian said.

The whole scene struck Nanée as comic. The toilet. The sink. The sad little mirror. The murmur of voices from beyond the door. Most of the people who worked in the office now had no idea of the illegal activities of the CAS; Varian had built up quite a staff of legitimate volunteers helping refugees in legal ways, as cover for his illegal rescue work.

"Oh, sure," Danny answered finally. "I'll just walk in and ask who is there and if they could leave with me."

Varian's eyes lit for a brief moment before he registered that Danny was being flip.

Nanée said, "If someone can find out who's there, I could try to get them out."

They both eyed her dubiously.

"You underestimate me, both of you," she said.

As VARIAN LEFT, Nanée held Danny back and opened the tap Varian had closed. Dagobert, with an impatient groan, sat dejectedly.

"How did you know that identity card was forged?" she asked. Gussie bought real cards from the *tabacs*, and Bill Freier, who doctored them, could imitate the official rubber stamp with just a few brush-strokes. Freier, who'd been arrested in Austria for anti-Nazi cartoons and caricatures and later escaped the French Le Vernet internment camp, lived under an alias in Cassis, creating forgeries in order to help fellow refugees and to keep his fiancé and himself alive while Varian tried to arrange US immigration for them. No one—*no one*—could tell Bill Freier's identity cards without a magnifying glass, and often not even then. His signature was awfully good too, and he did it for the CAS for fifty cents a card when others would charge three hundred times that.

Danny said, "What do you have in mind for getting refugees out of the camps, Nanée?"

"How did you know that identity card was forged?" she insisted.

"It won't be as easy as sweet-talking a single guard, if that's what you think," he said. "These camps come with fences and watchtowers and men with guns."

"The identity card, Danny."

He frowned. "It wasn't the card. It was the look on Fry's face when I picked it up."

Dagobert, hopeful, stood and wagged his tail as Nanée stepped to the sink, but she only idly dipped her fingers into the running water.

"Even if we could get these men out of the camps," Danny said, "they need passports, French transit and exit visas, Spanish and Portuguese transit visas, a final destination visa, and proof of passage out of Lisbon. Portugal doesn't want to be overrun with refugees when the music stops."

"For proof of passage, the venerable old Cook travel agency will provide false transatlantic tickets for two hundred francs," Nanée said. "For entry visas, the Chinese sell ones that say, 'It is strictly forbidden for the bearer of this document, under any circumstances and at any time, to set foot on Chinese soil.' Fortunately, neither the French nor the Portuguese read Chinese."

Dagobert lay down on the bathroom floor, head on paws. This was going to take some time.

Nanée said, "The other documents are complicated, but not impossible."

In recent weeks, the temporary Czech passports they'd relied on had been shut down. So had the Lithuanian ones they'd spent a fortune to get. The Dutch. The Panamanian. New Spanish and Portuguese rules made it nearly impossible to have transit visas from both countries at the same time too, and Varian's best guess was that every name telegraphed to Madrid for a Spanish transit visa was submitted to Gestapo agents operating in Spain. That meant refugees now could be sent through Spain only if they weren't well-known enough to be recognizable, and they had to travel under aliases until they got to Lisbon—another risk. The CAS had gone from sending people to the border on their own to having to escort them, increasing the danger to the staff. And try as Varian might, he couldn't get people out by ship; the harbor and coast were too closely guarded.

"There's a path over the Pyrenees that skirts French border guards." Nanée hoped this was still true, or true again. The escape route from Cerbère along the cemetery wall and over the border was so often watched now that it had become unusable.

Danny turned off the water, and Dagobert hopped up hopefully.

"You're changing your mind?" Nanée asked. She turned the water back on.

Dagobert let out a small, discouraged yip and settled back to the floor, head on paws.

"Most of these refugees are Jewish, Danny." The French now had an even broader definition of who was Jewish than the Germans did, and Pétain and Laval were trying to get Hitler's attention, to show they could contribute to his pet project—they could persecute Jews as well as any Nazi—and win a place for France in Hitler's Europe. "I know you think I know more than I ought to," she said, "but Varian hasn't told me anything. He is strictly need-to-know. You forget what a fine snoop I am."

"Don't imagine, Nanée, that you're a better snoop than the Gestapo, or even Vichy."

"So you'll join us." Not a question; after a decade of persuading Danny to do what she wanted him to, she could read acquiescence in his voice. She turned the tap off.

Dagobert bolted to her side, wagging his tail.

"We need to get T and Peterkin here," she said. "And we need to find you a place to live."

Friday, October 25, 1940
THE #14 TROLLEY, MARSEILLE

Nanée, T, and Miriam caught the #14 trolley east from the Noailles station, through the Plaine tunnel and past the Saint-Pierre cemetery; they'd left Dagobert behind lest he scare off potential landlords. Nanée had seen homes with space around them in the hills of La Pomme, a far better place for little Peterkin (now with Danny's mother near Cannes) than a lousy hotel or boardinghouse room in rat-infested, roach-ridden downtown Marseille. They hopped off the trolley to inquire at a café about rentals, then on a whim ducked through an underpass with enticing glimpses of the hills and valleys of Saint-Cyr, finding themselves on a long winding drive lined with plane trees and boxwoods, marked by brick pillars and a DO NOT ENTER sign. Carved into one of the limestone capitals were the words VILLA AIR-BEL—a name so like Miriam's fleabag hotel Paradis Bel-Air that they couldn't resist. It was so quiet. No traffic. No people shouting as they spilled from bars. No police whistles or harbor noise. Nothing but birdsong, the gentle shush of leaves fluttering in the wind, a trickle of water somewhere. It made Nanée a little nervous, as if noise were a drug she'd become dependent on to stave off her thoughts.

Just as they topped the long climb and spied through a phalanx of trees a villa atop the hill, white with green shutters, a voice called out, "This is private property!"

A stooped man was hurrying toward them across two wooden planks over an irrigation ditch. Nanée called to him that they were looking for a place to rent.

Dr. Balthazar Thumin, as the man introduced himself, feigned reluctance—it would be very expensive—but led them up a steep walk to a three-story villa with ivy climbing to a terra-cotta roof. He retrieved a huge key ring from a groom's cottage, opened a squeaky iron gate, and led them up an untended walk, the gravel poking at Nanée's feet; she'd had her shoes resoled, but she'd already worn them through again delivering messages for Varian.

The gardens were in disrepair, the oval pond covered in a foul-smelling green mold and surrounded by rangy hedges and geraniums, zinnias, and marigolds long past bloom, the paths distinguishable only by the difference between weeds fighting through gravel and ones thriving in loamy soil. The view from the belvedere, though—just an open gallery flanked by plane trees, but belvedere sounded so much more poetic—was wide and forever, begging for a painter to set up an easel. Sharp-needled pines and the soft silvers and gray-greens of olive trees stretched to the parallel railroad and trolley tracks and, beyond them, a stunning sea and cloud-dotted sky. For the briefest moment Nanée was standing on the belvedere of Marigold Lodge, looking down the manicured lawn-and-willow-tree stretch of Superior Point to Pine Creek Bay and Lake Macatawa.

As the doctor began opening the shutters on the villa's six sets of French doors, T whispered that even if the inside were as ruined as the gardens, Danny and she could never afford this. It didn't cost anything to look, though, and what was Nanée's wealth but an accident of birth, anyway? She might keep her downtown room too, but she wanted, suddenly, to have Peterkin grow up in a house like she'd grown up in, where he might settle into a window seat or the branches of one of these trees with a book about King Arthur or Joan of Arc, reading English with her the way she'd read French with her governess and piecing together a suit of armor from tin foil. She found herself longing to have room about her, quiet gardens to walk in, people she loved and who loved her sleeping under the same oddly meandering roof.

It must be her age—newly thirty-one—or perhaps this moment in time. She'd turned thirty in a world that had declared itself at war without really doing much about it. The Nazis had taken care of that,

occupying Paris and half of France and installing their Vichy lap-
dogs to run the rest of the country. Now, with peace declared, the war
seemed so much more real, and only begun. Just that morning they'd
woken to shocking newspaper photos of Pétain shaking Hitler's hand
at Montoire. Yet despite her American passport, France had become
the only home Nanée knew, the only one she wanted.

"Do let's have a look," she insisted. Then more loudly, for the doctor's hearing, "This reminds me of home, although of course it's much
smaller."

The doctor took a pack of Gauloises Bleues from his pocket and lit
one. He didn't offer them cigarettes. He was that kind of old-fashioned;
he couldn't imagine any decent woman would smoke.

"There are eighteen bedrooms," he said. "As I said, it will be very
expensive."

"You'll negotiate the price before you show us the place?" Nanée
asked.

Inside, a black-and-white-marble entry hall opened into the "Grand
Salon," one of three salons on the ground floor. It had a piano, an elab-
orate candelabra, plenty of Louis XV furniture, a stone fireplace as
tall as Nanée, cold now but with brass andirons welcoming new logs,
and ugly wires running along the baseboards everywhere. Electric-
ity! Nanée caught her own reflection in an age-spotted mirror over
the mantel, the thing huge and gilt and, if she wasn't careful, revealing
her absolute glee in its smoky glass. Beside the mirror, the unmoving
hands of a round brass clock read 11:45 although it was midafternoon.
Stairs to the second floor opened into a library much like the one back
in Evanston, with floor-to-ceiling bookshelves and a ladder to reach
the higher books. Doors from the library led to spacious bedrooms,
each with a mahogany double bed, a marble fireplace, an armoire, and,
Nanée was a bit discouraged to see, a washstand with chamber pot
discreetly tucked away. But there was, blessedly, a flush toilet on this

floor and one on the third floor too. And everything was in awfully good shape for a house that appeared to be inhabited by nothing but ghosts.

No, there was no telephone. No, no gas either. No central heat.

"And no tub," Nanée said. It wasn't a dealbreaker. Call it a hedge against being gouged simply for being American.

"Ah." Doctor Thumin took them back downstairs, through a break-fast room with a charming marble washbasin, and into a kitchen with a stove three times as long as Nanée was tall, a soapstone sink with running water, and utensils and china. There he threw open a door into a third bathroom—off the kitchen, for heaven's sake.

"This, it is a wedding present for my grandmère," the doctor said.

Nanée wasn't sure if he meant the beautiful zinc tub with a graceful bronze-doré swan's-neck faucet or the whole bathroom, but was afraid to ask for fear the delight in her voice would give her away.

As they stood again on the terrace looking toward the sea, she breathed in deeply of the country air. No rats here. No bar brawls. No thugs.

She startled at a swoop over the ruined garden—the mottled orange-brown of a beautiful wild creature spreading to white wings streaked with black.

"A booted eagle," Thumin said. "A Bonelli's eagle, he's sometimes called. You can tell he's young by his coloring. You must come see my collection, to see him up close."

"Up close?" Nanée said.

"I'm quite a fine taxidermist," he said. "I can show you as well a golden eagle, among the largest and most elusive of birds. They spend days perched motionless, impossible to spot. And they are among the finest hunters."

Nanée watched the eagle, trying to hide her disgust. Who would want to see such a wild creature gutted and stuffed, much less do it himself? And yet was any creature more beautiful than a mourning dove? That single, beautiful bird, so small and vulnerable. A true eye, her father always said of Nanée's ability with a shotgun. A steady hand. He'd showed her how to hold the dying bird's pale gray body, warm in her fingers, and smack its neck against the gun barrel. How to clean the blood from its pale peach breast and pick the lead shot from its flesh. How to dress the dead bird and cook it. He sat her beside him at one of the dining tables at Marigold Lodge, eating the dove for dinner that night because that's what hunters did, they ate what they killed. She cut the bird's flesh into tiny pieces and closed her eyes before each bite, remembering the feel of its heart racing against her fingertips. She swallowed without chewing, washing each devastating bite down with a big gulp of milk.

The doctor named his price, 1,300 francs a month.

A tiny bedroom with shared bath in a dump of a downtown hotel cost 450 francs. Nanée's room at the Continental cost nearly 1,300.

"You may think it is too much, but I will not be able to convince my sister to accept one franc less," Thumin said. "This price, we will not negotiate."

THEY MOVED INTO the villa together that Sunday: Nanée, Danny, and T, with Peterkin to be fetched from his grandmother the next day. Miriam joined them for the last few days before she went to get her fiancé in Yugoslavia. Varian's consiglieri, Maurice, took one of the rooms. And of course dear Gussie could not be left behind. Everyone else at the CAS was happy where they were living, with the possible exception of Varian; Miriam wanted to invite him, but Nanée found the prospect of living with him too daunting. They put sheets on the hand-carved beds and turned over their ration books to Madame Nouget, the cook T hired along with a maid named Rose, and they set up Nanée's radio in the Grand Salon, where it fit in nicely with the foggy mirror and the beautifully useless clock.

They had only begun unpacking when Varian dropped by, looking around in wide-eyed wonder as if he'd forgotten a world existed outside the office. Nanée was surprised to find her reserved boss not just rolling up his sleeves to help but as thrilled at the abundance of space as she was. They invited him to stay for dinner in the stained, leather-backed chairs at the dark dining table, along with Charlie Fawcett and their friend Leon Ball, an American lard salesman here in France, of all things, who'd both arrived with Varian. Charlie had been increasingly absent from guarding the CAS door for days at a time, leaving Nanée suspecting he was leading refugees over the Pyrenees to Spain, perhaps with this Leon Ball.

Over meager rations, Varian, with that disloyal Dagobert sitting under his chair rather than Nanée's, said they'd located André Breton hiding with his painter-wife and their daughter in an abandoned fisherman's cabin in Salon-de-Provence. "We've moved them to American vice consul Harry Bingham's villa out on the Corniche while we're trying to find a way to get them out of France, but that's dangerous for all concerned."

Miriam proposed they invite the Bretons to take two of the villa's extra rooms.

"Easy for you to say, since you're leaving," Nanée said, remembering André that night at her Paris apartment. *You spied on your father? Did you spy on anyone else?*

"André makes Nanée nervous," Danny said.

"Pffft, I don't even know him," Nanée protested.

"André has that effect on anyone with any sense," T said. "But he's French, and he isn't Jewish, is he?"

"The Vichy government finds his writings contrary to their 'révolution nationale,'" Varian said.

It would be only for a few weeks, until Varian got him out of France.

After dinner, they gathered in the Grand Salon over the newspapers—not the French collaborationist rags but the Swiss, which provided more information (although even they didn't criticize Vichy), and the single-sheet resistance newspapers like *Aujourd'hui.* Danny turned the chipped knob of Nanée's radio, searching for the signal-jammed BBC news.

"Wait!" Nanée said as faint music crackled.

Danny tuned the radio more carefully, and cranked up the volume. Big band music. "In the Mood," by Glenn Miller and his orchestra. But where was it coming from?

Charlie Fawcett, who played the jazz trumpet, stood and with delightful enthusiasm pretended to play Miller's trombone. Leon Ball joined him on the air saxophone.

Nanée stood and grabbed Gussie. "You know how to dance, kid? Come on!"

Varian scooped up Dagobert, took one of his paws in hand, and began to dance too. Then everyone was dancing—forbidden in Vichy France, as was jazz. They danced to Duke Ellington's "I Let a Song Go Out of My Heart" and "Frenesi" by Artie Shaw—Charlie playing air clarinet even as he danced with Nanée—and Judy Garland singing "I'm Nobody's Baby."

"That gal singing about nobody wanting to love her?" Charlie said. "That fits her like socks on a rooster."

He and Ball had a fine time joking about being more than happy to have Judy be their baby as Nanée wondered, as Garland did in the song, whether anyone other than good old Dagobert would ever take a chance with her in love, or she with them.

The music came, astonishingly, from a Boston shortwave radio station. On clear nights out here in the open countryside, they could get music all the way from the United States.

When they called it an evening, far later than they ought to have, Ball said he and Charlie would drop Varian on their way—evasive about where exactly they might be headed.

But Nanée said to Varian, "Why don't you take the blue room? We can get your things from Marseille after work tomorrow. But Dagobert sleeps with me."

Monday, October 28, 1940
THE PANIER DISTRICT, MARSEILLE

Nanée walked up a winding alleyway lined with decrepit brothels and bars, too close to the stinking muck in the sewage drain running down the middle, but she was determined to be seen disappearing if she was to disappear. A rat ambled along closer to the buildings, then climbed up onto a garbage pail and inside, less threatened by her than she was by him. Another crossed one of the lines of laundry strung from windows, dingy undergarments improbably mixed with brightly colored children's clothes. Nanée wished she'd brought Dagobert, but he would be yanking on his leash to stick his nose in the open sewer and racing off after those rats, running headlong into the garbage pail. She regretted too leaving her pearl-handled pistol back on the high armoire shelf in her new bedroom at the villa, thinking it would be incriminating if the police stopped her on her way to deliver this message whose meaning Varian would not even share with her. She'd understood without Varian having to say it that she couldn't be tortured into disclosing what she didn't know.

It was nearing evening, the sky as gray as the street. Old ladies on chairs in the doorways were wrapping their yarn around their knitting needles, preparing to go inside, while young whores emerged to shop their wares. At place des Moulins, a square with a café in which people sat sipping a last something before the chilly damp of the night settled in, a table of already-drunk men called out to her for her price. She swallowed back a smart retort and headed up the alley to the right, repeating the message to herself: *I'm afraid there will be no news from Paris.* She was to deliver it from outside the door. She was not to see who the recipients were. She was to leave immediately. *Not another moment beyond what you need to deliver the message, for their safety and your own.*

The hill crested to a view of the newer docks of the industrial port, filled with barrels and crates and massive dirty mounds of coal meant for Britain but going nowhere due to the blockade. A light drizzle began to fall on the coal and on the filthy street and on Nanée.

And there was the house she was looking for. The shutters Varian had described as pink were the color of the Pepto-Bismol her daddy used to take. A chunky woman in a high-slit skirt and wide-necked blouse adjusted her garter in the doorway, leaning low so her breasts were visible. Nanée glanced over her shoulder to see the whore's mark—one of the men from the table. Was he following her?

Poor Daddy. He was rolling over in his grave. But it was a sign of Varian's growing confidence in Nanée that he'd given her this delivery.

She pretended to search her pockets for something to keep the rain off her head as the man passed her. He slowed for a free look at the woman's breasts. After he carried on, Nanée slipped past her and through the door into a front room full of scantily clad women and attentive men. She found the stairway at the back, climbed dirty, deteriorating steps to the fourth floor, and knocked at the second door to the left, twice, then three times, then once.

The door creaked open, a chain affixed to keep anyone from barging in.

"Postmistress?"

"Indeed, yes," Nanée said. "I'm afraid there will be no news from Paris."

"No!" the woman wailed, a heart-wrenching sound. A low moan from behind her, a man's grief. Still, Nanée made herself turn back toward the nasty stairway.

"Please don't go." The woman was sobbing now. "Please don't leave us. We can't bear this."

Nanée hesitated at the rattle of the door chain. The poor woman was trying to open the door, so frazzled she didn't realize she had to close it to get the lock off.

"My husband can't bear this." The woman was sobbing even harder, the man keening.

Nanée longed to turn back to comfort her. Whenever she'd delivered bad news before, she'd been able to talk to the recipients, to assure them that it wasn't that they would never get their papers, never get over the border, but simply that there had been a delay.

Did this mean something more—"No news from Paris"? Not just that there was no help for these refugees now, but that there never would be? That a parent or a child or some other loved one they'd expected to escape with would have to be left behind? That someone was dead?

Could Nanée really not spend even one moment comforting this poor couple?

But already a nearby door was opening, drawn by the commotion even here in this place where nobody wanted to be seen. And Varian's voice was in her head, the look on his face when she'd asked him what the message meant. *Not one extra moment, Nanée. Not one word more. You deliver the message and you get out.*

Thursday, October 31, 1940

CAMP DES MILLES

Edouard pulled a sprig of crabgrass from a crack in the courtyard, the first bit of green he'd eaten in weeks. It was evening, the internees out for a last bit of fresh air, only Max still underground, chipping away at another brick as if art dug out of manufactured stone might save him.

"All indoors!" the bugler called.

As Edouard turned with the others to the black yawn of the factory doors, he caught sight of someone leaving the camp, already through the gate and headed to the train station.

"Danny!" he called out, hopeful for the briefest instant that the retreating back belonged to Danny Bénédite, although what Danny might look like after a year of war was anyone's guess.

The man didn't turn. And of course it couldn't be Danny. Danny had been at Dunkirk. That was the last Edouard had heard of his friend, and it was too much to hope that the man who'd saved him once might save him again.

IN THE WEAK light of the bare overhead bulb, Edouard took off his clothes, folded them neatly despite the dust, and set them in his suitcase. He put on nightclothes, then spread his blanket across the straw. Around him, hundreds of men were doing the same in the dim light. It was hard to say why they clung to this semblance of normalcy, but it paid to remember they were human, as Max had suggested that first night, even after all these months. The alternative was to begin to lose one's mind.

With a hand on his camera, he wrote his nightly few lines to Luki, words that grew increasingly honest as the likelihood of them ever reaching her dimmed. Other men chatted as they climbed under their blankets in every inch of space around him, but Edouard didn't want to talk. Seeing the man who probably wasn't Danny had brought back a trickle of hope—not that anyone might save him, but that someone he'd known somewhere along the way might save Luki. And with that hope came a flood of memories: the length of Elza in a silver dress the first time he saw her, at a speakeasy in Berlin when it was still possible to speak easy there; her delicate eyes looking up at him from behind delicate lace as he promised to keep and hold her, when the possibility of a forever had seemed real; the first touch of his finger to the squawking baby face—not the least bit delicate—of the child Elza named Lucca, after the walled city in Italy where Edouard had taken the first art photograph he'd ever sold. Elza had known him so well. Known how self-centered he was. She'd understood that memorializing his own moment of becoming an artist in Luki's tiny new soul would bind him to her. But she'd been wrong about what that photograph in Lucca meant. It was something that was hard to see until you had some measure of success, but it wasn't success that made one an artist. One was an artist. One was successful or not at selling work, but the sale of art no more made a man an artist than it made him a man. An artist simply was.

The men here who tromped down the steps to the bare, cold kilns in the basement each evening to paint or carve, to sing or play music, to rehearse, to write words or musical notes—the fact that Edouard himself had once made a living from his art didn't make him any more an artist than they were. It was the need to create art that made a person an artist. The need and the doing, the creating with whatever you had. And they were making art while his camera sat idle, the film he'd brought still unexposed. Yes, he dabbled in other mediums. He helped Max with a fresco. He chipped at a brick. But he did not turn to the photographs that were his own art.

"Lights out!" the bugler's voice called up the stairs, he too an artist.

Max had sketched him playing his bugle in the basement just hours earlier. Not the hard notes of reveille he played each morning, but a jazz piece so soft and sorrowful that Edouard might not have believed it came from a bugle if he hadn't heard it himself.

One bare overhead bulb blinked out. Then another. The last of the three glowed dimly over Edouard.

"I said lights out!" the bugler called, not angry, but with his own ass on the line and nothing to be gained in keeping the light on like there was in playing illegal jazz.

Max, on the other side of Edouard's suitcase, said, "It's your turn."

Edouard stood and pulled the string to turn off the light.

Someone closed a window across the room.

"Do leave it open, will you?" Max called out. "The stench over here is unbearable."

"We freeze with it open at night," someone near the window answered.

Voices from all around the room rose up in favor of or against the open window.

Max lowered his voice and said to Edouard, "Word is someone came today. Someone looking for artists and intellectuals Hitler means to silence. Specifically, you."

Edouard's heart crowded his throat, as it had that first moment he'd held Luki, as Elza had made him repeat her words, made him agree, *We'll call her Luki.*

"Any word whether it was friend or foe?" he managed.

Max's voice floated almost silently into the darkness. "If you have friends in this neighborhood, I should love to know them."

"But the Gestapo don't operate here, not in Vichy."

"Oh, Edouard, you are not so young as to be so naive."

Edouard lay back on his makeshift bed, the hope seeping out of his tired bones. It was a long time since he'd felt young.

"There's a group of them visiting camps to identify those of us they mean to deport to Germany," Max said.

Edouard closed his eyes, again considering how he might escape. He couldn't afford the risk. No one who escaped got any distance before they were caught, much less all the way to Paris, where he might or might not find Luki. But with the Gestapo coming for him, what choice did he have?

Friday, November 1, 1940
VILLA AIR-BEL

Nanée was surprised how quickly they settled into life together at Villa Air-Bel. Each morning, Madame Nouget or T or one of the others took the children to milk the clandestine cow they had acquired, named Madame LaVache-à-Lait for the gallons she produced daily. T—and after the Bretons arrived, Jacqueline too—gave their children big cups of milk each morning, still warm from the cow. They set aside another cup for each child for bedtime, so that even with the rationing—a half pound of pasta and six ounces of rice per person per month, ten ounces of meat and four of fats and cheese per week, and eight ounces of bread per day, all tallied on cheap paper ruled liked bingo cards—they wouldn't go to sleep hungry. They shared the rest of the milk with the neighborhood mothers who showed up each morning with jugs in hand, generosity born of concern for the children, but also some small insurance against anyone reporting the illegal cow.

Most mornings, Nanée and T and Miriam lingered together out on the belvedere over cups of ersatz, a nice-sounding word to describe a pale liquid brewed from acorns and twigs or, if you were lucky, roasted chicory root or barley made barely tolerable by a little grape-juice sweetener. Rose cleaned up, and Madame Nouget did the shopping, an hours-long chore given the scarcities resulting from so much of France's food going to the German war effort. A Spanish girl named Maria cared for Peterkin and for Aube Breton while André wrote in one of the greenhouses or the library, the only room in which they kept the fire lit all day, and Jacqueline laid out her paints, and everyone else took the trolley into the CAS office. Varian had taken so quickly to Danny that he'd already made him his chef de cabinet, in charge of the office, and the key person for locating refugees. T, with her flawless French and English, worked with them too.

They gathered again at seven for communal dinners at which the food might be meager but the company never was. Afterward, they read newspapers and listened to the radio, often until the BBC signed off with a rousing rendition of "God Save the King," for heaven's sake. They played made-up games, the favorite a simple listing of the ten people you most liked to fantasize being dead. They sang together, with Varian at the piano and Gussie singing enthusiastically. And if the night was clear enough, they returned to that Boston jazz station and rolled up the rugs and danced.

THE VERY DAY the Bretons moved into "the château," as they'd taken to calling the shabby old place, the Surrealists in the area got wind of it and began dropping by at all hours to pay homage to the founder of their movement, forever interrupting André's work. His solution was to send Gussie to spread the word that he would receive visitors only at a salon he would host, the first of which would be on La Toussaint, the French All Saints' Day, a holiday meant to honor the poor old saints who didn't merit their own special day. Anyone who cared to visit was to come between noon and seven to pray to the good saints of the arts, whoever they might be, through food and wine and games.

That morning—a Saint Martin's summer day, November but still warm enough for shirtsleeves—they set tables and chairs out on the belvedere, with white tablecloths, dishes, and silverware for the scant repast Madame Nouget was able to muster, and quantities of wine. Also long pads of paper, colored pencils and crayons and drawing pens, scissors and paste, and old magazines for the games André meant for everyone to play.

Danny climbed up a ladder Nanée held for him and out onto a branch of a tree. Nanée climbed to a lower rung and handed a painting up to him. Some of André's friends planning to attend this first salon had contributed works of art the two were now to hang from the trees. Danny took hold of the twine attached to the canvas, leaving the painting itself in Nanée's hands while he tied the twine around a branch.

"All right," he said.

"Are you sure it's secure?"

He gave her a look.

"It's a Miró, for heaven's sake," she said. "I'm not going to be the one to tell André I dropped it ten feet onto rough stone and I'm very sorry but it's now worthless, never mind how much money it might have fetched to help refugees."

She carefully let the painting go. It hung at a slight angle, but the ladder was too precarious for her to straighten it, and anyway, she rather liked the tilt.

From this height, she spotted Varian sitting with Dagobert, seeking his advice about whether he ought to get his own dog. Dagobert was as often with the children or one of the others as with Nanée now, as if he'd grown from a toddler always wanting his mother into a teenager who preferred his friends. And his best friend was, oddly, Varian.

Jacqueline Breton appeared below, her bangle bracelets jangling as if to announce the arrival of the mobile she handed up to Nanée—small, dangling black-and-white photos taken by Man Ray, who'd managed to flee Paris for Los Angeles. No color at all, not like the Calders Nanée loved, mobiles first envisioned in Mondrian's Paris studio thanks to light playing over colored cardboard tacked to the wall much like, Nanée imagined, the sunlight now reflecting from the colored glass adorning Jacqueline's blond hair.

"A bit of art actually *meant* to be hung," Jacqueline said, seeming so much more mature than Nanée even though they were the same age. Because she was married to André, who was fifteen years their senior? Because she was the mother of a five-year-old?

"I think we need to hang you, Jacqueline," Nanée said, meaning to compliment her hair, but sounding like a complete idiot. "I mean, you look like a work of art yourself."

"Of course if someone bid on me, we would have to sell me," Jacqueline answered brightly. "But then you never know. I might just make a fine whore!"

Even as Jacqueline turned back toward the house, Nanée said to Danny, "I have an idea how to get Edouard out of Camp des Milles."

Danny grinned. "'Edouard'? That's awfully chummy, isn't it?"

Danny had returned late the night before from a trip to Camp des Milles, where he'd managed to bribe one of the guards to allow him to see the list of prisoners. Several of the men on Varian's list were indeed being held there, including Max Ernst and Hans Bellmer, as was Edouard Moss. "Who is Edouard Moss?" Varian had asked. Moss was well-known in Europe, but not well enough known in the United States to have made Varian's list.

"We could threaten to go to the press if they don't release him," Danny said now. "It worked for Lion Feuchtwanger."

"Even my mother, who rarely reads, has read *The Oppermans,*" Nanée said. "Edouard Moss is not Lion Feuchtwanger."

Madame LaVache-à-Lait mooed somewhere in the distance. They were trying to teach her not to, since she was illegal, but it turned out she was even less compliant than Dagobert.

"We could get a group of artists to raise his visibility, like the French PEN club did for Walter Mehring," Danny suggested. PEN had written so many letters insisting on the release of Mehring that the writer had been freed.

"That was before Vichy and surrender on demand," Nanée said. "There aren't too many people more likely to be on a Gestapo list than Edouard Moss." Remembering again the individual hatreds Moss photographed that somehow struck more absolute terror in any decent heart than shots of vast Nazi crowds or military parades: the girl saluting Hitler; the man having his nose measured; the son cutting his Orthodox father's beard. Such ordinary people. They might be you.

With the mobile affixed to the branch, she again descended the ladder, chose another canvas from the stack leaning against the trunk, and climbed the ladder again.

"So listen," she said as she handed the canvas up to him.

Danny ignored the canvas. "You don't really imagine an internment camp commander will just hand over his prisoners to you."

"Not 'prisoners.' Just one." She supposed it was Jacqueline's little joke about being a fine whore that had put the idea in her head. "Varian won't like it, though," she said, already decided and wishing she could hurry down to the Marseille train station that very minute. But the effort would have to be more carefully planned.

"There is no chance, Nanée, that Varian would allow you to . . . to . . ."

"I believe the phrase you're seeking is 'jeopardize my virtue for the sake of nothing more than a man's life.'" She smiled and again offered the canvas.

He only stared at her through his round lenses. She could risk her life delivering messages, and that was fine with him, but her offering a man a little insincere affection made him uncomfortable?

"Perhaps it's prescient that I'm known as 'The Postmistress,'" she said. "I'll deliver the males." She smiled wryly. "But really, Danny, I promise you that whatever virtue I have intact will remain so."

She reached for a lower branch, affixed the twine herself, and eased the painting into place. Virtue was so relative, even in good times, and in any event not something she'd highly valued since she escaped that big house back in Evanston.

Friday, November 1, 1940
VILLA AIR-BEL

Nanée stood under the plane trees on the belvedere, watching André greet each of the forty-some writers and artists arriving on the tram for this first salon as if the château were his. Many were on Varian's list for American visas, including plenty who were radical in one way or another, while others, like André himself, were excluded as too left-wing to be palatable for Americans. "Villa Espère-Visa," the Russian writer Victor Serge dubbed Villa Air-Bel that afternoon. Hoping for a Visa.

André began the salon with a reading by Benjamin Péret of a scatological poem, which was met with raucous whistles and cheers. He then led them in playing the word-game version of Exquisite Corpse, blindly stringing together adjective, subject, verb, adjective, and object to form crazy sentences. A sentence years before had given the game its name: *Le cadavre | exquise | boira | le vin | nouveau.* The exquisite corpse will drink the new wine. When Nanée was in the subject spot, the word *kangaroo* came to mind. Knobby knees. Fig leaf. She didn't use any of them, choosing instead *train* and *station*, *hurry*, and *imprisoned*, thinking she ought to be leaving already to try to free Edouard Moss from Camp des Milles. But the game was unfailingly funny, and she too laughed. André would tack up anything that particularly pleased him on the tree trunk behind him. "So I'll be able to find it later," he said as he poured wine all around again.

They switched to the drawing version of Exquisite Corpse, creating bizarre composite characters—drawing but also using scissors and paste, fallen leaves and tree bark and twigs, a torn wine label, even scraps of food they incorporated into collages. One of the creatures looked so like a Surrealist version of the Vichy prime minister

Philippe Pétain that André labeled it "The Prime Collaborationist" and tacked it up on his tree.

He picked up a pencil himself then and created an entire character, half drawing, half collaging, using dry grass for a mustache and red-wine-stained bits of cork for eyes.

"Hitler," Jacqueline said, and everyone chimed in, *yes, Hitler*, setting Dagobert, who'd been left up in Nanée's room with a soup bone, barking like mad. It was indeed a comic Hitler——one that could get them all arrested if ever it was found. André labeled it Teppichfresser, "Carpet Chewer," for Hitler's rumored tendency to foam at the mouth, fall to the floor in his fury, and literally chew the carpet. André would have tacked it up beside the comic Pétain on his tree, but the glue wasn't dry.

They began putting together collages to form prominent people and guessing who each was meant to be. It was seldom obvious, and yet they never failed to guess. It was fun, and exciting, and dangerous.

Oscar Domínguez——the artist who, with Pablo Picasso, created *Never*, that gramophone devouring mannequin legs that had emitted the haunting laughter at the Surrealist exhibit in Paris——presented the group with Freud. It looked like a playing card, giving André the idea they ought to design a new deck. Not a Tarot deck, but an ordinary playing deck they could have fun with.

"We'll start with Oscar's Freud here."

"He can be our king," Varian said.

"Did you know the deck of cards has its roots in the military?" It was not a question, but rather knowledge André was going to share. "The clover suggests military pay, the heart soldiers' love. We'll have to do away with the military and royal slant for our game, though. No kings and queens and jacks we don't believe in."

They needed cards that would reflect their own heroes and values, they all agreed.

"Instead of king-queen-jack, we could have id-ego-superego," Jacqueline said.

"You're missing libido," Oscar Domínguez said.

"Genius," André said. "Freud can be our Genius."

"Instead of jacks, we could have jokers," Danny suggested. "Or magicians."

"Sorcerers," Nanée offered.

"Magus," André said. "Like sorcerer but without the evil."

"With a religious tone, though," Nanée said. "I thought you weren't much for religion, André."

"But I rather like the idea of wisdom," André insisted, and no one objected. It was Andre's idea. André's game. André's salon.

"If you don't mind religion, I nominate Joan of Arc for the third face card," Nanée said, remembering Joan of Arc and King Arthur and her failure of a tin-foil suit of armor. What protection had she meant to gain by it? "A warrior woman the Catholic Church refused to recognize for centuries and the English condemned for heresy and cross-dressing—which I'd think would stand her in good stead with any Surrealist."

"No saints," André said.

"Dosis sola facit venenum," Jacqueline said. "The poison is in the dose."

"Ah yes, Paracelsus," André said. "The Swiss doctor, alchemist, and philosopher of the German Renaissance, who gave us the value of observation in combination with wisdom."

Jacqueline proposed Paracelsus as the genius, rather than Freud, and soon they'd decided they could have a different genius for each suit, Freud *and* Paracelsus.

"How about a siren for the third character?" René Char offered.

"A singing temptress?" Nanée said doubtfully.

André said, "I would think you would like a siren, Nanée, for her power over us men."

She was outvoted. A siren it was to be.

They went on from there to reimagine the suits. In place of the spade, they considered a key of knowledge, then settled on the lock itself, the keyhole, the space that appeared empty but in fact held the hidden mechanics the key must turn. In place of the heart, the blood-red wheel of revolution.

"This begins to sound like a Communist game," Varian objected.

"You may call it 'the blood of change' in the United States," André assured him. "If you can get us there, we bequeath you renaming rights on the wheel."

Black stars for dreams—which seemed nonsensical to Nanée. "Stars aren't black; the sky that holds them is. And black would be for nightmares."

"Speaking of nightmares," Victor Serge said, "is it true Walter Benjamin's death was suicide?"

Benjamin had gone over the Spanish border in late September via a new route that had worked just days before for Lion Feuchtwanger. Despite admonitions to travel lightly so as not to attract attention, he'd insisted on carrying a suitcase full of manuscripts for the ten-hour mountain trek. He'd gotten out, but when he presented himself at the Spanish border post, they would no longer accept entry of stateless persons. He was taken under guard to a hotel near the Portbou police station, to be sent back to France. He died in that hotel room. A cerebral apoplexy, the attending doctor determined, but Benjamin had carried with him a quantity of morphine sufficient to take his own life. There was no safety for a refugee until he arrived on his final shore.

"We need a name for this game," Nanée said to change the subject.

"There will be more of that, suicides," Serge said, "with this new Kundt Commission going around. A fine little group of your fiercest Gestapo collecting for deportation to Germany anyone in Rivesaltes or Gurs or Camp des Milles who might have said an unkind word about the führer."

"We need one more suit," Nanée said, trying to push back the image of Edouard hanging himself by a noose made of his shirtsleeves from a rafter in some filthy room in some filthy camp. "For our game," she said.

André said, "Something to replace the diamond. Red."

"The hot flame of love?" Jacqueline suggested with a flirtatious glance to her husband. "We can call the game Le Jeu de l'Amour."

The Game of Love.

But André wanted to honor this moment, this place, this time.

"Le Jeu du Air-Bel?" Danny suggested. "Le Jeu des Nazis?"

"No saints, no sinners in this game," André declared. "No judgment."

"Le Jeu sans Compter?" T proposed.

Compter: to count, but also to reckon. A double entendre. André always did like wordplay.

"You are an optimist, T," Jacqueline said. "But I suggest we don't jinx ourselves by suggesting we won't meet our reckoning here in Marseille."

"Marseille," André said. "That's it. Let's call it simply Le Jeu de Marseille."

Every day in Marseille was a risk, Nanée thought. Every minute in Marseille was a moment in which a life might be lost. She ought to have gone that afternoon to Camp des Milles. She ought to have set off the moment the idea for getting Edouard out had come to her. It had to be done in the evening, anyway. She might be doing it now, instead of playing games under the nightmare stars of Marseille.

Saturday, November 2, 1940
VILLA AIR-BEL

Nanée put on the blue pinstripe Robert Piguet she'd worn when
she first met Varian, that to her said Evanston. "Convincing," T
called it, and although Nanée replied fliply, "Convincing of what?" she
knew the answer: that she was a woman of substance, used to being
listened to and taken seriously. And yet the suit wasn't as boring as
all that, either. Paired with a black belt and black gloves, it did draw a
man's eye. She pulled on her gray trench coat. She would like to wear
a hat, but a woman in a hat drew notice, and with no safe conduct pass
nor a way to get one without explaining where she meant to go, she
needed to move quietly until she was meeting the commandant at
Camp des Milles.

Varian wanted her to go and return in a single day, to plead a story
about Edouard's daughter and ask that he be allowed to come to Marseille to sort out the paperwork for a visa. Vichy would very occasionally allow this, albeit traveling with a guard, which would take
time to arrange. Nanée had balked, reluctant to risk calling attention
to Edouard unless she could expect him to walk out of the camp with
her, lest her visit leave him more vulnerable to the Gestapo's Kundt
Commission.

"I'm a terrible liar," she'd objected.

"We know what an excellent liar you are," Varian replied, "yet when
you deny it, it seems true even to me."

She added a diamond brooch and diamond cluster ring, gloves, and
a dab of Chanel N°5 at her throat, trying not to think about the fact
that it was the eve of the anniversary of her father's death. She packed
a change of underthings and a blouse and trousers. The pants would be
frowned at, but she'd be on her way back and she carried her American
passport and to hell with them all.

"But you'll be back tonight," T said when she saw the overnight case.

"Yes, that's the plan."

She was scared, no doubt about it. There was no guarantee her own plan would work any better than Varian's. But she'd left a life of guarantees in Evanston, and it was too late to be wanting them back.

"THERE IS AN earlier train. You don't wish to go earlier?" the ticket seller asked.

Nanée was buying a ticket to Arles to avoid suspicion, as there was no reason for her to travel to the little village of Les Milles other than to visit the internment camp. For her plan—not Danny's and Varian's, but hers—she needed to arrive at the camp in the early evening, and it would be easier to pass the time in Marseille than in tiny Les Milles, where she might draw attention.

"A ticket for the later train," she told the clerk. "Two tickets for the return."

Tickets in hand, she descended the wide white station stairs back to the boulevard d'Athènes and hurried past the pissoir with its Amer Picon aperitif ad, toward the splashing fountains of the Palais Long-champ. She passed shop after shop displaying the new ENTREPRISE FRANÇAISE signs meant to signal that they were French, not Jewish-owned, until she found a café without one, where she lingered half the day over cup after cup of ersatz coffee. If Danny or Varian knew she was taking a later train so she could appeal to the camp commandant in the soft hours of evening rather than the hard light of day, they might well prevent her from rescuing Edouard in the only way she could imagine would work.

A half hour before the train was to leave, she pulled the gray trench coat back over her suit and returned to the station. There, to avoid the attentive ticket puncher at the turnstile and the policeman beside him who might wish to see the French travel permit she didn't have, she went into the Buffet de la Gare. She bought yet another cup of ersatz coffee and, when she was sure no one was watching, slipped out the far door, which opened directly onto the train platform. She felt rather sly and clever about it, being illegal and all. Of course her papers might be checked anywhere along the way, and if she hadn't had the protection of her American passport, the consequences of being caught in transit without transit papers would be dire. But she did have her passport, and with it she hurried down the tunnel to the proper track, hopped on the proper train, and took a window seat, as any proper American woman traveling in France might do.

AT THE LES Milles train station, Nanée noted a modest hotel down the street where she could take rooms, then walked straight to the camp: ugly factory buildings behind an ugly fence, guards with guns staring down at her from atop hunting blinds, and filthy, emaciated men working in the yard, who unsettled her even more than the guards and guns.

"I'm here to see the commandant," she announced at the gate. She might be anyone. The camp commander's wife. His daughter. His sister. His mistress.

The guard hesitated.

She unbuttoned her coat with her black-gloved hand, as if heated from the exertion of the walk, to reveal her blue suit and the diamond brooch.

"One moment," he said, inviting her to step inside the yard and closing the gate behind her.

She studied the prisoners as she waited, hoping she might see Edouard or he might see her, but if he was among the men passing bricks from one pile to another for no purpose she could see, he was no longer someone she could recognize. Their conversations stopped. They watched her. But still, they moved those bricks.

Other prisoners crossed the courtyard with vats: the men's dinner, she supposed. Were there tables somewhere inside? A dining hall?

"What can I do for you?" a man asked, startling her.

The commandant was large for a Frenchman, with narrow eyes and what in Evanston might be called a prosperous middle. Encouragingly unattractive. Homely men, less inclined to arrogance, were so much easier to charm.

She smiled as sweetly as she could manage, knowing that even the worst of men were attracted to the nicest of girls, the ones they didn't imagine they could have.

"I'm sorry to descend upon you at dinnertime," she said.

He returned her smile and showed her into the guardhouse, where, as he said, she might be warmer.

Inside, she removed her coat. His eyes lingered. Yes, he liked the suit. Everyone in the guardhouse did.

She lowered her voice. "Is there perhaps somewhere more private? The matter I'm here about is . . . sensitive." She adjusted the brooch, wishing she had a hat to shadow her face.

"Perhaps you haven't had dinner yourself?" the man asked.

She smiled invitingly, but not too much so.

He turned to the guard. "I expect madame . . ."

"Mademoiselle," she said.

"Please have two dinners brought up to my private rooms," he said to the guard.

She hesitated. A good girl would hesitate. Make him want something he couldn't quite reach.

"I apologize," he said, "but I have no better dining facilities here to offer a lady."

She smiled her forgiveness and followed him.

Saturday, November 2, 1940
CAMP DES MILLES

Nanée and the commandant sat at a small table in the sitting room of a sort of apartment, not across from each other but rather more intimately cornered; if she wasn't careful to lean her folded legs away from him, they would touch his. She was carefully not careful as she removed first one black glove, then the other. She folded her hands, the diamond cluster ring facing him.

"This is so nice of you, to feed a weary traveler, Monsieur—"

"Robert," he insisted.

She looked demurely away lest he see the disgust in her eyes. What kind of Frenchman ran a camp like this? It would be revolting enough if he were German, to oversee men made to live so wretchedly. He was a Frenchman who ought to have fought to the death to save his country. Instead, he let prisoners starve while one of his men served him herb-roasted chicken, new potatoes, and delicate green beans on china, on a table set with real silver and a vase holding the last of the season's roses.

"Robert," she repeated, the name softer in French than in English. *Robe Heir. Bobby.* Imagining the sad, pathetic little boy he must have been, playing dress-up in an old robe that had been his grandfather's. Or his grandmother's. Yes, a sad little robe heir in his grandmother's ratty old robe.

He began to pour from a bottle of a local red.

She reached over and touched her hand to his, took the wine and poured first for him, then for herself, and set the bottle beside her own plate, in her control. She put the crystal to her lips, meeting his gaze over the glass and appearing to take a sip while merely wetting her lips with the wine.

Yes, this was going according to plan. But how well did he hold his liquor? Could she get him drunk enough that he might give her Edouard's residency permit and a camp release in exchange for nothing at all? Men were such absolute fools sometimes. Could she keep him drinking through some small affections until he fell drunkenly asleep, with no memory of the night beyond his own imagining of what they might have done?

They chatted easily. Or rather Nanée asked questions and let him talk about himself, which in all of society seemed to qualify for terrific conversation. Was there a man in this world whose favorite topic wasn't himself? The more the pathetic rooster puffed himself up, the more disgusted she became, but she was careful to appear attentive, to laugh lightly at jokes that were not the least bit funny and, as often as she could bear it, carefully allow her legs just the briefest bump against his.

A second bottle of wine was brought. She poured for the commandant and topped off her own glass. He handled his liquor unfortunately well.

"I have a friend here, Robert," she said. *Robe Heir.*

"Do you? But let's not talk of such things over dinner."

A stove was lit against the evening chill. Nanée glanced out the window; was smoke rising from chimneys elsewhere, to warm the prisoners? All that she could see was countryside; in these upper-story rooms, you had to stand at the window even to see the camp's encircling barbed-wire fence. But she didn't have to turn toward the window overlooking the yard and the factory to know that the only warmth for those imprisoned here would be the closeness of filthy bodies packed into inadequate space, in the company of fleas and lice, bedbugs, dysentery, and men dying in the night.

The server returned. He eyed her plate. Yes, she was finished, it was delicious, she said, wondering if the young man would eat the rest.

"You'd care for cognac?" Robert asked. "Dessert or cheese?"

The server was sent for cognac first, then to see what sweets might be available.

"Now, mademoiselle, perhaps you could tell me what I can do for you," Robert said as he offered her a cigarette.

She took it, forcing herself to touch his hand and lean close so he could smell her perfume before it was overwhelmed by tobacco. A small part of her wanted to giggle, as she might have if she were watching this moment played out on a movie screen. But that was just nerves. Nerves and disgust.

"I have a friend here," she said again.

Robert lit her cigarette. *Robe Heir.* "Do you? But I'm sure you know I cannot release a man simply because his pretty friend asks me to."

Nanée met his gaze as she took a first draw and gracefully exhaled.

Finally he said, "Perhaps you'll start by telling me your friend's name?"

She tapped her cigarette in the little silver ashtray set between them. Could she trust this man? If she gave his name, would that put Edouard in even more danger?

She unbuttoned her jacket as if to get more comfortable, revealing a peek at the short jacket's soft yellow silk lining and a view of the belt cinching her waist.

"It is not as you imagine," she said. "He is a friend."

He waited, watching, unconvinced.

"My friend is a father," Nanée continued. "His daughter's mother died some years ago. Now the daughter is in ill health. Truly, she needs her father. It's a difficult enough time for a child even when she is well."

Varian's plan, but on Nanée's own schedule. She had every intention of walking out of this camp with Edouard Moss at her side.

"It is a difficult time for all of France, of course," Robert said.

She uncrossed and recrossed her legs, making sure the silk stockings rustled softly, almost inaudibly, as thigh touched thigh under the conservative pin-striped skirt.

He looked away, his Adam's apple bobbing in his throat. "If I had his name, I might consider his file," he conceded.

The server returned with a bottle of Rémy Martin and two glasses. Robert told him, "I'll need you to bring me the file for . . ."

He looked to Nanée. The server looked with him.

Nanée hesitated, but what choice did she have but to plunge forward at this point? "Edouard Moss," she said quietly.

The commandant told the man he might leave the bottle on the table and dismissed him without thanks. He poured first his own glass, then one for her, the cognac sharp-smelling as it splashed into the crystal.

They drank and chatted about how very French it was to be short of everything and yet still have plenty of wine and cognac. She was beginning to imagine something dreadful—that the guard was punishing Edouard for her inquiry, or that Edouard wasn't there, that like Hasenclever or Benjamin, he might have given up hope and taken his own life—when finally the server returned with the file and a plate of madeleines.

Nanée waited for the server to leave, for the commandant to focus his attention again on her, then broke off a piece of madeleine and set it on her tongue.

His Adam's apple again bobbed in his neck.

The thing was gritty and sour in her mouth, like every bite of the dinner she'd managed to choke down. She reached for her cognac.

He invited her to join him on the sofa, where it would, he assured her, be easier for them to look at this file together. He moved himself, taking his glass and the file, leaving her little choice but to follow.

He opened the file and read quickly. He looked back up and considered Nanée. "And you are asking only for him to be allowed to come to . . . Where did you say this daughter is?" His voice pitched slightly higher now, excited. "It is possible I might arrange for guards to bring him for a brief visit if the girl is in Marseille with you."

Nanée took another cigarette and leaned forward for him to light it. She waited, not even imagining giggling this time.

She undid the top button of her crepe de chine blouse, as if to suggest how very warm it was in the generously heated room.

"You seem an honorable man, Robert," she said. "Are you an honorable man? One who keeps his promises?"

Sunday, November 3, 1940

CAMP DES MILLES

It was dark out, past midnight, but still a low murmur came from beyond the window. Nanée stood watching the men in the moonlight, waiting in line for the latrines. She pulled her suit coat closer around her, trying to imagine herself elsewhere as the commandant snored, asleep on the couch. What came to mind was that party at her apartment in Paris, Edouard Moss explaining why women in Surrealist art were so often naked and dismembered—because men were interested in exploring, without moral judgment, obsession, anxiety, fetish.

Without moral judgment, she told herself. With a life at stake. She believed this. She did.

But it had gone all wrong. They had been sitting on the sofa with Edouard's file and a camp release on the coffee table. Two chaste kisses, nothing more. She had put the pen in his hand. He seemed so pleased to be doing her this favor.

He set the pen back down beside the unsigned release then, and touched a finger to her shoulder, as if for one last kiss. He trailed it down a pinstripe toward her breast. She demurred.

He put his hand on the back of her neck and intertwined his fingers in her hair. He wanted another kiss, fine. One more kiss.

He didn't kiss her, though. He put his lips to her ear and whispered, "I want you to beg for this."

Had she laughed? No, she wanted to, but she saw how fraught that would be.

Then he was on top of her on that couch, shoving his hand inside her blouse, inside her brassiere. Did that hurt? Did she like that? He was drunk. He was drunk and he was big and the weight of his hand at her neck left her struggling for breath.

It was his shame, she told herself. Not hers. And yet she felt filthy. What had she done to allow him to believe the "games" that appealed to him might appeal to her? That's what it was for him—a game. He'd convinced himself she really did find his pig face and his paunch attractive. That she admired the power he had to humiliate others, to humiliate her. That she "liked it rough." Obsession. Anxiety. Fetish. As soon as it was over, he told her she knew how to please a man. He said it as if it were a compliment, a way of excusing his own fetish by projecting it onto her.

He was still snoring, still on the couch. She wanted to leave, to flee this horrible room and this horrible man. But if she gave him any hint that she hadn't enjoyed his attentions, if she left to return in the morning for Edouard, or even changed into her clean clothes before daylight, he might laugh at the idea that he had promised her anything. And what recourse would she have?

THE SUN WAS coming up, finally. Voices sounded in the courtyard outside, more than just the murmur of the men waiting in line at the latrine now. She tried to focus on them, to listen, to pick out from those thousands of voices Edouard's, which she'd heard on a single night nearly three years before.

Appalled, yes. Her father would be appalled. He might have shot the commandant to defend her honor, but it was her humiliation too, her shame—that was the way he would see it. Her mother too. Her brothers. Anyone who knew. She'd put herself in a compromising position. In doing so, she'd allowed this. Invited it, so many people would think. On a Sunday morning, no less. The Lord's own day. The very day, a dozen years ago, He'd taken her father.

Out in the yard, the roll call began—by number. She tried not to think about anything but the voices. Finally the guard called, "One hundred and thirty-two." Edouard's number. Danny had found out that much.

Silence.

Nausea washed through Nanée, the sense that she might have done this for nothing. But Danny had confirmed that Edouard Moss was here. Edouard's file was here.

"One hundred and thirty-two," a voice answered finally, uncertain. Was that Edouard's voice? She would have said he was younger-sounding, his voice deeper and warmer. But of course he would sound much older. Everyone now aged so fast.

She took her overnight case and her gray trench coat into the commandant's private bathroom. She longed to shower, but there was no lock on the door. She opened the case to the fresh brassiere and blouse, the panties and trousers and socks, and her flying scarf. Only when they were at the ready did she quickly strip off her jacket and blouse. She dampened the end of a sleeve of the soiled blouse, then stripped off her brassiere, wiped her chest, and pulled on the fresh brassiere and blouse. She pulled off her garters and stockings and panties and cleaned herself up as best she could with the blouse sleeve, only then shedding the skirt to pull on her trousers. She shrugged on the gray trench coat and looped the scarf once, loosely.

She might have left the clothes on the floor if she hadn't imagined the commandant fingering them again. Robe Heir. The sad little robe heir in his grandmother's ratty old robe. She stuffed them into the case, closed it, and washed her hands. She looked at herself in the mirror only then, when everything he'd touched had been washed off or stuffed away.

A bruise marked the base of her neck, already purple-blue. *I said I want you to beg.*

She adjusted her flying scarf to cover it, then pulled the collar of her coat up too. Nobody could know about this. It would change the way they saw her, whether they faulted her or not. They would stare at her, trying to see, imagining.

She returned to the bedroom and made enough noise that he couldn't help but wake.

"I need to get Monsieur Moss to his daughter," she said. She knew she ought to say something about enjoying the evening with him, but in spite of Varian's and Danny's confidence in her talent for lying, she knew it did not extend that far. *I hate to hurry your morning*, she tried to make herself say, but could not. *I'd be grateful if you would* . . . But she would be grateful to him for nothing, ever.

She fingered Edouard's residency permit in her coat pocket, where she'd put it after she freed herself from the sofa last night, after the commandant was asleep. The camp release sat on the table, still with the pen.

He scratched his hairy paunch under the shirt he still wore from the night before, eyeing her trousers with disapproval.

"You need to sign the release and get someone to take me to him," she said firmly. "You need to tell your men Edouard Moss is to leave with me."

Sunday, November 3, 1940
CAMP DES MILLES

Men clustered around vats of coffee being ladled into tin cups in the hard industrial space. The commandant hadn't brought Nanée himself, of course. He'd directed one of the guards to take her to Edouard Moss, who was to be released to her by his order.

"Edouard Moss?" she asked of the first prisoner she came to, working hard not to pull her scarf up against the stench of so many men living together on this uninhabitable factory floor. It wasn't their fault, she knew that, and yet it was unbearable.

A murmur rippled into a wave of silence, everyone staring at her.

"Edouard Moss?" she called out.

Nobody answered.

"Edouard Moss," she said. "I've come to get him. I have permission to take him to Marseille."

Another murmur arose, not spreading this time but all at once, many of the men looking toward the center, where one of three harsh lightbulbs lit the wretched space.

Still no one answered.

She made her way toward the lightbulb, afraid of what she would find. Edouard might have died in the night while she was with the commandant. Why had she waited? Why hadn't she demanded Edouard's release last night? But she'd had to tread so carefully; the commandant might as easily have changed his mind as not. He might even still.

The men parted to let her through. The guard remained near the stairs, unwilling to wade into the stench.

"I believe he's at the latrines," an old man said. He met Nanée's gaze, then looked to a suitcase sitting upright on the ground between his makeshift bed and another. A photograph sat propped on top of the case—Edouard and a woman so like Nanée herself that they might be sisters. Elza Moss, who would forever remain as confident and young as she was in this photo, even as the child she held grew up, as her husband's hair grayed, as Nanée herself saw the creep of fine lines at the corners of her eyes.

"Didn't someone say they saw Edouard in line at the latrine?" the man said to the others around him. And into the din of their response he whispered to Nanée, "He was here two nights ago, but not since yesterday morning."

Nanée felt she would retch from the loss and the grief and the fury. She was too late to save Edouard, just as she'd been too late to save her father on this same day twelve years ago, or even to see him. And the commandant, the vile little robe heir, had known she was too late. He'd purported to believe she wanted to offer what he wanted to take in exchange for the release of a man he knew to be dead.

"Someone was asking about him," the old man said. "The Gestapo."

The Gestapo? But no, that was Danny.

"The Gestapo are coming for him," the man said. "Don't let anyone know he isn't here. Give him as much time as you can."

"He's not dead?"

The alarm in the old man's face. She'd spoken too loudly.

He whispered, "They've allowed you to come in here to look for him, Nanée."

Nanée started at the sound of her name. How did he know who she was? She peered more closely: a long, familiar face, thinning hair, hooded eyes.

"I was afraid . . . ," he said. "Sometimes men die in the latrines at night and we don't even know they're gone. His photo, his wife and daughter. I was sure he was dead. I could imagine him leaving the suitcase, but not the photo. The fact that they've allowed you to come in here to look for him, though, suggests *they* think he's still here."

"He answered at roll call. I heard him." Realizing even as she spoke that it was this man's voice she'd heard. "I can't just leave without him," she whispered.

"If they find him, they'll send him to Dachau, as an example to the rest of us. Dachau. It's a German labor camp."

Far from helping Edouard, she'd put him in greater danger by exposing the fact that he'd escaped and was on the run.

"Come with me," she said. "Pretend you're Edouard."

The man looked at her, confused. "That would be too dangerous. I'm too well-known."

"Pretend you're Edouard," she insisted. "I'll get you out."

The guard called to Nanée, trying to signal her to bring her quarry along out of the godforsaken place.

"But . . . I'm Max Ernst," the internee said. "Even that fool of a guard knows exactly who I am."

Nanée tried to tamp down her astonishment, but she saw in his face that it was too late. Yes, that was the same roman nose, the same deep-set eyes. Max Ernst had been at her apartment on avenue Foch the night of the Surrealist exposition, with Leonora Carrington. Nanée had seen them both at later gatherings. His hair had been white and thin even then, but now it was nearly gone, as was his health.

"That guard isn't one to bend rules," he said.

The guard, seeing her look in his direction, motioned her again to move this along. She could defy him; there would likely be no consequence to her. But what about these men? What about Max Ernst?

"If you allow that Edouard isn't here," Ernst said, "all of Vichy will be looking for him."

But what choice was there?

"Make up something," he said. "Anything. Say you'll come back for him. If you tell them he's not here, he'll be found, and he'll be sent to Dachau. How far can he have gotten on foot in just a day?"

He took the photograph from the suitcase and thrust it toward her. "Take it," he said. "Find him. Give it to him, with regards from me."

"But if he's brought back, if he's captured and brought back, he'll need it more."

"I tell you, if he's captured, he will not be brought back here."

Sunday, November 3, 1940
CAMP DES MILLES

Only when the men were filing out to begin the day's work, when the courtyard would be full and she wouldn't be so obviously walking without Edouard across the empty courtyard, did Nanée rejoin the guard.

"Your prisoner?" he demanded.

She fingered the framed photograph in one coat pocket, Edouard's papers in the other. "At the latrines," she said. "He has dysentery, apparently such a bad case that he isn't able to travel."

The guard eyed her skeptically. She supposed the whole camp had heard by now how she'd spent the night.

"I will take you back to the commandant, then."

"I'm afraid I have to hurry or I'll miss my train."

No, he didn't believe her. She wasn't such a good liar as that. She glanced to Max Ernst, who was watching her as they'd planned. She leaned close to the guard and whispered, "It won't help any guard in this camp for the commandant to think a prisoner he's just agreed to release has already escaped. I don't imagine he likes to appear a fool." She let the thought sit there, register, alarm. "When no one is looking, you're going to open the gate, and I'm going to walk out." That way, if she could find Edouard, he would have his papers, and in any event it would seem he had left legally. But she couldn't be seen leaving alone, without him.

"How am I to arrange for no one to watch a woman like you?" the guard protested.

"I've taken care of that."

He stared at her. He saw his predicament. She might have felt sorry for him, but he was a Frenchman who knew how these men were forced to live, and would do nothing to help them. He would not even enter the space where they slept.

She touched her hand to her lips, the signal to Max, who was now headed out to the yard with the other men.

He nodded. Yes, he'd seen.

"All right, then," she said to the guard. "You're going to take me to collect my case from the guardhouse and get me as near as you can to the gate without me seeming to be leaving."

She took his arm, and he fell in beside her, heading out of the factory building.

"You will not punish the men who are going to save your skin with what they are about to do," she said. "You will persuade the commandant or the other guards or anyone else you need to persuade that you will deal with them, and if I hear so much as the faintest suggestion that they suffered any ill treatment, I will visit your commandant again. Do you understand?"

His Adams's apple bobbed in his throat. Desire and fear, they nestle so closely together in a weak man.

They entered the guardhouse, collected her overnight case, and emerged on the other side, nearer the gate. Max, watching from the line of brick-movers, saw her. A moment later he was swinging a fist at the fellow from the mat beside his in that filthy indoor space, just as they'd arranged. Everyone turned toward the fight, the other guards moving to intervene.

The guard with Nanée opened the gate, and she slipped out, with Edouard Moss's papers if not with the man himself.

Sunday, November 3, 1940
VILLA AIR-BEL

Nanée stood with her little suitcase in hand in her bedroom, finally, Dagobert licking her shoes, her ankles.

"It's okay, Daggs," she said. "I'm fine."

But she couldn't muster even the energy to pet him.

She'd slipped as quietly as she could into Villa Air-Bel, not wanting to answer anyone's questions about the camp or the long train ride back, showing the conductor only her American passport and her ticket and holding her breath, smiling innocently as he considered— Did she have no travel permit? And why was she only getting on at Les Milles with a ticket from Arles?—before he punched her ticket without question and moved on to the next passenger.

She closed her bedroom door and lit a fire in the fireplace, then stood watching it, soothed by Dagobert's busy tongue.

"It's okay," she said again, as much to herself as to him.

When the logs were caught, she set her case on the dresser and popped it open. She looked at herself in the mirror there, the dark circles under her eyes. She adjusted her scarf to better cover the deepening purple mark.

The panties and brassiere and blouse with the still-damp sleeve sat crumpled in the case, on top of the Robert Piguet suit.

She looked in the mirror again. It was his shame, not hers. Robe Heir.

She took the blouse out and set it on the fire, watched it slowly catch. Dagobert sat beside her, watching too. She added the panties, the brassiere. She took the silk stockings still attached to the garter out of the case next, tossed them too into the fire. Good silk stockings. Impossible to get these days. They seemed to shrink from the flames, giving off an odor of foul charred meat.

She stared at the suit. Somehow, the suit was the worst of it.

She'd just taken the jacket in hand when someone tapped lightly at the door.

"I'll be down in a bit," she said.

The door creaked open. T cautiously peered in. "Nanée, don't forget Miriam is leaving tomorrow."

Nanée tried to say of course she hadn't forgotten, but of course she had. This was Miriam's last night before she left for Yugoslavia, to try to get her fiancé back to the States.

"Nanée?" T said, registering the blouse in the fire, the stockings.

"I'll be down to help get ready for the party in a minute."

T took the suit jacket gently from Nanée's hands. "Wait, Nanée. Just wait."

"I'll never wear it again."

Even she could hear the anger in her voice.

T held the jacket out and examined it, the diamond brooch still on the lapel. She looked to Nanée—that frank, assessing gaze.

"Edouard wasn't there," Nanée said.

"Oh, Nan." T moved toward her, but Nanée stepped back. She couldn't bear to have anyone touch her.

T collected the skirt from the case and folded the two pieces carefully. She stood there holding them, watching the blouse and the stockings burn. "Do you want to tell me about it?"

Obsession. Anxiety. Fetish. But Nanée would never tell anyone. She couldn't have even T imagining this.

"What's to tell?" she said, embracing her rage. "I failed."

T set the suit aside and took Nanée's hand the way she did with Peterkin. Nanée wanted to object, but she didn't want to explain. She let T lead her to the little chair and sit her down.

"You're exhausted," T said. "Of course you are. It was a long trip, and you never have been any good at not getting exactly what you want. But you tried."

She picked up the suit.

"I won't ever wear it again," Nanée repeated.

"But someone else can. It's a convincing suit. At a time when so many people need to appear convincing. The suit of a woman of substance. At a time when we need so many more of you."

When Nanée didn't object, T looked at her oddly, differently. "Nanée?" She looked to the things in the fire again, then back to Nanée. "Oh, Nan."

Nanée looked out the window, to the long stretch of green and the train and trolley tracks, the sea.

"Are you sure you don't want to tell me about it?" T asked gently.

In the distance, a trolley crept across the tracks.

"I'm going to draw a warm bath for you down in the kitchen, okay?" T said. "A warm bath and a glass of something strong."

"Not cognac."

"I think there's some Calvados. Give me a few minutes, then . . . No, I'll come get you."

She stopped at the door and turned back. "You did a good thing, Nan," she said.

Sunday, November 3, 1940

A BROTHEL CELLAR

Edouard sat silently, his back to the wall, the cold wet of the cellar floor thick in his bones now. The bits of scamper in the dark no longer alarmed him, but the unfamiliar footsteps above now did. He quickly folded Luki's letter, words he couldn't see in the darkness but knew by heart, and tucked it back into his shirt pocket with the letters he'd written her. He wrapped his fingers around the knife he'd stolen from the upstairs brothel's kitchen early that morning, after the last of the clients left and the house quieted, just before the dawn.

Reluctantly he removed the iron grille over the hole in the cellar floor and climbed in, his feet instantly soaking in the foul water as he breathed in the underground stench.

The door at the top of the stairs creaked open. Light spilled down the rickety stairs. Not the cook come to get potatoes; the woman's hacking cough would have alerted him.

Edouard couldn't see the feet, but he could hear first one heavy step, then another.

He had the advantage, he told himself. His eyes were accustomed to the dark. If no second person followed, he had the advantage. He'd long ago given up the notion that he might not be able to kill another man.

He waded as quietly as he could through the low tunnel, away from the grate so that if it was opened, he wouldn't be visible from above. He emerged in an abandoned underground chapel, a small cavern at the other end that the brothel owner hiding him said dated from the Reign of Terror, when French revolutionaries visited the kind of violence on Roman Catholic clergy that the Nazis now visited on French Jews. It was odd, the things the mind turned to, to stave off fear. The bare stone here would have been the altar. Jesus on the cross behind it. He'd seen them when the madam sent him down with a flashlight so he would know where he was to hide if anyone came. No one unwilling to climb into the flooded well could know about the chapel. The only other person who knew it existed was the Russian Communist who'd hidden there before him.

Quiet, careful footsteps now in the basement. No light that Edouard could make out, but he wouldn't be able to see it from here unless it was pointed right down at the grate.

What could Edouard do if someone did climb into the well, if they did come down here to search? He might just submerge himself here. But better to wait at the edge of the tunnel, to have surprise on his side. Even if there were more than one of them, only one person at a time could emerge from that narrow tunnel.

Could hiding in this shit hole be better than Camp des Milles? What had he been thinking when he'd snuck onto Tater's truck as it carried away their garbage to feed to his pigs? He'd thought it his good luck when they stopped beside another truck loaded with wine, the two drivers sharing a friendly smoke and chat. He used the moment to slip from one truck to the other, with no idea where it was headed, only hoping it would take him farther than Tater's farm before he was discovered missing.

He ought to have waited for something he knew would take him toward Paris rather than away. That was his big mistake. He was farther from Luki now, not closer.

But in truth he didn't even know that; he didn't know where Luki was.

He had no money. No ration card for food. No papers at all. If he was found anywhere in France, he was doomed.

But with the Kundt Commission coming for him, it was better to be cowering in a foul-smelling abandoned chapel in a dank basement than to be a sitting duck. What choice did he have? He'd have been found if he'd wandered the landscape outside the camp. No one who did that lasted more than a day.

He'd been gone nearly two days now. This must be someone looking for him, or looking for refugees generally. There were rumored to
be hundreds or more hiding here, looking for a way to leave France.
That was why he'd come here when he realized where the truck had
brought him. If there were refugees here, there had to be people helping them. Nobody here had much affection for authority, most living
afoul of the law in one way or another.

Just one set of footsteps, alone. He was sure of it.

Why were they being so quiet, so careful?

The grate scraped across the cellar floor.

A flashlight shone down onto the black water.

Edouard stood perfectly still, holding the knife.

Sunday, November 3, 1940
VILLA AIR-BEL

Were you your father's favorite?" André asked Nanée. The question came out of nowhere. No one here knew this was the anniversary of her father's death. No one knew that she'd been in France when he died, that she'd insisted on going to Paris when he wanted her to come home, that she hadn't gone back even for his funeral.

They sat at a long table dragged out onto the belvedere for the warm November evening, Miriam's last with them. The antique tureen Madame Nouget had filled for the occasion with vegetables sculpted to look like a meat roast sat empty now, surrounded by wine bottles from which André kept refilling glasses as they played his favorite interrogation game. She wanted to tell him to turn his overbearing, overinsightful, overinsistent prying back on himself. But that was just her exhaustion talking, and she didn't want to ruin Miriam's last evening.

She rested a hand on Dagobert's head in her lap and whispered, "Hitler! Hitler!" and he barked the way he did, and they all laughed, their faces open and warm and happy as they sat in the semidarkness of moonlight, splashes of electric light spilling out through the French doors. How carefully Nanée tended to André's ego, and Varian's too, playing this game because both men loved the excuse to ask probing questions of others without ever answering any themselves. Truth, André called the game, but Nanée and T and Miriam secretly called it Sexual Confessions. That seemed the real truth André meant to get at. Nanée paid the expenses of the château; you'd think that would gain her some respect, but she was wise enough to understand that men who needed what you offered them tended to be less likely to respect you, not more. That was what had been going on the night before, too; the commandant had needed to believe he didn't need anything he couldn't have.

The commandant, she thought of him as now, stripping him of his name as if that might strip away her anger. She was trying so hard to shake it off for Miriam's sake, but she was awash in it, in the loss of Miriam's company, in the fear that her friend would never even get to Yugoslavia, or be unable to get out. In the loss of Daddy on this very day and her own inability to become the woman he wanted her to be. In her failure to save Edouard. Why in the world had she felt she should be the one to save him? Why had she imagined she could? Edouard, who'd drawn that head in flight goggles and a gilded birdcage that both was hers and wasn't, who even before they met had taken photos that made her feel understood.

"But were you?" André repeated as the laughter settled back into more pouring of wine. "Your father's favorite?"

You spied on your father? Did you spy on anyone else?

"I'm not sure Daddy had a favorite," she said, fingering her scarf just to confirm it was still there, still hiding her neck. She wished she had the excuse of getting a sweater against the growing evening chill, but she already had her favorite cashmere—a sweet pink, the color of innocent girlhood—draped over her shoulders. André didn't mean to make her uneasy. Already Nanée had come to recognize the peculiar look he turned on people he meant to make uncomfortable. The way he studied her before each careful, probing question was softer and kinder, yet as impossible to resist. She ought just to peel off her skin and lay it out on the table; he could see right into her mind and her heart.

He waited. He was good at that. Remaining silent. Waiting for more.

"That would suggest Daddy cared about who we were rather than how we reflected on him," she said finally. Bitter words. Why had she said them? Was it even true?

"And how did you 'reflect on' your father?" André asked.

Nanée smiled as she might have if Daddy were there. Evanston

Rules: a young woman must always tuck negative feelings out of sight. The odd thing was that some part of her wanted to answer André's question. She didn't want anyone to hear, but she felt somewhere deep inside a compulsion to answer.

"I was a good girl," she said.

André laughed. They all laughed. She'd meant them to, and yet the answer was also the truth.

"Were you really?" André's tone suggested that he did, in fact, believe her. He was so good at this. No one walked away from a game of Truth with André without having spilled their guts. He knew, somehow, what was true and what wasn't, and he believed he was doing you a service, that the truth really would set you free.

Nanée looked out across the dark landscape, the stars fading to nothing in the night mist nearer the sea. "Yes. In Evanston, I was a good girl."

André responded provocatively, "For your father?"

"Really, André!" Jacqueline said.

"I fear it's more common than we imagine," André said. "But I take it from the shock on Nanée's sweet face that the answer is no."

He returned his gaze to Nanée, clenching and unclenching his hands in that way he did. "And in Europe? Were you a good girl in Europe?"

Nanée ran a finger around the rim of her empty wineglass.

André lifted the bottle and poured the last of it for her.

"Were you a good girl in Europe?" he repeated.

She adjusted her sweater on her shoulders, feeling the chill of the night mist as she looked out to the long stretch of darkness. Was that sound a car? She peered out to the limestone-capped posts near the main road and the train and trolley tracks. Was that the dimmest glow of light peeking through blue-painted headlights? Was it her car? Hers was rarely used on account of the gas shortages, but Varian had asked her to loan it to Danny just after dinner, although neither would tell her why. Surely it was Danny. But what if it wasn't? What if it was someone the commandant had sent to arrest her? No one bringing good news came this late at night.

"Nothing I did here would embarrass Daddy," she said to André, "because no one he knew would know."

"So you were a bad girl in Europe?"

I said I want you to beg. Had it really been a game for the commandant, or had he seen in her expression that she might have laughed at him?

"In Italy?" André pressed. "That's where you first lived, yes?"

"No," she said. "I mean, yes, I lived in Italy. But . . . I was a good girl there. I *thought* I was being . . . daring." She slipped her arms into the sleeves of the sweater. Fingered her scarf, still in place. "The first time I bought a condom in Italy, I didn't know the Italian word for it, so I asked for *qualcosa per fermare la concezione,* something to stop conception." Offering to André the kind of little anecdote that might distract him, might allow her to spin this conversation in another direction. "The condom was for a friend, part of a complicated plan to convince a man she was quite in love with that her previously squandered virginity was intact. She'd told him she had never been with a man but rather 'did it herself,' with 'a sort of thingamajiggy.'"

André laughed.

"A thingamajiggy?" he repeated.

"Yes," she said, remembering the shock she'd felt at her friend's willingness to acknowledge such a thing as loss of virginity, and to suggest aloud a self-pleasuring alternative. "So we had to make a thingamajiggy to show the fellow. Hence the need for the condom."

André again laughed. Most of the table did.

"And this amour of your friend," he said, "he fell for your ploy?"

"He proposed that night."

The marriage hadn't lasted two years, but at the time they'd felt triumphant.

"And yet this 'daring' was for your friend."

Nanée met his gaze. "Yes, that's right."

"When did *you* become a 'bad girl,' then? Bad by Evanston Rules, which I gather means a girl has taken a lover?"

Taken a lover. It was what the European girls at the contessa's school had called it, too. So much more sophisticated than "gone the limit," and yet less true.

"When did *you* become such a terrific bad boy, André?" she responded.

"Ah, see, she tries to duck the question," he said, "and so we know there is something hiding here."

"In Switzerland," Nanée said, surprising herself at the ease with which the admission came. It had been after Daddy died, after Mother came to Paris and took up with Misha, after her brothers and Mother and Misha left to go back to the United States while she stayed to ski. She wondered why she was embarrassed by those details, unwilling to admit them. She wondered if André could read them on her face or hear them in her voice.

"And this first man, was he a good lover?"

"He was a bit of a scoundrel, André. I seem to be drawn to scoundrels."

T and Jacqueline and Miriam laughed. Lord, Nanée was going to miss Miriam's too-loud laughter.

"Again she avoids the question," André said to the table. He turned back to Nanée and repeated, "Was he a good lover?"

Was he? She'd imagined herself in love with him to justify going the limit, then dated one scoundrel after another as if to punish herself for being such a fool as to squander her virginity on a man to whom it meant precisely nothing. "At the time I had nothing to compare him to."

"But now you do."

Kind, understanding Tony in Barcelona had showed her how sex was meant to feel. She must have stumbled on him by mistake; he was a good bit more decent than her usual choices. But unlike the other men she'd dated, he wasn't "her class." He wasn't a man she could take home.

"Was Switzerland a good lover? I guess not, but then surprisingly few men are," she said, with a look that suggested perhaps André, too, was less satisfying than he might think.

Again, the women at the table laughed. But André simply clasped and unclasped his hands again, pleased with this confession, with the notion of a younger Nanée lying in that bed in Switzerland, not understanding what she was missing.

"And since then, you've had better lovers?"

Nanée looked again to the drive. Surely that was the dim glow of headlights? Danny, whose return would distract Varian, and with him André. But nobody else was looking.

"Perhaps even men you've loved?" André prodded.

"I've thought so," she said. Again fliply. Again the truth.

"Thought they were better in bed, or that they loved you?"

"That wasn't your question," she said. "Your question was whether *I* loved *them.*"

They all looked to the drive; yes, everyone now heard. They followed the slow progress of a shadow topping the hill.

"Your latest lover," André said, "was he better or worse than that first man?"

She lifted her glass and took a sip. She was glad of the darkness. She had imagined she could control the commandant, when there was nothing about the situation that she controlled. She had imagined she would rescue Edouard Moss, when she'd been putting him in more danger rather than less.

"I'm beat," T said. "You must be beat, Nan. Shall we head in to-gether?"

Nanée focused on the car headlights, their dim glow swinging to-ward them now as the car approached the gate. She stared, hoping to make out the car, but it was impossible to see anything with the head-lights still on, even dimmed.

"Better or worse?" André repeated.

"He wasn't a lover," Nanée managed.

"I think that's enough, André," Jacqueline said.

"How long ago was he?" André pressed.

"Leave it, André!" T said. "Bloody leave it alone!"

They all turned to T, startled. T didn't rise to anger, ever.

Her friend meant to help her, but it would be easier if she might just give some answer, some small truth that hid the rest.

"I . . . ," Nanée started.

The car stopped just beyond the gate. Doors opened. At the crunch of footsteps on gravel, Jacqueline was standing, saying with alarm, "Varian?"

Good god, it *was* someone sent from the camp. That fool of a guard hadn't kept quiet.

"It's okay," Varian said, rising as the gate creaked open and they heard the low murmur of voices—Danny's voice, thank goodness. Two sets of feet coming up the steps, not more. Two shadows crossing the belvedere in the spill of the light from the French doors.

Danny said, "Hey, you're all still out here?"

"Edouard," Varian said. "Welcome."

"Edouard Moss!" André said. "Good god, man, you gave us a fright. Danny, you might have let us know you were returning with company. We'd have opened the good stuff."

They were all standing now. Somehow, Nanée too was standing.

"Mr. Fry," Edouard was saying, declining to shake Varian's hand on account of his own filthy hands and clothes, his shoes and his pants looking and smelling as if he'd waded through sewage.

"Varian," Varian insisted, already pouring Edouard a glass of wine, insisting he take it. "I'm so glad we've got you here. Why don't you sit and have something to eat? I asked Madame Nouget to set something aside."

"André," Edouard said in greeting. "Jacqueline."

He kept his distance, embarrassed.

"You remember T," Danny said. "And Nanée."

Edouard stared, clearly as stunned to see Nanée as she was to see him.

"You might have been here yesterday if you hadn't fled, by the way," Danny said. "Nanée went to fetch you from Camp des Milles, only to find you weren't there."

Edouard looked from Nanée back to Danny. "I . . . Nanée, what a surprise. I . . . I had no idea you were still in France."

Nanée, with a hand to her scarf, said, "Wherever did Danny find you?"

"We got word at the office yesterday that Edouard was here," Varian said, "hidden in a cellar in the Panier."

Nanée, feeling dread sinking into her exhausted bones, managed, "Yesterday?"

"Not an hour after your train left," Varian said. "If we could have gotten word to you to call you off, we would have."

Yesterday, while she sat in her little blue suit at that café by the Palais Longchamp, passing the time until she could take the later train.

"We felt we'd better get him somewhere safer than the Panier," Danny said, "so we brought him here to the château."

"We fear, Nanée, that your visit may have alerted the camp to the fact that Edouard had escaped," Varian said. "Not your fault. Of course not your fault. Just bad luck. Danny tried to get him last night but the streets were teeming with police." He turned to Edouard.

"We've set aside one of the château's best rooms for you. Second floor. I'm afraid all the 'library suites' are booked this evening, but there is a nice room down the hall."

Still Edouard stared at Nanée as she stood in a splash of light from inside the house.

"You're shivering, Nanée," he said, stepping toward her and beginning to take off his jacket to give to her.

His face as the light hit it was even squarer than she remembered. Thinner. Far more deeply lined. His thin lips were even more set in sorrow than they had been that January she'd first met him, just after his wife had died. The mole at the end of his left eyebrow was the same, though. His eyes were the same compelling green even in this dim light.

He stopped himself just short of her.

He ought to be the one shivering, she thought. His pants were wet up to his knees.

"Danny, I'm filthy," he said. "Give Nanée your jacket, will you? She's shivering."

PART III

NOVEMBER 1940

We went, changing our country more often than our shoes.

—Bertolt Brecht, "An die Nachgeborenen"

Monday, November 4, 1940
VILLA AIR-BEL

Nanée watched little Peterkin carefully carry his mug of milk, still warm from the cow, to Edouard; even the child could see from the sharp bones of Edouard's face and shoulders and wrists that he was nearly starved to death, but he did look better this morning thanks to a bath and sleep in a decent bed. Miriam was off to Yugoslavia and most everyone else was off to their days, with only T, Peterkin, and Nanée lingering in the dining room while Varian and Edouard discussed with Bill Frier whether Edouard's documents ought to be under an alias. Nanée looked into her ersatz coffee, afraid the guilt would show on her face. She ought to have told them immediately that she had Edouard's real French residency permit and the release from Camp des Milles, but she'd had no idea that Varian had already set Bill Frier to the task of making Edouard forgeries, nor how she would explain having his real documents. To leave France, Edouard still needed so many documents she didn't have, anyway. French transit and exit passes, Spanish and Portuguese transit visas, a destination visa, and passage on a ship from Lisbon.

Varian was explaining that men younger than forty-two were often nabbed at the border even when their papers were in order, to prevent them fighting for the British. "We might explore getting you a demobilization certificate," he said.

"I wasn't in the military," Edouard replied.

Nanée petted Dagobert, who sat quietly in her lap, as Varian described the scheme. There had been a dear little sergeant at Fort St. Charles who, for two hundred francs, would set anyone up with a *certificat de démobilisation et route de marche*. You gave him a French-sounding alias and a few details about where you fought for France—although of course if you really fought, you wouldn't be talking to him—and he issued a certificate confirming that you were a French soldier whose residence was in North Africa. Voilà, not only were you in line to be transported "home," but your passage on a ship to Casablanca—neutral ground from which a refugee could get anywhere—was paid by the Vichy government.

"But I understood that escape route was shut down," Nanée said. "And that the sergeant was arrested, along with every 'soldier' showing up at the Port Administration to ask about available berths."

"There are always enterprising individuals looking to make an easy profit," Varian said. "We're hopeful someone will take up the task."

Thank heaven for Vichy contradictions and inefficiencies.

"Even if they do, what about Luki?" Edouard smiled apologetically. "She's only five, not quite old enough to enlist."

Varian looked to the empty plates around the table, not so much as a breadcrumb left behind. Madame Nouget had taken to weighing out the bread in even portions each morning and giving each person their share, to be eaten as wanted over the course of the day.

"Danny didn't tell me you had a daughter," Varian said. "And she's still in France?"

"I haven't seen Luki in over a year, since I put her on a train to Paris." Edouard's willow-green eyes were moist now. "She might be passing as a gentile, and I can't risk making inquiries in case she is."

He seemed to be suggesting he would go get her if only he knew where she was, but of course the Germans had forbidden Jews to return to the occupied zone since mid-August. For Edouard to try to retrieve his daughter from Paris would be suicide.

"I can't leave without Luki," Edouard said, seeming stronger each time he said her name.

"You're an escapee from an internment camp. It's too dangerous for you to stay here, not just for you but for all of us." Varian adjusted his glasses, a tic Nanée had come to see meant he was tamping down his irritation. "Let me explain to you what we have to do to get you out. For your American visa, I have to get your name from here to the US authorities without alerting Vichy to your whereabouts, lest you end up back in that camp or worse. I cannot simply send a telegram. Those days are over."

To smuggle the names for visas out, they now copied them onto long, thin strips of paper pasted end to end, which they wound tightly, encased in rubber, and inserted into the bottom end of tubes of tooth-paste, which they then re-crimped and sent with refugees; if their bags were searched, they would only be carrying clothes and toiletries.

"Someone in the States will have to submit an application for you to the Inter-Departmental Committee on Political Refugees, which is as cumbersome as it sounds—representatives from the FBI, the State De-partment, the intelligence divisions of the War Department and Navy, and the immigration section of the Justice Department. They present recommendations and provide assistance to the consuls in considering visa applications. You'll need affidavits in support of your application to have any hope of consideration by them, preferably from Americans of some stature."

"I've worked with some American journalists, years ago now, but they might vouch for me," Edouard offered.

"If the committee can be convinced," Varian said, "then the Ameri-can consul general *might* grant you an interview. He has his own opin-ion of things, and to be honest, he's a bit of a cold fish, with no affection for refugees. He thinks Germany will win this war, so why offend them? If he doesn't like your politics or your religion or haircut or the simple fact that you speak German, your visa request is denied. Maybe luck is with you, and the consul general can't be bothered, leaving Vice Consul Bingham to oversee your case." Bingham was a great ally for refugees; he'd housed André in his villa and rescued Lion Feucht-wanger from St. Nicola in the most extraordinary way, dressing the famous writer in a woman's coat, dark glasses, and a shawl over his head, and passing him off as his own ancient aunt. "We of course try to arrange for our applications to end up with Bingham, but we can't control when or how the committee sends your information to the consulate. And that is just the American visa—the easy part. The hard part is getting you out of France."

Varian again adjusted his glasses. "Let's do this. I have a visa list going out tomorrow. Let me have Lena add your name. And I can send a coded cable to initiate affidavit requests from your journalist friends. With the difficulty in communications, we won't necessarily know what progress is being made until the American consulate here calls you for an interview, if ever they do, but this will put the process in motion."

Nanée, watching Edouard's face, was reminded of him sitting in her apartment back in Paris. *You are thinking this is not an answer? But it is merely not the answer you wish to hear.*

"I appreciate that," Edouard said. "But I can't leave France without Luki."

NANÉE WAS SITTING alone in the small greenhouse later that day, tucked up onto a creaky old wicker chair beside the rusted garden tools, when someone tapped lightly at the glass door, startling her. She'd been staring down at her book, *Le morte d'Arthur,* as if she might make the words mean something, she might lose herself in Malory's stories of King Arthur, Lancelot and Merlin and Guinevere, and Tristan with the Belle Isolde, his uncle's wife, the dark side even to chivalry.

"I'm sorry to bother you," Edouard said as the door swung open. He stood there, not inside the greenhouse but not out of it either, as if he needed to speak with her but didn't relish the task. "I just . . . I wanted to thank you."

For one alarming moment, she was sure he somehow knew what had happened at Camp des Milles. She looked down to her book again, the hard black-and-white pages against the soft fur of her Schiaparelli bracelet. She couldn't say why she'd worn it today. She'd seen it there in her jewelry box, next to the diamond brooch.

"I have your papers," she said, the thought inadvertently finding voice. The papers were still in the pocket of her gray trench coat. They wouldn't help him get an American visa, and even with them he couldn't get a French exit visa, but they might help keep him from being arrested and thrown in a camp again before they could get him out of France.

"My real papers?" Behind the question, perhaps an accusation—it wouldn't help him to think false papers were real. "No, they can't be. My real papers are at Camp des Milles."

She turned again to the book, letter after letter collecting into sentences, paragraphs, pages, a story that wasn't real but that did reveal a truth. "I . . . The camp commandant gave them to me."

"He just gave them to you?"

"I did ask nicely," she said, trying for her best innocent smile, although she didn't feel innocent. Robe Heir. Bobby. The smell of him was still everywhere, despite the bath T had drawn for her yesterday and another she'd taken just that morning. It was on her hands and in her hair, in her nose and mouth, on the knees she'd crossed so enticingly in her silk stockings, and between her legs.

She looked out through the glass walls of the greenhouse to the outside, the bare branches of the climbing roses. When had the last of the leaves fallen?

"Vile men like him will do the most extraordinary things sometimes when they're sweet on a girl," she said.

Edouard studied her for a long moment, as if he could see that the papers were indeed real and what she might have done to get them.

She wished she had Dagobert with her, but he had been so happy to go out with the children.

"Well," he said, "it appears I can't leave under my real name, even with good forgeries. Vichy isn't going to let an escapee go so easily."

"The release is there too," she insisted, her sudden anger as thorny as the rose vines. "You don't have to worry that you're putting anyone here at risk by staying with us. I . . . I'll bring them to you when I come back in." Needing to have him leave before he did understand. "I . . . I'm just reading."

"Oh course," he said, an edge in his tone that she thought must be in his eyes and in the set of his square jaw, that single mole, but she stared down at her book, unable to meet his gaze.

"I'm sorry to have bothered you," he said.

"It's no bother," she said, still staring down at the letters on the page, black against white.

"Well," he said. "I'll leave you to your book, then."

Still he stood there. She could feel his gaze on her as she pretended to read.

Finally the light changed as he stepped back from the doorway, and the greenhouse door clicked quietly closed. The whole time, he hadn't even stepped inside.

Monday, November 4, 1940

VILLA AIR-BEL

Such a strange thing, to have walls around him and a door that closed, a fireplace to warm him, and food enough, eaten while sitting in a real chair at a real table with china and silverware and wine in a crystal glass rather than squatting at his straw mat on the concrete floor to sip gruel from a metal mug. That's what Edouard was thinking about—trying to compose in his head a letter to Luki describing this villa—when Nanée appeared at his bedroom door.

"Your papers," she said, holding them out as if they were indisputably real.

He hurried to stand, awkward as he saw her register the carefully made bed in the bare room. He had nothing anymore. Even the clothes he wore belonged to someone else. Rose, the maid, had been charged with burning his own clothes and the vermin that came in with him. She'd done it while he bathed last night. She'd spent a good hour combing lice from his hair too—him holding back the tears that threatened at the simple touch of her fingertips on his scalp. Today, Jacqueline was in town to get him new clothes that would fit. The kindness here was almost unbearable.

He crossed the few steps to Nanée, close enough to accept the papers but no closer, not wanting to offend her as he had somehow in the greenhouse. He ought to explore in his art this desire to touch Nanée's sweater just to feel its generous softness, his longing to feel the fur of the bracelet he'd once held to Luki's cheek. But he no longer had even a camera, and he hadn't taken a photo since that series of the caped woman he'd taken the day before Elza's death.

Luki. How would he find her?

"Thank you," he said, taking the papers and setting them on the dresser. When he turned back, the expression on her face so like Elza's had changed. Had she seen his doubt?

If the papers were forged and she knew it, she would tell him. She wasn't a fool. If they were forgeries, she would know that he needed to know when they might be used and when they might need to be destroyed. So either they were forged and she didn't know it, or they were real. But if they were real, how could she have gotten them?

She blinked back some emotion and offered a smile that was all bluster of some sort, hiding something. He wondered briefly where her dog was.

"This too," she said. "I didn't want to take it in case you ended up back at the camp. I didn't imagine I would ever see you again. But your friends assured me you wouldn't. Wouldn't end up back in that camp."

If he was caught, he'd be sent someplace much worse.

She held out the photo of Elza and Luki and him, the little frame he'd set atop his suitcase every night before he wrote all those letters to Luki that he couldn't send.

He'd thrown his arms around Nanée before he even realized what he was doing, how inappropriate it might seem, how presumptuous. Hell, what if Rose hadn't gotten all the lice?

"I'm sorry," he said, reluctantly loosening his hold.

She held tightly, almost as if she needed his touch as much as he needed hers. "It's okay," she said, her gentle voice a balm.

He realized he was weeping, then. Weeping at the simple touch of another human, someone not inadvertently bumping into him and apologizing for invading the tiny bit of space that was his. October 14, a year and twenty days ago—that was the last time he'd hugged someone. Luki at the station in Sanary-sur-Mer. A quick goodbye because he had so much packing to do, and he was to join her in Paris the next day.

"It's okay," Nanée repeated. "You're here. We're going to take care of you."

Somehow they'd moved to sitting on the edge of the bed, just talking. Then sitting side by side, their backs against the pillows. He wanted to touch her hand or her delicate eyelashes, but he didn't want to risk offending her in whatever way he had earlier.

The photo of Elza and Luki was on the table beside his bed—had he taken it from her hand? It was the only thing in the room other than the nightclothes André had loaned him, now hanging in the armoire, and the furniture.

"It's a bit empty, I know," he said, meaning the room, but seeing as he spoke that what he really meant was his life.

Luki was out there somewhere, though. Max was right. Edouard would know it if she were not. And this photograph belonged to him. A something. A family. A future.

"You . . . Would you like to be able to work?" Nanée asked. "To take photos?" Before he could answer, she rushed on, "You were in Sanary-sur-Mer? Did you leave your cameras with anyone? I could get them for you."

His cameras. The worn leather strap of his Rollei. The cold snap of its case. The smooth metal of his Speed Graphic's flash attachment. The thin edge of a filmstrip and the hard knob of his enlarger. The press of an eyepiece to his face.

"I can go to Sanary-sur-Mer," she offered. "I suppose the place you were staying was re-rented, but maybe—"

"It's mine," Edouard said. "The cottage. I bought it for Luki to have a home."

But was the cottage still his? The Vichy government had likely already confiscated it on the excuse that he was a foreigner, or a Jew, or simply because it was on the Mediterranean and so might pose a security risk, or on no excuse at all—just as they'd taken Edouard himself.

"I don't need my things," he said. "I need Luki."

"I'm sorry. Of course nothing else matters compared to finding Luki."

He touched a hand to his pocket, to Luki's letter to him and the ones he'd written but couldn't send. "My friend Berthe took Luki to Paris," he said, "but I don't even know if Berthe is still in France, or if Luki is with her. I can't write to them myself, not letters I can send. If Berthe is pretending Luki is her child, it would put them in danger."

"Of course," Nanée said. "I . . . Why don't I get some stationery and a pen, and I'll meet you in the library?"

So simple. So easy. They would compose a letter together, one woman who'd lived in Paris writing another who still did, like old friends. No one would suspect. This was how he could reach out to Berthe without putting Luki and her at risk.

But how would he get Luki out of the occupied zone? The Nazis would shoot them on sight.

One step, he thought. One step, then another, the way he'd survived the camp. Find Luki. Maybe she was already safely out of France.

He followed Nanée out to the library, where André and Jacqueline sat drawing at the little table in the corner. As Nanée went to fetch her stationery, Edouard studied the playing card Jacqueline was creating—bright red and yellow and blue triangles and swirls that might have been painted by Miró.

"It's Baudelaire," she explained.

Nanée, rejoining them, said, "And I suppose, André, that octopus is some 'marvelous' personage too?"

The tentacles so much like the drawing André had done that night in Paris, André's octopus body wedged between the head Edouard meant to be Nanée and his own legs she had drawn.

How had André come to be living here in Nanée's villa? With Jacqueline, but it wouldn't be the first time a Surrealist indulged in a ménage a trois.

"They're making a game," Nanée told him. "A card game which I suppose André will insist we play—after he makes up the rules to suit himself."

She smiled that way she did, softening her challenge, and sat down and took up that beautiful pen, moss-green agate with a gold clip and a gold band and bite marks at the end of the barrel. The pen he'd used to draw the face that wasn't Nanée's, that he'd boxed up in a hand-sketched birdcage; the eyes that weren't hers either, that he'd hidden behind her flight goggles as if his grief might so easily be captured and contained.

She set the pen to paper. "Now, let's find Luki, shall we?"

Tuesday, November 6, 1940

VILLA AIR-BEL

Edouard lingered over Madame Nouget's grape-juice-sweetened polenta pudding in the Grand Salon, needing to eat slowly what everyone else thought were meager rations, as Danny manned the radio dial and interpreted the BBC announcer's voice he alone was able to make out through the crackle. Roosevelt had won a third term in the States. The Germans had sunk the British merchant cruiser the *Jervis Bay*, while Ireland refused to allow Britain to use its ports. Jews from southwest Germany were being given thirty minutes' notice before being shipped to camps here in the French free zone, the French protesting they shouldn't be a dumping ground for Germany's Jews. This French need to label him, Edouard thought. An excuse to turn away. Before France lost the war, the label was "German," with the suggestion that he might sympathize with or even be a spy for the Nazis. Now that France aligned itself with Hitler, the label was "Jew."

"Now," André said, "the Murder Game." He'd already pulled out a jar filled with paper slips and was offering them around.

"See, this is the thing about André," Nanée said to Edouard. "He refuses to believe the whole world might not want exactly what he wants."

But already Jacqueline and T were taking the children up to bed, Peterkin with Dagobert, and Danny and Gussie were pulling the drapes to block out the moonlight.

The game was simple. Each of them imagined and wrote down an assassination scenario (a weapon or means of death and a motive), then drew slips from one jar to determine the assassin and the inspector, and from a second jar to determine the victim. Only the assassin knew who he and the victim were. They would turn off the lights and the assassin would make his way to the victim, to mimic his murder scenario in some appropriate way.

"A finger pistol to the head if your murder is by gun," Nanée explained. "Tap their lips if you're a poisoner."

"If you prefer to strangle, hands on the neck, yes, but please don't squeeze too hard," André said.

T, rejoining them, said, "Then the poor victim dies and the inspector begins the interrogation. True-or-false questions."

"There are no winners, no losers," André explained. "Only an exploration of the mind."

"We play to the death," Nanée said. "Then we keep playing."

Even Edouard laughed, though he found this unsettling. He wrote down a quick idea and put it in his pocket, then took his turn pulling a slip from the assassin/inspector jar: *The Assassin*. He folded the paper back up without, he hoped, giving himself away. The victim jar was offered and he drew from that: *Nanée*. Already, he felt exposed by this new game of André's.

As André hit the lights, Edouard noted Nanée standing beside the huge fireplace with its fat brass andirons, the foggy gilt mirror over the mantel, the untimely clock. They milled around in the darkness for a few minutes, until he reached her and tapped her on the neck, on the scarf at the dip in her collarbone where the nib of the pen his assassin wielded would go.

He backed quickly away from her as she fell, melodramatically screaming, to the floor.

Someone reached the light switch and turned it on. They all froze, everyone already laughing as André strode across the black-and-white marble to Nanée, pretending to be handing her a telephone receiver, saying, "Nanée, Hollywood for you."

He observed the room from his position standing over her.

Damn, Edouard thought. No one ever escaped André's inquisitions, in games or otherwise.

André offered a hand to Nanée, but she shook her head. "I'm too dead to get up." She coughed and gurgled, and was again dead.

Edouard considered André considering the room: Danny by the light switch. T a few feet away, with Maurice. Varian sitting casually on the couch, looking guilty, perhaps enjoying it for a change since in life he always had to play innocent. Jacqueline, too, looked guilty, but then beautiful women were always portrayed as angels or devils, with no room in between. And Gussie was, as he was so often, not far from Jacqueline.

"Edouard," André said, "you look even guiltier than normal. You're the assassin."

Edouard said, "You'd think you studied with Freud himself."

"You'll soon learn to be watching the others rather than the sleuth. It gives away your guilt."

The interrogation began.

"There was bloodshed?" André said.

"True," Edouard answered.

"Surely you see it there on the tiles, dear," Jacqueline said. "Perhaps we ought to mop it up before it stains the marble?"

"A knife?" André said.

"False."

"That level of cliché is mine alone," Varian said.

"I'd guess he bashed her head in with one of his cameras," André said, "but that would require he pick one up."

Edouard set a hand on the mantel, cool and steadying, as he watched the muddy, pitted reflection of André's face in the mirror.

"André," Jacqueline scolded, "Edouard hasn't even had time to gain his strength back, and he doesn't have a camera here."

Edouard looked to the bad landscapes covering the walls of the room, remembering the plays and sketches the internees had written and performed at Camp des Milles, the art made on the brick walls, the music they composed to play on whatever instruments they had. An artist was driven to create art even in the worst of times. Perhaps especially then.

He considered Nanée, still lying on the black-and-white floor where she'd fallen, a sickness in his gut as if he might really be seeing a dead body lying there, the pen with the bite marks at the end of the barrel not lodged in the long stretch of her neck because of course a good assassin would not leave it there as evidence, he would carefully wipe it clean and put it back in the desk. She was unscarred, though, except in his mind. It was Elza who was dead. Elza found on a street in Berlin, beaten to death by Nazi thugs. Her sister beside her, beaten to death too. Why had he let Elza return to Germany for her sister? They'd been in Vienna, in a country that was safe, although Hitler had been eyeing Austria too by then.

But of course he hadn't let Elza do anything. Elza wasn't a woman anyone controlled. She had promised to let him arrange to get her sister out of Germany, but she grew impatient. One afternoon, Edouard left to photograph a woman he saw leaving the Opera matinee in a red cape, and returned to find Luki having her dinner with the hired girl and Elza off to Germany. *A woman will be less likely to be questioned and suspected,* she'd written in a note for him. *The Nazis know who you are too. And I have no way to make a living here; if anything happens to you, your daughter and I will be left destitute, and this new child too.*

This new child.

Elza found her sister, only to have the Gestapo murder them both before they could get out of Germany. Edouard, still reeling, sent a telegram to André that same day, saying he would come to France immediately, with Luki and as much of his art as he could carry. If the Nazis would kill his wife and her sister because of the photographs he'd taken, they would kill Luki. It was their most hideous torture, to murder those you loved while leaving you to live.

Death was not a thing to be played at. Death was not an evening's amusement.

But there was Danny, laughter lingering still at the corners of his eyes. Danny, who'd watched so many die. Soldiers. Friends.

"You think this is cruel, Edouard," André said. "This pretending to violence. But it is in play that we access our own reprehensible depths, and unburden ourselves."

"André!" Jacqueline said.

Nanée too was rising, but André put a foot on her, to stop her.

"No, no, André is right," Edouard said. The cruelty was in his own imaginings, the violence inside himself, and it was a beautiful thing to hear Danny laughing. Danny, who needed to laugh as much as Edouard did. Even at Camp des Milles, there had been laughter. In laughter, you survived.

André leaned against the back of the couch. "There's blood on the scarf?" he asked.

Edouard studied him, trying to understand. Did André think *he'd* killed Elza? Thinking of Luki now. He ought to have had Luki baptized. What did it matter what he believed and what he didn't? What he believed was that he wanted Luki to live.

"At her throat where you stabbed her," André said. "True or false?"

"Oh." The game wasn't over. "Yes. True."

"Nanée hides her neck under this white scarf," André said, "knowing that it's what is hidden that drives us to obsession. We want to remove it, to see her bare skin."

"Good heavens," Nanée objected. "It's my flying scarf, is all."

"Is it?" André asked.

"I didn't know Nanée would be the victim when I wrote the scenario," Edouard protested.

André was right about him, though, if not about Nanée. He wanted to unwrap the scarf. He wanted to see the little dip at the base of her pale throat. Not to do her violence, but to touch her neck. The thought had been there under the surface since she'd shown up to dinner, as always, wearing that scarf.

"It is a pointed instrument?" André asked Edouard.

"True."

"Something from the kitchen?"

"False."

"The office?"

Edouard saw the pen in Nanée's fingers, the bite marks at the end of the barrel. Ink flowing onto quality stationery, *Dear Berthe.*

"Yes," he said. "True."

"A letter opener?"

"False."

André considered him with surprise, then smiled slightly. "A fountain pen."

"True."

"A pen?" Nanée said, fingering the white scarf at her neck. "Could you really do me in with a fountain pen?"

Danny said, "With enough force, you would pierce the windpipe."

"Doing violence with the tools of creativity," André said, "and yet not your own tools."

"Not my own tools," Edouard agreed.

"Indeed with my tool," André said provocatively. "And now, we must determine your motive, why you would kill poor Nanée by piercing her neck."

Edouard felt more exposed now than he had for some time. He couldn't even say why.

"It's a crime of passion?" André said.

"True."

"Hate," André said. "That isn't a question. That's a deduction."

Edouard watched him, feeling closed in, confined. André knew how Elza died.

"Revenge," André said, "for a wrong done to a woman you love. When you imagined your murder, you didn't imagine your victim was a woman. You can't imagine killing a woman. But you can imagine killing men."

Edouard nodded, thinking of Elza lying on that street in Berlin, and wanting to ask Nanée to please get up.

Nanée rose from the floor and dusted off the seat of her slacks. But of course she got up. The game was over.

"It's a barrier to creating," André said. "This discomfort with violence."

It wasn't a question, but still Edouard thought: true. So much of what he created came from violence, but the closer violence came to him personally, the less fascinating it became. He'd felt that even before Elza was murdered. He saw even then what a voyeur he was. And now? Now violence was there in the mirror every time he looked. Given a short moment with the men who had killed Elza and her sister, he would kill them with his bare hands and be glad of the chance. Up close so he could see their faces as the life bled out of them.

What had fascinated him when he saw it in others, he now abhorred in himself. And yet there it was. There it always had been. Evil in himself. Evil in everyone. In the beautiful Jacqueline and the more beautiful Nanée. In Varian, who imagined he was here only to do good. In Danny and T, who wanted to help Varian. In Elza. Yes, even in Elza. Not in Luki, though, he didn't think. Not in Luki, he hoped.

Sunday, November 10, 1940

VILLA AIR-BEL

It was there on the table in the entry hall, where the Chagall painting of a flying cow had been until just that morning. An envelope. Edouard was descending the stairs, headed outside to help set up for a Sunday Armistice Day salon, marking the anniversary the next day of the cease-fire on the Western Front at the eleventh hour of the eleventh day of the eleventh month, and with it France's victory over Germany in the Great War—which was of course no longer allowed to be celebrated, now that Germany ruled France. But they were having a salon, at which they were going to show the flying cow. Varian was trying to persuade Marc Chagall to leave France before the chaos of the Marseille government gave way to enforcement of the new Alibert anti-Jewish laws against French citizens as well as foreigners, but Chagall wouldn't believe his own government would turn against him, and he feared Varian's illegal routes out of France. He preferred, he said, "to stay safely on the right side of the law," but he'd given Varian the cow painting, and Nanée and Danny hung it from one of the plane trees that morning in preparation for the salon.

Edouard was whistling, actually, looking forward to seeing Max Ernst, who was on Varian's list and had, with some help from Vice Consul Bingham, been released from Camp des Milles. But he stopped abruptly when he saw the letter Nanée had written to Berthe in search of Luki, marked "addressee not found."

Wednesday, November 13, 1940
SANARY-SUR-MER

As the little wreck of a bus Nanée took from the Sanary-sur-Mer train station juddered away again, she set off on foot with an empty canvas bag big enough for her to sleep in, although that wasn't the plan. How dismayed her mother would be to see her traveling in such common ways, but they needed to husband gas for escaping refugees, and this was something she could do for Edouard—get his cameras, to give him something to do while he waited for responses from her friends she'd written in Paris after the letter to his friend Berthe was returned. Damn these little French coast towns and their nothing roads, though. She stumbled about and retraced her path until she found the yellow cottage with the sign on the gate, ATELIER-SUR-MER, and the key under the pot of dead plants by the door.

Inside, the place was so completely abandoned that it was possible to imagine Edouard's whole life might be shrouded in cobwebs and dust. A loaf of bread sat moldy on the round wicker table in the main room, yet hard as the clay tile floor. Badly fitted French windows were left unshuttered, the sun just now peeking through heavy clouds beyond the dirty glass. It was colder inside than out, where the sea, neither near nor far, rolled in darkly. A thought as dark as the water washed over Nanée, that she might find here the bones of Edouard's child.

She gathered from the front closet a Rolleiflex box camera, a larger Speed Graphic, a flash, a tripod, canisters of film that might be photographs he'd not yet developed, and assorted odds and ends the purposes of which she couldn't imagine. She loaded them into the bag. The gray felt fedora Edouard wore the night she first met him in Paris was on the shelf too, but there would be no room for a hat in the bag.

She pushed through the door into his bedroom, where his life was already in crates packed before his arrest. A life could not be boxed up in an hour unless one knew it had to be. She blew the dust from the nearest crate and looked through it. An address book. A few letters. Unframed photographs Edouard had told her to leave behind. "I don't need any of the prints," he'd said. "The negatives are together in a single crate. With the negatives, I can make new prints."

And there they were, underneath a stack of prints: sheaths of 4-by-5s and 35 mm strips, his work in miniature, sometimes separated by paper marked with rectangles and dotted lines, arrows and squiggles and letters that didn't make words.

She found shirts in the armoire to wrap around the photography gear. She considered the pants, too, but they were for a bigger man, one whose hips hadn't been whittled by a year of starvation rations in an internment camp.

The desk here was empty but for a single sheet of stationery and a framed 8-by-10 photograph propped against the wall the way *On Being an Angel* was on her dresser back at Villa Air-Bel. She blew the dust off the note first and read, *Dear Nanée.*

A letter to her?

What followed was the start of a thank-you note, unfinished, for the gathering she'd hosted after the Surrealist exposition nearly three years before. How impossibly odd.

She used a sleeve to wipe a layer of dust from the glass over the photo, to see the push-up man. Such an eerie photo. She remembered the look that had passed between Edouard and André when she'd mentioned it at that party, the embarrassment she'd felt under André's questioning. *Sometimes the viewer does not see all that is in the art.*

Was this photograph of Edouard himself? She considered taking it from its frame to save the weight of it and packing it, but it seemed wrong somehow to take the man from his pressed-silver home. A dark shadow hid the man's derrière at the bottom of the print. *Derrière.* The French word so much softer and more evocative than the English *buttocks* or *behind*. She peered more closely at the photo. It *was* a naked torso, wasn't it? Surely that was a waist, with the shoulders hunched forward awkwardly. Those bumps, was that the angle? Why was the photograph so unnerving? The man was naked, yes. Was that it? The reminder of the naked shoulders above her in bed, men who'd made love to her. No, not love. Men she'd gone the limit with, only imagining herself in love.

She looked at the back of the frame, to see if there was anything tucked into it. There was not.

She entered the cottage's windowless bathroom, where Edouard said she would find his developing gear. She used a kitchen cloth to wipe the cobwebs and dust from the big black bulby thing that was an enlarger for printing photos, and from its wooden baseboard and the metal-and-wood easel. She wrapped the bulb end in one of Edouard's shirts and repositioned the gear in the bag to accommodate its bulk.

A half dozen photos hung backside to her from wooden clothespins on a clothesline over a tub that held empty trays and bottles of developing chemicals he'd said to leave behind. She unclipped one, curious to see what Edouard had been working on before he was taken to the camp.

It was the same nude that was on his desk in the bedroom, but much darker. *Push-up man.*

She unclipped another of the photos: the same photograph, darker still. Another: again, the same photo. One after another, each darker or lighter, with more contrast or less, more light in one area of the print or another.

She examined one of the prints more closely. The slightly odd curve of the shoulders. The arms angled toward each other. The legs apart?

She peered more closely. Did she have it all wrong? Was it . . . ? Yes, the photograph was of a woman's torso, not a man's. A naked woman bent forward at the waist. The curves at the top that she'd thought were a man's curled shoulders were a woman's derrière. What Nanée had thought were the edges of a man's arms behind his shoulders were a hint of thigh, and at the bottom of the photograph a woman's spine disappeared into a shadow cast on her shoulders. The shadow of the photographer, of Edouard.

This photograph she'd seen as presenting a man's strength instead captured the opposite, a woman collapsing forward in grief or shame or loss, supplication. And yet there was her long, straight spine too. There was the sense that she would unbend and rise up again.

Nude, Bending—that's what Edouard had called that photograph back at her apartment in Paris. Or had that been André?

Ghost Wife. The vulnerability of the pose. The intimacy. Surely this was one lover photographing another? She looked over her shoulder, shivering at the impression she was being watched.

No one was there.

Still, she went out into the main room and looked around. She locked the front door. She retrieved the hat from the closet and fingered the inside leather band, softened by years of hair and skin oils but the tag still clean, the hat well cared for, the initials—ELM—only slightly faded. She took the hat back with her into the bathroom to put it in the bag after all, but already there was no room for it. She set it on her own head. Too big, but easy enough to carry that way. It smelled of Edouard, comforting.

Should she take one of the prints? *Nude Bending. Ghost Wife.* She peered at the photograph again. So intimate. It had been hanging in the exhibition, but Edouard had made André take it down. And he had been so clear about not needing any of his prints.

She wanted to take one for herself, but she carefully pinned the prints back up where she'd found them, on the line, and hauled the bag, heavy now, out of the little room.

She braced herself and opened the door into the last room, Luki's room, strewn with clothes and as full of dust and cobwebs as the rest of the cottage. She opened the window to the sound of waves against rocks, and gulls calling. Was that singing? She opened it wider and poked her head out to see a small area enclosed by a fence between the house and the sea. Surely that wasn't anyone singing, but rather some combination of the water and wind and birds.

She brushed away cobwebs and began sorting through things as she had in Edouard's bedroom, wanting to bring him something of his daughter. To leave behind all of Luki's belongings seemed to leave behind hope. She found the beautiful red coat trimmed with black velvet that Luki had worn in Paris, but the child was nearly three years older now; it would no longer fit. There was a cloth doll, clean and unloved. A book too young for Luki now.

They would have packed anything special except perhaps something bulky, like the coat, but how could she give Edouard this red coat his daughter couldn't wear, even if she could be found?

She tossed the coat back on the bed with the other clothes. A muffled tinkle of music sounded, as if some small musical instrument were in the pocket. But no, when she checked she found only a child-size pair of red gloves, soft leather that suggested the rich life they had left behind when they fled Austria. She started pulling the other clothes from the bed, feeling each carefully before setting it aside. Under a last little-girl white blouse was a tired old coat quite a bit larger than the red one. Bought secondhand, she supposed. Nothing else. She lifted the coat and felt inside its pockets. Pulled out a little wool thing that released another single note.

She held a tiny stuffed animal with a wind-up back.

She turned the key.

As the tinny notes sounded from the creature, Nanée was back in her own childhood, in her bedroom at the Evanston house. She was opening the lid of her music box, an exquisite round porcelain thing painted to look like a merry-go-round and inlaid with gold and pearls. When she lifted the lid, three miniature merry-go-round horses circled inside as this delicate music played. "Waltz of the Flowers," from *The Nutcracker*. A piece by Tchaikovsky that had been a failure in his lifetime, that had only succeeded after his death. Nanée couldn't have been much older than Luki was now when she first heard it, sitting in a dark theater in downtown Chicago. A special outing, just Daddy and her. He'd taken her hand when it looked like the Mouse King would kill the poor wounded Nutcracker, and assured her it was only pretend, and anyway, the Nutcracker would get that Mouse King. *Nasty creatures always get their comeuppance in the end.*

Nanée stared at the furry creature as its music wound down into the silence of the ocean beyond the open cottage windows, the waves lapping the rocks at the bottom of the palisades. It was a kangaroo, a baby one that must belong in the pouch of Luki's funny mohair mama that the motherless child had clung to at the gallery in Paris. Nanée tucked it into her pocket and, with Edouard's gray felt hat still on her head, closed the bag. She closed the window too, and walked out the front door. She locked the cottage and set the key back where she'd found it, under the pot of dead plants.

Wednesday, November 13, 1940
VILLA AIR-BEL

Edouard was sitting on a stone wall in the dark garden when he heard footsteps on the gravel—Nanée, identifiable even as a shadow in the moonlight.

"I've brought you something," she said, close enough now that her perfume mingled with the decay of the garden.

She had seen them, he thought. Of course she would have. All those prints of *Salvation*.

She handed him his Speed Graphic.

"Thank you," he said, relieved even with the weight of it, the burden heavy in his hands.

He let the lens bellow outward and peered through the viewfinder to the shadow of her face. He could not imagine ever taking a photograph again.

She put her hands in her jacket pockets and stood staring back at him, directly into the lens. "I brought as much as I could manage," she said. "All the negatives, like you asked. The enlarger and both cameras."

Both cameras. Yes, he had only two now, the Leica a casualty of his flight from Camp des Milles. The last thing to be left behind.

"Thank you," he said again, lowering the Speed Graphic and letting it hang from the strap around his neck.

She took his hand in hers and opened it, palm up, and set something in it, something from her jacket pocket. A single note escaped, a single pin plucking a single prong of the steel comb, a high note of the music he'd played every night for Luki, to make the transition from his own singing to the silence of the lonely nights after Elza died.

"Wherever did you find him?" he asked. "We looked everywhere."

"He was in a coat pocket," she said.

He wrapped his fingers around this familiar old softness, glad of the dark night, glad Nanée could not see the tears pooling in his eyes as he remembered the frantic search the morning Luki left for Paris, his own promise that he would find Joey. His promise to Elza's memory that he would keep Luki with him, always.

"We're going to find Luki too, wherever she is," Nanée said. "We're going to find her and we're going to get her here, to Villa Air-Bel."

He closed his eyes to the dormant garden and the still pond, the dark sky, the shadow of this woman who had no idea what she was saying. They couldn't even locate Luki, much less get her safely out of France. He hadn't been able to protect Elza, and he couldn't protect her daughter now.

An owl hooted in one of the plane trees, startling them both.

Nanée said, "I'll go to the American consulate tomorrow morning and . . . and see if I can arrange documents for Luki. And I have an American passport. I can go anywhere I want."

He hesitated. It was too dangerous for a man to smuggle someone out of the occupied zone, much less a woman.

"It's too big a risk for you," he said.

"Pffft," she said. "I risked my life once for a bird, you know. A beautiful black swan. I nearly crashed my plane into the frozen lake at Bois de Bologne avoiding him."

"A black swan," he repeated, remembering a better time with Elza, when they were in Paris just after they were married. Elza in a rented rowboat on that same lake, marveling at a black swan as it swooped in and settled on the water. "What an extraordinary creature," she'd said, and they sat for the longest time watching before he lifted his camera and photographed the bird. The image, though, was nothing of what he'd hoped it would be. He couldn't say why, except perhaps that the magic of the moment was not in the swan itself but in Elza's awe, which was nowhere in the frame.

"They're extraordinary creatures," he said, thinking he would get Luki himself, he would keep his promise to Elza.

"I couldn't bear to hit him," Nanée said quietly, a confession. Then more surely, "I was flying in his world. It was my duty to get out of his way."

BACK IN HIS room, Edouard found the bag of his gear at the end of his bed, where Nanée told him she'd put it. He carefully removed the things from the top, to uncover the enlarger. He set it on the floor, plugged it in, and turned it on. Yes, the negative was still in the carrier. Elza, bending forward, appeared in outline on the bare easel.

Why hadn't he stopped taking photographs when it might have saved them from everything? Why hadn't he stopped even after that first awful violation, which was nothing about Elza and everything about his work? The weeks turned into months, and Edouard spent more and more time away from her, working. Away all night because that was when the worst of the Nazi horror was done, he told himself. Neither of them said another word about what had happened after that first conversation. They were trying to ignore it, or he was. Trying to pretend it didn't exist.

That morning, the morning he took this photo, he'd arrived back home to Elza at the door. "Come with me," she said, the tone of her voice warning him not to defy her. She took his hand and she took him, still with his camera, into their bedroom. She pulled the drapes against the dim light of dawn, and she stood in front of him and began to remove her clothes.

"If you can't look at me, they will have taken everything that matters," she said. "You don't even have to touch me. Look at me through your camera. That will be easier for us both."

And he tried. He focused on her standing there, naked before him.

But he could not take the shot, could not forgive himself. She was the one to bend forward. In despair? In grief? He couldn't say, but a new fear washed over him, not for what had happened, but for how it might destroy them. She was right. She had been right from the first, when she'd begged him not to go to the authorities. No one even bothered to deny what had happened. They said Elza was "entertaining" the Nazis who had pulled her off her bicycle in the Tiergarten, and they couldn't help the fact that his wife preferred other men. They made sure he understood the details she had tried to spare him. Five men. On the route she rode home after she tutored each Tuesday night. They called her "Frau Moss."

Elza, bending before him, understanding somehow what he could not imagine, that taking this photograph would free him to touch her again, to take her into his arms, into their bed.

They stayed in Germany. He thought it was the right thing to do, to use his camera to fight to save his country, even still. That was his worst guilt until they murdered Elza and her sister—that he had stayed, that he continued to put her in danger. They never talked about the photo. He never developed the film, much less printed it, until he came home one evening to find Nazis in his own sitting room, Elza serving them beers, because what choice did she have? Luki watching, wide-eyed and afraid. He took them to Austria the next day. Fled to Vienna. He thought they would be safe there. He developed the negative and printed the photograph only then, *Salvation,* reclaiming Elza's love.

Thursday, November 14, 1940
THE AMERICAN CONSULATE, MARSEILLE

I knew your father, of course," Harry Bingham said.

"Did you?" Nanée responded to the American vice consul, trying to provoke a bit more detail and reexamining her story in light of this fact.

He sat observing her through round wire-rimmed glasses, more her own generation than her father's, his wavy light hair, straight nose, and round cheeks friendly-looking despite his small, thin-lipped mouth.

"My brother Dickey's daughter is here in France and in need of a passport," she said.

Bingham registered surprise. "I didn't know he was married."

She feigned the awkwardness a proper girl from Evanston would feel in making the suggestion that a brother might have an illegitimate child. "You can imagine what a great surprise this daughter was for us."

"I see," Bingham said.

"But his child is of course entitled to an American passport."

Bingham waited. She waited him out.

He said finally, "And the mother isn't American, I gather?"

"The mother has passed away," she said, sticking with the truth to the extent it could fit and even benefit her story.

Bingham said, "That's—"

Convenient, she thought, but she said, "You'd like to offer condolences, but the cold fact is that my brother is happy to be able to put his daughter into better care, if you understand what I mean."

The implication being that a man who took responsibility for his illegitimate child was honorable in some way the mother who bore the child would never be. Nanée hated the double standard of the wealthy, or perhaps of the entire world.

"I see," Bingham said. "And this daughter is . . ."

"Yes, unfortunately, she's in the occupied zone." Nanée had no idea where Luki was, but it would take Bingham time to get the child an American passport, if he would.

"You have a birth certificate?"

She extracted a baptismal certificate Father Pierre Marie-Benoît had provided, with Luki's real name and date of birth, listing her mother as Elza Moss and her father as Dickey.

"Ah, Père Barbiche," Bingham said, using the Capuchin friar's nickname, born of the man's long beard. The Catholic Church supported Pétain, who offered the possibility of restoring France to more "traditional" values that required women to stay home and be good wives, supporting their husbands, and assumed only Christians could have good values. The Vatican, being authoritarian itself, wasn't much bothered by Hitler; they'd reached a concordat with him only months after he was made German chancellor. But there were good people everywhere, including in the Church.

"I suppose the good friar must have been on a visit to Paris when the child was born," Bingham said. "He was at an Italian monastery until he fled Rome earlier this year."

"He's a friend of the mother's family," Nanée said, as the friar had suggested, should this question come up.

Bingham steepled his fingers. "You'll have to apply to the Germans, of course, to bring the girl out of the occupied zone."

"If I don't take her home directly from Paris," Nanée said, skirting the issue of the documents she would indeed need to apply to the Germans for to legitimately enter the occupied zone herself.

Bingham apparently appreciated the cleverness of this little twist, subterfuge being more likely to succeed when carefully planned. "It would be better if your brother applied from Chicago for this passport," he said.

"Dickey has no photograph of her, and with the post being what it is now . . . I rather hope to get her home quickly, and Varian tells me you occasionally expedite passports for friends."

"Varian?" Bingham said. "He didn't tell me you were coming."

She slid a photograph of Luki across his desk—an old one, but it was all they had. "It's a bit delicate, this business," she said. "My brother would prefer to keep the circle small until he can make things right."

Bingham said, "The occupied zone is a dangerous place. An American passport won't protect you there should you be caught defying Nazi law."

"I have many flaws, Mr. Bingham," she replied, "but being a fool is not one of them."

"It's the rare fool who recognizes himself as such."

She waited him out again, trying not to think of what a fool she'd been at Camp des Milles. She was going to tell Varian what she was doing this time, after she'd gotten this passport for Luki. She would apply to Vichy for a French transit visa for herself, but she wasn't sure whether to seek permission to enter the occupied zone, an application that would have to be made to the Nazis and would raise her visibility with them. Her inclination was not to; the harder part was getting out of the occupied zone with Luki, if that's where she was. And asking a refugee-friendly vice consul for an American passport for a German-born Jewish girl was one thing; drawing the Nazis' attention to herself as she went to smuggle that girl out was another thing entirely.

"Let me see what I can do for you," Bingham conceded. "Your brother's given name is Richard?"

"Samuel Dickey," she said.

"Of course. Your mother was a Dickey."

She tried to imagine how Dickey would react if this idea that he had an illegitimate French-born child got out. But she meant to have Luki safely out of France before any rumor got out of hand. Once Luki was in the States, the truth could be revealed. *Of course Dickey would put his reputation at risk to save a girl's life*, she imagined saying. *He's an honorable man.*

Friday, November 15, 1940
VILLA AIR-BEL

Nanée, back early from delivering messages in the Panier, settled
into the zinc tub in the ground-floor bathroom, as she now did
once a day and sometimes more. At the sound of someone entering the
kitchen—Madame Nouget beginning the dinner, she supposed—she
sank deeper, so the water in her ears muted the world. She scrubbed
and scrubbed, her skin and her hair too, and still she could smell the
stink of it all on her: the rats and the sewage in the streets, the despair
and failure and mistakes, the rotten stink of the commandant and that
camp, which, no matter how often she bathed, was always there. She
lay farther back, submerging her head and holding her breath until her
lungs nearly burst, letting the soap float out from her hair. When she
emerged, with her hair slicked away from her face and her eyes still
closed, she leaned her head back over the tub's edge.

"Oh! I'm so sorry!" Edouard's voice.

Already he was closing the door again, his voice from the other side
of the door now saying, "I knocked. There was no answer." Sounding
mortified.

She said, "I . . . I was just getting out. Give me a minute."

God, how cold the water had gotten.

She stood and wrung her hair out, brushed the water from her skin.

Was he still there, in the kitchen?

"Just a second," she called out.

She shrugged on her heavy terry-cloth robe and quickly toweled her
hair. She pulled the robe up around her neck to cover the mark there,
faded to yellow now, then flung the door open.

On the counter by the kitchen sink sat Edouard's enlarger and easel
she'd brought from Sanary-sur-Mer, a collection of roasting and sheet
pans, and the photographic paper and chemicals Danny bought for

him. Edouard himself, though, had retreated—never mind the claims of all these Surrealists that the human body was natural, or at least the woman's body was.

She hurried across the kitchen, through the dining room and the Grand Salon and up the stairs, looking for him, sure he must have taken some new photos now that she'd brought him his cameras.

SHE FOUND HIM in his bedroom, striking a match and lighting a candle on the dresser. The door was open, but she knocked on the jamb to let him know she was there.

"I'm sorry," she said, feeling her nakedness under her robe, pulling the heavy cotton tighter at her neck. Why hadn't she dressed first? "I monopolize that bathroom. It's such a luxury, a bath."

"No. No." He blew the match out. "I . . . That's what a bathroom is for, of course. I just thought . . . I had an idea. Some work I might do. I thought I might print some old film, and I need darkness and water to print, is the thing. But you did me a favor, putting me off by being . . ."

He held a negative up to the window light for her to see: a woman crossing a bridge, away from the camera, an opera cape blown open behind her so that it seemed she might lift off the pavement and take flight.

"So you're going to print something you've already taken?" she asked.

"André's comment about me not touching my camera has unsettled you."

"No," she said, only then aware of the disappointment he must have heard in her voice. "No of course not. Your art is your art. You have to come to it when you can."

"A photograph is art made in two parts," he said. "In the taking of it, and in the manipulation and development. The same negative can be so many things. The same sky can be light and joyous or dark and menacing, all in the wave of my hand between enlarger and paper." He took the negative to the burning candle on the dresser. "Ansel Adams says the negative is the score and the print the performance."

He held the negative over the candle flame.

"Wait! Don't destroy it!" she said. "I'll never forgive myself for having been in the bath when you meant to print it."

Still he held the negative there. She could see it getting hot, not melting or becoming misshapen, but the chemicals on the top side pooling so that even she could see the woman in the cape had lost her shape.

"I'm making her more haunting," he said.

Nanée said, "You're not destroying the negative?"

"Sometimes it is only in destroying a thing that we find what we create."

Friday, November 15, 1940

VILLA AIR-BEL

Edouard set his enlarger up in a makeshift bathroom darkroom. He lined up in the tub a roasting pan for the developer, sheet pans for the stop bath and fixer, and a deeper pan for the rinsing water. The zinc was still damp from Nanée's bath, the smell of the soap she used, citrus and verbena, bringing with it the glimpsed image: Nanée submerged in bathwater, the intoxicating stretch of her long, shadowed neck, her up-tilted chin. Always, what can be seen suggests what is hidden, the surface interesting not in what it is but in what it isn't. It was true in photographs and in life.

"Here I am." Nanée's voice disconcerting.

He might have been thinking it himself, *Here I am, finally, after all those months of being lost in that camp.*

She stood in the doorway, her hair still wet, her face clean and fresh. He wished he'd shown her the other negatives in this sequence so she could understand the long days he spent watching from their Vienna window while Elza tutored her math pupils, the full life they had and this, one of the last moments. That was, he supposed, why he'd needed to brûlage the negative, to mix the chemicals into something like loss, and grief, and guilt.

He poured his chemicals into the pans and put the Kindermann globe over the bathroom's single bulb, less daunted at the dim ruby glow now that he wouldn't be alone with his demons. If Nanée weren't there, he might explore dozens of crops and manipulations and exposures, but she'd never been in a darkroom, and what excitement was there in seeing a test strip emerge in the tray? He felt good about the brûlage too. In melting the emulsion, in leaving that to chance, perhaps he had created something. He would leave this printing of the caped woman too to chance.

He put the negative in the carrier, emulsion facedown lest the photograph print with what was right as left and what was left as right, the way it seemed his life had been for so long now, everything the opposite of what it should be. He adjusted the enlarger until the image came into focus on the easel, the clear lines of the operagoer's billowing cape now melted and reformed into ethereal waves, her face more goddess than woman.

"Who is she?" Nanée asked, her own face goddesslike in the red light. "This woman in the dramatic cape, who you've inexplicably melted."

The smallest bit of a laugh bubbled up from somewhere deep inside him as he inserted paper into the easel and set the timer. He had laughed at Camp des Milles, but that laughter had come from a place behind his eyes that wanted to be tears.

When the timer's metal bell tinged, he moved the paper from the easel into the developer and rocked the roasting pan back and forth.

"Look, there she is," Nanée said, her voice full of awe as the woman began to take shape, the wavy edges of her cape as haunting as he'd imagined when, seeing just the hint of Nanée's body wavy in the bathwater, he'd remembered this image.

"The Goddess of the Château, despairing for a visa to America, like the rest of us," Edouard said.

He ran the print through the stop bath and fixer, then set her in the water to rinse. He carried her in the water tray out into the light of the kitchen and set her on the counter for Nanée to better see. The print was dark, but that only added to her haunting quality.

"It's like she's us," Nanée said. "Not us how we look but . . . but how I *feel*."

She is you. The thought so sudden and true that Edouard was afraid he'd given it voice.

"Would you like to see who she was before?" he asked, thinking again of the full sequence of photos he'd taken: an elegant Viennese woman emerging from a matinee at the Opera to find the street blocked by a Nazi pop-up protest. Her face startled. Disgusted. Turning. Walking away. These were the kind of photographs he took, or used to. A watcher. A woman who never imagined she was involved. He'd followed her—stalked her, really—all the way to the little bridge crossing the canal in the Stadtpark where he'd taken this shot, her strides no less angry for the distance she put between herself and the Nazis by then being dispersed by the Vienna police. He couldn't say even now why he'd followed her.

Nanée said, "I think if I saw her in other photos, it would spoil this quality, this light on myself."

This light on myself. He wondered what it was of herself that she saw in the caped woman. Her proud anger, he thought. Her pride at her anger. He too saw himself in this photo, his fingers focusing the lens as Elza would have been writing that note back in the apartment, explaining that she had to go to Germany to get her sister. He'd believed his own proud anger set him above others. It was something he realized only after Elza was murdered, an unconscious assumption on which his work was based.

He said to Nanée, "This is what makes a photograph compelling, or shocking, or moving. We all imagine ourselves innocent. Aghast at cruelty. Empathetic. Human. We don't imagine that in simply watching we provide an audience."

We cheered or jeered, or perhaps we only stared. He wasn't sure it mattered. In being there to watch, we encouraged. This was what he photographed: the genteel society from which violence seeped up.

He said, "We don't imagine our own slovenly posture, our lurking eyes, our glee as we witness shame. The camera records that which we would never recognize in our own hearts, and yet when we see it in the faces and postures of others, we see it too in ourselves."

"But there's nothing slovenly or lurking in her."

"We don't see that our own proud anger allows us to feel superior."

"Do you feel yourself superior, Edouard?"

His name warm in her voice.

"Do you not, Nanée?"

"Think you superior?" The slightest teasing smile on her lips. "Might we not learn even more from looking at photographs of ourselves?"

"We never believe the camera has truly captured us unless we appear beautiful. We think photographs showing our ugliness are distortions, bad angles, bad moments. Not who we are."

He looked to the kitchen sink and the copper pans, the jug they used to collect milk from Madam LaVache. "Beauty, it isn't interesting to me," he said. "It's the face we present to the world. I wish to capture what we hide. That which brings us shame."

"And now?" Nanée asked gently. "There is so much violence and shame, slouching and lurking. So much hiding, saying we're one thing while doing another. Why can you not photograph now?"

Edouard studied her face in the bright daylight streaming through the windows. "And now? Why do you stay in France?"

She crossed her arms.

He hadn't meant to offend her. He never meant to offend her. But she could leave France any time she wanted.

"I suppose I prefer being in the thick of it," she said.

It was some kind of truth, if not the whole of it; he could see that in her direct gaze.

"I find," he said, "that if I'm to turn the camera to the watchers now, I must turn it to myself. I don't know how I ever imagined I was anything else."

"But in photographing—"

"No. This is what I told myself for so many years, that I'm different because I have a camera, I turn it to show the watchers that, in giving evil an audience, they encourage violence. But in doing so I too give evil the audience it craves. I . . . I now think this is what people fear more than anything: not that they will be revealed as horrible, but that they won't be revealed at all, that they will be nothing."

Nanée peered down into the water again, to this goddess who was once simply a woman in an opera cape.

"I have to see inside myself first," Edouard said. "I have to rid myself of this need to be seen."

"You don't do that by refusing to take photographs. You don't even do that by refusing to publish them. There is no way out if nobody shows the truth. And maybe it's in knowing that we're watched that we behave our best. Maybe we need to be watched more, rather than less."

He'd followed the caped woman because he wanted to be like her, to refuse evil an audience. And yet Nanée was right too. Evil unchecked by the world's response might be even more ruinous.

"To be watching others," he said, "I would have to venture out into the world, which would make it more dangerous for Varian to help Luki and me. I . . . I'm afraid it might make him less inclined to help us get out of France."

Saturday, November 17, 1940
VILLA AIR-BEL

Edouard was huddled near the fireplace and the smoky mirror and the untimely clock in the Grand Salon with everyone, Danny fiddling with the radio dial, when a terrific crash sounded in the entry hall. Edouard bolted from his chair to find Rose, the maid who had so gently combed the lice from his hair, sprawled on the black-and-white tiles at the bottom of the stairs, surrounded by an alarming amount of foul-smelling liquid the color of dirty blood. Had the girl had a seizure?

André was beside Edouard now, taking the girl's pulse, saying she was unconscious, but that was probably from the alcohol rather than the fall. "Red wine," he said of the vomit around them as he lifted Rose. "I'm not sure why we put up with her, but Nanée has a soft spot for drunkards."

He carried her up the stairs, headed for her room on the top floor.

"André is a doctor," Jacqueline explained. "It's so easy to forget, but there it is. He's the right person to help her. He'll let us know if he needs any of us."

Already Nanée and T were emerging from the kitchen with rags to clean up, stooping to the floor as Dagobert sniffed the vomit.

"Let me do this much, at least," Edouard said, taking the rag from T and kneeling on the hard marble tiles. How often had he done this at Camp des Milles, cleaning up after someone? How often had others cleaned up after him?

"Edouard," Nanée said with some emotion in her voice.

She was examining something with the keys and the matches that had spilled from Rose's pocket. She handed him a preprinted interzonal postcard, a form on which the sender checked boxes and filled in short blanks, which was the only mail the Nazis now allowed from the occupied zone.

"That girl, I don't mind her drinking," she said, "but I sure as hell wish she wouldn't forget to give us our mail."

It was addressed to Nanée, from a friend of hers in Paris she'd sent to Berthe's apartment there, to see if she could find out anything about where Luki might be. Because the friend's responses were limited to the choices on the form, he would have to parse what they might mean.

Her friend was healthy—that box was checked and "tired," "seriously ill," "injured," "killed," "imprisoned," and "dead" were all crossed out. "The family is fine" was checked. She didn't need supplies, but she needed money "for rent." No job news. No new school information. But the line that read "___ aller à ___ de ___" was filled in to say that Berthe had gone to an address in Dinard, to live with her brother.

Dinard was in Brittany, on the north coast. Berthe must be there, on the English Channel, far into occupied France.

"I'll leave at once to get her," Edouard said, already imagining Luki running on a windy Brittany beach. It was all he could do not to weep for this bit of maybe-news.

"You don't even know if your daughter is still with Berthe," Nanée said gently. "And even if she is, Edouard, you would never make it there and back."

Edouard stared down at the card. He wiped off the little bit of vomit splatter with his finger. If he were caught in the occupied zone, or even traveling without papers on this side of the divide, Camp des Milles would look like a spa retreat compared to where they would send him. But he had to get to Luki.

"One step at a time," Nanée said. "Let's write to Berthe. Let's find out if Luki is there."

"Right now? You'll write to her now?"

"As soon as we get this cleaned up. But you do know the post doesn't come at nine in the evening?"

Edouard looked at the card again, the miracle of those words, _Berthe aller à 3 boulevard de la Mer, Dinard_.

"What does your friend mean, that she needs money for rent?" Edouard asked, focusing on the checkmark beside that line.

"That someone is renting Berthe's flat?" Then, more certainly, "That the information is probably pretty good, as that is the address to which the person who now lives in Berthe's apartment sends the rent check."

"How do you get that from two words?" Edouard asked.

Nanée shrugged. "My friend needs money for absolutely nothing, so it must mean something. What else could it mean?"

Edouard nodded. "So we could resend the returned letter to Berthe at this Dinard address."

Nanée finished wiping the vomit from the marble tiles and stood. Edouard too stood, and he took a strand of her hair to wipe off a bit of vomit sticking it to her cheek.

"Thank you," he said.

She kept his gaze.

He nearly kissed her, she with one vomit-drenched rag in hand and he with the other and the vomit-splattered postcard too.

"Thank you," he repeated. "I can't thank you enough for what you're doing for Luki and me."

Sunday, November 24, 1940
VILLA AIR-BEL

The Villa Air-Bel gang and the usual gaggle of artists and writers had been playing Truth for hours out on the belvedere in what had become a regular Sunday salon. Jacqueline and T called to Peterkin and Aube, playing their own made-up game around one of the trees hung with art. It was the moment of the day when Edouard most missed Luki, as the children headed for bed. Nanée had somehow obtained an American passport for her, but it had been eight days now since they received the postcard suggesting Berthe was in Dinard, and there'd been no response to the letter they'd sent by the very next post.

He fingered his camera on the table in front of him, the new Leica everyone at the château had chipped in to buy and surprised him with the night before, moving him to tears even as Danny slid it across the big dining room table. Again and again today he'd lifted it to frame a shot, but never pressed the shutter release. And now it was too dark. There was enough light on the table to see each other, but nothing to spare.

Nanée, the interrogator in this round of Truth, touched a hand to her neck—bare tonight, that's what was different, she wasn't wearing her flying scarf. She said to Varian, her victim, "And if the Emergency Rescue Committee does send someone new from the States to replace you, will you go home?"

"I don't imagine it will come to that," Varian objected.

Edouard and Max shared a look. One never imagined a thing would "come to that" until it did. But the Vichy government didn't want Varian in France, and the US government seemed intent on avoiding any appearance of offending them.

Danny launched into a joke on himself, and Nanée beside him laughed, tipping her head back that way she did when she was truly amused and not just being polite. Edouard hardly knew what he was doing, raising the camera, adjusting the f-stop to minimize the depth of field.

Nanée looked to him, her eyes surprisingly dark in the dark evening. Good lord, he could not do this with her watching him.

And now everyone was watching them watch each other.

How had he thought it would be easier to take a photo at this salon than to stage some bizarre composition of things, like Bellmer and his dolls, with no one there to judge or care?

"You won't make me horribly ugly, will you?" Nanée said.

He smiled at the preposterousness of the idea, or perhaps at the worry that went with the question, the fear of our own ugliness. "I warned you that beauty doesn't interest me. Tip your head back again, will you? Lift your chin to the stars?"

"Lift my chin!"

He felt André watching him. God, he hated the way André watched a person. If there was an audience that would make a man stop what he was doing, it was André Breton.

"Your neck is beautiful, Nanée," André said. "Do let him take the photograph he wants to take."

She set a hand to her throat again, her expression uneasy, or even ashamed, as if André had just provoked her to confess something about herself she didn't want known, or perhaps hadn't known herself. "Even Lee Miller's beautiful eye looks eerie and ugly when isolated from her face," she said.

"But Nanée, beauty is convulsive," André said. "A disorienting and shocking disordering of the senses."

"I'm not sure I care to have whatever beauty I might have disordered," Nanée said, "much less shockingly." Joking, and yet not. Her hand still at her throat.

Veiled-erotic. André's term. Did André use it to seduce women? Had he seduced Nanée? Was he seducing her now, in front of his own wife?

André still watching.

"Close your eyes," Edouard said.

"Close my eyes?"

"Imagine you're that black swan."

"What black swan?" André asked.

Damn him for crowding in, making the impossible more so.

"Close your eyes and lean your head back. Stretch your neck as long as the swan's, and don't think about anything but that beautiful bird."

She smiled uncomfortably, but she closed her eyes as if to test whether she could trust him. She slowly tipped back her head.

"Your hand," he said.

She hesitated, then lowered her hand so that the long stretch of her neck was exposed. Vulnerable. Veiled-erotic.

He wanted to reach over and set a fingertip at the dip between her collarbones.

"I do hope you're not the throat-slitting type," she said.

Everyone around the table laughed, a welcome break in the tension.

"But of course we know he is," André said.

"He didn't slit her neck that night," Danny said. "He plunged a fountain pen into it."

"A little more, Nanée," Edouard said. "A little farther back. Now stretch your chin up toward the stars."

Her chest arched with the motion, the way Elza's used to arch when they made love. *Go ahead, Edouard. I want you to*, Elza had said that first time, on a blanket on the ground in broad daylight. They had gone on a picnic. The lovemaking had surprised them both, and yet it hadn't really.

Elza had been dead so many years now. Elza had died only yesterday.

"Right there," he said. "Hold that."

He pressed the shutter release.

"All right," he said. "Thank you."

Nanée sat forward as if brought back from a dream.

"That's all? Just one?" she asked, puzzled, but also perhaps relieved. She put her hand to her throat again, gently, as if an explanation might be felt in the touch of her neck.

"Yes," he said.

"Just me, leaning my head back?"

"Yes."

"I don't understand."

"No," he said. "Neither do I."

He held her gaze, remembering her beautiful neck tilted back against the zinc tub, wet from the bath. He'd wanted to touch it then too. He wondered if she would think the photograph he'd just taken obscene. He wondered if he would show it to her, or to anyone. He couldn't say why he'd needed to take it, why he imagined taking this very shot might free him.

"It's a way to see myself," he said.

He stood then, and took his camera, and he backed away. He knew the whole long table was watching him, but it didn't matter, the others didn't matter.

Nanée didn't say a word, either. She just watched him go. She wasn't a watcher, but she was watching him.

Monday, November 25, 1940

VILLA AIR-BEL

Madame Nouget was measuring the day's bread into equal portions and the children were just in from milking the cow, with
Dagobert tagging along, when Edouard entered the kitchen. He was
headed for the bathroom darkroom, but Peterkin's face lit up the way
it did, and the boy insisted he would share his cup of warm milk with
Edouard. T split her son's milk in two portions, and Peterkin brought
the second cup to him, carrying it so carefully.

"It will make your belly warm for the day," the boy said.

They were all hungry, always. This was a way T cared for her son,
feeding him something warm and soothing, loving, as the day started
and again before she tucked him into bed. Edouard didn't want to de-
prive the boy of a drop, but he imagined Luki handing this cup to him,
how much it pleased both of these children to share what they had.

"Thank you," he said, relieved to see as he accepted the cup that T
was surreptitiously topping up Peterkin's own cup from the milk set
aside for the neighbors.

He took the first warming sip. It was morning. The day barely begun. Another morning in which he had awoken not on straw in a room
crowded with a thousand men snoring and coughing and groaning,
the smell of sweat and vomit and excrement, but in a bed in a room
filled with sunshine, a view of open countryside and mountains, the
smell of coffee, albeit ersatz.

The door to the bathroom was open behind them, the edge of the
zinc tub just visible. Not a latrine, but a real bathroom. No line to stand
in. No stench.

He felt clean. So clean, after so many months of never being clean.

Clean and warm, he thought. Clean and warm.

He knelt to Peterkin's level. "You are such a good, generous friend,

Peterkin," he said, and he hugged the boy, Dagobert licking his shoe as if reading his mind as the tears welled. He closed his eyes and allowed himself to imagine these were Luki's small, thin shoulders, that Luki and he were together again, holding each other in some place where he could keep her as safe and warm as this soothing milk.

He would wait until the house had emptied for the day, he decided. Until Varian, Danny, T, Maurice, Gussie, and Nanée left for the CAS office, with Dagobert or without him, depending on what Nanée had in store for the day. Until Jacqueline took Aube to school and Maria had Peterkin occupied. Until Rose had finished cleaning the breakfast dishes and Madame Nouget was off to the daily shopping, all those lines to stand in. Then he would develop the photograph of Nanée's neck.

THAT AFTERNOON HE found Nanée reading in the small greenhouse, as she so often was, her book not the usual pretty French paperback with an elegantly lettered plain white cover, but something heavy and brown and British.

"I developed it this morning," he said. "I'm going to print it. Your neck. Would you like to help?" The invitation out before he lost his nerve.

In the bathroom darkroom with her a few minutes later, he inserted the negative into the enlarger carrier and adjusted the f-stop and enlarger head. *Who is she, this woman in the dramatic cape, who you've inexplicably melted?* she'd asked him the last time they were together in this red darkness. *Who are you?* he wanted to ask her now.

He'd developed the photo and run a test strip that morning, so he would have some idea what exposure he wanted. He meant to solarize the image in the manner Lee Miller had stumbled upon by accidentally letting light onto a developing print, partially reversing the blacks and whites into eerie silvers. If he did it well, re-exposing and redeveloping the print, the boundaries between dark and light at the neck and under the jawline would appear brightly outlined, the photograph more dramatic and surreal, otherworldly.

The neck, not *her* neck, he realized he was thinking, the art stepping in, taking over.

He took a deep breath—the scent of citrus and verbena, of Nanée beside him, watching. He set the timer and turned on the machine.

Someone knocked on the door just then. Of course they did.

"I'm developing a photograph," he called out. "Could you use one of the upstairs loos?"

They heard Maria's voice gently asking Peterkin if he could hold it while she carried him upstairs, then the girl scooping him up and hurrying away.

When the exposure was done, Edouard placed the paper in the roasting pan of developer. As soon as the image began to appear, he removed the print from the pan and submerged it in water.

"But you can barely even see the outlines," Nanée protested.

He waited ten seconds, then held the flashlight above the print and turned it on for just a second.

"Edouard! But won't that ruin it?"

Already, the flashlight was off again, and he was setting the paper back into the developer, his mind on the art, on this image but also on another one, a self-portrait he had taken years ago. It would be interesting to see what might happen if he solarized that one. Not who was she, but who was he? The negative should be in the ones she brought from the cottage. He hadn't realized until she brought him his work how much he needed the reminder of all he had created to believe he could create again.

As the image began to rise from the print, Nanée made a little sound. Surprise, he thought. Not mirth but something else. Discomfort? Had he misread her? He had imagined she would be amused. *We play to the death. Then we keep playing*, she'd said with such spunk when he first played the murder game with them. He'd hoped this photograph would make her laugh.

He set the tray down in the bathtub.

"She's stunning," he said, wanting to reassure her as they watched the image grow bolder on the paper. Just Nanée's chin stretched high so that, in the eerie silvers, the image—nothing but her neck and the line of her jaw up to the underside of her chin—created a Rorschach test of a photograph. Was it a woman's neck tipped back provocatively, or a man's penis?

She touched her hand to her collarbone, where in the image there was a small discoloration that might be a shadow or something on the lens, and she laughed. She did laugh. "Is that obscene, or am I obscene for thinking it might be? At least you can't tell it's me!"

"Ah, but of course it will be titled *Nanée's Beautiful Neck*."

He hesitated, then reached out to her. Touched her neck. Her skin.

He kissed her there, at the base of her throat. Up her neck. Underneath her chin. On her jaw. Her sensuous lips.

She groaned almost inaudibly.

Someone again knocked on the door. Good god, what timing.

Nanée called out, her voice deep now, "We're developing something in here. Could you use one of the upstairs loos?"

Rose grumbled on the other side of the closed door that there was no pleasing anyone in this house.

And already Nanée was untucking his shirt, her hands warm on his skin.

"Wait," he said, realizing there was no proper place to make love and not wanting this first time to be up against the damn toilet.

He lifted the trays one at a time, carefully, so that no chemicals spilled, and stacked them in the sink.

"The photograph," she objected.

But the photograph he could print again.

"Are you sure?" he whispered. "I don't . . ."

She hesitated, then whispered something back, her breath warm. "I'd rather be wild than broken," it sounded like.

He skinned off his shoes, dropped his pants, knelt to remove her shoes, her slacks, her panties that were the smooth white of her flying scarf. She pulled his shirt off. He pulled the soft cashmere over her head, unhooked her brassiere, and lifted her so that her legs straddled his waist. He carried her into the zinc tub and sat with his back against the cold metal, her warm body on his in the red light and chemical smell, with the single photograph, not yet fixed or rinsed, growing darker and darker, to become nothing at all. And that was fine. That was somehow as it should be. A thing that could be redone again, anytime.

Monday, November 25, 1940
VILLA AIR-BEL

Nanée had her clothes back on before she emerged from the darkroom bathroom with Edouard, but still she felt stripped bare. Edouard must have seen it in her face, because he touched her arm, he started to ask if she was okay. She turned away, not wanting him to see, just as she had turned away so briefly as he lifted her into the tub, as she felt the extent of the damage his body had suffered: his bony shoulders, bony hips, knees as bony as she had imagined them in that Exquisite Corpse drawing she'd done the night they met.

There was a new interzonal postcard waiting there on the kitchen counter where Rose must have left it, addressed to her but meant for him, from his friend Berthe. From Dinard, in Brittany. *La Famille __X__ va bien.*

"Luki is in Amboise," Edouard said, the words coming like the release of a long-held breath. He stood beside her, holding the card so she too could read the second line, *Mon autre fille va entrer à l'ecole d'Église Saint-Denis en Amboise.* Berthe's "other daughter" would enter school at the Saint-Denis church in Amboise.

"Amboise," Nanée repeated, more exhale than word. For two days after Pétain had begged for peace, some of the last and bravest of the French had fought the Germans from the entrance to the Château d'Amboise, a castle that had welcomed the likes of Leonardo da Vinci in centuries past. For two nights the Germans had shelled the town, tons of explosives leveling large parts of it. If Luki had been long in Amboise, she might not have survived.

The damned Germans. The damned Vichy. The damned commandant.

"We could send a letter," she said. "To Amboise. To the school."

But they didn't know anything about the people at the school. They didn't know if anyone there knew Luki was Jewish, or even that Luki was Luki. And a third letter would add delay, with every day Edouard spent in France a danger.

If she could get Luki and bring her to Marseille, Edouard could leave. Edouard would have to leave.

Nanée could leave with him, though. She was American. She could always go back to Evanston, to hell with their ideas about who a girl ought to love.

She was moving too fast; she knew that. The moment in the tub was a moment captured, like one of his photographs. What went before and what came after were unfixed, ungrounded, unreal. To have expectations was to open your heart to breaking.

But Amboise. It was in the occupied zone, yes, but just the other side of the demarcation line. Not more than ten miles, she didn't think.

"I could go get her," she said. "We have an American passport for her. I have an American passport. No one would suspect an American woman my age traveling with a child."

Wednesday, November 27, 1940

AMBOISE

It took Nanée all of Tuesday to get the nearly five hundred miles from Marseille to Tours, where she caught the first bus Wednesday morning to Amboise, the easy part of this journey to find Luki. She came alone, traveling on a valid French transit visa, with more francs than she would need in her pocket but without the German-issued *ausweis* or *passierschein* necessary to enter the occupied zone. She did, though, still have a Paris apartment, as she explained to the nice young border guard to whom she handed her American passport with a bribe discreetly tucked inside. Monday night Varian had helped persuade Edouard that she ought to be the one to find Luki and bring her to Villa Air-Bel. Then after they turned the radio off and everyone went to bed, Edouard tapped lightly at her door, and climbed into her bed, and made love to her again. She woke Tuesday before dawn to him still beside her, wanting to tell her more about Luki, to share with her his love for this child he'd been separated from for so very long.

The bus dropped her in a rubble pile of a town, mansard roofs collapsed into crumbling facades, or intact but hanging out over lopsided walls and shattered windows, or in heaps of nothing that would ever be anything again. All that remained of what had been a church—perhaps the Église Saint-Denis of Luki's school?—were high pillars of unroofed stone. Yet along the Loire here a winter market offered the last of the fall produce spread on tables, stalls of tablecloths and napkins, and plenty of local wine.

Nanée hadn't eaten much since she left Marseille, but the attention she drew in the market made her uncomfortable. No one trusted a stranger these days. So she asked the woman at the first market stall to point her to the school.

"The school?" The woman frowned suspiciously and pointed back across the main road, mercifully away from the bombed-out church. "Église Saint-Denis is two blocks up and to the right. White-and-brown Tudor. But there is no school."

Nanée held herself hard against the tears threatening. "The school was destroyed?"

The old woman stepped back and, with fear in her eyes now, repeated, "There is no school."

NANÉE STOOD LOOKING up at the stone and slate and mercifully unbroken stained glass of Église Saint-Denis, trying to imagine what Edouard's friend could have meant to send them looking for Luki at a school that didn't exist. But the interzonal card form left little room for providing information. She was just about to pull the church doors open when a young nun emerged, as startled by Nanée as Nanée was by her.

Nanée asked if the nun could point her to the school.

"The school?"

The nun took Nanée to the Mother Superior of her order, a bull of a woman dressed, like the younger nun, in heavy black robes with a simple black drape of fabric over her head, her face and shoulders encased so tightly in white that all you saw was her guarded face, surprising clear skin, and plain-brown-paper eyes. Her face in all that fabric was disconcerting. *Face Floating in White and Black*, Eduard might name the photograph he might take.

"I'm looking for a girl I believe to be at school here, a five-year-old," Nanée said. "The child of a friend. They were . . . separated. Her family are frantic to find her."

The Reverend Mother stood and calmly closed her door. "You are not the girl's mother?" She blinked long lashes the same faded brown as her eyebrows and eyes. Could Nanée trust her? Was Luki here, and if so, did they know her as Luki?

"I come at the request of her father," Nanée said.

"And he is where?"

Nanée simply met her gaze. She was in occupied France. She couldn't assume anyone here was on her side, much less anyone in a position of authority in the Catholic Church.

"It is complicated to trust in this moment," the nun said. "I find that if I put my trust in the Lord, he guides me. Perhaps we could start with this missing child's name?"

Nanée wasn't sure she believed in any lord, but then her childhood had been marked by no real trauma. It was hard now to see what she had been running from when she left Evanston.

She chose her words carefully so that anything she said could be explained as something less illegal than coming to smuggle a Jewish girl over a border even Nanée herself wasn't permitted to cross.

"We call her Luki." Not Luki Moss, but *we call her Luki*, leaving open the possibility of a nickname that had no bearing on an actual name.

"This girl would know you?" the nun asked.

"I have something her father thinks she'll recognize, although what such a young child remembers and what she forgets after so long is hard to know."

The nun again waited.

"A drawing of a stuffed animal the girl had when she left."

"When she left? But you suggested they were separated."

Nanée again simply met her gaze.

The nun said, "You will know the name?"

"I'm sorry," Nanée said. "Did I not say? Luki."

"The name of this stuffed friend?"

Nanée considered what harm might come from disclosing this fact. "Professor Ellie-Mouse," she said.

"And the child's father . . . ? You'll tell me at least how you mean to get the child to him?"

Nanée waited.

The Reverend Mother fingered the heavy rosary that hung underneath the white cowl almost to her waist, then rang a bell on her desk, calling in another nun.

"Sister Amélie," the Reverend Mother said, "I have word the château wishes to contribute some greenery for the altar this Sunday. I'd like you to collect it from the château's farm, and tell the foreman I've set aside two places in the chapel, but I would appreciate knowing whether we should expect his friends tomorrow or later in the week."

The Reverend Mother spoke as if this was nothing more than a chore she'd forgotten to discharge, but Nanée suspected it was something more, a coded message. And so many of the châteaux in the occupied zone had been confiscated by the Germans that she couldn't help but feel alarmed. In Paris, they'd taken over all of the buildings at 82, 84, and 86 avenue Foch, nearly next door to her own apartment. She'd heard that 84 was being used for "interrogations," that passersby could hear people screaming in French, and in English too.

Wednesday, November 27, 1940
VILLA AIR-BEL

Edouard, at the table in the Grand Salon, made his way through the negatives Nanée brought from Sanary-sur-Mer, looking for a self-portrait he'd taken a decade before, the night in November 1929 when Germany voted the Communists and the Nazis into power. The Berlin police had stood ready for mass riots that didn't materialize, but there were rock throwings and arrests enough for Edouard to capture on film. And here it was—his own face leaning so closely into the lens that the shot was of nothing but one eye with the mole he hated, his nose, and part of his mouth and chin.

"Edouard?"

Edouard looked up from the negative to Varian joining him, Dagobert at his heels.

"The American consulate has granted you an interview," Varian said. "And you're in luck. The consul general has taken a few days' leave. Vice Consul Bingham will see you Friday."

As Edouard absorbed this news, Varian leaned down to pet Dagobert. *If I don't return, he's yours*, Nanée had told the man just before she left for Amboise, making light of it, but the words had echoed in Edouard's mind half the night. Had she made it safely over the border into Occupied France? And how in the world would she get back out?

"We'll have to send you through France and Spain under an alias," Varian said. "Even if what Nanée says is true, that your camp release is legitimate, if it was issued under the false belief you were still in the camp, it's . . . compromised at best. And it won't protect you if your name is on a Gestapo list. Again, even without a young girl—"

"Luki is awfully competent despite her age."

Was she? He knew so little about her now. He hadn't seen her in more than a year. And her memory of her mother had faded so quickly;

he'd kept a photograph of Elza beside Luki's bed and talked about her all the time, and still what Luki remembered was the smell of her mother, "like caramel and the white flowers in the garden, and also bread."

He ought to have gone for Luki himself, the risk be damned. But it wasn't just a risk to him; it was a risk to her if she were caught with him.

"Maurice is meeting now with a German couple, Hans and Lisa Fittko, who are rumored to be getting refugees out over the Pyrenees on an ancient smuggler's route from Banyuls-sur-Mer," Varian said. "It's ten steep and perilous miles, often in freezing temperatures and fierce winds—too difficult for many refugees—but with the gardes mobiles watching the Cerbère cemetery route so closely now, there's no alternative."

Edouard looked down at the stack of negatives, work that had put them all at risk, that had already caused Elza's death. Perhaps Luki was safer wherever she was than she would be with him. But to leave France without her would be to dig his own heart from his chest and set it out on a rocky path over the border, to dry up and die.

"She needs a father. She needs you," Elza had said when she first placed Luki in his arms. "Now, what shall we name her?" And when he didn't answer, "I think we should name her Lucca," binding this child to him through his art, through his arrogance. "We'll call her Luki," Elza said. Luki. This child Edouard had struggled to embrace. Elza had understood that, even as Edouard refused to. She'd written in that last note, explaining why she, rather than he, had to rescue her sister from Germany, *If anything happens to you, Edouard, your daughter and I will be left destitute.* Not Luki but "your daughter." Not "my daughter." Not "our daughter." His. *And this new child too,* she'd written, as if she knew how often he imagined this new baby she was carrying would be a son with his eyes or nose or jaw. How horrible was he to have thought that? How much must it have grieved Elza to know what a horrible man he was. *If anything happens to me, promise me you will keep Luki with you and take care of her, always,* she'd written. *Promise me you will put her before everything else, and make her know how very much she is loved.* A promise Elza ought not to have had to ask of him. If he were a better man, his love for Luki would have been something Elza could count on, and not the last thing she'd needed to ask of him in her life.

"Edouard?" Varian said.

Edouard stared at him blankly.

"I was suggesting we might send Luki out by train, given her American passport. We do worry that applying for a French exit visa under the name Moss might draw attention to you, but—"

"You'd have us go separately?" Remembering Berthe holding Luki up to that train window more than a year ago. "No. I'll carry her over the border."

Varian adjusted his glasses. "We dress those we send over the border as day laborers. A man doesn't cart his young daughter on his back all day as he harvests grapes."

"No one would watch us the whole way."

"Yet nor will they send word to let you know when they'll be watching so you can set the child down before they see you carrying her. And it's not only the French border patrol who might be watching. Free France is not so free as all that. The Kundt Commission—the Gestapo in France—have free rein over refugees, and like to make examples of those they find on the wrong side of the law."

"Terrific," Edouard said, a Nanée word, one of the peculiar choices that made the way she spoke so fresh and lively, so full of hope. But he said it sarcastically, with the opposite of hope.

Varian looked into the cold fireplace. "The Gestapo are as happy to make an example of a woman as of a man. Perhaps happier. And time is running out for refugees in France."

Edouard looked to the clock on the mantel, the hands that never did move and yet at the moment were probably pretty close to right. Luki was just a child. Surely even the Gestapo wouldn't subject a child to what they had done to Elza.

"I promised Elza I would keep Luki with me, always," he said. A promise he'd already broken.

Wednesday, November 27, 1940
AMBOISE

L uki heaved open the heavy church door, careful not to get dirt on
the white dress that used to be Brigitte's and the blue cape Sister
Therese had made her so she would be just like the Lady Mary, and
the Lady Mary would love her more. Inside, she held Pemmy tightly,
waiting until it wasn't so dark anymore and she could see the window
colors. She walked carefully along the center aisle, not looking up at
the bleeding man with the thorns on his head. She crossed to the pew
that faced sideways, to the stone Lady Mary, whose robe was chipped
now from the noisy, scary, hiding-in-the-basement time when everywhere things were broken, houses and cars and the big bridge across
the river, and Sister Josephina disappeared. She knelt in the pew
and put her hands together, with Pemmy's too, and closed her eyes.
"Lady Mary," she whispered, "will you please ask Papa to come get
Pemmy and take her home?" You didn't have to speak loudly in the
church because God could hear you even if you were only thinking.
And the Lady Mary was God's mutti. Probably she would just tell
God for you.

She was still praying to the Lady Mary when she heard a whisper.

"She's an angel, isn't she?" The Reverend Mother's voice.

She opened her eyes, remembering to say "Amen" even as she pulled
Pemmy to her. She knew she ought not to stare, but she imagined the
Lady Mary, in answering her prayer, would understand and explain it
to God.

"Mutti?" she said.

"Child," Reverend Mother said gently, "your *maman* is with the angels."

Luki touched Pemmy's pouch where Joey should be. The photograph Pemmy wasn't supposed to have, of Mutti and Papa and Luki

from before Mutti went to live with the angels, was there with Flat Joey Letters, where Luki could always find them but no one else ever did.

The Mutti Angel stooped to her level the way Papa used to, and said, "I'm not your mutti, but I promise I will take you to your papa."

Luki considered this. Maybe it was like with God, who was three people who were the same, and one of them was a father and one was a son who didn't even look like his father, and another was a ghost Luki had never seen even in a picture.

The angel said, "Look, I've brought a letter from him."

She smelled like a flower as she handed Luki an envelope. Luki put it to her nose. It smelled like the angel.

Her own name was on the envelope. Luki.

She held it right against her heart. Papa could write a letter to her. And when you went to be with the angels, you couldn't write letters. Papa hadn't gone to be with Mutti. Papa had stayed here, to be with her.

The tears poured out then. It was like with the pee-pee when she was hiding in the trunk when she still lived with Tante Berthe and Brigitte. She couldn't stop.

"How come Papa doesn't come?" she asked—the question she never said aloud because she was afraid Papa had gone to be with Mutti and hadn't taken her with him; she was afraid if she said it aloud, it would be true.

"Oh, sweetheart." Reverend Mother lifted Luki into her big, soft arms, and Pemmy, too, and sat in the pew. She smelled like the stew from lunch. "Your papa loves you so much," she said. "He would come if he could. But he might get hurt on the way here, or taking you back with him. So he sent his friend. Now go ahead, open the letter."

On the envelope, still: Luki. The letters shaped just like her name on Flat Joey Letters.

She carefully opened the flap, like she used to after Papa didn't come to Paris and Tante Berthe would read letters to her, then let Luki read them one word at a time until she had each word inside her and she could take the letters out any time she wanted and read them to Pemmy.

Inside the envelope was a folded paper. Luki put the paper to her nose. It smelled like the same flower. She unfolded it carefully, not letting even Pemmy see.

It was a drawing of Pemmy and her on the dreaming log.

She remembered, then, the warmth of Papa's arms, the tinny smell of chemicals on his hands sometimes when he touched her cheek, the songs they sang, with Mutti and the angels singing too in the splash of the sea.

"Mutti is with the angels," she said. "They all sing to me."

"Your *maman* is in heaven," Reverend Mother agreed.

"But Papa isn't with her?"

"Your papa is at my house," the angel said. "He's fixing up the bedroom right next to his for you. He's looking out the window every minute, hoping you've come."

She wondered if the house was in heaven, with Papa and Mutti both, and how they would get there. Was the long white thing at the angel's neck her wings?

"Does Papa still sing at the dreaming log?"

Mutti Angel examined Papa's drawing. "The dreaming log is too far away now, but we dance and sing together almost every night. We have another girl living with us too. Her name is Aube. She's your age. And a boy named Peterkin."

"Peterkin." Luki giggled. "He sounds like he should be in a storybook!"

"We have a cow, too. A nice cow. Aube and Peterkin like to milk her."

"Is it hard?"

"To milk Madame LaVache?"

Luki giggled again. What a funny name for a cow—Madame the

Cow. "Could Pemmy milk Madame LaVache? Can you milk a cow if you don't have fingers?"

The angel laughed, all tingly and every color of the church windows mixed together, like in Sister Therese's kaleidoscope that she let Luki look into whenever she wanted because Luki was very careful with special things.

"I bet she could," the angel said.

"So Pemmy can come too?"

"Of course. We would never leave Pemmy behind."

Luki folded the dreaming log drawing back into the envelope and tucked it into Pemmy's pouch, behind Flat Joey Letters and the photograph.

"Oh! I almost forgot," the angel said, and she reached into her pocket and there he was: Joey, sitting on her hand.

"Pemmy, look!" Luki said. Then to the angel, "He isn't an angel either?"

"The baby kangaroo?"

"Not a baby, a joey," Luki said. "If I touch him, he won't disappear?"

"Heavens, no!"

Luki took Joey and turned his key so he sang. She opened Pemmy's pouch and set him inside it, next to Flat Joey Letters and the photograph and the dreaming-log drawing.

The angel offered her hand.

Luki said, "If you disappear, can you still take me to Papa?"

The angel smiled. She had a pretty smile, but different from Mutti's smile in the picture. "Wouldn't that be terrific, if we could disappear? That would make it easier for us to get you to your papa. Now, why don't you call me 'Tante Nanée'?"

Thursday, November 28, 1940

AMBOISE

Nanée climbed from the cart and brushed the hay from her borrowed peasant clothes. It was a chilly morning, the temperate weather giving way to a threatening storm more appropriate to what, back home, was Thanksgiving Day—at least for those who, like the gang at Villa Air-Bel, her family back in the US, and a third of the forty-eight states, ignored Roosevelt's decree setting it a week early this year just to extend holiday shopping, for goodness' sakes. She understood what she had to do now, and the storm might work to their benefit. The driver would take them to a château that bridged the river forming the demarcation line here, with its front door in the occupied zone but the south door from its gallery, which spanned the river, opening onto the far bank, in the free zone. The Reverend Mother's message, sent by Sister Amélie, had been code that meant the convent was sending two people who needed to escape.

Nanée reentered the convent through the service door to find Luki in Sister Therese's lap, holding her kangaroo and looking as earnest as when they'd found her kneeling in that pew in the transept, her kangaroo's hands held together with hers in prayer. She was so small, Edouard's daughter. So young. So very earnest. Had Nanée ever been that earnest? "This one spends an inordinate amount of time praying to the Virgin Mary," the Reverend Mother had told Nanée. "I would dissuade her, but it brings her such comfort, so I settled on allowing her to borrow our Mary for as long as she stayed with us." Leaving Nanée herself longing to be someone who could be comforted by prayer. "I would have told her she would return of course to being a Jewish girl when she rejoined her papa," the Reverend Mother had said, "but I'm not sure she understands that she is Jewish, and in this time it's safer for her not to."

Luki had been brought to her by the Reverend Mother's sister, Berthe, when Berthe could no longer keep Luki safe. The Reverend Mother had been afraid to hold out much hope to Luki, with her father in a camp.

"You are a good person, Reverend Mother," Nanée said to her now.

"It is the way of Amboise," the nun responded. "Even fallen to the Germans, we continue to fight." She turned to Luki. "Remember, child, you must be absolutely silent from the moment you get into the cart until Tante Nanée invites you to speak. Not a whisper. But you can say anything to me now. Do you want to say anything?"

"I don't want to be locked in," the girl said.

Nanée, wondering what hell had provoked that comment and the sudden fear in the girl's sea-bottom eyes, assured her, "The driver has a secret hiding place hollowed out in the hay for us."

But people betrayed others in this new world for the smallest personal gain, and what did she know of this driver?

Luki said to Sister Therese, "Pemmy forgot to thank the Lady Mary, but I told her it was okay because the Lady Mary is God's maman, and she knows everything."

"Yes, that's what we believe in our religion," the Reverend Mother said. "But our Mother Mary is so happy now that you are going to your papa, who will take care of you and teach you from now on."

"I'm not scared, but Pemmy is."

"I've always said Pemmy is one very wise kangaroo. I suppose that's why she gets to be a professor. Now, we must get you on your way. Your papa will be impatient to have you back with him."

"We're not going to fly?" Luki said to Nanée. "We're going to ride on the cart, under the hay?"

"Indeed, yes," Nanée said, wondering how the child knew she flew.

"And later we'll fly?"

"Not fly, no. We'll take a train."

"Because you don't have your wings."

"No, not anymore."

Sister Therese stooped to Luki's level and took her hands and, with them, the kangaroo's. "It has been one of the great pleasures of my life to have spent this time with you, Luki. Now Tante Nanée will take great care of you until you get to your papa. And he'll be the happiest papa in the world, to see you again."

The child turned her big, dark eyes to Nanée. "Will you hold Pemmy's hand all the way?"

Nanée hesitated. She felt so inadequate to step into the shoes of the Virgin Mary and the Reverend Mother and this lovely young Sister Therese, and unsure whether to admit to Luki that she was scared too, or if knowing a grown-up was scared would make Luki more so.

She said finally, "I'll hold Pemmy's hand all the way, but will you hold mine?"

NANÉE FELT ODDLY comforted by the slightly scratchy mohair kangaroo hand and the child's warm fingers in hers under the scratchy hay. The jostle of the wagon was uncomfortable, the borrowed peasant garb uncomfortable too. But she'd become so used to discomfort that she was more comfortable being uncomfortable than not. She only wished she could do more to comfort the girl.

It seemed to take forever to cover the eight miles from Amboise to Château de Chenonceau, their heads together on Nanée's overnight case, which was awkward to have on this part of the journey but would help them avoid suspicion as they traveled in the free zone. (Who trained across half of France without luggage?) The cart would turn, and slow, and even stop, and Nanée would hope finally that they were there. But it would be only an intersection or another cart or a dog in the road.

Again, they stopped. She listened. They were at the château's gate-house, finally. But even at the château only a very few knew of Madame's efforts to help people escape occupied France: the foreman of the château's farm operation, his wife and grown daughters, who worked in the kitchens, and his son who served as Madame's chauffeur. One couldn't know who might keep a secret and who might use it to better his own place.

The gate tender circled the cart, then said to the driver, "I'll need to examine the hay."

Nanée wished they'd thought to add some manure to the hay just in case, to make the examination more unpleasant. She was a woman hiding in a hay cart, smuggling a Jewish girl into an estate that was an escape route. If they were found, Nanée would have to claim to have slipped under the hay when the driver wasn't looking, to save him or at least give him a chance.

"Shall I do it for you? I can run a pitchfork through it," the driver offered, already climbing up onto the back of the cart, his feet close to Nanée.

She let him know by her touch where they were, as they'd practiced. She held Luki tightly, protecting her in case the driver misjudged as she listened to the slice of the pitchfork above her head, the rustle of hay being tossed.

"Again," the gate tender said.

Again, the driver dug in the pitchfork, farther up the truck bed now. He tossed the hay perhaps a dozen times.

The man, satisfied, allowed the cart to pass on into the estate, and a moment later they turned again. The cart slowed and came to a stop amid the sounds of people in the early morning beginning a day of work.

Their driver said to someone, "I have extra with the hay this morning, at Madame Menier's request."

Menier? The chocolate family?

They would have to hurry, the man replied; Madame had requested one of the cars in just a few minutes.

Nanée squeezed Luki's hand, their signal to remain silent.

A moment later, a small Frenchman with protruding, close-set eyes hurried Nanée and Luki from the hay wagon to a Bugatti Coupé Spécial, the same rare model with the same royal-blue cab that Nanée's mother preferred to be chauffeured around in when she was in France. A younger man stood beside the car in a tidy chauffeur's uniform. Beyond the garage, steep-roofed little cottages clustered into a tiny village, each with three sets of steps up to three red-door entrances, where those who worked the château farm must live, and perhaps the house staff as well.

"The rain be just beginning," the older man whispered. "With a bit of luck it will blow in a big 'un."

He popped the trunk. "At the house, me wife and daughters'll bring things to load in the trunk for Madame to take into town. As the first girl goes back inside, you go with her. Pretend you're kitchen girls. Leave everything behind. Just you and the girl."

It was all happening so much faster than Nanée had expected, on account of the storm. The wind was blowing something fierce as the foreman closed the trunk over them, and his son drove them off in the first burst of rain, which soon washed so thickly over the car that Nanée could hear nothing else.

Luki touched her face to get her attention. Nanée whispered right into her ear, "Quickly. The rain will hide your voice."

"Pemmy and Joey can come too?" Luki whispered. "They don't want to stay in here alone. It's scary."

Nanée tightened her hand over Luki's. "I'm not sure they can pass as kitchen workers," she said. "But if Pemmy and Joey stay in the car, they'll get to go in with the lady of the château, like a princess and a prince."

"Do you think the lady of the château is quiet and still and listening, like the Lady Mary?" Luki asked.

"I think the lady of the château answers prayers," Nanée said.

A few moments later, the car came to a stop, and the trunk opened. Someone was shouting. German words.

Thursday, November 28, 1940
VILLA AIR-BEL

E douard took the print from the developer: his own younger face, the man he'd been even before he met Elza, when he'd first tried to capture the watchers Hitler fed on. He submerged it in the water, waited ten seconds, then flicked the flashlight on and off several feet above it. Sometimes a little extra light on a thing showed it for what it was, showed him for who he was.

Voices sounded outside the bathroom door, Aube and Peterkin returning from milking Madame LaVache. They were going to celebrate the American Thanksgiving today, so Madame Nouget would need her pans back for her feast—if you could call anything pulled together on rationing a feast.

Where was Nanée now? Had she found Luki? Were they out of the occupied zone?

He set the print back in the developer, and the image began to rise up, his own face becoming something different, not black and white but eerie silvers that, set against each other, appeared darker and lighter than they were. Sometimes you had to embrace the fact that not everything was as it seemed, even inside yourself. Accept it. Learn to live with it.

He ran the solarized self-portrait through the stop bath and fixer, then submerged it in the pan of water to rinse. He removed the negative from the enlarger then, and inserted another, the real ghost of his own past that had lurked in the enlarger carrier all the time he was in Camp des Milles, that had been there still when Nanée brought it to him. *Salvation.*

Thursday, November 28, 1940
CHÂTEAU DE CHENONCEAU

Luki, still in the car trunk with Tante Nanée, kissed Pemmy's fore-head and set her hand on her pouch, where Joey now snuggled safely with the photograph of Papa and Mutti and her and the dreaming log letter from Papa that meant he wasn't an angel. She didn't understand. She was supposed to pretend she was a cooker for the castle while Pemmy waited in the car with Joey for her princess entrance, but someone closed her back in before she could get out. Now they weren't even at the castle, they were back in the garage. The old man with the bulgy eyes was lifting her from the trunk.

"A German patrol came up in the moat just as the car crossed to the door, but they did manage to get your fancy little case into the big house," he said as he took them into some plain rooms like the nuns lived in.

"You strike me as a good bluffer," he said to Tante Nanée. "Once the storm's past, we might slip you through the Orangerie on foot and let you cross through the gardens as if you're bringing flowers for the house."

"You have flowers this time of year?" Tante Nanée asked.

"The cottage in the center there, that's where we grow 'em. Year-round, so's the château is always welcoming. You'll need nerves for this, though, as you might be questioned by a patrol. Not a lot of folks can stand up to German questioning."

"I can stand up," Tante Nanée assured him.

"And the girl?"

Tante Nanée said, "If we go for a walk, Luki, can you promise not to say a word to anyone, not even to me, until we get to the château? We might meet some men who aren't nice, and you will just have to pretend you don't talk. Can you do that?"

She nodded.

"Not a word?"

She shook her head.

The foreman squatted to her level. "What's your kangaroo's name, honey?"

She pulled Pemmy closer and didn't say a word.

"Would you like a candy?" the man asked.

She just kept looking at him.

"All right then," he said to Tante Nanée. "Soon as the rain stops. You pretend the girl is your daughter. A girl that age could be helping her maman. We do here. You'll not know our ways, so you'll be telling them you're new, if there is any telling to be done."

THE MUD FELT heavy on her shoes as they walked a path through trees; they were going to a castle, not through the front door like a princess but she wasn't a princess anyway. Tante Nanée couldn't hold her hand because she was carrying the pretty flowers the man brought, but Luki held Pemmy tightly, with Joey tucked down in her pouch so he wouldn't be scared. Pemmy could come with them, but she couldn't talk. No matter what, only Tante Nanée could talk.

No matter what, Tante Nanée would take her to Papa; she wouldn't take her to the angels or make her disappear. Reverend Mother said so, and Reverend Mother didn't lie because a lie was a sin and if you sinned you didn't get to go to heaven to be with Mutti and God.

The man with the funny eyes walked with them to a magical glass house all full of trees. It smelled like the oranges Luki used to get at special times. She had forgotten about oranges, but now she remembered. Mutti loved oranges.

The man reached up to one of the trees and twisted off an orange. He didn't say anything. Even Tante Nanée and the man were quiet in here, just like if they were hiding. But he smiled, which made his eyes nice even though they were bulgy. He held the orange out to her, and she took it. He pulled another one down and tucked it in her coat pocket. He didn't say anything, but he touched Pemmy gently. He meant for Pemmy to have that orange because kangaroos love oranges.

Luki made Joey peek out from Pemmy's pouch. The man laughed without making a sound, just with his funny eyes, and he pulled down a third orange and tucked it in her other pocket, then touched Joey the way he had touched Pemmy. Joey got his own orange too!

The man pulled a scissory thing from his pocket and cut a single branch with pretty red berries. It had prickles, but he put it in Pemmy's hands and wrapped them around the branch, then wrapped Luki's hand that held Pemmy over it, so the prickles wouldn't bite into Luki's fingers. Pemmy didn't have any fingers, so the branch wouldn't hurt her. He touched one of the berries, then touched his lips and shook his head. She shouldn't eat them.

They left the magical glass house through a different door, with the branches and the oranges and the flowers and with Pemmy and Joey, but without the man with the funny eyes. Tante Nanée couldn't take Pemmy's hand, but they were in such a beautiful garden now—with fences and paths and a fountain that looked like they belonged in a storybook—that even Pemmy wasn't scared.

And there were *two* castles! One was a baby castle, just a circle with a round-y pointy roof and windows only at the top, but the other one was huge and magical, with circle parts like the baby castle at every corner and big blue roofs and chimneys and windows and more windows and more. It sat right in a river, with water all around it. A long skinny part that was almost all windows stretched the whole way across to the other shore. That was where they were going—to that big castle! There was a scary monster spitting water from the bridge, but Luki walked right beside Tante Nanée toward the castle doors they weren't supposed to go through because they weren't princesses.

A voice called to them to stop. Luki thought at first it was the water monster, but it was a man below it. He was a soldier in a uniform, in a boat. He used the old words. He didn't sound nice like a prince would sound.

There was another man in the boat with him. He wasn't a prince either. They were German, and she was German, but she didn't like them anyway.

Tante Nanée showed them her flowers and Pemmy's prickly branch. "We've got flowers and greens for the mistress," she said.

Luki wanted to say *and oranges*, but she wasn't supposed to talk.

The man didn't understand Tante Nanée. Luki could understand the words he said, but Tante Nanée just repeated with her own words that they were getting decorations for the house.

Dekorationen für das Haus. Luki used to help Mutti decorate, things that made the rooms smell good. Pemmy helped too.

The other man in the boat pointed a gun at them.

Luki was startled. She knew the German men had guns, but they never pointed them at her.

She looked to Tante Nanée. She wanted to explain to the not-nice man in his words that they were just bringing pretty things to the castle, so his friend would put his gun away and they could go inside. Pemmy seemed to think this was what the man with the funny eyes meant about not talking, but Luki wasn't sure. The scary man wasn't asking Luki a question. He wasn't offering her a candy she wasn't supposed to have. He was asking Tante Nanée something, and Tante Nanée couldn't make him understand, and Luki could make him understand because she knew these kinds of words.

And Pemmy did not like that gun being pointed at her.

Thursday, November 28, 1940
VILLA AIR-BEL

After a midday Thanksgiving supper of the roasted chicken Madame Nouget had managed to find, they took Varian's nut pie (with plenty of whipped cream, thanks to Madame LaVache) into the Grand Salon. Edouard forked a bite, imagining Luki warmed by this fire, and carrying her upstairs to tuck her in at night, milking Madame LaVache with her in the morning, and dancing to music all the way from Boston. His thoughts of the future were here, in a place he could see in his mind. What was a place like Boston or New York or Chicago like? Who would they know? How would he manage to house and clothe and feed Luki there?

"Perhaps Nanée might put Luki on the train," Varian said, continuing a conversation started as they were cutting the pie. "You could meet her in Portbou, on the far side?"

The nuts were gravel between Edouard's teeth. "I've done this before, though. I sent Luki with a friend on a train to Paris, meaning to follow." It had been well over a year now since he'd hugged Luki.

"Look, let me lay this out for you as clearly as I can," Varian said, getting testy. "When we started this, yes, it might have been possible to get you out on the train with your daughter. But border guards willing to look the other way can no longer be counted on or even hoped for. And the Gestapo in Spain are checking every request for a Spanish transit visa, and picking up refugees with no apparent resistance from Franco."

Edouard went to the window, to the long empty stretch to the sea in the distance, no one coming. He knew he and Luki had to leave as soon as they could. Escapes were increasingly dangerous, and might soon end altogether. Captain Dubois of the Marseille police, a connection Vice Consul Bingham had made for Varian, had just days earlier let Varian know the Marseille police had now been charged with gathering evidence enough to eject Varian himself from France. Varian's passport was good until January, but his French visa had expired, and he had no ability to get it renewed for want of a letter that the American embassy refused to give him. "How many times do we have to tell you there is nothing we can do for you?" the embassy insisted. "Even your wife wants you to go home." And the CAS's own Charlie Fawcett had just been arrested in Spain, and with a secret list of refugees who needed visas too. The list was hidden in the third valve of Charlie's trumpet, on which he'd learned to play songs that didn't need that valve. Other documents were sealed inside plaster heads that appeared to be works of art in progress. Neither the list nor the documents had been found on Charlie yet, as far as anyone knew. But everyone at the CAS office now meticulously destroyed anything incriminating once it was no longer needed, and Varian brought the remaining documents back to the château each night.

"Luki can cross the border on foot with me," Edouard said to Varian.

"I'm not offering you this alternative, Edouard," Varian said. "I'm telling you that if you wish to leave France, this is the way we will help you do so. We'll provide you documents under an alias to get to Portugal—"

"Forged documents."

"Yes. Ones that will not match your daughter's name. The two of you traveling together in France—that's not a risk we're willing to take. There will be some risk with you traveling together through Spain too. Once you get to Portugal, you can use your real name and your American visa."

Edouard fingered the window glass, the view as limited as that through the lens. Whatever he did put Luki and everyone else in danger. He was a watcher, and he was watched.

Thursday, November 28, 1940
CHÂTEAU DE CHENONCEAU

N anée tried to appear as meek as a servant girl to the Germans. "To decorate the house," she said again. *Haus*—that was the word in German, but would a servant girl know that? She pointed to the château, the servants' entrance just across the forecourt, if only they could reach it. Luki, mercifully quiet, only stared at the soldier on the moat and his gun.

"Du arbeitest hier?" the German demanded.

"To decorate the château," she repeated, not knowing what else to say.

A woman appeared at the servants' door, calling, "You'd best hurry! The mistress is impatient!"

The Germans conversed with each other, but didn't lower the gun.

Nanée said to Luki, "Come, sweetheart." She nodded toward the woman standing there. She might just walk on if she were sure the child would follow, but she couldn't risk leaving her standing there alone.

Luki looked to her, then walked on across the bridge.

What a brave girl you are.

Nanée hurried after her, wishing they could enter through the closer main door and hoping even a German wouldn't shoot a child in the back.

Nanée tripped on the servants'-door threshold, sending the flowers flying as she sprawled onto the hard stone floor, but already the woman was kicking her feet out of the way and pulling the arched wooden door closed before the German soldiers fired that gun. She helped Nanée stand again, then scooped up the flowers and shepherded Nanée and Luki farther into a kitchen, which was warm and dry and smelled of yeasty bread.

Nanée was startled by a bell rung just above her. Six bells hung from the wall there, much like back in Evanston, each to summon staff to a different part of the house. The woman whispered for them to wait and disappeared, leaving them in a kitchen with arched stone ceilings, a huge fireplace with a smaller oven built into the wall beside it, and cabinets full of brass pots and pans and crockery, with more hanging on the walls, along with garlic and herbs. There was a water pump in one corner, a wide butchering table against a wall studded with all sizes of cleavers, and a side room filled with cabinets of china and food. In the center of it all stood a black iron oven four times the size even of the one at the house back in Evanston, where her parents threw parties for a hundred or more. Nanée wondered where the cooks and maids and other staff who must usually bring the place alive were now.

A clock ticked. A leaded window gave a view through a narrow stone arch to water. Was it the moat? The river itself? It was barely below them. Anyone who drew near in a boat could see right inside.

Luki looked up at her, still silent.

"Whisper," Nanée whispered as quietly as possible.

Luki whispered, "Pemmy likes castles."

The woman returned and hurried them up a staircase, past an extravagant gallery with a black-and-white marble floor and perhaps twenty huge arched windows all stretching across the river Cher. The dark doors at the far end were the doors to the free zone.

They continued on, though, up to a higher floor, where the woman tucked them into a hidden room not much bigger than a closet, with a single window crossed with iron.

"Talk in whispers," the woman cautioned. "Stay away from the window. I've put your pretty bag in here so you can change your clothes. We'll come get you when it's safe to cross."

Nanée nodded, already helping Luki out of the peasant clothes and into more appropriate attire for the niece of a wealthy American woman traveling to Marseille.

"You'll walk fast as you can away from the river," the woman said. "Don't linger on the riverbank. If there are Germans, they'll like as not shoot. A narrow footpath leads to the tomb of Madame Dupin, who they say enlisted Rousseau to help her write down the history of womankind, and perhaps she did and perhaps it's here somewhere or perhaps some gentleman burned it up two hundred years ago, but her tomb—that's what you're looking for. Madame Dupin will be your guide to a path to the right that will take you to a farm. They won't be surprised to see you. If it's early in the day, they might be able to take you straight on to the train, but there's no telling till it's told."

"Thank you for all you're doing," Nanée said, changing her own clothes now so the woman could take the case, wanting to ask the woman's name, to thank her properly, but it was safer, always, to leave names unknown.

As the woman slipped quietly out, leaving Nanée and Luki in the little room with the single window that looked over a huge formal garden seeming to float on the water, about to break free and drift away, Luki pointed to the orange still in her hand. Nanée hesitated. Would the smell of an orange give them away to some less sympathetic porter or maid? But the whole château smelled of flowers, and of the river out the window. She took the orange and dug her nails in to peel it, releasing the crisp citrus scent.

LUKI WAS FAST asleep when a woman's voice startled Nanée.

"This new German patrol seems to have set up on the river for the night, so we're going to move you to a proper room," the woman, who introduced herself as Simone Menier, said. She'd brought no light with her. "I don't generally ask for names, Nanée, but I suppose you will know who I am, and the fact is, I know your mother."

Nanée lifted Luki over her shoulder and followed Simone Menier down the stairs, past the gallery, which was lit now only by moonlight, and through a windowless entry hall with a vaulted ceiling carved with roses and cherubs and cornucopia, where Nanée could see in the electric light that Simone Menier was as elegantly beautiful as her home. As they ducked up a stunning staircase, the pitched ceiling here too carved with keys and faces, flowers and fruit, it occurred to Nanée to wonder how this lady of the château knew who she was.

Simone Menier hurried past the windows at the turn in the staircase, overlooking the river. They were backlit. Anyone out there could see them. She showed them into a bedroom with an elaborately painted joist ceiling, a cold fireplace, and an inviting four-poster bed. The drapes were closed, the room lit only by the spill of light from the hallway.

"We're reluctant to light the fire, as both the light and the chimney smoke might alert the Germans to a fuller house," she explained, already pulling back the bedcovers so Nanée could lay Luki down.

The kangaroo was not in the girl's arms. They must have dropped her.

Simone Menier was off to fetch Pemmy before Nanée could say another word, only pausing at the door to insist that Nanée call her Simone and to offer her cognac. Nanée hesitated, torn between the recollection of drinking cognac with the commandant at Camp des Milles and the opportunity to sit and chat with this brave, generous woman.

"The only staff in the house now are my housekeeper and her son," Simone said. "They'll both go to the gallows with me should it come to that. If you don't prefer cognac, perhaps champagne? I'm sorry not to be able to send you on your way to the free zone this very moment, but selfishly . . . good female companionship is such a rare thing in this time."

Nanée thought of T giving Peterkin his nightly milk back at Villa Air-Bel. "The château," they called that old place, but it was nothing like this one. She thought of Miriam, now gone off to Yugoslavia and her fiancé.

"Good female companionship is a rare thing in any time," she said.

Simone returned with a tray of champagne and chocolates, Pemmy, and a book. She set down the tray and tucked the kangaroo in with Luki, and they settled into chairs.

"Bibliothèque Rose!" Nanée exclaimed as Simone handed her the book. The Pink Library. "I read the whole series again and again with my French governesses when I was a child. *Les malheurs de Sophie. Dans la bonne voie.* And this, of course." *Thérèse à Sainte-Domingue,* about a little girl who helps free slaves. "These books may have been my first step toward moving to Paris." Stories of girls who were as brave as she'd once believed her father imagined her, only to see in retrospect that his words that night at the bonfire at Marigold Lodge were nothing more than an offhand remark meant to soothe an injured child. "These heroic French girls were a grand improvement on the pigs and rats and horses offered in English books," she said.

Simone laughed gently as she poured the champagne into ordinary wine goblets. "I hate to disappoint you, but I'm afraid these 'classic French tales' were written by a Russian—Sophie Rostopchine, writing as 'the Countess de Ségur.'" She smiled warmly. "You've a long journey ahead. The girl isn't your daughter, I gather?" Said not in the way André Breton might, not prying, but only trying to understand.

"She's the daughter of a friend," Nanée answered, remembering Luki setting off toward the door to the château with that gun pointed at her, as brave as any of the girls in these books. Thinking of the child in her father's arms back in Paris too, thinking Nanée was the mother she had lost. *Mutti, will you sing to me?*

The champagne and chocolate combination was surprisingly delicious, the peachy, orangey, slightly sweet champagne complementing the edge of citrus she tasted in the rich chocolate, although that might be the orange peel under her nails.

She thanked Simone for all she was doing.

"This is nothing," Simone demurred. "During the Great War, we treated well over two thousand men in a makeshift military hospital in the gallery. Of course, everything was easier with my father-in-law. They're both gone now, my father-in-law and my husband. Like your father. I sometimes wonder if all the good men in the world are gone."

"How do you even know who I am?" Nanée asked, the question ruder than she'd intended.

"I saw you as my housekeeper brought you up from the kitchens. You won't remember, but we met briefly in Paris some years ago. I happened to be at a restaurant where you and your mother and a gentleman friend were dining."

Misha, Nanée thought. Misha and her mother drunk and making a scene, as they were wont to do.

Simone looked to the bed, where Luki remained fast asleep. "Will you take the child and her father back to the United States with you?"

"Her father and I aren't . . ." But she was in love with Edouard even if he wasn't in love with her. Perhaps she had been since that first night in Paris. "I . . . Maybe. I don't know."

Friday, November 29, 1940
CHÂTEAU DE CHENONCEAU

N anée startled awake to Simone Menier whispering, "It's time. We have to hurry before the morning traffic on the river begins and the staff arrive."

Nanée was immediately alert, climbing from the bed still in her traveling clothes, pulling on her shoes. "Luki," she whispered, nuzzling the kangaroo into the child's cheek. "It's time to go to your papa."

Luki, with the softest sound of half-asleep contentment, pulled the mohair kangaroo close to her. "Pemmy, the angel is taking us to Papa."

At the gallery, the dawn peeked gray and overcast through the arched windows, good weather for escape, but still the long stretch of black-and-white tiles loomed ominous. Nanée and Luki might so easily be watched from outside until they exited, then taken into custody or worse. They stood waiting, watching the chauffeur at the far end peering out the last window before the doors, Nanée's little case in his hand.

He held up a single finger, then signaled them to come.

"Joey!" Luki cried out.

Pemmy's kangaroo pouch was empty.

Nanée looked to the chauffeur, who shook his head. No, there was no time to find a baby kangaroo.

She knelt to Luki's level. "Joey will have to stay here, sweetheart, but Simone will take good care of him and send him when she can."

Luki whispered to Simone, "Are you a queen?"

"Ah, my husband always said I was. Your Pemmy can write Joey letters. I'm sure he would write her back."

"He can't write. He's only little."

The chauffeur waved impatiently. Really, they needed to go.

"Could Pemmy stay with Joey and be a princess?" Luki asked. "I'll have Papa. Joey doesn't have a papa."

"It's up to you, Luki, but you have to decide now," Nanée said. "It's time to go."

Simone met Nanée's gaze over the child's head, but Nanée had no idea which would be worse for Luki, to leave Pemmy behind or to carry the mother kangaroo away from her baby. She gave Simone the address of Villa Air-Bel as Luki hugged the kangaroo tightly, then kissed her again and again and again.

Nanée took the things from the kangaroo's pouch—the photograph and Edouard's letter with the drawing of the dreaming log—so that Luki wouldn't have to. "Pemmy would want you to have them," she said. "She won't forget you, ever."

The child kissed her kangaroo one last time and handed her to Simone. "Pemmy can't go backward," she said. "Kangaroos can't. They can only go forward."

Nanée, holding Luki's hand, hurried across the gallery to the doors, which the chauffeur slipped open. He poked his head out and looked around, then handed Nanée her traveling case.

She ducked out and hurried Luki up the path, away from the river toward the tomb—a huge old stone thing dripping green and black with moss, carved with a robed woman sitting with one hand on a knee and the other to her cheek as if contemplating . . . not a sadness, but something weightier than the decaying leaves covering the tomb's base and stairs.

Birdsong rose behind them, alarming Nanée. Someone coming?

Someone shouted, frighteningly guttural words.

She grabbed Luki and ducked up the stairs on the tomb's far side, even as the birds fell into a frightening silence. She meant to tuck up against the mold-slimed stone, but on further thought ducked into the woods so they might move without being so exposed.

Two German soldiers came running, guns drawn. Germans, although this was free France. Were they the men from yesterday? Would they recognize Nanée and Luki?

The Germans stopped at the tomb, then cautiously circled it. Nanée kept a hand to Luki's mouth, willing her to be silent, wishing she'd brought the Webley, and rehearsing in her mind the story she'd devised in that first little room at the château.

A red squirrel crouching absolutely still a few trees over shot off, zigzagging. The Germans fired their guns again and again.

One of the Germans began to laugh. "Es ist zu schnell für uns!"

The two of them, now laughing together, settled in on the steps to the tomb, just where Nanée and Luki would have been, and lit cigarettes.

They had just holstered their guns when one of the soldiers saw Luki. Nanée motioned her to stay where she was. Leaving the traveling case on the forest floor so she wouldn't have to explain it, she stood, drawing their astonished looks off of Luki and onto her.

One drew his pistol again and pointed it at her. The other returned his gaze to Luki.

Friday, November 29, 1940

THE AMERICAN CONSULATE, MARSEILLE

Y ou're not a Communist, I hope, and never have been?" Vice Consul Bingham asked Edouard. He had a file open on his desk.

"Never," Edouard confirmed.

"And the French Republic interned you in Camp des Milles, then Vichy let you go?"

Edouard hesitated.

"If you escaped, that's better," Bingham offered. "We don't have to wonder if your release means you're a Nazi sympathizer or even a spy."

"I did escape," he said, a truth, if a partial one. He'd both escaped and been released, if Nanée was to be believed.

Bingham examined one document, then another. "You have good friends among the American press."

Those must be the affidavits in support of his application.

"Married?" Bingham asked.

"Widowed."

"I'm sorry for your loss."

Edouard nodded. "My Lucca—"

"Lucca Moss?" Harry Bingham smiled troublingly, and set his pen down. "Ah, now, that is interesting. I recently issued a passport for a girl in Paris named Lucca Moss. An American girl. What an odd coincidence."

Edouard sat silently.

"Such an unusual name," Bingham said.

Edouard wasn't sure whether to agree or not.

"An adorable child, if a photograph doesn't lie." Bingham smiled, his cheeks becoming even rounder.

He set aside another document then, to reveal a visa with Edouard's photograph attached on the bottom left. The top left corner was blank, to mark the details of Edouard's arrival in the United States, but the top right side was filled in: *American Consulate at Marseille, France. Date November 29, 1940. Seen: This bearer, Edouard Moss, who is without nationality . . . The validity of this Immigration Visa expires on March 29, 1941.*

At the bottom right, listed as other travel documents: *This Affidavit in Lieu of Passport issued to Edouard Moss by the American Consulate at Marseille, France, dated November 29 and valid indefinitely.*

Luki had an American passport. Edouard now had a visa. If Nanée could get Luki to Marseille and they could get out of France and to Lisbon, they could get to America, and they could stay.

Friday, November 29, 1940
MADAME DUPIN'S TOMB

The man pointing the gun spoke the words of Mutti and Papa. Tante Nanée didn't understand him. She said she had come to visit the tomb.

"Das Mädchen soll auch stehen," he said. *The girl should also stand.*

"The tomb," Tante Nanée repeated. She took a step toward the man.

The German cocked the gun. "Das Mädchen!"

Luki stood slowly.

"Was machst ihr hier?" the soldier demanded. *What are you doing here?*

Tante Nanée hid Luki behind her. "The tomb," she repeated. "We came to pay respects."

Das Grab, Luki thought. Like Mutti. Mutti went to a tomb, which was the way she got to the angels. Papa had told her that, or Reverend Mother had.

"Das Mädchen!" the man repeated. Did he want Luki to answer? Did he know she understood his words?

"Sie ist deine Mutter?" the man demanded.

Luki looked up at Tante Nanée. "Maman is with the angels," she said.

Both the soldiers' faces softened.

Tante Nanée squeezed her hand. This was like when they walked to the castle. She was supposed to pretend she didn't talk.

"Das ist das Grab deiner Mutter?" the one with the gun asked.

It wasn't. It wasn't her mother's tomb, but Luki didn't say that. She wished Pemmy were here to help her be brave.

He approached them. Tante Nanée tried to keep between Luki and him, but he knelt down to her level. He looked right at her.

"Ich habe eine Tochter in deinem Alter." He had a daughter who was her age.

He put his gun away. He put his hand in his pocket and drew out a hard candy. It smelled of lemons, even over the forest and mossy tomb smells.

Luki looked up at Tante Nanée, who nodded.

The man unwrapped the candy, and Luki took it and set it on her tongue.

Danke, she thought, but she said, "Thank you."

"Danke?" the soldier asked, and he nodded as if he knew he was right.

Tante Nanée's hand tightened over hers again.

Luki nodded too, but she didn't say another word.

Friday, November 29, 1940
VICHY

Nanée and Luki were well settled in a first-class sleeper compartment with a private bath, just a wealthy American and her niece who was raised in France by her mother, now deceased. The full bed was already made, and Nanée had declined turn-down service. The sitting room had a sofa, a chair, and a table at which they could take meals so they wouldn't be seen in the dining car. It was late, somehow still the same day that Luki, with the German's lemon candy in her mouth at that tomb, had taken Nanée's hand and waved goodbye to the soldiers. It hadn't been a long walk, nor was the man repairing equipment at the farm to which Simone Menier sent them surprised to see them. He drove them to a town several miles away, each inch from the demarcation line distance well gained. There they caught a local train to Vichy, where they transferred to this night train to Marseille.

"Pemmy would like this," Luki said. "A princess train."

Outside the train widow: the Vichy station. It was past time to leave. Still the train didn't move.

Nanée tried not to worry. They'd cleared their documents before they boarded, simply handing the two American passports over with the single transit pass as if of course the child didn't need her own. She hadn't been questioned.

She opened the book Simone Menier had given Luki, and pulled the girl closer. They admired the perfectly detailed illustration facing the title page, young Thérèse and her mother in rich fabrics and gorgeous hats walking together along a harbor. "'It was 1789,'" she read. "'A cold autumn rain darkened the city of Le Havre. And yet a great stir reigned on the quays because one of the vessels which made the crossing to America was preparing to set sail.'" *Thérèse à Sainte-Domingue*— Nanée had read this a hundred times. A French girl with her family in Haiti was terrified by the dark-skinned slaves. *She almost dared not touch the black hands reaching out to her.* By the final page, though, Thérèse would be helping her mother end slavery on the island, which had always left Nanée longing to do something more important than reading books in a dull house in a dull town where she was to master nothing beyond the foxtrot and needlepoint.

A knock at the door startled them. "We have need of checking your papers before the train can depart," a Frenchman called out.

Their papers specifically, or were they double-checking everyone? Nanée squeezed Luki's hand, then opened the door slightly and said they'd cleared documents before they boarded.

"It is an extra precaution due to Maréchal Petain's visit," the attendant apologized.

She handed him her passport and the French transit visa that allowed her to move about the free zone.

"And the child's papers?"

"Pétain isn't to visit Marseille until Tuesday," Nanée said. "It's only Friday."

"It will be Saturday when the train arrives," the man said. "We must take precautions. I'm sure you will understand. The lengths these troublemakers go to. An anarchist put a bomb in an underpass near la Pomme in hopes of killing the Prince of Wales."

Nanée tried to hide her alarm: La Pomme was where Villa Air-Bel was. "Was nobody hurt?"

The man smiled indulgently. "I'm afraid the Prince of Wales has not visited France lately. This was perhaps eight years ago."

"I see." She laughed more easily than she felt, wondering what an attempted bombing nearly a decade ago could have to do with anything. "Well, you don't imagine a five-year-old girl will blow up a bridge, I hope!"

"Truly, we must check everyone," he apologized.

She fetched Luki's passport, tamping back the temptation to ask how an anarchist attack years ago could possibly cause him to now need to confirm a child's passport, far too aware that Luki had no French transit visa.

He gave the passport a cursory glance and handed it back. "I apologize that you may be bothered once or twice again on the journey."

Nanée wondered how many stops there would be along the way, how many document checks, really. She would have to order coffee to keep herself awake. She couldn't afford to be caught off guard along the way. But at least they were out of occupied France, with only Frenchmen now to be fooled or bribed.

"How long we will be delayed?" she asked.

The man shrugged. "You will arrive when you arrive, and not a moment earlier."

Nanée snuggled again with Luki, who'd turned the book's pages to an illustration of two jaguars. In the background, a dark-skinned boy held a baby jaguar by the back of its neck as a white man pointed a rifle at the poor thing.

"What are they doing to the baby?" Luki asked.

Nanée flipped pages, looking for a gentler illustration, only to come upon a jaguar on his back. Was he dead?

"That man is a bad man," Luki said.

On the facing page, a man stripped to the waist and tied to a tree was being caned.

Nanée flipped pages more quickly, saying, "Now where did we leave off?" Perhaps the illustrations made sense in the context of the story, or perhaps she could finish the page and close the book.

Luki stopped her at a drawing of a man with arms tied behind a tree trunk as another man aimed a cat-o'-nine-tails at his bare chest.

"He's a bad man, so he has to be punished," Luki said, meaning the man being beaten.

How did you explain to a child that some people were unforgivably cruel? She remembered another illustration in another Pink Library volume, of a woman flogging a child. How terribly proper and yet brutal these books were, all manners and morals, with virtue always triumphant while bad children got the switch. What a beast she must have been as a child, to love them.

"The Germans are bad men," Luki said. "I'm a German. That's why I know the words the bad men say. But I'm a girl."

Nanée nodded, trying to see where her mind was headed.

"Papa is a German."

"Oh, sweetheart." Nanée hugged Luki close and kissed the top of her head. "Your papa isn't a German like that. Your papa is a very good man. He'd never hurt anyone."

"Even if they were bad men, like in the picture?"

"The bad man here is this one," Nanée said, pointing to the horrible one wielding the whip. "But Thérèse helps them, so they can't be hurt anymore."

Nanée flipped further backward. Why couldn't this be the Pink Library story with the toy store and the beautiful rocking horse?

She glanced out the window, wishing the train would set out before some bad man somewhere changed his mind about letting them go.

She read on, watching out the window too and thinking of the replica of that rocking horse her father had had made for her one Christmas. She'd been too big for it, really, even then. Would home be easier to negotiate now, without Daddy there to disappoint? But it would be impossible to bear Misha in his place.

She turned to the next, mercifully illustration-free page, hoping Luki might fall asleep before they got much further.

"Were the men after we left the castle good men, even though they said the German words?" Luki looked to Nanée with her big dark eyes, which had seen so much more than a five-year-old ought to.

"I don't know," Nanée admitted. Had the German soldiers known they were escaping and let them go?

"They gave me candy. Sister Therese used to give me candy. Her name is the same as the girl in the story."

"It is."

"Sister Therese is a good person."

"Yes."

"She isn't German."

"No."

"Reverend Mother is a good person."

"Very good."

"The Lady Mary is good even though she's stone."

Nanée wasn't sure how Edouard would feel about his daughter's infatuation with the Christ mother he didn't believe in. Or did he? Nanée wasn't even sure what she believed herself. Faith. What did the word mean? Her faith was in the selflessness of people like the nuns, the hay wagon driver, the caretaker's family, Simone Menier. People like Miriam, T and Danny, Varian, Gussie, and Maurice.

"I asked the Lady Mary to ask God to send someone to take Pemmy to Papa," Luki said. "Then you were standing with Reverend Mother."

Nanée smoothed Luki's hair and closed the book. "Your papa is the one who sent me to get you."

"You're not an angel?"

"I'm afraid not. I'm just a girl, like you."

"The queen of the castle is a good person," Luki said. "She'll take care of Pemmy and Joey."

"She will."

"She'll send them to live with me and Papa."

"Yes."

"Sister Therese says someday Papa and I will be with Mutti again, but we have to wait for God to call us." The child took the drawing Edouard had given Nanée from her pocket and studied it. "Do you think God calls on the telephone?"

Nanée allowed that she wasn't sure.

"Papa says Mutti still loves me."

"Yes."

"He told me that at the dreaming log."

Nanée smiled sadly, imagining Edouard on that log overlooking the sea at the cottage at Sanary-sur-Mer, trying to help his young daughter understand what Nanée, at thirty-one, still could not: how she was to spend the rest of her life never able to speak with the parent who'd had a rocking horse made for her just because she wanted it.

"Your papa is a very good person," Nanée said.

Luki burrowed into Nanée and closed her eyes, her warmth spreading through Nanée, who used to snuggle against her father this way by the bonfire at Marigold Lodge—the Michigan house that belonged to her now but would always belong to the rest of her family too. Her mother and her brothers would be there now, the day after Thanksgiving, playing bridge or charades or backgammon and getting on each other's nerves. They'd be overfull of leftovers, turkey and mashed potatoes with gravy, pecan pie or pumpkin or some of each, in a world where you could still eat more than you needed and sleep without fear, a world in which one day was lived much like the days before and after, where it still mattered what you wore and who you socialized with, whether they were "our class." Where a girl was to wear white and become a happy wife to a man who spent his spare time at his club, a mother to children who would bicker and disappoint. Was that why she came to France? Why she stayed, even though there was never enough food and no one, really, was safe?

She watched out the window, stroking Luki's hair and willing the train to leave. She ought to keep the girl awake to have dinner. They'd barely eaten all day, and there would be plenty here in first class. When they got to Villa Air-Bel, it would be back to rationing.

"I love Papa," Luki said.

Yes, Nanée thought. I do too.

She might have been thinking of her own father, or Edouard, or both men.

She began quietly singing words she'd all but forgotten, that her father used to sing:

> *Angels watching ever round thee*
> *All through the night.*
> *They will of all fears disarm thee,*
> *No forebodings should alarm thee,*
> *They will let no peril harm thee*
> *All through the night.*

The train whistle sounded, and the train began slowly, slowly, slowly to move, its gentle sway rocking them as, outside the window, the station gave way to poles and swooping wires, to an empty, moonlit road and empty, moonlit fields, and in the distance, a dark shadow of woods.

Friday, November 29, 1940
LYON

Luki was with Mutti. She wished Papa would come, but Mutti said they must leave Papa to make his photographs. A man came, but he wasn't Papa. He wasn't an angel and he wasn't God, and he wasn't God's son, the bleeding Jesus who wore the crown of thorns that Luki wanted him to take off so his head wouldn't be so scary, and he didn't speak the bad-men words, but he held a whip and he held Pemmy by the neck!

She startled awake. In a bed. She wasn't with the nuns. Where was she? Where was Pemmy?

A bit of light came through the window, and the door was ajar, with the Mutti Angel who wasn't Mutti and wasn't an angel standing in silhouette.

Why was the bad man here? That was who was speaking, the bad man who captured Pemmy. She couldn't see him, but it was his voice.

She was too afraid to move. She pretended to sleep. If she was sleeping, it might not be real, or maybe the bad man wouldn't see her.

The bad man said, "But you must have a French transit visa for the child also. We are under the strictest protocol for all trains bound for Marseille." He was using the regular words. He wasn't a German man.

Luki peeked just a little. She was on the beautiful princess train, on her way to Papa. Tante Nanée wouldn't make her disappear, because Reverend Mother had said so, and to lie is a sin.

She peeked a little more. They were at a train station. It was night-time. Outside the window, people stood in pools of electric light. Tante Nanée was saying something, but her voice was too quiet to hear the words.

The bad man said, "No one without every document in order may be allowed to continue on. Not even a child."

Tante Nanée stepped out of the room and closed the door behind her. Luki stared at the door, her eyes wide open now. She wanted to call out to Tante Nanée please not to leave her. She didn't want to be alone in the dark, without even Tante Berthe's voice outside the hiding trunk. Papa wasn't here. Mutti was with the angels. Even Pemmy was gone. Pemmy was a princess, and Joey was a prince. No one would hurt them because they were with the queen in the castle. But without Tante Nanée, Luki didn't know how to get to Papa. Papa wasn't at the dreaming log. Luki didn't know where Papa was.

Saturday, November 30, 1940
VILLA AIR-BEL

Edouard held Luki in a long, desperate hug, afraid to let go, afraid to crush her, to suffocate her, to lose her again. Luki held on as tightly, his every concern that she might not remember him washed away in her embrace. He held her just a little bit away, finally, to see in the light splashing out from the villa onto the belvedere the same caramel hair and startling blue-black eyes. She had been old for her years ever since Elza's death, but now she looked like an ancient soul peering out from a child's face. She was exhausted. He needed to get her something to eat and tuck her in bed. He might stay up all night, watching her sleep.

Behind him at the French doors to the villa, everyone stood watching. They had just finished dinner and were moving into the Grand Salon to listen to the radio when Edouard saw Luki and Nanée from the window, in the moon shadow as they walked across the car park. Only Dagobert ran out with him, the little dog now climbing all over Nanée, a few feet away.

Luki threw her arms around him again and began sobbing. He kissed her head, breathing in the slightly sour scent of a child too long on the road. "It's okay," he said. "We're together now. That's all that matters."

"I didn't disappear," she blubbered.

"No," he said. "No. You're here with me."

"I wanted to see Mutti, but I was afraid to disappear," she said, or that's what it sounded like, but it was hard to make out, her words so racked with sobs.

He held her for a long time, repeating "You're here with me" over and over.

She didn't have Pemmy. Had she outgrown the kangaroo? The idea made him inexplicably devastated. He held her back a little and looked her straight in the eyes, pulled a handkerchief from his pocket, and wiped her face.

"Did Pemmy take a bath and have to ride in your suitcase again?" he asked.

She giggled a little. He had never heard a sound so glorious.

"Pemmy stayed with Joey," she answered, wiping her running nose with her sleeve. "They're going to be a princess and a prince until the queen can send them to us. She'll help them write letters. We had a suitcase, but we left it behind in the woods by the tomb."

Edouard looked over her head to Nanée, with Dagobert now in her arms.

"We slept on the train, in a whole big bed!" Luki said. "Much bigger than when I left Paris with Tante Berthe. The train was supposed to come this morning, but it was very late. Tante Nanée took me a secret way after we got off the train. Did we surprise you?"

Without waiting for him to answer, she turned to Nanée. "Will you live here with us, Tante Nanée?"

Nanée laughed her easy, deep laugh. "This is my house, Luki. Look, this is my dog, Dagobert. Remember, I told you about him?"

Luki smiled now, and looked into Edouard's face. "Like in the song," she said, and she began to sing the nursery rhyme, "'The good king Dagobert put his pants on inside out.'" She giggled and exclaimed, "Except this Dagobert doesn't even *wear* pants!"

God, this girl would break his heart.

Nanée set Dagobert on the ground and said, "Daggs, this is our new friend, Luki."

The dog looked from Nanée to Luki, then approached Luki carefully, as if he meant to be sure not to scare her. Luki touched Dagobert's ear the way she forever touched Professor Ellie-Mouse's kangaroo one. Dagobert shook his head quickly a few times, which startled Luki. She laughed, and the dog put his paws up to her and began licking her face, and she laughed even more.

Edouard said, "Shall we show you your room?" Luki was wound up now, but would soon crash. "Mind you," he said, "it might not be your room for long. We're going to go on a grand adventure together, you and I. Very soon."

"But this time, you'll come with me on the train," Luki said.

Edouard hesitated.

"The princess train me and Tante Nanée took was very pretty," Luki said, "but every time we stopped, a man banged on our door."

"Every time the train stopped?" Edouard asked Nanée.

"Pffft, extra security, because Pétain will be here Tuesday. They were quite concerned Luki might be planning to blow a bridge just to embarrass the man, but of course a smile and a few francs are so often all that's needed to address such concerns."

"Well, Moppelchen," he said, "we may not even take a train. We might just walk to Spain!"

"To Spain?" Luki said. "That's a different country!"

"It is," he said. "You are a very smart girl."

"Can Dagobert come to Spain with me?"

Nanée knelt down to Luki's level. "You haven't even met Madame LaVache yet, and already you're planning to leave?"

"Madame LaVache!" Luki exclaimed. "Papa, can we meet Madame LaVache now? Tante Nanée said I can milk her."

Edouard wished he had a camera with him, wished he could capture this moment. He scooped her up and stood, basking in the touch of her arms around his neck, her legs wrapped around his waist, her breath on his cheek.

"I suppose the moon is bright enough to light our way out to visit Madame LaVache."

He pulled Luki to him again and hugged her tightly, suddenly desperate. To leave, yes. To get this child somewhere safe.

"THIS COW WILL be awfully confused, us coming to haunt her in the dark," André said, but it was clear in the way he said it that the adventure amused him. Edouard trooped with everyone across the uneven field toward the little milking shed and Madame LaVache, Aube and Peterkin continually asking Luki if she still had the sugar cube, and teaching her to call to Madame LaVache, "Woooo, cow!" Jacqueline admonished Aube again and again to watch for cow patties—impossible to do in the moonlight—before Varian found one with his foot. As they neared the fenced enclosure and the shed, a dark mound rose. Ah Madame, we disturb your slumber.

The cow looked friendly enough, but she was nearly five feet tall at the withers and weighed well over a thousand pounds, and she had those little horns too, and there really wasn't much to that rail fence. The old girl never failed to stand docilely as the children approached, though, her pure white face now nearly glowing in the moonlight, her funny brown ears sticking straight out the side from her massive and comical head.

Luki stretched out her arm and opened her palm so that the sugar cube sat there as an offering. The cow took one slow, small step forward to bridge the divide, then stretched her neck over the fence and gently tongued the sugar cube into her mouth.

Luki laughed and laughed.

The cow stood there, watching her. Surely that was a cow-smile on the animal's face.

Then Aube and Peterkin were on either side of Luki, petting Madame LaVache's long white face and wet pink nose, as untroubled by those horns as if they were simply another set of ears.

"Who ever knew a cow could be such a gentle creature," Nanée said. "She could teach my mother a thing or two."

Edouard wondered what Nanée's mother was like. Her family. Her home. Why she was here in France, risking her life. He ought to be the one staying here. He ought to be taking photographs to show what was happening in the camps and in the streets. Nanée was like the woman in the cape who had so fascinated him. Or better. She took messages to hidden refugees. She went to internment camps to free men like him. She'd gone over the border into occupied France to rescue a girl she'd barely met, while he'd stayed here on the excuse that he didn't want to put Varian and those who helped him at risk. It was the same reason he didn't take photos. But the truth was, they were already endangering themselves. The truth was, it was Luki he was unwilling to endanger. He knew revealing the truth of what the Nazis were doing here was more important than any one girl's happiness, even than any one girl's life. But he couldn't bring himself to risk Luki.

THE CHILDREN HAD been put to bed, even Luki fast asleep now, her bedroom door open so that she could call to Edouard if she needed him. They'd brought the radio upstairs to the library so that she could see him as the adults visited. It was a clear night, and Danny found them the Boston station.

"May I have this dance?" Edouard asked Nanée.

She put a hand in his, her other on his shoulder. He set his own hand at her waist. Her hair was still wet from the bath she'd taken after the visit to Madame LaVache, while he had tucked Luki in and sung to her, and sat there for the longest time just watching her sleep.

"You smell good," he whispered, and he pulled her closer. Citrus and verbena, from the soap she said Varian had brought from Portugal.

André Breton, dancing with Jacqueline beside them, raised an eyebrow.

Edouard danced Nanée away from him, toward the open door to Luki's room.

"She calls you an angel sometimes," he said.

"I'll tell you about that tomorrow, when I'm competent to string words together."

"I'm sorry," he said. "Of course you're exhausted. I ought to let you go to bed."

"I'm not tired," she said as unconvincingly as Luki had when he'd tucked her in.

He smiled a little, his heart light for the first time in forever. "Thank you for bringing Luki back to me."

She looked up at him. I missed you, he thought. He wanted to kiss her, but not here, not in front of everyone. Bing Crosby sang on the radio about wanting to be with someone as the years come and go.

Edouard whispered to Nanée, "Do you ever think about going home?"

She set her head on his shoulder and swayed with him to the music coming all the way from Boston, all the way from the far side of the world.

PART IV

December 1940

The sad truth of the matter is that most evil is done by people who never made up their minds to be or do either evil or good.

—Hannah Arendt, *The Life of the Mind*

Sunday, December 1, 1940
VILLA AIR-BEL

It was Sunday. Salon day. Voices drifted up from the belvedere, the guests arriving, with Edouard and Luki not even quite dressed. They'd slept through breakfast, but Madame Nouget brought them a tray with bowls of thin porridge, ersatz coffee for him, and milk for Luki—which she was quite devastated not to have coaxed from the cow herself. He pulled on his jacket and tie, then fixed a ribbon Aube had given Luki into hair lighter than her mother's, but with the same luster and wave. She smiled her gummy smile, one of her bottom front teeth loose. She could read now too. She could write. Already, he had missed so much.

"You're beautiful," he said.

"You're handsome, Papa."

He hugged her. Truly, he could not get enough of hugging her. He hadn't realized how much she completed him until she'd arrived back in his physical life.

Outside, Edouard introduced Luki to everyone.

"Marcel, this is Luki. Luki, this is Monsieur Duchamp, who paints and sculpts, and is awfully good at chess." Duchamp had routed Edouard whenever they played at Camp des Milles, on that board scratched into the floor.

"I can beat my papa at checkers," Luki said.

Duchamp said, "That does not surprise me!"

Edouard was particularly moved to introduce Luki to Max, who was talking with Nanée but knelt down to Luki's level and told her he felt like he knew her. "From all the stories your papa told me about you when we were at Camp des Milles."

"You were with Papa?"

Max said, "I slept right next to him, and I will tell you I watched him say he loved you to your picture every night, and kiss you every morning. He missed you so much."

Luki was silent for a long moment, her hand warm and small in Edouard's. "He slept next to me all night long last night," she said.

Max smiled. "I hope he didn't snore so loudly that he woke you!"

Luki giggled. "Papa doesn't snore!"

"Doesn't he?" Max said. "Ah well, it was hard to say who was making what noise back then. We did some paintings together, your papa and I did. Did you know that?"

"Papa does the best pictures."

"Yes, he tells me that too."

"Look, a horse," she said.

"Is there a horse here as well as a cow?" Max asked.

"In the tree!" She pointed to one of the plane trees flanking the belvedere.

Edouard's photograph of that horse on that empty merry-go-round, distorted and out of kilter—who'd hung it there? His own anger from that morning in Berlin was reflected in the image, the manufactured horse rearing back from the photo's bottom left corner, as if as startled by the photographer as Edouard had been when Luki was refused a seat on the empty ride. Elza hated this photo, hated the memory of her daughter being denied on account of being something she wasn't, really. But Edouard felt the photograph said something people ought to know. That was why he'd given it to André, who'd made it a centerpiece of the Surrealist exposition in Paris.

It wasn't the only one of his photos displayed in the art trees. There was his solarized self-portrait, unframed but nestled in the branches. And *The Caped Woman, Brûlaged*—Edouard couldn't see it now without thinking of Nanée's words. *I think if I saw her in other photos, it would spoil this quality, this light on myself.* Her pride at her anger, like his own, he'd thought. She hadn't answered his question about what of herself she saw in it, just as she never answered his question last night about whether she might consider going home. She was good at remaining silent when asked a question she didn't want to answer, when her answer would bring a hurt she didn't want to bring.

Underneath the art tree, an assembled group began laughing together—friendly, appreciative laughter as one of them pointed to a photograph high in the tree: *Nanée's Beautiful Neck*.

"This was your idea?" he said to Danny. "To hang my photos?"

Danny grinned, guilty. "But I had a coconspirator."

They looked to Nanée, with Luki, who was telling her, "Papa saves my memories for me."

"Saves your memories," Nanée repeated. "Oh, that's such a beautiful way to put it, Luki."

He thought of Nanée in the bathwater, her head tilted back against the zinc of the tub. He thought of her naked in the tub that second time, as they made love. It was clear from her soft expression under the charming bowler hat she wore today that Luki had succeeded where he hadn't yet: Luki had won Nanée's heart.

"When I forget Mutti's voice singing to me, I look at my photograph." Luki pulled out from a pocket the photograph of Elza and Luki and him he'd tucked into her kangaroo's pouch just before he put her on that train in Sanary-sur-Mer. "Then I can hear her again."

And Edouard could hear Elza now too, as he looked at the photo. Elza singing to Luki. This child who was so much wiser sometimes than he was. All the photographs he hadn't taken these last years since Elza died, they were moments lost, moments that would be ignored, forgotten, with no mirror held up to reality, no hammer shaping it.

He looked back to the solarized self-portrait, himself as a young man. Accentuated in the high contrast: a hint of wariness underlying his young man's confidence in what he could and ought to do, how he would change the world. Something in the sideways cut of his eye toward the lens, the straight set of his mouth. He'd been afraid of what he was doing even then. He'd been afraid so many times, to be taking photos of Hitler's fanatics that would blow back on him if the world turned out to be exactly as it now was. It had never occurred to him, though, not to take the shots he needed to take.

Was he afraid to see whatever his lens might reveal inside himself? Why hadn't he taken a photograph since Elza died, not even at Camp des Milles? Why wasn't he taking photographs now, capturing this moment of what it meant to be trapped in a world that didn't want you but would not allow you to escape? All these people living together, some desperate for a visa, others desperate to help them find a way out. André going off every morning to the table in the library or to his greenhouse, to write. Jacqueline painting. Artists gathering every Sunday to celebrate what little they had. Even in the darkest times at Camp des Milles, the men kept making art and music, literature, theater. It was how they stayed alive. How they helped the world right itself.

Nanée was right: if his camera didn't relieve him of the guilt of being a watcher—an audience for those who, like Hitler, could not bear to be thought of as nobody—it did at least help expose them. Them and his own ugliness. The camera did record that which we would never recognize in our hearts and yet can see in the faces and postures of others. And wasn't that how we started to heal the world, by digging through our own faults to find the best in ourselves?

He'd told Nanée that he couldn't turn the camera on the watchers now, he needed to turn it on himself, but in that first self-portrait a decade ago he'd turned his camera to the watchers, only to see his own face staring back at him. Art was a hammer, after all. One to shatter his own hard shell, his own untrue vision of himself.

Sunday, December 1, 1940
VILLA AIR-BEL

The only lights on in the whole big place were here, in Nanée's own bedroom, the rest of the château already turned in. She sat in her terry-cloth robe at the edge of her bed, with her hair up, her back to Edouard and his new Leica on his tripod by the door.

A shiver ran through her, although the room was warm enough.

"Can I ask you something first?" she whispered.

"Of course. What is it?"

"The photo, the one—" The one I think of as *Ghost Wife*, she'd nearly said. One lover photographing another. Edouard might have had affairs when he was married, of course; the Surrealists were quite free about sex. But she didn't like to imagine him as a man who could profess to love one woman while tasting another, not in any event, and certainly not when one of the women was the one in that photograph.

"*Nude, Bending,*" she managed, but then found she couldn't finish the question. She didn't want to know who *Caped Woman* was; she wanted to be able to imagine herself in that photograph. But *Nude, Bending?*

"Yes," he said, his inflection on the word leaving her unsure what he meant. Was it a question: Yes, what is it you want to know? Or was it an answer: Yes, the photograph was of his wife.

Nanée couldn't say the word *wife*, much less her name. Elza. She didn't want to step too far into his private grief, to make him talk about things he might not want to share, the gut-wrenching emotion captured in the photograph. She didn't want to know it was Elza, and yet she wanted to know if he'd photographed other women too before this moment of her own vulnerability.

He whispered, "It . . . it was something she wanted to do. A demon she needed to rid herself of. No, a . . . a demon she needed to rid me of. One she knew I needed to purge from myself."

His voice full of some pain Nanée had been trying not to touch.
Some shame.

That photo—the woman bending over so vulnerably. What would
drive a woman to wish to be photographed like that, or a man to want
to do it? What kind of wound might that heal?

He whispered, "Can I ask you a question?"

She nodded.

"I only ask because Varian says we might leave as soon as this
week."

This week. The weight of it sinking through her. Edouard gone
from her life. She'd thought for the briefest moment last night as
they were dancing that he was going to ask her to go home with him.
She could leave any time she wanted; she could present herself at the
American embassy, and they'd help her arrange it. But could she live
under Evanston Rules again? It would be a different thing too, to go
with Edouard and Luki, with the ghost of Elza. And she had already
failed at her sole attempt to mother a child; T had given Peterkin over
for her to take to the States before France fell, but she was so unlikely
a mother that even the damned bureaucrats in Biarritz could not be
convinced.

"There's a new path over the Pyrenees into Spain," Edouard said.
"I want to believe my release papers are real, but I think the only way
they might be . . ."

She looked to the window, the darkness outside. She had to tell him.
Like her, he couldn't ask, but while she didn't need to know whose
body was in the photograph, he did need to understand how his release
papers could be real.

"Yes," she whispered.

She tried to make herself say the words he couldn't ask—how she'd
gained Edouard's papers, if not his freedom, or what passed for freedom for a Jewish refugee in Vichy France. She didn't want him to be as

confused by her answer as she was by his. But he would see her differently if she told him about the night with the commandant. How could he not? She saw herself differently.

She shrugged off the top of her robe so that the soft terry cloth pooled at her hips.

Edouard was silent for a long moment. Perhaps he meant to tell her what his *yes* meant. Perhaps he meant to ask her to say more directly what hers did.

He murmured, "I expect this will be a little cold."

She nodded again.

She waited in the quiet of a paint tube being opened. The chemical smell as he squirted it onto a painter's palette he'd borrowed from Jacqueline. The paint cap being replaced.

He set the palette beside her on the bed.

The paintbrush on the skin of her back shocked, the contrast of the cold of the paint and the warmth of his touch. He used one hand to steady himself, or her, as he painted something just to the left of the small of her back.

He didn't speak, but his breath was warm.

His other hand slid down, touching her rear, not erotically but only to steady himself as he painted.

Rear. What a prudish way to think of it.

Mon derrière. The word masculine despite her own derrière being distinctly female. Not bare. The robe pooled around it. Her arms together over her bare breasts.

Ma poitrine. My chest. Even the French saw that one as feminine.

Another shiver ran through her. How disappointed her father would be that, just like her mother, she'd fallen for a refugee without a penny to his name.

"Are you cold?" he whispered. "I'll be quick."

He was already painting the same thing on her right side, the same

even swirls to make a second fleur-de-lis—the symbol of French royalty and Catholic saints, of the Virgin Mary.

The Lady Mary, Luki called her.

"I'm almost done."

The palette and brush set on a cloth on a tray on her dresser. Edouard
at his camera on the other side of the bed. "Whenever you're ready."

She sat as straight as she could, squaring her bare shoulders. She
turned her head to the left, so that her face would appear to him in
profile, not all the way but enough so that he could see her jawline,
the hint of her lips and nose and eyes. Her left side, which was her best
side, although she didn't suppose anyone else would see any difference.

"Perfect."

The hush of his voice a reminder of all the others sleeping in this big
old house, their borrowed family.

The whisper of the shutter. One shot. A second. A third.

"Thank you. That will do it."

She smiled a little.

The whisper of the shutter again.

"I thought you were done."

"I couldn't resist that expression."

"You told me to keep a neutral expression."

"Even I, sometimes, am wrong."

She felt his hand on her back again, then a cloth wiping the paint off
before it could dry.

"You're beautiful," he said, his voice so low she might be imagining
it. "Do you know that? Do you know how beautiful you are?"

She turned to him, inhaling the wet paint smell that was him, and
that was her now too.

Sunday, December 1, 1940

VILLA AIR-BEL

Nanée was lying in bed—Edouard returned to his room in case Luki looked for him in the middle of the night but Nanée still naked under the sheets, lingering in the memory of their bodies together, belonging—when she heard something. The click of the villa's front door opening? At this hour?

She threw on her robe and grabbed her Webley from the top shelf of her armoire.

They did sometimes have late-night visitors. Nanée had once returned well after midnight to find the dining-room door closed, and British voices, then Varian emerging, as startled by her as she was by him. He'd nodded acknowledgment and asked her to muster up something to eat, then received the wine and a sausage of dubious origin through a door opened only wide enough for her to hand him the chipped wooden tray—protecting her, she realized only later, from the dangerous knowledge of having as "guests" British soldiers trying to escape France.

Now, she slipped quietly out to the library. Varian's voice, in a low murmur, rose from the entryway at the bottom of the stairs. "Roundups?" He stood just inside the front door with Captain Dubois, their friend in the Marseille police, who'd brought news just that morning that Bill Freier had been caught with the false identity papers he was forging for Edouard in his possession.

"Roundups," Dubois confirmed. "Because Pétain is coming. We're to conduct roundups to clear the streets of any possible trouble. They'll begin at dawn."

Monday, December 2, 1940
VILLA AIR-BEL

Edouard watched Luki at the soapstone sink with Aube and Peter-kin, T placing the jug of milk in the sink and pulling three cups from the open shelves. None of them saw him. He raised his Leica and focused his lens on Luki accepting the cup of fresh milk from T and holding it, letting its warmth seep into her little fingers. She was five now, and in the year they'd been apart, she'd somehow lost so much of what had been Elza in her. She had her own eyes, her own mouth and jaw and gap-toothed smile. Even the square width of her bony shoulders was different from Elza's finer bones. It was as if he were losing Elza again. Or perhaps finally beginning to let go.

He took the shot.

They all four turned at the whisper of the shutter. He shot again, the four of them at the sink. The children drinking milk as if life were normal. Family.

"Papa," Luki said, "Madame LaVache has so much milk that we had to bring the jug in before it got too heavy. But we get to go back out and milk her some more. And we saw an eagle who wears boots."

"A booted eagle," T explained. "He must have a nest nearby."

Luki grinned, that loose tooth even more so. "Dagobert barked and barked at him!"

Monday, December 2, 1940
VILLA AIR-BEL

W here the devil are Danny and Lena?" Varian asked Nanée.
They were working in the warmth of the library's porcelain
stove, Nanée trying to fill Lena's role while Gussie did what Gussie
did. Varian was cranky, snapping about the particularly vile batch of
ersatz coffee, Edouard's photo-taking, and her own inability to take
dictation, a skill she had never claimed, and her lack of knowledge
about how much money the CAS had on hand, information she wasn't
privy to even though she'd just contributed another $2,000 on top of
the $5,000 in September. They had for weeks now brought every-
thing incriminating at the CAS office back to the château at night, but
on Dubois's warning about the roundups, Varian sent Danny on the
first trolley to close the office and bring Lena back with him. Here,
they were far enough away from the city center that they would be
caught only in the most widely cast of nets.

Lena arrived without Danny, saying, "A thousand pardons!" as if she
weren't the most competent and loyal assistant in existence. The roundups had started, enormous *râfles* all over the city. She'd been arrested
on her way to the office and taken to the Évêché, the former bishop's
palace that was now a police facility at the edge of the Panier. They let
her go, but it wasn't an indulgence they were generally granting. The
police had already filled the prisons and some of the military barracks,
rounding up people just to be doing something so that they wouldn't
be blamed should anything go wrong while Pétain was in Marseille.

Varian sent Lena directly back to the office to fetch Danny, and
Nanée was again taking notes as Varian talked with Edouard, when T
called up as calmly as if she were announcing lunch, "Nanée, police."

Nanée, her every nerve buzzing, asked, "For me?"

"At the door. They say we'll all need to show them our papers."

Nanée set a hand on Edouard's arm, then put a finger to her lips. T had directed her comment to her so as not to alert the police to Edouard's presence. Could they slip him out? Gussie too would be at risk as a Polish Jew, but he did at least have identification forged by Bill Freier.

She hurried to her room and looked out the window. Down beyond the green gate, a squad car and a paddy wagon waited. Police surrounded the house.

She signaled to the gang in the library, which now included André and Jacqueline. Varian, with only the slightest hesitation, set into the flames in the porcelain stove his address book with the records of everyone he was trying to help, everyone trying to help him, and every illegal money exchange they had made. Nanée did the same with her notes.

André indicated with a gesture that he and Jacqueline would go downstairs and stall for time. Nanée tried to stop him; with his writings banned by Vichy, was he the best face to present? But he did have his charming way, and he was French and not Jewish, and Varian and Nanée and Gussie needed time to destroy everything.

Nanée grabbed her Webley from the armoire and hid it in the chamber pot in the washstand. She gathered a few bits of paper that would be better not found. She pulled the little drawing she'd tucked up behind *On Being an Angel* and opened it, that drawing from the first game of Exquisite Corpse she'd ever played: a head in a birdcage that might or might not be hers, the octopus body holding the bloody Hitler head, the knobby knees and kangaroo. She tore off the top third, the birdcage head Edouard had drawn, and tucked it again behind the frame, then hurried back to the library to add André's Hitler-head-holding octopus to the fire, the legs and kangaroo she'd drawn going with it.

She poked Varian's journal deeper into the flames.

"Even Bill Frier," Varian whispered to Edouard, "who disdains everyone else's work, thought the papers Nanée got for you were authentic."

"The papers *are* real. I . . . I bribed the camp commandant," Nanée insisted quietly. Varian would assume she had used money, even if Edouard might know better.

"The chaos of Pétain's visit will work in our favor," Varian said to Edouard. "With so many arrests, they can't be looking very closely at anyone. Stay near me. Follow my lead."

André came up the stairs and calmly announced that the police requested everyone's company in the Grand Salon, indicating with a subtle shake of his head that he could put them off no longer. But perhaps Edouard's papers *would* be honored. They were real papers, if gotten under false pretenses. Had the guard at the camp kept Nanée's secret? If he hadn't, would the commandant see it was in his own interest to let Edouard remain free? The papers did include the commandant's legitimate signature. But if the police didn't see it that way, everyone at the château would be at risk.

She whispered to Varian, "Anything else in your briefcase?" Focusing on what they could do something about.

Varian was flipping through his own papers when Gussie noticed on the writing table André's manuscript in his elegant lettering and trademark bright-green ink—no more flattering to Vichy than his octopus drawing that Nanée had just burned. But a plainclothes policeman appeared at the top of the stairs just as Gussie was collecting it. Varian took the pages from the boy and set them in his briefcase as if they were his. The decision whether the greater risk was to leave the briefcase behind in hopes it wouldn't be searched or to take it with them was made by the officer, who instructed him to hand it over.

"WHAT'S THIS ABOUT?" Varian demanded to Nanée's relief as they descended the stairs with Edouard and Gussie and their police chaperone. His words put the oversize commissaire and his companions on the defensive, the only way to manage these bullies.

T, with André and Jacqueline, waited on the black-and-white marble of the entryway, along with Madame Nouget and Rose. After some discussion, the police decided they could wait to fetch Maria and Luki and Peterkin from outside. That accounted for everyone save Danny, who had not yet returned from the office, Maurice, who was "traveling"—taking refugees over the border, Nanée suspected—and Aube, who was at school.

"We must see your papers," the commissaire said.

"Our papers," Nanée objected, worried for Edouard. "For pity's sake. In our own home?"

The police meant to search the house, too. They had an order.

"You'll show it to us, then?" Varian said.

The man handed over a crumpled carbon copy of a general order to search any premises suspected of Communist activity. Not even André, a committed Marxist, had belonged to the French Communist Party since Stalin's Moscow show trials five years before.

"We protest and reserve all rights," Varian said, which sounded like a line he'd rehearsed at the urging of some lawyer somewhere just in case this very circumstance arose.

"You may take that up with the judge," the commissaire replied.

Nanée suspected any judge they might see would be days or weeks away.

The commissaire said, "We know there has been a suitcase brought from the train station. We will search this place from top to bottom until it is turned up."

"But that's my sister's suitcase," Jacqueline objected. She explained to her friends, "She's just come down from Paris. She left her bigger bag here while she looks for a place to live."

"And what is in the suitcase?" the commissaire said surprisingly politely. Beauty had its privileges.

"Her clothes, for heaven's sake," Jacqueline said. "Her toiletries and jewelry and perfume."

Nanée felt a little relieved; if this was just about a suitcase, it would soon be over.

A plainclothes officer ushered Jacqueline upstairs to get the suitcase, the appreciative gaze of the other officers following her. The police herded the rest of them into the dining room, where a clerk had already set up a typewriter on the dining room table. He set out printed forms beside it and asked T to take a seat.

"Me?" T replied.

"Your papers," he said.

She handed them over to him. She did not sit.

He began putting questions to her as she stood beside him, straight and proud. He typed her answers into the form.

The officer and Jacqueline returned with the suitcase, which was opened to reveal women's clothes.

"What did you expect to find?" Jacqueline demanded.

The officer, startled, said, "A bomb."

"A *bomb*? Don't be ridiculous."

"It is not ridiculous," the man objected. "It was right here, at the end of Dr. Thumin's property—right where the Maréchal's train will pass—that an anarchist tried to murder the Prince of Wales by—"

"I promise you, we have no bombs here," Nanée said, wondering why in heaven's name all of France was so obsessed with a single bombing nearly a decade ago.

"We will see for ourselves," the officer said.

"Again, we protest and reserve all rights," Varian said.

The officer took André up to search his room.

Madame Nouget and Rose were allowed to return to the kitchen, but directed to collect Maria and the children and send them in.

"The children! For pity's sake," Nanée said. But it was Maria they were interested in. Maria was a foreigner.

"I'm sure Madame Nouget would stay with the children," T suggested. "Surely there is no need to subject them to this."

Her suggestion was ignored.

One of the police went with the staff to search the kitchen. You could hear him rattling through the cupboards as André returned, the search of his room having produced his service revolver, which seemed to bring the fat commissaire satisfaction. Nanée was pretty sure it was legal for André to have it; he'd been in the French army.

Varian talked his way upstairs on the excuse of using the toilet. Nanée supposed this was a ploy to destroy something else; the nearest bathroom was off the kitchen. She had no idea what Varian might need to get rid of, only that it would be too easy for the only remaining incriminating material in the whole house to be the manuscript in his briefcase, which was already downstairs.

Maria came in with Peterkin and Luki, who clung to their parents, and Dagobert.

Nanée said, "Perhaps you could search my room next?" She meant to buy Varian time and to be up on that floor to help him if she could. "I'm sure you'd like to get through this as quickly as we would, and there are quite a few rooms upstairs." She'd be back in the dining room before the typist finished with T and André and Jacqueline and moved on to Edouard and Gussie—not that there was anything for her to do to help them except to hold her breath with everyone else.

She climbed the stairs to her room with a policeman, Dagobert at her side. As the man pawed through her drawers, she listened to Varian in the hallway chatting up the man accompanying him, commiserating with him as the fellow confessed that, yes, the commissaire was always this unpleasant. The bathroom door clicked closed. A moment later, the toilet flushed.

Varian emerged again, saying he needed to get a handkerchief. Nanée was just about to whisper "Hitler, Hitler" to Dagobert, to set him barking and distract everyone from whatever Varian meant to do, when she heard the fellow assure Varian there was no hurry. A single set of steps entered Varian's room.

While her police escort examined the books stacked around her room, she again looked out to the paddy wagon parked beyond the gate. "We must be awfully important to merit our own van," she said, making noise to cover whatever Varian was doing and distract the man from his own search, but also hoping the fellow would assure her the paddy wagon wasn't for them. No assurance came.

He approached the washstand, where she'd hidden the Webley. She had never used the chamber pot there, but she feigned mortification, saying, "I'm sorry. I'm not sure my chamber pot from last night has been emptied."

She was back in the dining room before the typist asked for Edouard's papers and confirmed the information on his French residency permit. Luki sat in his lap now, snuggled into his chest as if to put as much distance between that typewriter and her as she could.

"Your home is in Sanary-sur-Mer?" the clerk asked Edouard.

"Yes," Edouard answered without offering anything about the fact that he hadn't been there in a year thanks to a stay at Camp des Milles, compliments of the French.

"Sanary-sur-Mer," the clerk repeated.

"Yes," Edouard answered again.

"My brother-in-law is on the force there. Perhaps you know him?"

"I mean no offense," Edouard said cautiously as Nanée too tried to gauge whether this might be some kind of trap, "but I hope you'll understand that I try not to make a habit of becoming acquainted with police."

The clerk laughed easily, then offered a name.

"Ah," Edouard said. "A fine man, I'm sure." Hedging his response so that if there were no such man, he would not have claimed to know him.

Just then, the policeman searching the kitchen emerged waving a piece of paper. "Hidden between two of the plates!" he exclaimed.

Dagobert, startled, barked and barked at him.

It was a drawing from the prior day's salon games, an Exquisite Corpse rendering that had particularly amused André. He'd labeled it "Le Crétin Pétain," the Moron Pétain. It must have been underneath one of the plates Rose put away that morning.

"This," the commissaire said, "is treason."

"Le Crétin Putain?" André replied nonchalantly, suggesting the French leader's name clearly written in André's careful green ink was instead the French word for "whore." The Moron Whore. It had never before struck Nanée how close the spellings were.

Monday, December 2, 1940
VILLA AIR-BEL

E douard stood on the belvedere, Luki in his arms. It had been a grueling few hours, with nothing but a tray of coffee and stale bread for lunch, as Madame Nouget had been detained from her morning shopping. Luki hadn't left his side since she'd been brought in with Maria. He'd spent every possible moment attending to her so that, if anything happened, her last memory of him would not be of his scattered attention, as it had been when he'd put her on the train to Paris, but of nothing in the world being more important than her.

"I talk to the Lady Mary even though she isn't here in stone," she was saying. "I ask her if she could ask God to put Pemmy and Joey on the princess train, like Tante Nanée and me, to come here."

Edouard looked out to the mist over the valley, the sea nowhere to be seen today. The fact that the police had left them on the belvedere for the moment, the staff watching from behind the French doors, allowed him a small hope that he was wrong about where this police business was headed. He still had his camera too. But he sure could use a Lady Mary to believe in himself.

"Everyone into the van now," the oversize commissaire said.

Edouard tried to appear calm for Luki's sake as André protested that he and Jacqueline were French, and everyone's papers were in order. Anger directed at men who knew what they were doing was wrong was invariably met not with acknowledgment or apology but with anger; he'd seen that time and again at Camp des Milles.

"You don't really mean to take the children," T said.

"Papa, I want to stay with you," Luki whispered.

Edouard too wanted to believe the French wouldn't take children, but the French could be more German even than the Germans. And a small part of him wanted to keep Luki with him, no matter where he went. But if they were taken to a camp, the children would be sent with the women. Luki would go with T or Nanée or Jacqueline, although none of them were Jewish—surely they wouldn't be sent to camps.

Nanée said to the commissaire, "Varian and I are American. I'm afraid you might be sorry to have taken us when it comes down to it. And surely our word that these young children and their parents have planned no nefarious Communist plot against Pétain ought to be good enough?"

"It will be only for a short while," the fat little functionary insisted, a lousy liar.

"Do you have children yourself, monsieur?" T asked.

The man looked to Peterkin, holding T's hand, then to Luki in Edouard's own arms.

"Madame Breton has a daughter who is at school, you say?" he asked Nanée, too awed by the beautiful Jacqueline to address her himself, apparently. Then, looking to Gussie, "And the boy is hers too?"

Gussie looked surprised, as if he didn't realize how young he looked, nor that he was as fair and beautiful as Jaqueline. That did explain why they hadn't asked to see his papers.

"I will allow Madame Breton to stay with the children," the commissaire said, chancing a smile at Jacqueline.

Nanée said, "But T's son and Edouard's daughter—"

"Madame Bénédite must come; she works at the Centre Américain de Secours. And monsieur is a refugee. I'm sure Madame Breton can attend to the children until you return."

Edouard hugged Luki to him.

"I want to stay with you, Papa," she repeated.

"I know. I want to stay with you too, my love," he whispered, stroking her hair. "But it won't be any fun. You'll have a much better time here with Madame Breton and Peterkin and Aube."

T was similarly soothing Peterkin, and Madame Nouget had

emerged from the house to help, leaving Rose and Maria cowering inside.

Edouard whispered to Luki, "Maybe Pemmy and Joey will arrive today. Maybe the queen has already sent them. They'd like you to be here to greet them."

"But the last time, you said you would come the next day."

He hugged her to him, choking back his grief. "I know," he managed. "I know."

Luki began sobbing, and Edouard nuzzled into her neck.

"I love you, Luki," he said.

She began wailing then, "Don't leave me, Papa! Don't leave me!"

He could not do this again, and yet he had no choice.

"I love you more than anything," he said, nodding for Jacqueline to take her, as Madame Nouget was taking Peterkin from T. "I love you to the ends of the earth."

She clung so desperately to him that he had to peel her hands from his neck and hand her, kicking and screaming in terror, over to Jacqueline, who wrapped her up as if in a straitjacket as he hurried away. Even the guards saw they had to let him go ahead if they were really going to put Luki through being separated from him again.

He could still hear her screaming as he hurried to climb into the paddy wagon, to get out of her sight. The others followed, the commissaire at the last minute remembering Varian's briefcase. Damn. They waited in the back of the van as the officer who'd taken Varian upstairs was sent to fetch it. He returned and handed the case to Varian, who tried to hide his surprise. Was this inadvertent or intentional? There were friends of their effort everywhere.

The officer closed the door, the metal click solid and final.

"Don't worry," Varian said. "When Danny gets word of this, he'll get us released somehow."

Nanée opened the briefcase, retrieved André's incriminating

manuscript, and stuffed it under her blouse, against her back, where it was caught by the waistband of her slacks and well hidden under her coat.

"If it comes to it, I'll find a way to dump it at the police station," she said as they headed down the long driveway.

The van pulled to a sudden stop. Some kind of skirmish was going on. A moment later, the back of the van opened, and Danny was pushed inside.

Edouard took a single photograph before the doors slammed shut again.

"Lena advised me to come back to the château," Danny said. "I thought she said so I *wouldn't* be arrested."

Edouard looked out through the grated window to the villa behind them, the belvedere empty now, Luki mercifully inside and no longer able to see him again abandoning her.

Monday, December 2, 1940
THE ÉVÊCHÉ, MARSEILLE

The paddy wagon entered the Évêché police station in the old Bishop's Palace through a surprisingly beautiful courtyard not far from the cellar where Edouard first hid here in the Panier. They pulled into an old stable that had been converted into a motorcycle garage. The gate clanged shut behind them, eerily like the gate at Camp des Milles, and they were herded across a courtyard and up a creaky old staircase into an overcrowded, low-ceilinged attic room. Chalked on a board at the front: VIVE LE MARÉCHAL.

Already Nanée was sweet-talking a young clerk. No, please, she and T didn't want to be separated from their friends, but she did need to use the restroom. She was gone an awfully long time, but returned with a smile that Edouard took to mean that André's incriminating green-ink manuscript had been torn up and flushed away.

The commissaire flew into a rage on learning that Varian had the briefcase. Varian merely handed it to him.

They were held all day, Edouard growing increasingly alarmed. He knew as well as anyone that an hour of questions could stretch into days or months or years in a camp. How could Varian hold on to his American naivete even now?

He pulled Nanée aside, finally, not wanting to ask but needing to know. "Nanée, the release and my papers. I . . . It's hard to imagine how you could have gotten them."

She looked across the crowded little room. "The camp commander didn't know you'd escaped," she said finally. "I didn't know you'd escaped."

A newsboy interrupted with the evening papers, the headlines announcing the upcoming visit by Pétain, "Victor of Verdun." Varian bought several, and handed him one to share with Nanée, then offered the boy money with the promise of more if he would fetch them some sandwiches and drinks.

Edouard studied Nanée's face, her head tilted toward the newspaper. "I . . . If I understood . . ." He made himself say it as directly as he could. "The commandant isn't a man who releases prisoners just because a pretty woman asks him to."

Nanée smoothed her hand over the newsprint as if the gesture might make the news disappear. "I entertained him," she said, not looking up.

He looked away, but already he was seeing in his mind Nanée bent forward, in grief and shame. Edouard's own shame, his unworthiness.

Nanée, still focused on the newspaper, whispered, "It wasn't like you're thinking. I did stay the night, yes, but only to . . . I got him drunk so that . . . So he wouldn't remember. So he would imagine he owed me something."

He longed to tip her chin up the way he had Elza's after he'd photographed her, before he touched her bare cheek and her shoulder, before he made love to her because he could not let them succeed in taking everything. He wanted to see in Nanée's eyes the truth of what she was saying. But he was afraid to touch her. He was afraid to see in her eyes that this was only a story meant to ease him into the reality he was left to live with, only tolerable if left unvoiced.

They were interviewed one at a time, pro forma conversations after which T was allowed to leave. Varian pleaded Edouard's case as Luki's only parent, and the interviewer said he would take the request to the commissaire. The clock kept ticking. The man didn't return.

At seven, knowing Luki would be terrified if bedtime came and he wasn't back, Edouard implored Varian to inquire again.

The commissaire had gone home for the day.

They'd been moved to a bigger, equally crowded room on the

ground floor, and it was nearly ten o'clock, when a detective approached Edouard, saying, "We have more questions for you."

"Me?" Edouard said, shifting his Leica to his side to be less obtrusive.

"You are Monsieur Breton?"

André reluctantly identified himself, and permitted the man to take him to a table in the corner for further questioning. Something in the still confidence of André's lion head moved Edouard to photograph the two of them walking away through the crowded room.

André returned not much later, having gotten more information than he gave up. "They're taking us to the SS *Sinaïa*," he said.

Varian said, "I came to Europe on that very ship some years ago."

Edouard wasn't sure what kind of omen that was. He couldn't imagine any way that being put on a ship in the middle of the night could be anything but bad.

ON DECK, THEY were issued burlap-and-straw beds and blankets—six hundred guests of the Vichy government, in the not-so-deluxe accommodations of the SS *Sinaïa* at quai du Président Wilson. They had no idea why they were there, or whether the ship was meant actually to set sail, to take Edouard away from Luki, or when or under what circumstances they might be released. Nanée protested when she was culled from their little herd, but she was ushered away at gunpoint to join the women and the elderly in the third-class cabins. Edouard hurried down into the hold and grabbed an upper iron bunk by a porthole, in view of one of the mooring lines on the quay side. If anyone began to make way to set sail, he would try to get back up to the deck and jump ship without being shot.

Varian settled on the bunk beside him, Danny below, and André next to Danny, below Varian.

Edouard lay huddled on the straw mat under the thin, rough blanket, looking up through the porthole to a cold, starry sky. He wished he'd had the sense to grab a photograph of Luki. He understood the despair that led Walter Benjamin to suicide, to have escaped incarceration only to be imprisoned again. He would leave France as soon as he got out of here, if he got out of here. He would find a way, and he and Luki would leave. He and Luki and Nanée.

The thought caught him off guard. That was why he'd been silently relieved when Nanée was made to go with the women. Edouard had lived this life before. He knew how hateful it could get, how unforgivable people could be under stress. He wasn't sure who he hoped to protect by the separation. He'd endured this once before, and managed to keep his friends. She was a rich girl, used to luxury.

And yet here she was, choosing to stay in a France occupied by Germany when she might leave any day. Choosing a life that left her prisoner on a ship off the coast of France when she might be climbing into fine cotton sheets in a mansion in someplace called Evanston, in the peacetime luxury of the United States.

He raised his Leica, which, surprisingly, no one had taken from him, and photographed the men in the bunks.

They looked at him, surprised.

"Forgive me," he said. "I'm only documenting this life. I don't know what I'll do with the photos, whether I'll do anything with them. I only know that they need to be taken."

Tuesday, December 3, 1940
ON THE SS *SINAÏA*

E douard tidied himself as best he could before Nanée rejoined them
on deck the next morning while André, elected for the purpose,
went to fetch their breakfast from the galley—so much like Camp des
Milles.

"It is the way of incarceration," Edouard assured the others, feign-
ing less fear than he felt at being held here. "Everything requires waiting in line."

André returned finally with black bread, faux coffee, and the news
that not one among them would be allowed to communicate with anyone outside. Not Varian or Nanée. Not the other furious Americans.
Not even the prominent French journalist who was taking copious
notes.

After lunch—beef still quite frozen in the middle and, this being
France, plenty of wine—they were loaded into the hull without explanation. This time Nanée was allowed to accompany them. A pock-
faced, gawky guard at the hatch beamed shyly, like the teenage boy
he probably was, when she wandered over to chat him up from below.

"I'm Nanée," she said.

The poor fellow only stared mutely at her.

"Wouldn't you like to tell me your name?" she asked.

"I'm . . . I'm Paul," the boy stammered.

"Paul," she repeated. "You're quite adorable, Paul. Has anyone ever
told you that?"

The boy answered, "My mother."

Nanée smiled gently as those watching the interchange worked hard
not to laugh.

"Paul," she said, "I don't suppose you have any idea how long they
mean to keep us here?"

Paul shook his head.

Nanée thanked him, and returned to join them.

"That went well," Danny said. "You didn't want to ask him to find out?"

"The sad sacks are the easiest to bamboozle, but you can't do everything on the first hello," she said. "I did learn from voices overhead, though, that Pétain is about to come by in a coast-guard cutter."

André said cheerily, "Can't have the old man faced with the prisoners taken on his behalf."

WHEN THEY WERE let up to the deck again, Varian wrote a message for Vice Consul Bingham, wrapped it around a ten-franc coin, waited carefully until it seemed no one was looking, and tossed it onto the dock, toward some delivery boys. "Maybe one chance in ten that some boy doesn't pocket the coin and toss the note," he said.

"What an optimist you are," André replied. "I wouldn't take that bet at a hundred to one."

But a few hours later, a package arrived, addressed to Varian—a good number of decent sandwiches, with Bingham's calling card.

"What exactly did you tell him in that note, Varian?" André asked.

"I said, given a choice between freedom and a good roast beef and tomato on rye, I'd take the roast beef, of course. What did you think I would write?"

André said, "Next time, make clear you need a fifth of good whiskey with that, would you?"

Edouard laughed with them. Laughter was, like art, a way to survive.

Wednesday, December 4, 1940
VILLA AIR-BEL

Luki wanted to cry with Peterkin as the men put the rope around Madame LaVache's big neck, but Aube wasn't crying and Luki was bigger than her. For two nights now, Papa had been gone, and Aube and Peterkin's papas too. Peterkin's maman, who'd gone with Papa but then came back, was like Sister Therese. She poured Luki milk and tucked her in at night and sang to her, and when Luki woke to the bad men coming, she came into her room—with Dagobert too—and promised her the bad men weren't real. But Peterkin's maman wasn't Papa. Luki wished Papa would come back. Papa had promised he wouldn't go away again, and now he was gone.

She fingered the ribbon Aube's mother had put in her hair, a green one she'd picked because it was almost the color of the ribbon at Pemmy's neck and of Papa's eyes. She wished Pemmy would grow tired of being a princess and ask the queen to send her to Luki. She wished she could ask the stone Lady Mary to bring Papa back, and Mutti too. She wished they could all sit together on the dreaming log and sing.

She blinked, trying to make the tears go away.

Cold fingers intertwined with hers, Aube's maman's hand. Madame Nouget took her other hand as Peterkin's maman hugged him. Rose and Maria too watched the men make the cow walk up the plank onto their truck.

"Goodbye, Madame LaVache-à-Lait," Luki whispered. "You're a good cow." She would have waved to her, but she didn't want to let go of the hands holding hers.

Wednesday, December 4, 1940
ON THE SS *SINAÏA*

On their third day, Nanée managed to persuade the poor pock-faced, gawky boy-guard to take a note to the captain. To their astonishment, she and Varian received in response an invitation to the captain's cabin. He poured them beer, apologizing that he didn't have anything better, nor any way to help them.

"The administration has requisitioned my boat," he said. "The matter is not in my hands."

Nanée, even after days on board with no real opportunity to clean up, didn't fear this captivity, exactly. She didn't imagine they would send an American woman to a camp. And no one relied on her except Dagobert, who would be well cared for by T and loved by Peterkin and Aube and Luki, although he must be as confused as when she'd left him in Brive with T just before France fell. How much more horrible it must be for Edouard, to have a five-year-old daughter missing him.

Really, she didn't see why this captain couldn't at least let them send word to the consulate, and she was just suggesting that when the cabin boy showed up at the door to announce a visitor, and Harry Bingham entered as if Nanée had miraculously summoned him.

"Varian," the vice consul said, "how the devil did you get caught up in this mess?" He registered Nanée, and chuckled. "Nanée," he said as they exchanged kisses despite her disreputable state. "The last time I saw you, you were off to Paris. I thought you meant to go home directly from there."

"Pffft. And leave this extraordinary hospitality?"

"Hospitality," the captain said, unlocking a cupboard and extracting a bottle of good whiskey and four crystal glasses. So much for having nothing but beer. "A votre santé," he said.

Bingham had been trying to find someone with authority to release them since Gussie came to him with the news they'd been arrested. With so many arrests, it was impossible to determine where they'd been taken, though. And even after he got Varian's note, his influence was limited, as the French were falling all over themselves to avoid blame for anything that might go wrong while Pétain was in town. The Vichy leader was leaving the next day, though, and Bingham hoped to have more luck come morning.

"Couldn't you move my friends up to decent first-class cabins in the meantime?" he asked the captain.

Alas, there were not enough guards to accommodate that. But at least someone now knew they were here.

DETECTIVES ARMED WITH files took up residence in the first-class lounge the next morning, and soldiers on deck began calling names. One by one, the prisoners were being let go, with only a few sent into the lounge for some further indignity, all of them foreigners.

Danny said to Edouard, "Take my papers. Pretend you're me. They don't seem to be doing anything but checking names to a list."

They were huddled, quietly discussing whether it would be safer for Edouard to take Danny's French passport or use his own residency permit, which Nanée again assured them was authentic, when Danny's name was called and a decision had to be made.

Danny went off to present himself. They watched as the boy-guard Nanée had befriended scanned his list, found Danny's name, and checked it off. But rather than sending him down to shore, the guard sent him in the other direction, into the lounge.

Nanée was already trying to devise some intervention—surely she could sweet-talk this boy Paul—when he called out Edouard's name.

Nanée watched Edouard cross the deck. It seemed forever until the boy found his name, even though he'd just called it, for heaven's sake.

The poor kid seemed puzzled. He'd made a mistake and was sorting out how to cover it up, Nanée thought.

She joined them, saying, "Paul, don't you have my name on that list too?"

He blanched, the distraction she wanted.

"No," he said. "I sure wish I did, but someone else has the list with the ladies."

"I'll see you onshore then," she said to Edouard, who took her cue and set off before the boy could see she'd made his decision for him.

She stayed, chatting easily now, as Edouard made his way down the plank, off the boat, and out of sight. Only when he was gone did she set about getting a better look at the boy's list: Danny's name, and below it, Edouard's—names and a very few details, and a final column in which there was a checkmark for Edouard but not for Danny. She scanned up the page to another name with a checkmark.

"What's that mean, Paul?" she asked.

He looked to the checkmark she was indicating.

"That's the ones we can't let go."

He hadn't followed the line across the page properly. Danny was meant to be let go, and Edouard to be kept.

"Is the ship to take them somewhere?" she asked, needing to determine how much time they might have to get Danny off, and what the detectives in the lounge might want Edouard for.

The boy shrugged. "I don't think so. But I just send them one way or the other. That's all I know."

BY MIDAFTERNOON, NANÉE and everyone but Danny were released and on the trolley, Edouard and André headed for Villa Air-Bel and their daughters while Nanée went into town with Varian to see what could be done about Danny. The streets of Marseille remained festooned with flags and tired bunting. Some of the Garde Pétain still swaggered down streets where the street sweepers were hard at work. The roundups had nothing to do with illegal activity; they'd simply cleared the streets of anyone who might cause a ruckus while Pétain was in town. If it hadn't been for Jacqueline's sister's suitcase, they too might have been spared.

Danny had succeeded in closing the office the morning of the raids so that none of the other employees had been taken into custody. The legal activity of the CAS was in full swing again when Nanée and Varian arrived. A stranger sat in Varian's office with his feet up on the desk. Varian was so calm about it. So unfazed. He had been expecting this moment, and, in typical Varian form, had already thought through how he would play it. Even as Jay Allen—a newspaper man sent by the Emergency Rescue Committee in New York to replace him— explained that he would be running the CAS part-time and leaving his assistant in charge while he traveled around Europe, reporting the news, Varian nodded as if that suited him just fine. He suggested that Nanée find Captain Dubois to see about getting Danny released from the boat while he turned his desk over to Mr. Allen and Miss Palmer— giving the appearance of helping transition the office to their care, Nanée saw, while buying himself time before he would be forced to return to the States.

Allen was not prepared to allow Nanée to leave quite yet, though. A package had arrived for her that morning, with no return address, and he meant to have her open it in front of them. He clearly wasn't someone who would break rules or risk his own safety to help refugees.

Nanée suggested that Allen open the package himself, so it was he who pulled Pemmy from the box. When little Joey fell from the stuffed kangaroo's pocket, startling him, it was all she could do not to laugh. Varian too, judging from his expression.

"It belongs to a young girl I was traveling with," Nanée explained, staying with the truth.

Who brought it? She had no idea. Also true.

"How do we know it isn't being used to smuggle something?" Allen demanded.

"In a child's toy?" Miss Palmer said.

"You're welcome to examine the poor, overloved kangaroo and her baby," Nanée said, "to see if you can find any seam that has been tampered with."

Allen scowled. "I have a train to catch. Miss Palmer, you can deal with this."

As Nanée, Varian, and Miss Palmer watched him go, even Miss Palmer seemed relieved. Nanée picked up the joey from the floor and offered it to the woman, who declined to take it.

"I'm sure the child it belongs to will be very glad to have it," she said.

Nanée hesitated. "Do be careful here, Miss Palmer. Not everyone in Marseille is well-intentioned."

Varian wasn't about to disclose to Allen and Palmer their secret routes, the places they hid refugees, or how they converted Nanée's dollar contributions into francs. Nanée could see that. He would transition to these newcomers the legitimate work of providing assistance to refugees in the limited ways Vichy allowed, while his own people continued the work of getting refugees out of France from Villa Air-Bel.

Nanée left Varian with Miss Palmer and went to find Captain Dubois, who was incensed that anyone working at the CAS had been arrested in the roundups. And why hadn't they contacted him for help? She rode with him back to the boat, but waited onshore. A few minutes later, Danny emerged. He had no more idea why he'd been kept than any of them had as to why they'd been arrested in the first place.

"Just Vichy efficiency," Nanée said.

Thursday, December 5, 1940
VILLA AIR-BEL

Luki held Pemmy up, then Joey, for Papa to kiss good night. They were all tucked under the warm covers, Papa just finished reading to them from the letters he'd written her even when he couldn't send them.

"Now, Pemmy," Papa said, "you keep Luki company, and don't let her lose another tooth for a few minutes. I have some things to talk about with Mr. Fry."

Luki nodded. "About going to America."

"Yes."

"Together."

Papa looked the way he did when he was making up his mind. "Together, yes."

"And we'll go on a train?"

"We'll leave on a train. We might have to walk some of the way. And we'll be on a boat for a long time too."

"America is very far away."

"Yes."

"It's where the angels live."

"The angels?"

"Tante Nanée lives there, except she lives here now. That's what she told me on the train. This is her house. We'll go on the same train?"

Papa went quiet in that way that always made Pemmy nervous.

"Yes," he said finally, "this time we'll leave on the same train."

"We could take the train Tante Nanée and I rode. It had a whole big bed, and a place to sit, and our own toilet. Will she come too?"

"Nanée?" Papa stroked her hair.

She closed her eyes, his hand gentle on her forehead. She touched Pemmy's forehead the same way, so she would feel warm and cozy too.

"Would you like that?" he whispered.

Would she like Tante Nanée to come with them? She was afraid both that Tante Nanée wasn't an angel and that she might be, that she could fly her to Mutti, but then she would have to leave Papa behind.

She whispered, "I wish Mutti could come with us."

Papa pulled her close. Luki could feel him crying even though he didn't make a noise.

She whispered, "Do they have dreaming logs in America?"

Papa put his hands on her cheeks and looked right inside her, the way he did when he was sad and she was sad. He kissed her cheek, then, and he whispered, "We'll find a dreaming log there."

Friday, December 6, 1940
VILLA AIR-BEL

The damned police had taken the cow. Nanée was glad to be again sleeping in her own bed, eating meager rations, and soaking in the zinc tub, but without Madame LaVache's milk, there wasn't food enough for the children. Danny and T decided they'd have to send Peterkin back to Danny's mother in Juan-les-Pins. The Bretons might do the same if they had family to send Aube to and didn't need to have her nearby when their American visas came through. It would not be an issue for Luki. That boy-guard had made a mistake and kept Danny rather than Edouard, but the Marseille police had taken down all of Edouard's information in the roundup. They knew he was here at the château, and if the Gestapo weren't on to that fact yet, they would be soon.

"We're sending Edouard by the F route," Varian told Nanée the morning after they were released from the boat.

She understood the heightened urgency of getting Edouard out, but why was Varian telling her? With Varian, everything was need-to-know.

He'd asked her to join him in the library with Maurice, who'd just returned from the border with the alarming news that Azéma, the mayor of Banyuls—known for his easy way of greeting people on the beach or at the harbor while quietly helping smuggle refugees across the border—had been replaced and hadn't been seen since. Maurice hoped the mayor had gotten himself into Spain on the same route he'd drawn for them, but there was no way to know. And his replacement was a Pétain loyalist.

"What about our other friends there?" Varian asked.

Maurice explained to Nanée that Hans and Lisa Fittko were running a new escape route over the Pyrenees from Banyuls. "Hans and

Lisa are still in place," he told Varian. "The new mayor called Lisa in and told her he wasn't fooled; he knows exactly who she is."

Varian looked alarmed. "And does he?"

"He imagines her a British spy. He said he could see right through her, but that he could also 'keep silent' if she didn't 'give him any trouble'—perhaps an invitation for a bribe or perhaps merely staking his ground to ward off charges of being a collaborator should the winds change. I don't have to tell you that Hans and Lisa are nervous. They'll be happy to have the last of our refugees out of France and the American visas you promised them in hand."

"I don't know how Edouard will get a child over the Pyrenees," Varian said. "We can't risk asking to expedite travel or exit papers for Luki; that would attract too much attention, with Edouard's name already on the Gestapo list." That was, they'd determined, the reason for those on the ship being detained while the rest were let free—they were wanted by the Gestapo. "And there isn't time anyway. We need to get them out now. The child makes passing them off as farm laborers improbable, so they'll have to set out as weekend picnickers or something. They won't be able to take out anything more than a string bag of the type that might hold a loaf of bread and a bottle of wine. But the Fittkos might be able to get some of Edouard's work out on the train."

Varian handed Nanée half of a torn strip of colored paper with numbers written on it.

"The Fittkos have the other half?" Nanée hadn't thought about the details of how this was done, how the Fittkos could be sure the people who showed up were legitimate CAS protégés and not impostors meant to flush them out.

Varian stood and poked the fire, which sparked and crackled. "A man traveling alone with a daughter like Luki will draw attention."

"I see." She was to take Luki. "Just to the border?"

"That will be up to you, Nanée."

Her French transit visa was still good, but she didn't have a French exit visa, or time enough to get one. If she left illegally, she would not easily return to France.

"Everyone here would understand if you chose to go," Varian said.

Dagobert made a little whining sound, and Varian reached down and pet his head. "I've been thinking I might like a dog myself," he said. "Do you suppose Dagobert here would tolerate sharing the château with another dog?"

"Villa Espère un Ami Chien," Nanée said. Yes, Varian would do well with a dog.

"We have Edouard's American visa, and Luki's passport," Varian continued. "Edouard will have to travel under an alias to Portugal; those documents are in process."

They had a line on an identity card for someone who'd died that morning, whose description would be close enough to Edouard's for him to use the deceased's documents.

"So with any luck, Sunday," Varian said.

"The day after tomorrow? I . . . What about . . ." She glanced down at Dagobert, who looked up at her expectantly.

Varian reached down and rubbed the dog's ears the way only Nanée ever did, and Dagobert shook his head. "I'm afraid he'd draw too much attention to you and Luki." Varian too knew not to say Dagobert's name aloud.

Saturday, December 7, 1940
VILLA AIR-BEL

Nanée stopped a few paces outside the door to Edouard's bedroom. She'd come to get Luki's things, which were to go in her own suitcase until they got to Banyuls. Edouard would be traveling as prosperous businessman Henri Roux, the wealthy being so much less likely to be questioned than the poor, while Nanée was Nanée, and Luki was her niece. Edouard would have the first-class cabin adjacent to theirs—tickets Varian had already arranged. It was safer for Nanée and Luki to travel separately, in case Edouard's alias was discovered, but the proximity would allow Luki the comfort of her father just the other side of the wall and give Nanée some chance to help him if he found himself in a fix and sent up a flare by, say, tapping his fingers on the adjoining wall.

Edouard's bedroom door was ajar. He was packing, his back to her, his bony shoulders curled forward under a shirt with the sleeves rolled up, bony hips under pants that he would not have begun to fit into that night she first met him, before the internment camps that were first French and then Vichy. He'd neatly laid out on his bed the espadrilles Varian had brought for better purchase on the rocky path over the Pyrenees, the uppers leather to keep them warmer. One pair for him and one for Luki. In small piles next to the shoes were thick wool socks and warm clothes for the climb through the mountains, and his Leica, eight film canisters full of as many negatives as he could fit, a stale baguette, and a Bibliothèque Rose book—the one with the rocking horse, which Nanée had found in Marseille and bought for the excuse of sitting alone with Luki, just the two of them reading together. Also, the letter from Luki he'd brought from Camp des Milles, and the ones he'd written to Luki but never sent.

He held a photograph.

Varian had suggested Edouard might pack some of his work, although he needed to be careful which photos to risk being caught with. "You won't be able to carry them with you over the Pyrenees," Varian told him, "but there's a chance the Fittkos might find someone to ferry them for you—a small chance, but some is better than none."

It was Nanée who had the idea to load some of Edouard's 35 mm film canisters with negatives and hide them inside a hollowed-out baguette they could then wrap in paper and carry in Edouard's musette bag. He could bring much of his work that way, to reprint it when he got to the US, without the higher risk of a stack of photos being found on him. Nanée wondered which he was taking. Negatives she'd brought from Sanary-sur-Mer? The shots he'd taken in the last few weeks? The ones from being confined in the Évêché and on the boat?

Yes, the images from the Évêché and the boat. Their publication would help open the world's eyes to what was happening here, the lives of those frantic to escape France, refugees who could not find refuge. Perhaps he'd also take the negatives from here, their life at Villa Air-Bel—a place Edouard might love, but still a kind of confinement. He could hold those until Varian was ejected from France so he wouldn't jeopardize protégés like André, whose status as a former Communist was holding up his American visa. If Danny could carry on their work after Varian was inevitably forced to leave, the Villa Air-Bel images might not be published for months or even years. But when that work could no longer be done, Edouard could publish them too. It was what he ought to do. What she wanted him to do.

If he were caught trying to leave France with these negatives, though, he would be arrested for crimes against Vichy and France. Treason. If he were caught just carrying them, not even trying to leave, that would be enough to sentence him to death.

Edouard bent his head forward, revealing the raggedness of his haircut and the hairs growing on his neck, above his collar.

If no one else could be found to take the suitcase over the border, Nanée could do it. She could apply for an expedited French exit visa and take them when she had it. Her luggage might be searched at the border, of course. They might find the negatives of this moment Vichy was hiding from the world. What would they do then? Would they keep the work and let her go on, or would they arrest her?

Edouard ran a hand over the back of his neck as if to rub out a tough decision, turning slightly with the gesture so that Nanée could see the photograph in his hands.

Nude, Bending. Ghost Wife. The photograph he'd printed so many times in Sanary-sur-Mer. She'd pinned all those prints back in place and left them at the cottage. He must have printed it again here, at Villa Air-Bel. Did he mean to take it with him? Would he risk his life, and perhaps Luki's and hers too, for that single photograph? A naked woman. If found in a search, it would be considered indecent, cause for arrest no matter who he might otherwise have succeeded in pretending to be.

Saturday, December 7, 1940
VILLA AIR-BEL

Edouard stood in his bedroom, staring at *Salvation*, every sense awash in the grief of leaving behind the only world Elza had ever known, the only world they had ever shared. He breathed deeply, trying to gather himself. It would be for the best, for him and Luki both. To start over. To begin the new life he'd imagined they would begin in Sanary-sur-Mer, only to find himself still mired in their loss. Even now, Elza's memory was so real that he could smell her in this photo, and with the smell of her, taste her, hear her breath.

He turned then, realizing it was not Elza's breath he was hearing, not Elza's perfume, but Nanée's.

Nanée was there, down the hall, beyond Luki's door. She was disappearing through her own doorway into her own room, where they'd made love last night and the night before, where he'd painted her back and photographed her after she brought Luki to him. Was that really only a week ago?

He turned back to the photo, *Salvation*. He folded it in half, and when he heard the click of Nanée's door closing, he took it out to the fire in the library and set it on the flames. The negative was already sequestered in the baguette, in one of the film canisters. He might print the image again someday, when he thought he could do it right, when it really would heal him.

He set the letters, the one from Luki and the ones he wrote her, in the empty suitcase. He ought to burn them too; they contained too much detail about life in the camps to be carried safely. He removed them from the suitcase and placed them in the pocket of the shirt hanging in his armoire, one Jacqueline had bought for him the day after he arrived at Villa Air-Bel. He would wear it the next day, when they left.

Saturday, December 7, 1940
VILLA AIR-BEL

Nanée returned to her own room, still thinking about Edouard's photo. *Ghost Wife.* She was surprised to find the door open; she was trying to be so careful, trying not to signal to those who didn't need to know that she would be taking him to the border. But everyone at Villa Air-Bel knew that Edouard and Luki were leaving.

T was sitting at the edge of the bed, the Robert Piguet suit folded neatly in her lap. "Wear it for me, Nan," she said. "The only other decent clothes you have are trousers, and they'll draw the wrong kind of attention. You need a convincing suit. What you're doing, it's so dangerous."

"Whatever do you think I'm doing?" Nanée protested. T was not someone who needed to know.

T gave her a look. "You're taking a German refugee wanted by the Gestapo illegally across half of France, if not across the border."

Nanée closed the door behind her.

"So you do mean to leave France with him then?" T said.

Nanée considered her friend, so much smaller than she was, and somehow so much more accomplished. A wife. A mother. A woman of substance on whom Danny relied.

"You should," T said. "You should go with Edouard. Take a chance for once in your life. Don't use the excuse of needing to stay to help Varian. Varian's days here are numbered."

Edouard's voice drifted in from the room next door. He was tucking Luki in, reading from the letters he'd written her, as he did every night. Always funny bits. Light bits. Nanée wondered if that was all he'd written, or only what he now chose to read.

"You'd have me leave France for a man I barely know?" she said with a lightness she didn't feel. Edouard had been at Villa Air-Bel for barely a month.

"All the work we do here will end soon, whether you stay or you go."

Would it? Or when Varian left, would Danny take charge and carry on? Nanée closed her eyes, listening to Edouard's voice, wondering if he would come to her again tonight, if he would whisper her name and make love to her before slipping back to his own room lest Luki wake and find him missing.

"I don't think it would be good for Luki," she said.

"For you to go, or for you to stay here? I ought to have pushed you to get to know him better in Paris."

"He was leaving that day for Sanary-sur-Mer."

"You might have written him letters, like Danny and me. And Sanary-sur-Mer isn't that far for a girl who flies airplanes."

If Edouard had sent that bread-and-butter note she'd found on his desk in Sanary, she would have written him back. Why hadn't he? Why hadn't she written first? How could they know anything about each other, really, in the few weeks they'd had together? Could she take him back to a world where she would be forever judged for not being the kind of woman she couldn't stand to be, where everyone she knew would assume he was a penniless refugee who loved not her but her wealth? And once she left France, she would not be allowed to return.

"After the war, Edouard will not want the memory of his wife that he sees in me now."

"You might let him decide that."

"Luki—"

"Luki already thinks of you as her mother."

"And yet I am not."

T smiled gently. "And yet you're saying goodbye here. You're fixing this home in your memory."

Nanée wanted to object, to say she hadn't been doing exactly that, saying goodbye to the zinc tub and the little chair in the greenhouse

where she liked to read, the clock on the mantel that refused to recognize the passage of time, the pond they'd rescued from ruin, and the
view from the belvedere to the sea, the trees so often hung with art.

"In case," she admitted. "In case I decide to go . . ." Not home. This
villa was more home than anywhere she had ever lived, their makeshift family more family to her than anyone back in Evanston. "In case
I decide to go back."

T wiped away a tear. "How will I bear it here without you? I know
you should go. I want you to. But I want you to stay too. Selfishly, I
want you to stay. I ask myself, Who could get away with all you get
away with? Who will manage the money exchanges? Who will glide
through the Marseille streets to deliver messages? But in my heart,
it's, Who will light the fire every night and start us singing? Never
mind that you can't carry a tune. Who will make Danny laugh?"

"I can too carry a tune."

"You can't, but I love the way you sing anyway. We all love the
way you sing." T smoothed the suit still in her hands. "I can let you go,
but I can't lose you. And this is . . . You might . . . You'll need to appear
as convincing as you possibly can. A woman of substance. A woman
no one would—"

"I don't have any stockings."

"Nan, nobody has stockings anymore."

"That suit would hardly be appropriate for hiking over the Pyrenees." Again with a lightness she didn't feel.

"It's not Aero-Chanel, I'll give you that. But you've never been
one for dressing appropriately. You just like to pretend you are."

How comfortable she'd felt in that Chanel dress and flight jacket,
even at the Surrealist exposition that had so discomfited her. And of
course T was right. The skirts Nanée wore to deliver messages in the
Panier were not appropriate for a wealthy American woman traveling
first class. Her trousers, elegant enough, would draw the wrong kind

of attention. And she was too big to borrow anything of T's, too small for Jacqueline's.

She walked away from the damn suit in T's lap, to the window. It was dark outside and light in the bedroom, so that the windowglass reflected a dim version of her own face back at her. "I didn't even free him," she said.

"Edouard?" T's voice turning toward her. "But you had no way to know he wasn't at that camp."

"I didn't even free him," she repeated.

"It was still a brave thing you did, Nan. Brave and selfless. Giving yourself to that man there. You were saving a man's life."

"I didn't give myself to him." Wanting to tell T, to set down her anger and her shame.

"But . . ."

Nanée watched as T, reflected in the window, held the suit to her chest.

"I don't mean to . . . I'm sorry. I just . . . I thought you had sex with him. I thought that's how you got Edouard's release."

Nanée kept her gaze focused on their reflections as T stood, looking from the suit jacket in her hands to the cold fireplace where it might have burned. "Pffft," she said after a moment, that handy little noise she'd learned from the French girls, a way to dismiss something you lacked the words to address.

T set the suit on the bed, came to stand beside her, and put her arms around her. "Oh, Nan," she whispered.

Her body felt so slight, her friendship so warm.

"I'm sorry," T said. "I'm sorry. I didn't . . ."

She put one hand on each cheek then and made Nanée meet her gaze, the way she had done with Peterkin when she said goodbye to him in Brive, when she needed him to know how much he was loved.

"I promise you, Nan, that isn't your shame." She wiped a tear from Nanée's cheek. "That's his shame. It's all his."

Saturday, December 7, 1940
VILLA AIR-BEL

Nanée stood at her bedroom window, staring out into the moonlight on the plane trees and the belvedere and the garden, trying not to think of the Robert Piguet suit in her armoire, her suitcase packed now with her own things and Luki's, which would be less dangerous in her possession than in Edouard's. In the quiet of the late night, she remembered that first time she'd listened to the quiet here, out on the belvedere with Miriam and T.

If Edouard didn't come tonight, that would be his choice. His daughter. His decision. Luki still wanted her mother to return from heaven. He would have to decide what was right for them all.

Just when she had decided that he wouldn't come, that that would make her decision easy—whatever they had was over; there would be no last night together, and if she went back to the United States she would be going alone—his quiet knock sounded on her door.

The shadow of Edouard entering, closing the door behind him. Not climbing under the covers like he usually did, but sitting silently at the edge of the bed.

"I'm over here," she said.

He looked toward her voice, but didn't speak. In the silence, a train whistle sounded far in the distance.

"Can I ask . . . ," he said finally. "It's more than I can ask, but . . ."

Yes, she wanted to say.

"Anything," she said.

He stood and came to the window, and tucked a small bundle of paper in her hands—his letters.

"Take Luki?" he whispered. "If anything happens tomorrow, leave me behind, but please take Luki? Make her go with you."

"Edouard, nothing is—"

"She isn't Jewish," he said. "You will be at no real risk. Let Luki believe you're an angel. Let her think anything that will convince her to go with you, to get to the United States, to be safe."

She reached to his face in the moonlight, his skin as damp with tears as hers had been with T.

He leaned forward, kissed her forehead, and left, closing the door as silently as he'd come.

Sunday, December 8, 1940

VILLA AIR-BEL

Nanée stopped halfway down the stairs to the entry hall, where everyone was saying goodbye to Edouard and Luki. The girl's hair was tucked into two tidy caramel braids. Nanée wondered how many men knew how to braid a little girl's hair.

This is real, she thought. They were leaving.

Dagobert trailed at her side, not on a leash.

As T looked up, Nanée tried to see herself as she did. Her new traveling case in hand—very like the old one she'd left at Madame Dupin's tomb—with Luki's things and her own, including her own espadrilles. "In case Hans and Lisa need your help getting them out; you'll need the better foothold on the stony paths," Varian had said when he gave them to her, although when he'd told everyone at the breakfast table that Edouard and Luki were indeed leaving that morning, he hadn't mentioned Nanée. She wore her gray coat unbuttoned and, underneath it, the blue suit with the soft yellow pinstripes that she hadn't believed she could ever wear again. She would trade them for the trousers, flight jacket, and scarf in her traveling case when they arrived at the Fittkos' in Banyuls.

She took the last stairs carefully, remembering Rose sprawled on the entry floor, André lifting the maid and carrying her up to her room, herself on her knees, cleaning up, and the postcard she'd found on the floor, suggesting Berthe was in Brittany. She fingered the things in her own coat pockets. How empty the house would seem without Luki's gentle giggle, without the trace of developing chemicals, the occasional sound of a shutter when you least expected it, the apology that forever followed, Edouard's gentle voice saying he was only documenting this life, that he didn't know what he would do with the photos but that he needed to take them.

Dagobert nuzzled her leg as if he sensed what was to happen here, that she would, as she had in Brive, take this child and leave him behind.

Gussie shyly offered Nanée his lucky copy of *L'envers et l'endroit*. "Carry it under your left arm, not your right," he said.

"But you still need the luck yourself."

"Knowing you're carrying it will bring me more luck."

"Gussie—" Nanée kissed his cheek, unable to finish giving voice to her thoughts. If she were ten years younger and had half an ounce of sense, she would fall for him.

"Are you ready?" she asked Luki.

The girl nodded. Solemn. Resolved. How devastating that a child so young had to know so much of the ugliness of the world. When Nanée was Luki's age, she'd slept in a four-poster bed draped in lace, with no idea that anything in the world would interrupt her night, much less her whole life. She chose each morning from a closet full of clothes, and played on the sands of Lake Michigan, and read any book she wanted, and learned French from her governess. She summered at the beautiful Marigold Lodge that was now hers, and spent long days on the family yacht, and never gave a thought to the milk she drank. And yet her father had never braided her hair. A life of wealth and a life of riches aren't always the same.

She looked to Edouard: his square face, the mole at the end of his left brow, the startling willow-green eyes as steeped in sadness as they had been the night she first met him, at that exposition she hadn't wanted to attend. His Leica, slung by its strap around his neck, hung at his side. He nodded as solemnly as his daughter had. His suitcase, the negatives hidden in the baguette inside it, sat on the floor by the door. No rucksack. Only Germans carried rucksacks, and he would need to pass as anything but German on the path over the Pyrenees.

Edouard said he'd like to take a group photograph to remember everyone by, so they gathered on the belvedere for the natural light, arms around one another to fit more tightly together. Nanée scooped Dagobert up and held him, then set a hand on Luki's shoulder and looked out to the long, wide stretch of France framed by the neat row of boxwoods and the tree trunks and the lacy branches: the pine and olive trees, the red-tiled roofs, the paths of the railroad and the trolley, and, this morning, a gorgeous blue sea. It was somehow easier to imagine leaving it in the bright light. She loved France, but she could leave it, if only she could take Danny and T and Dagobert with her, if only she could take this feeling of being useful, of being intrepid, of doing good.

Edouard set his camera on the tripod he would leave behind. He framed the shot, adjusted the settings, and showed Madame Nouget what to press. He joined them then, sliding one arm around Nanée's waist and setting his free hand on Luki's other shoulder. Nanée let go of Luki now that her father was beside her, to get Dagobert to look toward Madame Nouget as she pressed the shutter release.

Edouard took back the camera and slung it around his neck, then put on his gray felt fedora. "All right then," he said.

"Wait." Nanée set Dagobert down, took the hat from Edouard's head, and looked at the leather sweatband inside, his initials there, ELM. He was to be traveling as Henri Roux.

She took the fountain pen that had been her father's from her coat pocket and used the nib to scratch Edouard's initials out.

"I'm obliged to act the criminal," Edouard said.

At the pain in his voice, Nanée lifted hers. "Misbehavior can be awfully fun if you embrace it," she said. She wanted to set the hat on his head and kiss him, but she only handed it back to him and slid the pen into her coat pocket.

"I almost forgot, I have something for Pemmy," she said, pulling out the oversize safety-pin brooch, silver and Bakelite red, she'd tucked in her pocket first thing that morning. She knelt in front of Luki the way she'd knelt that night to clean up after Rose, and she pinned the baby kangaroo safely to his mother. "So Pemmy won't lose Joey on her way to America."

This is real, she thought again. They were leaving.

"That makes Joey so happy that he wants to sing for you," Luki said, and she wound the key on the baby kangaroo and let it go so that the little music box buried inside him played "The Waltz of the Flowers."

Nanée smiled at Edouard, wishing she had a way to similarly connect him and Luki. "It makes Pemmy happy too, I bet."

"Yes, Pemmy too," Edouard agreed.

"Except Pemmy doesn't sing," Luki said. "Only Joey sings."

They began the goodbyes again, all of them hugging Edouard and Luki and wishing luck to Nanée, no one but T and Varian with any idea that she might not return.

"I'll see you in New York, then," Varian said, the send-off Nanée had come to see less as a sign of Varian's optimism than as a way for him to inspire confidence in his protégés as they embarked on this perilous journey.

Only T hugged her. T hugged her and whispered, "Ask Lisa to send the suit back to me if she can. It will remind me to be selfless and brave."

"Now remember," Edouard said to Luki, "Nanée is going to hold your hand the whole way. I'll be with you, just behind you or just ahead."

"But I want to go with you, Papa. I want to be on the train with you."

"I'll be in the compartment just next to you. You'll follow me as we board so you can see where I am. You can knock on the wall anytime, and I'll knock back."

Luki looked dubious, but she turned to Nanée. "Can we read to-gether, like we did on the train before? Will you teach me the words?"

"I would like that," Nanée said.

She stooped down to Dagobert's level. He licked her bare wrist, then her face. This is real, she thought once again. They were leaving. She would go with them to a place that didn't feel like home. She would leave Dagobert here in France, which wasn't her home and yet felt more like a home than anywhere she had ever lived.

She petted the mess of his fur and kissed him twice again. "You are the best dog ever," she whispered, burying her face in his, opening her mouth wide so that she would taste him, taste his fur and his little black nose, his eyes, that would never stop loving her.

PART V

DECEMBER 1940

Unfortunately, the way along the Cerbère cemetery wall had become too dangerous . . . Now it was being closely watched by the *gardes mobiles*. This was apparently on orders from the German Kundt Commission, which was the Gestapo agency in that part of still unoccupied France . . . That meant that we had to cross the Pyrenees farther west, where the mountain crests were higher and thus the climb more strenuous.

—Lisa Fittko, *Escape through the Pyrenees*

Sunday, December 8, 1940
MARSEILLE

Edouard followed Nanée, who was holding tightly to Luki's hand and carrying her elegant little case, up the wide white steps and into the Gare de Marseille-Saint-Charles. They bypassed the ticket counter and the ticket taker, and entered for the station café, which Nanée said had an exit directly onto the train platforms; they could avoid document checks here simply by stopping for a bad cup of fake coffee. He was in her hands now. He and Luki were in her hands.

He took a seat at one table, Luki and Nanée at another, maintaining the facade of traveling separately. They separately ordered coffees, and separately sat listening, waiting for their train to be called. Edouard opened Gussie's book, which he'd carried in his left hand per the boy's instruction; Nanée had given it to him once they were out of Gussie's sight, saying she couldn't possibly carry it herself and still carry her suitcase and hold Luki's hand, and anyway, he needed luck even more than she did.

Was that policeman watching him, or was he admiring Nanée? She wore a plain gray coat to avoid attention, but a woman like her would draw looks even wrapped in butcher paper.

Yes, Nanée too saw the man. The policeman was headed right for them, as if he knew exactly who Edouard was. Was he one of the policemen from that long day at the Évêché, before they were imprisoned on that boat just to ensure that nobody would embarrass Pétain?

He slid his Leica toward his hip, away from the approaching officer. This was not a time to invite scrutiny. His suitcase with his work was tucked under the table; he would just leave it there if this man wanted to take him in for questioning. Nanée would retrieve it, so his photographs wouldn't be lost.

The officer hesitated just as he reached Edouard, then passed him and approached Nanée.

Nanée took Luki's hand and squeezed it. Luki held Pemmy more tightly as she looked up at Nanée, some understanding passing between them.

Nanée met the policeman's gaze with startling ease and a quizzical expression—not unkind, and yet Edouard saw she meant to brush back any idea the man might have of paying her notice.

"I'm sorry," the policeman said. "I mistook you for someone else."

Nanée smiled, and returned to her coffee.

The policeman took in Luki. He said to Nanée, "But you are American, yes?"

"Pffft. Is it so obvious? I've lived in France for a decade."

"Ah, but the look in your eyes. You American girls have a different confidence than that of a Frenchwoman. More direct. A Frenchwoman, she is always trying to charm."

Nanée laughed easily. "So you're saying I lack charm."

"No, no, not at all." Trying to regain his composure, he asked Luki, "What's your kangaroo's name?"

Edouard tried not to show his alarm. Luki remained mercifully silent. *Moppelchen*, he thought. My little fatso, now so thin.

"Where are you going?" the man asked. Still, Luki said nothing. She only looked to Nanée as if she were the parent rather than him. Nanée smiled ever so slightly.

"Perhaps you would like a bit of chocolate?" the man offered Luki, fishing in his pocket and holding out a small bar of Chocolat Menier.

Still, Luki only met his gaze.

"I believe that's our train they're calling," Nanée said, although Edouard hadn't heard any train being called. "She's shy, but I'll take it for her, thank you." She rose and collected her travel case. "Have a good day, Officer," she said. Then to Luki, "This way, darling," nodding as if to show Luki the way out to the platform, so that Edouard would see and walk out ahead of them to the train, which was, indeed, just arriving.

He boarded first so Luki could see him, and took his first-class cabin, alone. He tucked his suitcase away so as not to invite a search, and listened to Luki's voice drifting from the adjoining cabin. Would his forged papers be good enough if he had to produce them here on the train? The real US visa that also served as a document in lieu of passport in his own name was sewn into the lining of his jacket, along with his real French residency permit and camp release. He had a French identity card, also real, in his coat pocket; it had belonged to an Henri Roux, whose photograph had been carefully replaced with one of Edouard by Varian's new forger. Edouard had memorized everything handwritten into the form, the details of the real Henri Roux, recently deceased: born December 9 of the year before Edouard was born, in the Dordogne, to parents Pierre and Marie Roux. Height: 70 inches, to Eduard's 71. All the other details stated on the card were close enough that they might describe Edouard, with the exception of the last line, *Signes particuliers: Néant*. Distinguishing marks: None. The real Henri Roux had no defining mole at his left eyebrow. If the line had been left blank, like the line for facial hair, the forger might have written in Edouard's mole, but *None* was written clearly there. Bill Frier might have been able to transform the single word into something suggesting Edouard's mole, but that was beyond the skill of this new forger. Still, this was, Varian had assured him, the safest kind of alias. Any check would show Henri Roux as a real French businessman, and wouldn't likely turn up his death only two days earlier.

A few moments later they departed, without any document check.

The train would take all day to get to Perpignan, where they would change to a local train to Banyuls-sur-Mer. The threat of discovery would remain every minute. There might be a document check anywhere along the way. Still, as Edouard watched Marseille disappear out the window, he wondered if luck might finally be on his side.

Sunday, December 8, 1940
MONTPELLIER

W here are you going, Monsieur Roux?" the uniformed train
attendant at the door to Edouard's compartment asked—
demanded, Edouard would have said, but he was trying not to seem
defensive. They were at the station in Montpellier, quite far to have
gotten without their documents being checked, and the man was Vichy, that was clear from his words, his attitude, even his bearing. Better
Vichy than German.

Edouard handed him the ticket to Banyuls, a real ticket but in Henri
Roux's name. As the man glanced at it, punched it, and handed it back,
Edouard tried to appear relaxed.

"And your documents?"

Edouard handed over the identity card with its fingerprints of a
dead man not yet buried.

"What business have you in Banyuls?" the attendant asked. Again,
demanded. "And what need have you of a camera?"

Edouard smiled and raised the Leica slightly, unsure whether the
man would be flattered to have his photograph taken, or suspicious.

"I'm exploring Banyuls as a location for business expansion," he
said. "Photographs are so often helpful for remembering."

The man frowned, unconvinced.

To Edouard's horror, he began ticking through the details listed on
Henri Roux's identity card, reading each under his breath and looking
up at Edouard to confirm.

"Height: 70."

Edouard sunk into his heels, hoping to shrink that extra inch.

"Face shape: Square."

"Complexion: Brown."

"Hair: Brown."

"No mustaches."

No mustaches, Edouard thought. But not no distinguishing marks. Was there any chance the inspector could be convinced Edouard's mole was not distinct enough or had been inadvertently left off?

"Forehead: Ordinary."

"Eyes: Green."

"Nose: Medium."

The man considered Edouard's nose, leaving Edouard remembering that shot he'd taken so many years ago now, of the Nazi measuring a man's nose with a caliper.

"Mouth: Medium."

The next line would be his chin, and then there would be nothing left but *Signes particuliers: Néant.*

Edouard moved his Leica aside, in the process deliberately clipping one of the cabin's lamps with his elbow so that it hit the man's arm before tumbling to the ground with a gratifying commotion.

"Terribly sorry," Edouard apologized, stooping to retrieve the Henri Roux documents that had fallen to the floor and righting the lamp as, already from next door, Nanée could be heard calling out in fear.

The attendant went running. Edouard set the forged identification on the table in his compartment and followed.

Nanée stood cowering in her cabin, holding Luki close, already exclaiming to the inspector about a spider. "Right there," she insisted. "He was right there."

Much fuss was made moving cushions and searching everywhere.

No spider surfaced. There was, Edouard knew, no spider.

"There is an empty compartment at the far end of the carriage that perhaps would better suit?" the attendant offered.

Nanée, holding Luki's hand, squeezed it and said to her, "Did it frighten you, sweetheart?"

Luki shook her head.

"It didn't? But it was as big as my hand. And hairy. Did you see it? I hate hairy spiders."

Again, Luki shook her head.

"You didn't see it?" Nanée said, seeming astonished. "It was like something from a Surrealist painting." She looked quite confused. "Was I . . . Was I sleeping?" Then to the inspector, apologetic now, "I'm terribly sorry. Perhaps I dozed off? It does seem, now that I think of it, that it was too impossibly terrible to be real. I . . . How mortifying."

The inspector said it was no trouble at all, he was there to serve her. But perhaps if she was truly all right, then he might check her travel papers?

Edouard backed away, only to have the inspector say, "Oh yes, I do still need to see your documents, sir."

Edouard was astonished to hear himself say, "But you did just examine them. My ticket to Banyuls? My identity card and French transit visa. If you need to see them again, though, they're in my cabin."

"I did, yes, of course," the inspector said, and Nanée apologized for being such a terrific pest as a neighbor, saying she would promise to have better dreams if she dropped off again. Edouard waved his hand as if to say it was no bother and backed out of Nanée's compartment.

Luki smiled a little as she watched him go. The whole time, Nanée had held tightly to her hand, and she hadn't said a word.

Sunday, December 8, 1940
PERPIGNAN

If there was anyone at the Perpignan train station who wasn't a refugee on the run, you could have fooled Nanée. A fierce wind bit at her fingertips even down here on the plain, making her wonder how cold it must be in the mountains already tipped with snow. Still, the nearby cafés were full, with hawkers openly shouting out black-market dollar exchange rates—outrageous ones—and even the people-smugglers openly offering for a price personal guides over the border, diplomatic limousines, and passages on ships to Gibraltar, from which one was expected to jump off and swim the last leg of the trip. Everyone here hoped to leave quickly; the few remaining ways to escape France might close any day, any minute. But of course one had to be careful. More than one of the hawkers would take you up the mountain, strip you of your possessions, and leave you stranded. More than one would collect payment for the promise of transit over the border, then turn you over to Vichy to collect a reward.

Nanée sat next to Luki on a bench in front of the brick-and-limestone station, waiting for the local train on to Banyuls-sur-Mer. Edouard sat at the far end of the bench as if he had nothing to do with them. Gussie's book was open on his lap, but he was watching the pétanque players in the square, men laughing together as the little balls they tossed rolled toward the smaller target ball, and chattering in Catalan—Spaniards who'd escaped Franco. Were they headed back now, the threat of Hitler in France worse than the fascist ruling Spain?

Edouard stood and raised his Leica. He photographed the bowlers. He walked a few paces, then turned back to frame a shot of the bench and the station behind it—an excuse, Nanée assumed, to photograph his daughter.

Nanée breathed deeply, sea air with an undertone of the lingering coal exhaust from the trains and the human smell of travelers too long on the road. She huddled closer to Luki, to keep her warm as they waited. So much of the journey through life is spent waiting.

"They have different words," Luki said.

Nanée looked again to the bowlers. "Yes, they're speaking Catalan."

"How come some people have one kind of words and other people have another?"

"I'm not sure," Nanée admitted.

"Some of their words are like the words we use now. Not like the words Maman used."

Edouard moved closer, looking at them through his camera. Too familiar, Nanée thought. But perhaps she knew too much. Perhaps others who noticed them, if anyone did, would think him photographing the station and, with it, strangers on a bench.

"In America," Luki said, "we'll use different words than here."

"In America, people use different words," Nanée agreed.

"Tante Nanée taught me some," Luki said to Edouard. Nanée took Luki's hand in hers and squeezed it, but Luki was already saying in English, "I love you, Father."

Edouard lowered his camera, his smile sweet and warm. Far too familiar.

A gull landed a few feet away, in search of crumbs the pétanque players might drop. Luki hopped from the bench and approached the creature as carefully as she had always approached Madame LaVache-à-Lait, leaving Pemmy behind on the bench.

Edouard resumed his seat beside his suitcase at the bench's end, as if the abandoned kangaroo somehow reminded him that he wasn't supposed to be traveling with them. He picked up Gussie's book. A distant whistle sounded, the train bound for Banyuls-sur-Mer arriving.

Nanée smoothed her conservative, calf-length blue skirt with its soft yellow pinstripes, thinking how empty her own traveling case was compared to his. No negatives. No photographs. Not much more than a pair of slacks, a clean blouse and sweater, and her flight jacket for the trek, her espadrilles, her silk flying scarf. Luki's things, yes, but they weren't hers.

"Can I ask you a question?" she asked into the train whistle and the cheer of the game ending, one team winning while the other lost. Edouard kept his gaze on the bowlers already tossing out the little target ball to begin a new game. She and he might be two strangers continuing a conversation started over the child traveling with her. *Nude, Bending*, she wanted to say. *Ghost Wife*. But she only watched silently as a ball lofted through the air and fell back to the ground, far away from the target.

The train whistle sounded again, much nearer now. They watched another ball loft through the air and hit the dirt, and keep rolling, farther and farther away from its mark, as the train pulled into the station. He stood, and she stood too, and she called to Luki as if she really were her own niece. Luki abandoned her bird and took Nanée's hand. Nanée gave her Pemmy, with Joey still safely pinned into her pouch, and again took up her traveling case. She headed through one of the limestone archways back into the station, where they boarded a single-class local train for which no one even asked to see their tickets. She and Luki took seats on one side of the aisle while Edouard sat alone on the other, beginning the last long hour to Banyuls-sur-Mer.

Sunday, December 8, 1940
BANYULS-SUR-MER

It was evening. Banyuls-sur-Mer had the deserted feel of a place no one wanted to stop. The tiny station was nothing more than a small stucco building with an outdoor platform, on the side of town farthest from the house on the sea where they were to find Hans and Lisa Fittko. Edouard, with his suitcase in his right hand and Gussie's book in his left, disembarked from the train ahead of Luki and Nanée so that Luki would be able to see him, always. It would be harder to remain apart here. If all looked well, Nanée and Luki would join him as if they were a family traveling together.

They were the only passengers to step off the train into a cold, biting wind.

"All right then," he said to Nanée as she joined him. He handed her Gussie's book, and he knelt and kissed Luki, then buttoned her coat and helped her pull on her gloves. "Here we are," he said. "Here we are."

"Can I carry the lucky book now?" Luki asked, and Nanée helped her manage both Pemmy and the book.

He pulled on his own gloves and buttoned his own coat, and they set off downhill through the little fishermen's village, the vineyard hills disappearing as they wound along narrow roads through colorful buildings, pink and yellow stucco with bright blue shutters so like Sanary-sur-Mer.

In just a few minutes they reached the sea, the palm trees blowing and trails of sand dancing across the empty stretch of beach, electric lights from the waterfront buildings reflecting off the water, which was white-capped and turbulent in the wind. The town's little square was as alive with pétanque players as the station in Perpignan had been—players laughing so enthusiastically that Edouard let go of Luki's hand to photograph them. He didn't register the sound of wheels on pavement until a car was just behind them. Such an unusual sound, an automobile.

A large black limousine pulled to a stop, then a second one, the headlights on him for a moment before they dimmed. He turned instinctively toward Luki as already men piled out, bracing themselves against the wind. Black boots. Black uniforms. One after another after another. Gestapo from the Kundt Commission, tasked with finding wanted Germans in free France and arresting them under the authority of the Article 19 surrender-on-demand provision of the armistice agreement. A dozen or more.

Luki was twenty paces ahead of him, with Nanée, both of them safer without him. There was nowhere to go, nothing to do but act as if he were alone and these men of no concern to him.

If they arrested him, Nanée would take Luki to the States.

The bowlers too grew silent, attending only to their little metal balls, pretending innocence and indifference, but their quiet was telling. Edouard's instinct was to photograph them, the watchers pretending not to watch, but he didn't dare draw attention to himself.

The Gestapo took a tour around the square, intimidating merely by their presence. One fell into step with Nanée, who held tightly to Luki's hand. It was all Edouard could do to keep his distance as the man asked her in German if she would like to join them for the evening. She appeared to understand his intent, if not his words.

She set her suitcase down and, with her free hand, smoothed her blue pin-striped lapel above the top button of her coat as if drawing power from the fabric. "I understand that when I wear a *short* skirt, the party will come to me," she responded in English, "but if you could see beneath my coat, you'd realize my skirt is rather long."

The man tried to puzzle out what she was saying. "Amerikanerin?" he asked.

"I'm afraid so," she said. "Not the master race."

He said, "Ich heiße Robert."

Nanée hesitated, then scooped up Luki and settled her on her hip. What the devil was she doing? She took Gussie's book in her left hand.

"Robert," she repeated, pronouncing the name in the French way rather than the German. "Of course you are." She seemed to gather herself somehow, then said, "Are you an honorable man, Robert?" Repeating his name again as if it were French.

She said to Luki, "Sweetheart, I wonder if this man has a chocolate for you?"

Luki fixed a shockingly steady gaze on the man.

"Schokolade?" the German repeated. "Nein ich . . ."

He called ahead to his Gestapo friends who were circling the bowlers on the square. "Hat jemand Schokolade für das Kind?"

Not a single bowler looked up. They continued studying the little silver balls intently, no one making a sound. But the German's friends laughed at him and told him to come along.

Nanée put Gussie's book in Luki's left hand, took up her suitcase, and walked on, still with Luki on her hip. A mother and daughter headed home from the train station, perhaps.

The Gestapo toured the square and returned to their cars. They pulled forward only a short way, to the nicest hotel in town.

Sunday, December 8, 1940

BANYULS-SUR-MER

Edouard knocked on the door of a well-kept three-story house directly on the beach just across from the public toilets, not far enough away from the hotel the Germans had stopped at for comfort. The place looked even more deserted than the train station, but Varian had warned them that this might be the case. Maurice came every couple weeks to let the Fittkos know who would be coming and when, but matters had been complicated by the change of mayors. In the event that Hans and Lisa weren't there, Varian had told Edouard and Nanée to take Luki down to the beach and watch for their return.

They left their suitcases and Gussie's book tucked up against a wall by the door, enough out of sight, and carried on along to the beach, away from town; they didn't want to be visible to a Nazi looking out his hotel window. They found a suitable bench and settled in to wait. Just a family on an evening stroll, stopping at a bench to watch the sea. In wintertime. In the dark. In a cold wind. But at least they now didn't have the suitcases to give them away.

"I love you, Father," Luki said, practicing that line of English Nanée had taught her.

"I think you can call me 'Papa' even in English," he said.

"I don't want to say it wrong," Luki said. "Reverend Mother told me I mustn't use any of Mutti's words. I mustn't even call Mutti Mutti. I must use the Lady Mary's language. I must call her Maman."

Edouard looked around. There seemed no better option than this for waiting. He pulled Luki into his lap and stroked her hair.

He said to Nanée, "The Virgin Mary speaks French?"

Nanée laughed a little, and Edouard laughed with her. It felt good to laugh off the tension.

"My understanding is the *Lady* Mary speaks to us in whatever language we prefer," Nanée said.

Luki said, "When the bad men use Mutti's words, does the Lady Mary understand what they're saying like I do?"

Edouard looked to the crashing sea, searching for a way to help her understand something he didn't understand himself. He took her face in his hands and met her direct gaze. "The German language isn't bad, Moppelchen. Understanding it and being able to speak it doesn't make us bad. It's the men who use the words badly who are bad. Bad men are bad in any language."

"So I can still use Mutti's words?"

"You can, only you have to understand that . . . that most of the people you'll speak to now won't understand those words. And . . . and some people think anyone who speaks German is bad. They're wrong, but it's what they think."

"So it's better if I use the other words, like Reverend Mother said."

"Yes, I think I have to agree with the Reverend Mother on this one."

"I like it when you call me Moppelchen, like Mutti used to."

She yawned and closed her eyes, and in a moment she was sleeping, lulled by the steady rhythm of the crashing waves.

He sat with Nanée, looking not to the sea but to the door of the three-story house. "You wanted to ask me something?"

When she didn't answer, he said, "Back in Perpignan? But then the train came."

"It was nothing," she said. "I was just . . . I was thinking about *Nude, Bending*. How I thought it was a man's body. A man doing a push-up."

He studied her in the darkness, the moonlight reflected on the sea. Did she remember the photograph from the exhibition, or had she seen all those prints of that single image in the bathroom at Sanary? Hung to dry facing the wall so Luki wouldn't see them, or perhaps so he wouldn't have to face them himself.

"*Nude, Bending* isn't its title," he said. "That was André's title for it."

"What is it meant to be called?" she asked.

"It isn't," he said. "That photograph was never meant to be shown." The words harsher than he'd meant them.

"I'm sorry," he said. "That wasn't . . ."

She waved him off. No offense taken. And yet he sensed in her stiffer posture that he had again offended her.

They sat quietly together for a long time, watching the house while trying to appear not to be doing so, Edouard now unable to shake that photo, that morning he took it.

He spotted, finally, a sorry-looking man walking in the dark toward the house. Was that Hans Fittko? He half hoped it wasn't. The man paused, apparently struggling simply to walk down the road, and not just because of the wind. How could he hike a mountain?

The man turned in at the house, now coughing so hard he had to pause even before keying his door. As he straightened again, he saw the suitcases.

He looked first in the other direction, then toward Edouard and Luki and Nanée.

Edouard rose, lifting Luki to his shoulder.

"*Salvation*," he said to Nanée. "I call it *Salvation*."

Sunday, December 8, 1940
BANYULS-SUR-MER

Edouard hurried to join the man at the door, Luki waking in his arms with the motion. Nanée followed with Pemmy and Joey.

"We're looking for Jean and Lise," she said, the code names they'd been told to ask for, and she handed him the scrap of torn paper Varian had given them.

The Fittkos were meant to produce the other half of the paper, but the man only handed the scrap back to Nanée. Perhaps they had the wrong man? He fit the description Varian had given them, but so many men would have, just as Edouard conveniently fit the description of the dead Henri Roux. Medium everything. Medium age, thirty years old, give or take. Hair enough for his age, but no more, in a typical brown. A sharp wedge of nose under a sturdy brow. If there was anything unusual about Hans Fittko, Varian had said, it was his ears. But then it was better to be nondescript in France these days.

This had to be the right house, though, three stories on the sea, right across from the public toilets. And the man didn't seem surprised by their presence or the paper scrap. He seemed simply exhausted.

"My wife is in hospital," he said.

"I'm so sorry," Nanée said. "What's happened?"

"She's jaundiced," the man said. "Her fever kept climbing,"

Edouard looked uneasily to Nanée. They ought not to say a thing until they saw the matching scrap of paper. But Nanée was saying nothing about them. She was simply showing the kind of sympathy anyone would.

"The doctor wouldn't come because the boy told him we were German," the man continued. "Thank the lord for Hermant."

"I'm so sorry," Nanée said again, relaxing a little at the sound of

Hermant's name, as Edouard himself was. Hermant—Beamish—was one of them, long trusted by Varian with couriering refugees.

"I'm sorry," Hans said. "Forgive me. Do come inside."

Still, Nanée hesitated.

"Again, my apologies," Hans said. "I forget myself. Wait a moment."

He disappeared into the house, coughing again. A quick moment later he emerged with the companion paper scrap, and he again invited them in.

"But I cannot take you over the border," he said. "Even under the best of circumstances, I couldn't make the trek alone with you."

Nanée handed Pemmy to Luki. Edouard grabbed his suitcase, glad to get Luki out of the wind and cold. Nanée reluctantly allowed the exhausted Hans Fittko to carry her case. She took Gussie's book, carrying it in her left hand.

THE HOUSE INSIDE was room after room of fine wood paneling and beautiful fireplaces and views right on the sea, with not a single bathroom. "I'm afraid we don't even have running water," Hans Fittko apologized, "but there are the public toilets across the street."

The place didn't belong to the Fittkos, but to a doctor no one had seen or heard from since he went off to war. The mayor himself—Azéma, the old mayor—had suggested the Fittkos take it over. It had plenty of rooms in which to house refugees until they could get across the border. He'd given the Fittkos handwritten statements on his letterhead, certifying that they were residents of Banyuls, too, and entered them in the town register so that they didn't have to use the fake identity cards Varian had gotten them in Marseille. He'd even issued them ration cards and given them extra food stamps for the refugees. Those days had ended, though, with the new, Vichy-installed mayor.

"Please," Hans Fittko said, "just choose whatever rooms you like. I'll get you something to eat, although I'm afraid our larder is less full now than it once was."

Edouard suggested Luki and Pemmy might explore the house and choose a room, but Luki hesitated.

"You can choose a room where you can hear the sea," he said.

"Like from the dreaming log."

"But don't go outside without me. Choose a room for you and one right next door to it for me. That way, you won't have to hear me snore."

Luki grinned, that tooth she'd lost while he was on the boat a re-minder of so much he'd missed, and she said she didn't mind his snor-ing, but it woke Pemmy and Joey. "We can leave our doors open? And you'll be right here all the time, so I can come find you?"

"I will be right here," he assured her.

"Can I choose a room for Tante Nanée too?"

"Perhaps I could have the room on the other side of yours, just like at Villa Air-Bel?" Nanée replied.

After Luki set off to explore, Edouard and Nanée shed their coats and hats. Hans poured them glasses of wine, along with one for him-self, and offered them a bit of stale bread.

"There are linens and blankets in the cupboards in most of the rooms," he said. "I would help you, but . . ."

"You must be exhausted," Nanée said.

"You cannot stay here long," Hans said. "It isn't good for the child. My Lisa, she washed her hair in the cold, and now . . . She needed to be taken to the hospital in Perpignan at once, but if I took her myself, without travel papers, they would have arrested me. Hermant arrived just then, as if he knew we needed him. He took her to the hospital, and returned to tell me she was there, but that it would be three days before the doctor came."

Edouard listened to Nanée assure him that it wasn't his fault or his wife's, that jaundice came from poor nourishment, and she was sure they were too generous in giving their food to refugees.

"We won't stay one moment longer than necessary, for Luki's sake and for yours," she said.

"You are American?" Hans said. "Perhaps you could visit my Lisa at the hospital in Perpignan, and let me know how she does?"

"We changed trains there," Nanée said. "I wish I had known."

But of course she couldn't have stopped there, not when she was traveling with Luki and him.

He hated even to raise it with the man's wife in the hospital, but it had to be asked. "I . . . I understand you can't possibly take anyone over the border right now, but perhaps you have a map of the route?"

Hans excused himself, and returned in a moment with a pencil and a thin square of paper. "My Lisa," he said, "she is the one who knows the way. We cannot keep a map here. It isn't safe."

He set about drawing a map as best he could.

"Here, just past the creek," he said, "you will go through the Puig del Mas. It is on the outskirts now, but it is where the town of Banyuls began. You must be here when the vineyard workers go out for the day, as often there are border guards here. You will try to blend in." He indicated Edouard's hat. "It is too nice for a worker, you see? You must seem to belong. If you are very lucky, perhaps the morning will be too cold for anyone who does not have to be there."

He continued drawing the path, going through the markers and the risks.

"Here the route passes an empty stable. After this, there will be seven pine trees on the plateau that will indicate the right direction. They will be always to your right.

"Here the path follows a low stone wall.

"A boulder marks the path here.

"Here, you will cross a clearing, and there will follow a steep vine-yard where there will be no path at all, where you must clamber up through the vines."

Edouard took a shot with his Leica: Hans drawing a map of escape. This is what they did. Clandestine. Forbidden. This was a man who risked his life for others. A Jewish German, like Edouard himself.

"Here, you must be very careful. The path is precarious. It will not be easy. There is a narrow ridge at the top, where you will need to rest if you can, but look carefully first."

He marked on the little map a point where it was very easy to lose the way if you weren't careful, as the path would be barely visible and at the same time the seven pines would be hidden behind a hill.

"Here the path is very close to the road," he said. "You must be absolutely silent and listen for traffic. You cannot easily be seen from the road just above, but you can be heard. You will not wish to invite a closer look over the edge."

From there, the path would rise more gradually, but it wouldn't feel much easier that long into the hike.

"There is a gray stone that marks the border," Hans said. "Beyond that, Lisa and I do not go, but the path continues on directly to the town of Portbou. You will come to a pond, and if your canteens are empty you will want to drink, but you must not do so. The water will make you sick. Typhoid. You understand this?"

Edouard nodded. Typhoid caused high fevers, diarrhea, and vomiting. It could kill a person, even one in the best of health.

"You must carry on along the cliff wall until you see the valley and the town. The road there will take you past the Spanish border station, where you must register. Show them your travel documents, your Spanish and Portuguese transit visas. It is possible still that, as you will have no French border stamp, they will turn you back. It is possible even that they will take you into custody, to be handed over to the Gestapo. It varies from one day to the next. If all else fails, you will offer them money."

"A bribe?" Edouard clarified.

Hans shrugged as if to say there was no point in calling out bad behavior as such if it might work in your favor.

"In any event," he said, "you must have a Spanish entry stamp or you will not be allowed on the Spanish trains or into Portugal. From the border post, you will go directly to the train station and take the first train to Lisbon. If the last train to Lisbon is gone, take some other. You must try to get a train out the same night, before the rules change or anyone simply changes his mind."

"Yes, of course," Edouard said. "Now, you said it's best to leave in the morning, to blend in with the workers. But if we left midday—"

"Both of you?" Hans said, confused. He looked to Nanée. "But you are working with Varian. And what about the child?" Then to Edouard, "No, only you are going over the mountain?"

"I can't leave France without Luki," Edouard said.

"But this, it is not—a child? No. The path up, at best it is three or four hours. Sometimes it is ten or more. The mountain, it can destroy a grown man. Even for you alone, it would be better if you had a forward person and a rear, in case the Kundt Commission are out. So that someone can distract them while you hurry forward or back. You cannot be caught."

"If it comes to that, I can delay them," Nanée said. "I have an American passport. Luki and I both do."

"But the girl is Edouard's daughter?" Hans said, confused.

"Yes," Nanée said.

"Yet she has an American passport?"

"Yes."

"Well, then, it is easy enough. We can send the girl on the train, and send you over the border, Edouard. I can perhaps arrange it with the friend who helps us get luggage out. And Nanée can take the train back to Perpignan and send me word about Lisa."

"Luki is not a piece of luggage," Edouard said.

Hans looked affronted, of course he did.

"I'm sorry," Edouard apologized. "It's been a long day for us, too. But I can't send Luki any way other than with me."

"You cannot go by train," Hans said.

"Luki can't go alone."

"No," Hans said. "She is so young. This is why I am proposing to arrange it with—"

"We don't have a French exit visa for her," Nanée said.

Hans frowned. "But she does have an American passport?"

If anything happens to me, promise me you will keep Luki with you and take care of her, always. The last thing Elza had asked of him, a promise he'd made—too late for her to know of it as she was dying, but no less a promise. Perhaps more. A promise he'd broken once already. He wouldn't break it again.

"Luki unfortunately shares my name," Edouard said. "Varian feared applying for an exit visa for her would endanger me. And there wasn't time."

Hans nodded. Yes, he understood the difficulty.

"Varian suggested that, with Luki, perhaps we could pass as picnickers?"

"In the bright light of day? No, this you cannot do. The greatest risk is here, leaving Banyuls."

The Gestapo sleeping in the hotel just down the way, the Kundt Commission here to patrol the border.

"The only way is to leave before dawn, to blend in with the vineyard workers," Hans insisted. "In the dark, so the sentries can't tell that one isn't a worker. But children don't work in the vineyards. Not children this young, no. Do you really mean to take the child over the mountain?"

"I can carry Luki," Edouard said.

"I do not mean to challenge you," Hans said, "but sometimes the fog is so thick that you cannot see your way. You cannot see that the path is slippery, or even that there is a path. And again, it can take ten hours or more. We might send you first, and let your daughter follow on the train. If we arranged an exit visa for her after you left—"

"Walter Benjamin made it over this route carrying a suitcase full of manuscripts that likely weighed more than Luki. I'm younger and stronger than he was."

Hans looked dubious, but conceded, "Then it would be best to go as soon as possible."

He devolved into another fit of coughing.

"Yes," Nanée agreed. "We'll go as soon as we're able."

Hans didn't like the idea of them going later than early morning, or going without him, and he didn't like to have them stay another night in Banyuls, allowing more time for Edouard to be caught or the Spanish to decide to close their border. Everything was a risk, but he insisted, finally, that the biggest risks were daylight and time.

"I can get you started," he said. "But it must be before dawn."

"You're sick," Nanée said. "You're exhausted."

He said to Edouard, "If you are going to take the child, you must let me get you to the plateau. I know better what to watch for, how to keep you safe. Edouard, you must keep her close to your side, especially at the beginning. The guards tend to be on the town side. Keep her close to you, on the mountainside, so that perhaps, in your shadow, she won't be seen. We will go very early."

When Hans finished drawing the tiny map, he handed it to Nanée. "If you are stopped, it is rice paper, and small enough to eat. You might manage to do so, as the attention will likely be on Edouard. And as you say, you have the American passport."

They would leave well before dawn. Hans would go with them as long as he was able. It was much quicker and easier coming down than going up, so he could turn back when he began to tire. He didn't know if he could go as far as the border, but with the map they could find their way. Beyond the border, he could not go. He couldn't risk being trapped outside France with his wife in the hospital here.

"Now we all must sleep," he said, "or you will never make the trek."

Sunday, December 8, 1940

BANYULS-SUR-MER

Nanée lay awake, listening for the quiet knock on her door but hearing only the pop of the burning wood and the steady crash of the sea, the wind, and occasionally the sound of Hans coughing somewhere else in the house. The Robert Piguet suit sat neatly folded atop her traveling case with Gussie's book and a note asking Hans to have Beamish take them back to T.

The light knocking came finally, and her door opened slightly.

"Nanée?" Edouard whispered.

"Yes," she said, not a question but an answer, an invitation.

The door creaked slightly on its hinges, the shadow of Edouard appearing in the doorway, illuminated by the firelight, followed by the quiet sound of the door touching the jamb again.

She watched the shadow of him standing there. His arms lifting to his face. The whisper of a shutter.

"I don't know that I'll get anything in this light," he whispered, "or what I'll do with it if I do."

He set the camera on the bureau, beside Gussie's book and the neatly folded suit. The shadow of him moved between her bed and the fire. Then he was lifting the covers and climbing in with her.

"Luki?" she whispered.

"Fast asleep."

He touched her hair, her face, her chin, her neck. The length of him beside her was first cold, then warmer. Her body moved to him, responded, wanted.

He lifted the hair at her neck, his breath on her skin.

She touched the mole at the end of his eyebrow, which was sturdy and straight. She closed her eyes and listened to the howl of the wind and the crash of the sea, half expecting a torrent of rain to fall, the way it would when this kind of weather blew in over the point and Marigold Lodge.

"I have a house in Michigan," she said. "On a lake. It's my family's summer house, but it belongs to me now. My father left it to me."

He looked at her, but didn't say anything.

She traced one of the lines on his forehead, another at the edge of his mouth. "There's plenty of room. It would be an easy place to start over. Luki would like it there."

He put a finger to her mouth and traced her lips. To caress her, or to silence?

She put her own lips to his, and she kissed him.

He kissed her back, as desperately as she kissed him. He didn't say anything. He kissed her and she kissed him, and he pulled his shirt off over his head.

She felt his hand under her nightclothes. His skin on her skin.

They made love silently, as intensely as the wind now rattling the windowpanes.

Monday, December 9, 1940

BANYULS-SUR-MER

It was still dark when they left for the long walk with Tante Nanée and the sad man with the wide hair and the pokey-outy ears.

"Stay right up against me," Papa said. They were passing the place where the men who spoke the bad words had disappeared the night before. Papa picked her up and walked very fast until they reached the place where the long black cars stopped and the man didn't have any chocolate to give her. Luki was a little afraid.

They kept walking, out of sight of the building with the bad men, before Papa set her down again.

"Stay right next to me. You'll be warmer right up against me."

"Pemmy is cold," Luki said.

"Do you want me to button your top button, Luki?"

"No, Pemmy. She doesn't have a coat."

Tante Nanée took the white angel wings from her neck and tied them around Pemmy's neck. She had to wrap it and wrap it, because Pemmy was small, especially at her head.

"It is amazing how much warmer a scarf keeps you," Tante Nanée said. "That's why I always wear this when I fly."

"You wear this to fly?" Luki said.

"I do. I'm not sure I could fly without it!"

Luki touched the white, which was soft and flowy. "Can Pemmy fly?"

"Can Pemmy fly?" Tante Nanée laughed her colored-church-window laugh. "Well, I suppose she would need flight lessons. That would be something, wouldn't it? A flying kangaroo?"

Luki nodded. She wanted to ask how hard the lessons were, and if she could fly too.

"If you fly as high as the angels," she said, "can you come back again?"

Tante Nanée knelt and looked into her face the way Papa did. "The thing about flying," she said, "is that it's always hard to return to earth, no matter where you've flown."

Monday, December 9, 1940
BANYULS-SUR-MER

E douard carried nothing but the musette bag Hans Fittko had filled with bread and jam substitute, in which he'd also stowed the Leica, several rolls of film, two canteens of water, and the stale baguette in which his negatives were hidden. Nanée's held sandwiches and more water. The four of them—Edouard and Luki and Nanée, led by Hans Fittko—crossed a little creek at the edge of Banyuls-sur-Mer, then made their way through a group of houses among towering trees— the area Hans had told them was often thick with border guards, but they saw none. Hans was coughing less this morning and, he said, perhaps able to take them all the way to the border.

They folded in with workers speaking Catalan and carrying spades and baskets, headed uphill to the vineyards. Hans said a few words to two of the workers, who handed over their baskets, one to Hans and one to Edouard.

Hans gave the men several cigarettes, which they tucked into shirt pockets as they carried on, walking basketless now on the outer edge of the vineyard workers.

They were walking along a low, overgrown stone wall when Hans nudged Edouard deeper into the trail of workers.

"On the left," Hans said. "Don't turn your heads."

Two caped shadows stood in the gap between trees and bushes. Not, Edouard didn't think, the Gestapo from last night. French border guards. They were danger enough. He kept Luki close at his side so his own body and the other workers might block her from view.

The workers who'd given Hans their baskets stepped up to the shadows. A match flared. One cigarette glowed red, then a second and a third before the match was extinguished. A distraction, Edouard saw. Yes, a cigarette. A polite request for a light.

The day, when it dawned, was beautifully clear, thanks to the wind still howling this morning, which Hans said was more of a blessing than it seemed. It wasn't as cold as a tramontane often was, and as long as it blew, they wouldn't have to worry about finding the path in the fog.

"This is the third day of the winds," Hans said. "According to the ancients, if the tramontane blows after three days, it will blow for another three, and so on up to twelve days." Even the howling could be a blessing if one could stand it, Hans said, as it would hide any noise they made.

The path turned left. Here was the boulder Hans had described as he drew the map. So far, Luki hadn't slowed them much, leaning into the wind in her little espadrilles, asking Edouard at the boulder if they could stop for a rest.

"If Pemmy and Joey had ropey shoes, they could walk," she said.

Hans subtly shook his head.

Edouard said to Luki, "We'll stop to rest, but not yet."

They reached the first clearing in about two hours. It was a third of the way—but the easiest third, Edouard concluded as he looked behind them, the land sloping gently down to the rooftops and the shore and the sea. Ahead were mountain peaks.

They'd left the workers behind now.

"Pemmy is tired of walking," Luki said. "And she's very tired of the wind noise."

Edouard lifted her onto his shoulders.

"This will draw attention," Hans Fittko said.

Edouard looked down to the town below them. Crawling slowly along the waterfront, like an all-seeing Surrealist beetle searching for prey, was one of the Gestapo's dark limousines. The distance that had taken them hours on foot could be traveled in minutes on the road by those who could afford the attention an automobile brought. He swung Luki down.

Hans, reaching to help her, caught his foot on a tree root and went sprawling, holding tightly to Luki and rolling to the side to protect her from the fall. Edouard, trying to catch them both, fell with them. Luki was so surprised she didn't even cry.

Edouard hurried to scoop her up, saying, "You're fine, you're fine."

He looked around, hoping the ruckus hadn't drawn any attention.

There was a thin line of red on Hans's forehead.

Edouard set Luki on her feet, then turned back to Hans. "Are you okay?" he asked. "Let me give you a hand up."

He brushed the gravel from the palms of his gloves.

Hans took a small first-aid kit from his musette bag. He cut off a length of bandage and wrapped his own already-swelling ankle, then returned the remaining bandage to the kit.

"When you get to the plateau," he said, "you will see the seven pine trees."

"We can't leave you alone," Edouard protested. "You'll need help getting down the hill."

"Keep those pines always on your right," Hans insisted, handing him the medical kit, "so you won't go too far north and lose the path."

Nanée gathered Pemmy from several feet ahead, still with Joey sturdily pinned to her, the musical baby kangaroo sounding a single note when she picked them up.

Edouard met her gaze, knowing what she was going to say before she said it and wanting to stop her, as unforgivably selfish as that was.

"I could take Hans down," she said. "I have an American passport. I can leave anytime." She handed the kangaroos to Luki.

"You need to bring up the rear until you reach the border," Hans said. "If anyone follows, you can delay them. As you say, you have an American passport."

Luki said, "Pemmy and Joey could go with you, Monsieur Fittko."

Hans smiled. "I've managed far worse than a short downhill hike on an ankle that is little more than twisted, I'm sure. Anyway, without espadrilles I'm not sure your kangaroos will be much help for me, and they'd be terribly sad to be parted from you, as will I."

To Nanée and Edouard, he said, "Walter Benjamin told Lisa as she took him this route that it was best to pause before you become exhausted, to preserve strength."

There is nothing which can overcome my patience, Benjamin had written in "Agesilaus Santander," an essay about a Paul Klee oil transfer and watercolor of an angel he'd had to leave behind, which represented to him everything from which he'd had to part. But Benjamin had chosen a lethal dose of morphine rather than be returned to the Gestapo. A thing was so often nothing until it happened to you.

The sense of belonging Edouard would leave behind. A hat in which the initials that had always been his were scratched out. The hat itself now left behind too.

"Remember," Hans said, "the path will parallel the official road over the ridge. It's an old smuggler's path that runs below the road, mostly concealed from it by an overhang, so again, the border patrol can't readily see you. But if they hear you, they need do little more than peer over the edge to see you as well."

He turned to Nanée. "Near the top of the mountain, there's the vineyard that will lead you right to the point at which you can climb over the crest."

"The vineyard," Nanée repeated, and Hans assured her again that yes, even at the top of the mountains here, grapes were grown.

"Be careful. Keep on alert. There are wild bulls in these mountains, and smugglers. You don't have provisions enough for a smuggler to bother with you, but they won't know that when they see you."

"The border guards and the Kundt Commission—are they likely to venture this high?" Edouard asked, thinking of that limousine.

"I'm afraid so," Hans said.

Edouard found a fallen branch and broke it off to a slightly shorter length for Hans to use as a walking stick. "Thank you for all you're doing for all of us, Hans," he said. "For everybody like me. I hope . . . I'm sure Lisa will be fine, but . . ."

"Yes," Hans said. "She has to be."

As Hans set off, limping back down the hill, Edouard raised his Leica and took the shot: *Portrait of the Man I Ought to Be.*

Monday, December 9, 1940

THE PYRENEES

The climb grew steeper after they left Hans and the clearing. It was hard to have any sense of where they were due to the hills on either side, golden in the morning light, and the cliff ahead. What had been little more than a steep, rocky goat path—goat skulls being, Edouard gathered, what the sun-bleached ones that littered the path were—narrowed to boulders with small trails of gravel in between. More and more often they had to stop and take the measure of what was path and what wasn't. So much of it was crumbling shale and slippery gravel. A misstep, and you might slide off the side and into the deep ravines. He held so tightly to Luki's gloved hand that more than once she complained, "Papa, you're hurting me."

What had he been thinking, to insist Luki come this way with him?

They could see now the vineyards in the distance—wintering and windblown grapevines on ground sloping so steeply that it seemed to Edouard almost vertical. The sun was full on now, and surprisingly warming. The wind seemed to be letting up, but that might be the deception of hope.

Together he and Nanée eyed the way forward, searching for the path to get uphill from where they stood.

"Up there," Nanée said.

He could see it now: the path on the mountainside above. But there was no way to get up to it.

He eyed the rocky cliff, then hoisted Luki onto his back. Nanée took Pemmy so Luki could hold more tightly to Edouard.

A spray of gravel rained down on him before he'd even set a hand in place to begin the climb, loose dirt blowing into his eyes. Behind him, Nanée grew suddenly quiet. Luki, too, was now completely still, clinging tightly to him.

He looked up. Heard a rustling above even over the wind, which was definitely less fierce now. He hoped that wasn't just the shelter of the hill.

A few more bits of gravel spilled downhill.

Was that a man in the shadow of that overhang above, near the top? Near the vineyard they needed to reach? He quietly turned so that Luki would be hidden behind him, protected, albeit with her legs still wrapped at his waist.

Yes, Nanée too had seen the man. She'd seen him first and was already moving, motioning him silently to follow.

More rocks spilled from above, less cautiously now. The man was headed for them. His cap appeared over the top of a boulder, then disappeared again.

They started as the man spilled down onto the path in another spray of rock. A lean, sun-worn man with packages tied all over his body.

"What are you doing here?" the stranger demanded, taking them in. They were not professional smugglers. They were no threat to him, just an opportunity.

The smuggler glanced to Nanée, standing with the kangaroos in one hand and her other in the pocket of her flight jacket. She looked like she might spring at the man.

"I can show you the way over the mountain," he offered—for a price, he meant. "No one knows these paths like I do."

He saw Luki then. "You're taking a child over the mountain?" He backed away.

Edouard adjusted Luki and told her to hold on to him tightly, then returned his attention to the climb. The smuggler, reaching for one of his packages, moved toward them. Eduard turned to fend him off.

The smuggler stopped where he was. Put his hands up to show he meant no harm. "For the girl," he said.

He untied one of his packages and unwrapped a length of dried sausage, the smell of it mixing with the faint scent of thyme and rosemary and lavender that must be strong here in summertime. The man didn't hand him the sausage, though. He offered him the length of dirty cloth that had held it to his body.

"For the girl," he insisted. "She'll be safer."

Edouard hesitated.

"Like that," the man insisted, pointing to the kangaroos Nanée still held, Joey fallen out of Pemmy's pouch but still pinned to her.

The cloth flapped once in what was now more breeze than wind.

Edouard took it from the man and used it to tie Luki to him at his waist.

"A child. *Bon chance.*" The smuggler shook his head as he set off down the path they'd come up, the sausage still in his hand.

Edouard reached for one of the rocks above him, set a foot on a low one, and began to climb.

Monday, December 9, 1940
THE PYRENEES

They were close to the road now, on a narrow path between a cliff edge and a wall of rock, not easily visible from the road thanks to the overhang but close enough that they might be heard. They were moving as silently as possible, listening intently. Edouard held tightly to Luki's hand, worried with each step that he might slip, or Luki might. He would have kept her tied to him the whole rest of the way if she allowed it, but she was her mother's child, she had her own mind.

They followed Nanée, he and Luki. He and Luki and Pemmy and Joey, Luki might have said. How thankful he was for Madam Menier sending the kangaroos. How thankful he was for her helping Nanée get Luki out of occupied France. For the foreman and the housekeeper and the chauffeur who helped her. For the nuns who kept her safe before that. For Berthe. For everyone who had protected Luki when he couldn't.

Nanée stopped. She stood absolutely still. He heard what she heard then. Not voices but something lower, something that quickly took shape as the sound of footsteps. Not just one person but several, it sounded like.

Nanée backed away from the cliff edge, to the wall of rock, for the protection of the overhang.

He did the same, pulling Luki with him, wishing the awful howl of the wind would return so they wouldn't be heard.

A small, muted note sounded.

Edouard listened in fear, horrified to see that Pemmy and the little musical joey had fallen onto the ground on the other side of the path. An inch or two farther, and they would tumble into the chasm.

"Was war das?" a voice above them demanded. *What was that?*

Monday, December 9, 1940
THE PYRENEES

Nanée squatted carefully, silently. The footsteps overhead had stopped, the voices so close that she could reach up and pass them a canteen for a sip of water. She didn't think they could see Edouard and Luki and her, but if they looked over the edge, they would see the kangaroos.

Voices responded to that first familiar voice, Robert's voice—the German from the Kundt Commission who'd tried to charm her the night before in Banyuls-sur-Mer. The soldiers spoke among themselves, German she couldn't begin to understand.

Could she get the stuffed kangaroos before the Germans caught sight of them? Her flying scarf around Pemmy's neck was so close she could almost reach it from where she was.

"Musik," Robert said. "Ich höre Musik."

Nanée grabbed the kangaroos. She tried to move carefully, but still the music sounded again, a single note from Tchaikovsky's *Nutcracker*, "Waltz of the Flowers." *Nasty creatures always get their comeuppance in the end*, Daddy had assured her.

But that had been pretend. This wasn't pretend.

Another quiet metallic plink sounded.

"Hört ihr das?" Robert insisted. "Musik."

The soldiers went silent just above them.

Nanée held her breath and listened, thinking *Robe Heir*. Thinking *little Bobby* and imagining this Robert too as she'd imagined the commandant, as a pathetic little boy playing dress-up in a ratty old robe that had been his grandmother's. *Are you an honorable man?*

Several of the men on the road above were talking at once now, all looking for the source of Robert's music.

She racked her mind for a plan. She had an American passport.

Luki had an American passport. But Edouard was a stateless refugee, with one set of documents that were forged and another under his own name, which was on the Gestapo list for deportation to Germany.

How many of these men had there been the night before? In their black boots and their black uniforms, their black limousines, their black hearts. Were they all there now?

She fingered the kangaroo's mohair ear the way she so often fondled Dagobert's. Would she ever see him again?

What a brave girl you are. You don't even cry.

"Die Musik ist in deinem Kopf," one of the other Gestapo above them said. Not Robe Heir.

There was much hilarity in response.

"Die Musik muss aus der Tiefe der Höhle kommen. Mach weiter, Robert. Springen!"

They laughed and laughed at that.

Voices again, and the sound of scrambling above. One of them climbing down?

Nanée looked about, but there was nowhere for Edouard and Luki and her to hide, nowhere to escape. Just the narrow, rocky path in either direction, and the long drop off the cliff ledge.

More scrambling. A tussle?

More words. More laughter.

Boys taunting each other, like they had when Robe Heir had stopped to flirt with her last night. Like Dickey and his friends had taunted her that time she went dove hunting with Daddy and them.

The Gestapo moved on, still laughing.

They appeared up ahead on the curving road, three men in black boots and black uniforms. Only three.

If she could see them, they could see her. Their backs were to her, walking away, but if they turned now and looked, they would see Edouard and Luki and her.

She signaled for Edouard to stay up against the cliff wall behind her. She was already removing her gloves and reaching into the pocket of her flight jacket for her pearl-handled Webley.

There were only three Germans.

She tucked the kangaroos between her thighs to free her hands, and silently readied the gun.

The Nazis kept moving forward, kept laughing.

She pointed the gun, both hands on the grip and her finger on the trigger, her arms straight out in front of her, the way her father taught her.

Focusing on the target.

Wishing she could do something else with the kangaroos so she could widen her stance.

Wishing she had a longer-barreled gun for the better shot.

Willing the men not to turn back, not to see them.

Perfectly still and focused.

She had a clean line of sight.

They weren't far away now, but with each passing moment they were expanding the distance.

Luki, behind her, remained quieter than Nanée had ever imagined a child could be as Nanée clutched the gun while keeping the kangaroos wedged between her thighs, praying to the Lady Mary that no further music would sound. Praying for the wind to howl again.

The men kept walking, kept laughing.

The growing distance was a good thing. Perhaps they would just keep walking. But with each step, the difficulty of the shot was growing too.

The one named Robert glanced back.

Did he see them?

No, he was turning again to his comrades. He was still walking.

The pearl handle of the gun was cold against her fingers. Like the cold grip of her shotgun, the pieces of shot warm as she dug them from the dove's fragile breast.

Robert's head turned to look again, registering what he couldn't quite believe he'd seen. Astonishment in his face.

She willed him to pretend not to see her. To let them go, as the Germans at Madame Dupin's tomb had done.

It seemed forever, him standing there, deciding.

The sun sharp on her face. Her bare fingers on the gun.

Just pretend you don't see us, Robe Heir.

His mouth opening. Yelling to the others.

She pulled the trigger.

Good god, she'd missed.

She widened her stance for better aim even as the Nazi was reaching for his own gun.

And now his comrades were turning to her, to the sound of the shot.

They were drawing their guns.

She pulled the trigger a second time.

He crumpled. Had she killed him?

Another gun pointed straight at her. Firing.

She shot again, now at the other Nazi shooting at her.

A burning sting. Searing pain.

She shot again, a fourth shot.

And again, pushing away the pain.

And again.

Aiming now at the man landing on the path up ahead of her. Good god, where had he come from?

The firing pin clicked dully, striking the empty cartridge.

Monday, December 9, 1940
THE PYRENEES

Luki's face was buried in Papa's chest. He stooped to the ground, holding her against him so she couldn't see.

The scary bangs had stopped. She felt Papa's chest pounding, and also shaking the way it did when he was sad. She wanted to look at him, to see him still there even though she could feel his heart, but he held her head so firmly that she couldn't see, she could only hear someone calling faintly for his mutti, in the old words. Then nothing but the quiet *shhhhh* of the wind.

"Luki," Papa whispered, "I want you to keep your eyes closed. Promise me you'll keep your eyes closed?"

She nodded, her head still pressed to his chest.

She felt the scratchy mohair of Pemmy being placed into her hands, the smooth slidiness of the angel wings at her neck. One of the bad men had heard Joey singing. Joey hadn't meant to sing. It was Luki's fault. Luki had dropped him. She didn't mean to drop him, and he didn't mean to sing.

Papa lifted her, still holding her like that, so she couldn't see, and he carried her as he walked.

Monday, December 9, 1940
THE PYRENEES

They moved fast, carrying on along the cliff wall, putting distance behind them before anyone came along the road and found the Gestapo. They stopped only when they were out of sight of the men. Nanée had been walking with the edge of her flight jacket sleeve pressed to the side of her head, and she hesitated to let go. So much blood, as if it were bleeding from inside her head and pooling in her ear.

She removed her hand to let Edouard see. If it was a serious wound, she wouldn't survive anyway.

It was her ear—not exactly a superficial wound, but more blood than guts.

"A single inch from deadly," Edouard said.

Deadly.

"Do you think . . . all three of them?" Nanée asked.

"Even the one calling for his mother went quiet before we were out of earshot," Edouard said, relief rather than regret in his voice.

"Earshot," she said. "Ear. Shot." Making a joke of it as Edouard dressed her wound with provisions from Hans's medical kit. They laughed and laughed, not because it was funny but because Nanée had just shot three Gestapo dead. Shock expressing itself.

She thought Edouard was right, the men were dead, but it had all happened so fast, in just seconds. Robert, on the path, was certainly dead—shot right in the center of his chest. His dead body sliding over the cliff's edge onto their path even as she was shooting the others. She and Edouard laughed and laughed at that too, after they had her ear bandaged: Nanée firing an empty pistol at a man who was already dead.

They stopped for a slightly longer rest, finally, at a narrow ridge near the top of the climb. Nanée was shivering despite the exertion of moving so fast. This was shock too, she supposed. She needed something to eat. She might have pulled a few sweet grapes from the vines here, but they were bare, saving her from the ingratitude of stealing fruit from a path left open to freedom. She took a canteen from her musette bag and gave it to Luki.

"You need to drink too," Edouard said. "You're awfully pale."

Nanée pretended to sip without actually drinking anything. They were running low.

Edouard gave Luki another sip.

The wind was so much gentler now, but the cold bit at her face. Or maybe that was the pain of her wound.

There was snow up here. Not so much that you sank into it, but enough to make the path slippery.

They carried on, turning with the path, which rose more slowly now. They trudged on as quickly as they could manage for perhaps another hour.

When they crested the summit, they stopped altogether. The steep cliffs fell away to a little town with red tile roofs far in the distance, and just beyond, the white-capped blue of the Mediterranean, all the way until it met the blue of the sky. Was that the Spanish coast?

In the other direction, the path they'd come up stretched down to Banyuls and what seemed to be a second sea. Behind them, an arc of higher peaks—Catalonia's Roussillon—was dotted with snow.

It was breathtaking, truly. Edouard must think so too; he stood taking it in. Even Luki simply looked.

"It's like there are two seas here," Nanée said.

Were they on the right path? In all the explanation Hans had given as he drew the map for them, he hadn't mentioned this stunning vista.

"Papa, a dreaming log." Luki scrambled down from Edouard's back and hurried off, slipping a little on the snow but recovering her balance and carrying on.

"Moppelchen, we can't stop here," Edouard said. "We can't stop again until we're in Spain."

"I don't remember Hans talking about a vista like this," Nanée said. "Do you? We need to consult the map, to make sure we're where he meant us to be."

She watched Luki climb onto the log, remembering her big brother on the log sofa in Michigan, laughing at her when she tried to scramble up to join him, and her father lifting her up onto the log and sitting beside her, putting his arm around her so she wouldn't fall off. Was it a real memory? It seemed both unreal and undeniable at the same time. She'd spent a lifetime trying to please him, trying to become the brave girl she'd imagined he wanted her to be.

But she wasn't in Michigan now. She wasn't in Evanston. She wasn't a child reading stories about girls as extraordinary as she wanted to be, stories that always had happy endings and had never been real. She was in France. She was smuggling a German refugee and his daughter over the border. The penalty for shooting even a single Gestapo was the least forgiving kind of death.

They hadn't been able to see the two men still on the road above them. They weren't standing. Would knowing they were dead make her feel better, or worse? They were someone's sons, maybe someone's brothers or husbands. Someone's fathers. And she had killed them. But they would have killed her. They would have killed Edouard. They would have killed Luki. Wouldn't they have?

They sat in the sunshine, the wind gentle now and almost silent, with no canyon to howl down up here on this peak. Edouard sat beside Luki, and Nanée beside him. She dug from her musette bag a bit of bread. She took the smallest bite possible, to seem to be eating while leaving the bread for them. She passed it to Edouard, careful to make sure he had it before she let go, lest it fall to the ground. He didn't even pretend to eat any before holding it for Luki to take a bite.

"You need to eat," Nanée said. He was visibly exhausted from carrying Luki. "You need to keep your strength up."

"You need to eat," he said. "You . . ."

"I'm okay."

She made herself meet his gaze, his startling green eyes that were sad and weary still, but also wild and alert, watching, aware. Full of compassion.

"They would have killed us," he said. "You did the right thing. They would have killed us."

She nodded.

She removed her gloves and pulled from her pocket the little rice-paper map she was meant to swallow if they ran into trouble, but then she just held it in her cold fingers.

Edouard kissed the top of Luki's head.

Nanée sat silently beside them as a large bird, a hawk or an eagle, floated high overhead. Would the Germans have shot first if she hadn't? She didn't know. She couldn't even say that in that moment she had thought about it, that she had considered that she couldn't risk what those men might have done. She'd only focused the way her father taught her. She imagined a bull's-eye, a target like the one from that first pistol shooting contest she'd won. She fired on instinct, as she'd once shot that dove who hadn't done anything, who was only flying up in a sky in which he belonged.

"She was pregnant," Edouard said quietly. "In the photo."

Nude, Bending. Ghost Wife. Salvation.

He didn't say Elza's name, or Luki's. His gaze remained on the bird floating higher now, growing smaller in the sky before turning and swooping down toward the earth.

She waited, silent.

"After . . . after she'd been . . ."

What word couldn't he say? Or wouldn't he say with his daughter there?

"It was a way of . . . of . . . I don't know. She wanted me to take the photograph. She thought it would help heal me."

After she'd been unfaithful? But then why would he keep the photograph?

"Us," he said. "Heal us."

She glanced to his face, not wanting to make him uncomfortable but needing to see as well as hear what he was saying, to understand. Elza was pregnant with Luki in the photo, but Elza had never been unfaithful to Edouard. That was what he'd meant when he told her Luki wasn't Jewish. That Luki wasn't his daughter.

A child under German law was not Jewish if one of her parents was not. That was the . . . not just shame, but grief she felt herself, even when she first saw that photograph, *Salvation*, when she thought it was a man rather than a woman. It was, she saw now, both: Edouard capturing his own shame and grief in this photograph of a woman he had loved but had been unable to protect. A photograph that, in capturing their grief, somehow revealed Nanée's own very different grief, her own very different loss.

Luki snuggled up to Edouard, her kangaroos forgotten in the moment, falling to the snowy ground. He pulled her closer as, in the cold blue sky, the lone creature spread its wings wide, riding low on the wind.

"Because of your work?" she said. "Because of your photographs?"

"Yes."

"And still you keep taking them." The girl saluting Hitler. The boy forced to cut his father's beard. The people held prisoner on the SS *Sinaïa*.

"She said some things were important, and other things were not.

She said the test of who we are doesn't come in easy times; it comes in times like these."

Nanée set a hand on the log beside him, thinking a thing wasn't anything if you didn't allow it to be. Thinking shame was too powerful a force to leave its control in the hands of those who would manipulate it. Shame and expectation both. Thinking the person she had become here was the only person she wanted to be.

She slid her hand over until her bare finger bumped up against his already resting there. After a moment, he lapped his little finger over hers.

She looked out to the two seas that were the same thing, feeling the warmth of his single finger on hers as she focused on the stunning blue-green, the whitecaps, the single bird a black shadow against the light. And he looked with her. They watched the lone eagle arcing gracefully toward them, its wings stretching wide and magnificent. They watched together as, beyond him, the wild waters lapped against the shores of two different countries, connecting somewhere beyond the horizon, in a place they couldn't yet see.

Monday, December 9, 1940
THE PYRENEES

E douard stood to set off again, looking to the horizon but still scraping his heart over the past. *I'm pregnant*, Elza had told him. Pregnant with the child who would become Luki. He hadn't been able to touch her. Hadn't been able to ask. But of course she wouldn't have known any more than he did whose child she was carrying. *I want you to photograph me*, she'd said. *Photograph us. I know you. I know this will be easier for you if you take me back into your heart through your art. If you take this child, too, into your heart through your art.*

He took the small rice-paper map from Nanée, who was standing too now, beside him. She picked Pemmy and Joey up from the snow and handed them to Luki as he focused on the markings Hans had drawn. His future, and Luki's, and Nanée's.

Were they here? Or here? Or here?

It was a long moment before he could get control of his voice.

"I think we're here," he said finally.

"Where?"

He pointed to the place on the little map where Hans had indicated the path would fall away to the Spanish border station.

"Here?" Nanée said.

"Yes."

"But that's in Spain."

"Yes."

He indicated the line of the path down to the Spanish border station, where they would have to register, to show their travel documents and hope not to be turned away or worse.

Luki said, "We're in Spain, Papa?"

"Yes," Edouard said. "We are out of France. We are out of France.

We still must get the people in Spain to allow us to pass through to Portugal. But we are out of France."

Luki hugged her kangaroos to her, and began to sob. She was exhausted. Of course she was.

"Moppelchen," he said. "My Moppelchen." He pulled her to him, kissed the top of her head, and stroked her hair. He lifted her and sat again on the log, and he rocked her for a few minutes, thinking, as he did so often, of how he'd failed Elza and Luki both, and imaging Elza writing that last note to him—*If anything happens to me, promise me you will keep Luki with you and take care of her, always*—when his love for Luki should have been absolute from the day she was born.

But he saw as he looked out to the two seas, Luki warm in his arms, that Elza's note hadn't been a request; it had been a reminder. Elza had been sure of his love for Luki even when he doubted his own heart. She would never have risked leaving her daughter behind to return to Germany for her sister if she hadn't been sure of that love.

He watched Nanée watching Luki as Luki wound down, her fear settling out through her tears. Yes, this child had already won her heart too.

"We'd better go," he said finally. "We don't want to miss the last train out of Portbou."

Nanée looked directly at him, watching. "Yes," she said.

She set a hand on Luki's. "I'm going to miss you, Luki," she said.

Words meant for him too. He heard that in her voice, felt the blow. Her gentle way of saying goodbye to Luki, and to him.

He stared down at the markings on the map. How had he convinced himself that Nanée belonged with him? That she had chosen him. That she would leave everything she loved behind to come with him. To go home, he'd thought, but where he was going was no more home to her than it was to him.

He searched for a reason he might offer to change her mind: It was too dangerous for her to stay, more dangerous for her even than for him, because she'd shot the Germans; if any of them had survived, they would be looking for the woman who had planted two feet firmly on that path and shot them, not the man and the child tucked up against the cliff behind her. Varian would surely be evicted from France soon too, and what would she do then, even if she was allowed to stay? Luki would want her to come with them. He wanted her to come.

He said, "If those Germans have been found—"

"I know, but I'll be able to see the approach from above, I think."

She'd thought it through, then, this turning back.

"It's too dangerous," he insisted.

"No one suspects American women of anything but needlepoint. Men so seldom imagine us capable of the things we're capable of."

"I—"

"Everything good I've ever done," she said, "I've done here."

She looked at him then, watching him so closely in this moment of freedom and despair, the way he'd watched her all that first night they'd met, from that moment after he'd demanded André take *Salvation* down.

He wanted to ask if she would leave France when Varian did. But nobody could replace her. He knew that. The work she did as the Postmistress put her life at risk every day, and nobody else at the CAS could do what she did.

He held the tiny map out to her, wanting to ask if he would ever see her again.

"You'll need it to find your way," she said, refusing it. "Me, I would only have to eat it."

He laughed a little. How had she known that would make him laugh? And that he needed either to laugh or to cry.

All the life he was leaving behind. The sense of belonging.

"I could stay too," he said. Nobody could do what he did either, really. If he stayed, the photographs he could take would make the world see. He had always been afraid; it was there in that first self-portrait, and still he'd taken his photographs and published them, knowing he was taking impossible risks even if he couldn't imagine the consequences: that he would lose Elza and the child they made together, that he would have to abandon everything of the life they'd built, taking only his cameras and as much of his work as he could gather, and Luki. He was carrying his photos with him even now.

He said, "I ought to stay."

"You would endanger everyone who knows you," she said. "Varian. Danny and T. Gussie and Lena and Maurice and Beamish."

Her cheeks were red from the wind and the cold, and her nose too, and she had never looked more beautiful.

And you, he thought. If I stayed, I would endanger you.

She took her canteen from her musette bag and made him take it. "For Luki," she said.

"I—"

"The photos you've taken already tell the story here."

She took from her musette bag his letters, and she handed them to him. "These too. Use them for good whenever you can."

Luki said to Nanée, "The angels still need you," as if she had sorted this out in her own way.

"Yes," Nanée said. "Yes, I suppose the angels do need me here in France. They appear to need all the help they can get."

Luki said, "And Dagobert."

"Yes," Nanée said. "Yes, Dagobert needs me."

"He will take care of you, like I take care of Papa and he takes care of me." Looking to him now.

"Yes," Nanée agreed.

"But you will watch over us, like the Lady Mary?"

Nanée touched a finger to Luki's cheek, then trailed it down her arm to Joey and to Pemmy, to her scarf around Pemmy's neck. "I will always be thinking of you, Luki," she said.

Luki began to unwrap Nanée's white silk scarf from her kangaroo's neck, but Nanée stopped her.

"You keep it," Nanée said. "I would like you to have it, so Pemmy won't get cold."

"But you can't fly without it."

Nanée pulled Luki to her then, and hugged her desperately. "You keep it for me, Luki," she managed. "You keep it for me, and someday when this madness ends, I'll find you and I'll take you flying with me."

Luki said, "And Papa?"

Edouard looked to the hawk floating on the wind, lest Nanée see his devastation, lest Luki too see it.

"And your papa," Nanée said, "if he wants to come."

"But not to heaven," Luki said. "We would come back to earth."

"I'm afraid we always do come back to earth."

Nanée stood then, and said to Edouard, "Be careful. The rest of the way, be careful. The Gestapo are in Spain too."

"Let me . . ." He looked to the pocket of her flight jacket, where she had the pistol. "You don't want to be found with it."

"You can't show up armed at the Spanish border check."

"There's that foul pond up ahead that Hans warned us not to drink from."

Nanée stooped to Luki's level again and pointed to the sky. "Look," she said. "I think it's a golden eagle. The most elusive of creatures. They can spend hours or even days perched in a tree. Motionless. Impossible to spot."

As Luki peered up to the bird, Nanée slipped the pearl-handled pistol from her pocket.

He took it from her, and slid it into his own pocket.

Nanée said to Luki, "They're the best flyers, golden eagles, but they also build nests high up in the cliffs, which they return to year after year."

She kissed the top of Luki's head and stood again. "I really am going to miss you something terrific, Luki Moss."

Edouard picked up her nearly empty canteen and his musette bag with the stale bread hiding his film, awash now in what he was leaving, what he was losing: the world he knew, the places he'd shared with Elza, and with this woman who, improbably, had taught him to love again.

Nanée smiled sadly, a lovely smile without the least trace of co-quetry in the arch of her brow or the curve of her cheek, her slightly impish mouth.

He raised his Leica and took the shot: Nanée standing on the moun-taintop with the two seas behind her that were the same sea, the bird swooping toward her that was not the hawk he'd thought, he saw now, but rather the golden eagle Nanée told Luki it was.

He took Luki's hand, his daughter's hand. He managed, finally, "Goodbye, Nanée."

"In France, we say *au revoir*," she said. "Until we see each other again."

Tuesday, December 10, 1940
VILLA AIR-BEL

N anée held Dagobert for a long time there in the entry hall, letting him lick her hands and her neck and her face, and saying over and over again that she'd missed him too as Varian and the others congratulated her on her successful trip. Varian had received word from his contacts in Madrid that Edouard and Luki had made it that far, and ought to reach Lisbon the following day.

She gave Gussie back his book, and kissed him once on each cheek, bee kisses, and told him it was awfully lucky and she might ask to borrow it again. Then she pleaded exhaustion and headed up to her room, Dagobert at her heels.

T followed.

Nanée set her traveling case on her bed. Dagobert hopped up and sat beside it as she opened it, took out the suit, and handed it to T.

"Don't bring it back to me this time," she said.

T didn't answer.

"I really will burn it if—"

Nanée saw it then, what T had already seen. Propped up on her dresser, against the wall beside the photograph of the naked woman swimming up through murky water: a man's face, photographed in three-quarter profile and so close to the camera that the first time she'd seen it, as she helped Danny hang it from a tree for that Sunday salon, it took her a minute to make out that that was part of a chin in one corner of the print, an earlobe in the corner above it. One eye. One eyebrow that looked more like a silverfish than anything else. Part of a nose. Part of two lips. Eduard's solarized photograph of himself as a young man.

It was unframed, and propped up against it was an envelope on which her name was written in André Breton's trademark green ink. Nanée imagined it then: Edouard, sitting at the table where André so often wrote, using a pen André would have left there.

She touched a finger to the photograph, at Edouard's mole. "I suppose you're right, T. I suppose I do push the good ones away."

"Oh, for heaven's sake, open the note, Nan," T said. She set down the suit and opened the envelope herself, unfolded the sheet of notepaper inside, and put it in Nanée's hand, Edouard's words in André's green ink:

My Nanée,

I suppose I have known all along that you would read this, that Luki and I would go alone to Spain. To Portugal. To America. I suppose that's why I fell in love with you, because you won't choose Luki and me over so many people you can save by staying in France. Not won't, even. Can't. Because you are who you are.

If it weren't too much to ask, I would tell you that I will wait for you until you come back to America, or until Hitler is defeated and I can return to France and to you.

Instead, I leave you this self-portrait, so that you might be reminded of what you have done for me, and for Luki too. You have taken the dark places in our life and brought light in again. You have allowed me to see that there is darkness in all of us. That is simply who we are.

—ELM

Nanée held the note out to T, who took it and read it. "This Edouard Moss is much cleverer than your usual 'terrific lout,' Nan—heading to America without you," she said. "Someone once told me there's an advantage to an overseas love. 'Make her want something she can't quite reach.'" She smiled and said, "I do think even your father would have liked this one, not that you should care."

Nanée took the photograph of the swimming woman from its frame and put the self-portrait of Edouard in its place. She closed up the frame again and tucked the little sketch back into the back corner, the top third of that Exquisite Corpse. The head in a birdcage. A face that might or might not be hers. Did it matter? The cage door had always been open.

"Varian didn't like to say it before he welcomed you back home," T said, "but he has a delivery he needs you to do."

She left then, taking the suit and saying just before she closed the door behind her, "It's good to have you home."

Wednesday, December 11, 1940

LISBON

The hotel clerk found their reservation under Edouard's real name, which he could use now that they'd reached Portugal, exhausted but safe, finally.

"Welcome to Lisbon, Mr. Moss," the man said. He smiled down at Luki, then pulled a beautiful brass key from one of the wooden pigeonholes and offered it to her.

"With your permission, I'll send word to our mutual friend Mr. Fry that you and Miss Moss have arrived," he said to Edouard. "And so often these days our guests collect mail for others. Shall I be directing packages and mail under any other names to you?"

Edouard allowed that the clerk might watch for anything arriving for his friend Henri Roux.

"Ah yes, I believe . . ." The clerk opened a drawer and flipped through some envelopes and sheets of paper. "Here it is." He set a telegram on the reception desk, addressed to Henri Roux. "It arrived from Marseille this morning. I'll trust you to get it to your friend."

Sunday, February 2, 1941
MARIGOLD LODGE, MICHIGAN

Edouard sat with Luki on the big log Nanée had told him about, the "log sofa," looking out to the lake, to this new shore in the red morning light.

"Sometimes I lose what Mutti sounded like," Luki said, "but I can remember when she sings to me."

Edouard listened to the lapping of the waters of Lake Macatawa, frozen only at the shoreline despite a thick new snow quieting the ground and the willow trees.

"And sometimes I can't remember exactly what she looked like," Luki said. "I can't remember which face is Mutti and which is the angel."

Edouard set a hand on the wool hat on her head, unsure whether to correct her, to say "Nanée," or simply to let it go.

"Maybe it's like with the Lady Mary," she said, "or like the three gods who are all the same. Reverend Mother's gods that aren't ours."

He thought: Nanée is doing god's work under any definition of god, or none at all.

Next week, he was to go to Ypsilanti, where the Ford Motor Company was building a facility to assemble airplanes. He was to photograph the construction for his first assignment in this new life. The following week, his photos capturing what it meant to be among the six hundred guests of the Vichy government in the not-so-deluxe accommodations of the SS *Sinaïa* would run. They would appear in a major magazine here in the United States, where they might change minds and hearts.

"After the angels don't need her anymore," Luki said, "do you think they could give her back to us?"

Edouard studied her inquisitive face. "Who?"

"Tante Nanée."

"Would you like that?"

Luki nodded.

He touched a finger to the telegram from Nanée that had been waiting for Henri Roux in Portugal, which he kept now in his shirt pocket with the letter Luki had written to him at Camp des Milles. *It isn't too much to ask.*

"I hope so," he said. "I think so."

He looked out to the stretch of willow trees and the lake, imaging the young girl Nanée once was here, summers spent reading up in the trees. He closed his eyes, remembering Nanée's neck stretched out in the zinc tub at Villa Air-Bel. The curve of her back at the edge of her bed as he painted those fleurs-de-lis. Her square shoulders in her leather flight jacket as she headed back down the mountain, toward Banyuls-sur-Mer and the train back to Marseille, the trolley back to Villa Air-Bel.

"Yes," he said. "I believe we will get Nanée back."

In the silence, he picked up the kangaroo pair that Luki had dropped to the ground when they first sat down. He brushed the snow off and handed them to her. She wound up the smaller kangaroo and set him free to play—a waltz, which the Viennese claimed as their own.

"We might go back to France when it's safe for us to do so," he said.

"Tante Nanée could sing with us on the dreaming log."

Edouard hugged her close, imagining too what Nanée might be doing now. It was afternoon in Marseille. She would be out making deliveries for Varian, winding her way through the filthy alleyways of the Panier to some refugee holed up there, as he had once been. Maybe she'd finished early and was back at the château, stooping low to receive Dagobert's slobbery love. Filling the tub and sinking into the water. Maybe it would be a clear night, and Danny would find that Boston station, and she would dance to music from over here, from this world that was hers, and was now Luki's and his too.

"Someday she will take flying lessons," Luki said.

"Nanée?"

Luki gave him a look, so much like Elza. "Pemmy! And me too. Do you think Tante Nanée would teach me to fly?"

He unwrapped the white silk flight scarf from the kangaroo's neck, then tipped his daughter's chin up so that he could look into her deep-sea eyes. He wrapped the scarf once around her neck, loosely, leaving long tails that caught in the wind.

"I believe she would love that." He pulled her close, to keep her warm, and himself too. "My Moppelchen," he said.

Together they watched a plump little cardinal land on a willow branch hanging just above them, bright red against the white lace of tree branches. The bird tilted its head, its little black face observing them curiously. It chirped once, a delightful sound, then lifted off into the sky, floating gracefully over the lake.

AUTHOR'S NOTE AND ACKNOWLEDGMENTS

Here are a few things that are true about Mary Jayne Gold, the American heiress whose real courage inspired that of my fictional Nanée: She grew up in an Evanston mansion and summered at Marigold Lodge in Western Michigan, went to finishing school in Italy, and flew a red Vega Gull (which did not in fact have a stall horn). She was friends with Danny Bénédite, who really did use his position with the Paris police to arrange French residency permits for refugee artists. She stayed in France after Hitler invaded, and fled Paris with Theo Bénédite, and tried to get their son out of France by claiming him as her illegitimate child. After the armistice, Mary Jayne went to Marseille, intending to leave France. She instead stayed, and joined Varian Fry's effort to help refugees, contributing her time and thousands of dollars. She rented a place called Villa Air-Bel, where she lived with, among others, the Bénédites, Fry, the Bretons, and Dagobert. They hosted salons there at which they played Surrealist games and hung art from the trees.

But this is not Mary Jayne Gold's personal story. She did not fall in love with an artist named Edouard Moss, who does not exist except in my mind, on the page and, if I've done my job well, in your mind and perhaps your heart. She did not as far as I know travel into occupied France to rescue a Jewish girl. I don't know if she could shoot a pistol, much less do it so well.

This book did, though, begin for me with Mary Jayne Gold, Villa Air-Bel, the artists and intellectuals at Camp des Milles outside Aix-en-Provence, and the efforts of Varian Fry and the *Centre Américain de Secours*, as well as those of Hans and Lisa Fittko. Other characters inspired by real people include Miriam Davenport, Justus "Gussie" Rosenberg, Marcel "Maurice" Verzeanu, Charles Fawcett and Leon Ball, Lena Fischmann, Bill Freier, and Hiram "Harry" Bingham IV. With the exception of Edouard Moss, the artists and writers named in the novel, including André and Jacqueline Breton and Max Ernst, are based on real people. The depictions here are meant to honor those involved in these rescues, but all, including Varian Fry, are to some extent products of my imagination.

I hope readers will be inspired by this novel to learn more about the real stories that underpin it. Some of the sources on which I relied include Mary Jayne Gold's *Crossroads Marseille, 1940*; Varian Fry's *Surrender on Demand*; Miriam Davenport's unpublished "An Unsentimental Education"; Justus Rosenberg's *The Art of Resistance*; and Lisa Fittko's *Escape through the Pyrenees*. I also relied on the writings of real artists and intellectuals who were rescued, including Lion Feuchtwanger's *The Devil in France*; André Breton's *Letters to Aube*; Victor Serge's *Notebooks 1936–1947*; and Hans Sahl's *The Few and the Many*.

Other sources I found particularly useful include the oral history interview with Mary Jayne Gold on the US Holocaust Memorial Museum website; *Villa Air-Bel* by Rosemary Sullivan; *Surrealism* by Amy Dempsey; *The Holocaust & the Jews of Marseille* by Donna F. Ryan; *In Defiance of Hitler* by Carla Killough McClafferty; *A Quiet American* by Andy Marino; *André Breton in Exile* by Victoria Clouston; *Marseille • New York* by Bernard Noël; and the many wonderful resources made available by the Varian Fry Foundation at varianfry.org, as well as those at AndréBreton.fr, and villaairbel1940.fr.

I am so often inspired by photos. For this book, the single photo called variously *Nude Bending*, *The Ghost Wife*, and *Salvation* was inspired by Lee Miller's 1930 photo *Nude Bent Forward*. The photo Nanée purchases when she can't buy that one is inspired by Francesca Woodman's haunting 1977 photo *On Being an Angel #1, Providence, Rhode*

Island, the title of which I did not know when I chose it as the model for a photograph I did not intend to title. The scene in which Edouard paints on Nanée's back was inspired by Man Ray's 1924 photo *Ingres' Violin*; the paint is my own. Edouard's self-portrait is inspired by Maurice Tabard's *Untitled (solarized face)*. The caped woman is drawn from a photograph Mac Clayton took in Paris, and the brûlaged version of it by Raoul Ubac's *The Nebula*. And *Nanée's Beautiful Neck* bears an uncanny resemblance to Man Ray's 1929 *Lee Miller ("The Necklace")*.

Gratitude to so many people on this one, starting with my editor, Sara Nelson, whose indefatigable dedication and good humor are a writer's dream, and the whole gang at Harper Books who support me so amazingly, including Jonathan Burnham, Doug Jones, Leah Wasielewski, Robin Bilardello, Katie O'Callahan, Katherine Beitner, Juliette Shapland, Carolyn Bodkin, Virginia Stanley, and Mary Gaule, as well as everyone at HarperCollins Holland and the other foreign offices. Thanks to Joanne O'Neill for the stunning cover, and for her patience. And to my agent, Marly Rusoff, and the intrepid Mihai Radelescu, who help me in so many ways.

To the many booksellers who have been so kind to me and so enthusiastic on behalf of my books—I would call you out individually, but that would make this a very long book. Ditto to everyone at the Jewish Book Council and the many book festivals that have given me a chance to connect with readers.

My Flight Team—Captain Christopher Keck and crew Dylan Rich and Brittney Kaniecki—took me on a virtual flight over Paris to show me Nanée's view and help me understand what avoiding a bird and nearly stalling a plane at low altitude over the lake in the Bois de Boulogne might be like. Thanks also to Sue Hulme, whose father, David Hulme, owned and piloted a Vega Gull, for sharing with me photos, video, and technical details.

I was so sorry to have missed a hike over the Pyrenees myself despite three planned trips canceled due to flu, record heat, and Covid travel restrictions. I'm grateful to Patrick Jouhanneau and Tom Pfister, who shared their time and photographs with me. Tom also sent me his *Eva and Otto*, written with Kathy and Peter Pfister, about their parents' escapes from France; the emotional impact of their stunning book echoes through Edouard's journey. I commend it to everyone.

I'm grateful for the Camp des Milles Memorial and everyone who had a hand in preserving this history. Also to the many people who made my research in various places as comfortable as home and far more interesting, especially Robin and David Young, who allowed me to stay in their beautiful Paris apartment, and Thomas Chase, who was such a great help there.

The enormously talented Adrienne Defendi helped me with passages on photography. Mynda Barenholtz helped with research. Brenda Rickman Vantrease and Jenn DuChene read for me.

I am so grateful to The Brothers Four—Pat, Mike, Mark, and Dave Waite—for helping our parents in a difficult time as I was writing this book, and to Mom and Dad for so very much support in every way. My sons, Chris and Nick, provided moral support and, in being their wonderfully steady and safe selves, allowed me to set aside a mother's worries and get words onto the page.

As always, the company of my amazing partner in life, Mac Clayton, made the research trips to France great fun, even as the Berthillon melted faster than we could eat it in that long stretch of record Paris heat. He tirelessly read draft after draft, always providing great suggestions. Truly, without his help, I could not have completed this novel on the schedule I did. His company, love, and patience saw me through the long days of writing this novel in the midst of a pandemic, which I hope will be in our rearview mirror as you are reading this. (Knock wood; Nanée does draw her superstition from my own.)

ABOUT THE AUTHOR

MEG WAITE CLAYTON is a *New York Times* and internationally bestselling author of seven prior novels, most recently the Jewish Book Award finalist *The Last Train to London*. Her novels include the Langum Prize–honored *The Race for Paris; The Language of Light*, a finalist for the Bellwether Prize for Socially Engaged Fiction (now the PEN/Bellwether); and *The Wednesday Sisters*, one of *Entertainment Weekly*'s 25 Essential Best Friend Novels of all time. A graduate of the University of Michigan and its law school, Meg has written for the *San Francisco Chronicle*, the *Los Angeles Times*, the *New York Times*, the *Washington Post, Forbes, Runner's World*, and public radio. Her work has been translated into more than twenty languages. She lives in northern California.